S.J. Deas was born in 1968. 〰〰〰〰〰〰 ⌄o Wales. Well, one bit of Wales. Twice. Whei〰〰〰urning principalities he managed to study theoretical physics at Cambridge, get a job at BAE, marry and have two children. He now lives in Essex.

Praise for *The Royalist*:

'A page-turning novel, unpredictable and suspenseful, haunted by intriguing twists and turns . . . The characters are vividly portrayed, three-dimensional and convincing' *Historical Novels Review*

'Deas writes at a furious pace . . . It is his wonderful descriptions and his creation of a powerfully charged atmosphere that really capture the reader' *We Love This Book*

'Deliciously atmospheric . . . a fine novel . . . I look forward enormously to the next' *For Winter Nights*

'I take my hat off to the author for his ability and desire to portray all of this horror and dirt . . . Highly recommended' *Parmenion Books*

'Vivid and atmospheric . . . A very enjoyable and refreshing read that gave you a new understanding of the time and the New Model army and how it was anything but united' *Reality's A Bore*

S.J. DEAS

the Royalist

headline

First published in Great Britain 2014 by
HEADLINE PUBLISHING GROUP

First published in Great Britain in paperback in 2015 by
HEADLINE PUBLISHING GROUP

2

Cataloguing in Publication Data is available from the British Library

ISBN 978 1 4722 1697 7

Typeset in Sabon by Avon DataSet Ltd,
Bidford-on-Avon, Warwickshire

Printed and bound in Great Britain by Clays Ltd, St Ives plc

MIX
Paper from
responsible sources
FSC® C104740

Headline's policy is to use papers that are natural, renewable and recyclable
products and made from wood grown in well-managed forests and other
controlled sources. The logging and manufacturing processes are expected to
conform to the environmental regulations of the country of origin.

HEADLINE PUBLISHING GROUP
An Hachette UK Company
338 Euston Road
London NW1 3BH

www.headline.co.uk
www.hachette.co.uk

To Jane and Ginni and Wakefield and Quin,
who persuaded me to pick up a pike.

CHAPTER 1

Three times they tried to kill me. They came for me on those blasted northern moors and I lived. They cut swathes through my fellows at Edgehill and somehow, deep in dead men, I came through. They routed my company outside Abingdon and cornered me in the thick of night when I had nowhere to run to and nobody to watch my back. Yes, three times they tried to kill me.

Third time lucky.

I strained to see. There was no window in the cell but somewhere there was candlelight and it was enough to show that I was alone now. There had been three others in here with me when I closed my eyes but it was no surprise they were gone. They were Irishmen, all three, and I found out long ago what they do to Irishmen here. Sooner or later the same was coming for me. I found myself bewildered that I'd slept through it but felt little else save to be all the more sickened at how far I'd fallen. I'd listened to those men cry and talk of the homes, the families they'd left behind, lovers and wives and sisters and sons. Now they were gone and I couldn't even remember their names. That's what they bring you to in a place like this.

I rolled onto my side and sat cross-legged in the gloom,

picking tacky damp stalks of straw from the rags that were left of my clothes. I had no doubt that I stank. The cells festered with sweat and filth and urine but I'd been here so long that I didn't notice any more. I thought of my wife, my beautiful Caro, of the scent of her hair when she stood close with her head pressed to my chest. I waited for the shudder of loss and longing to come but it didn't. I was nothing now but numb.

I didn't suppose it mattered. I wasn't getting out of there alive and all those promises I'd made to the three Irishmen, to take away messages for wives and brothers and sons, well, we'd all known they were empty words. Sometimes you say what you've got to say and even if the other man knows it's a lie, he's still glad to hear it. Sometimes, flying in the face of everything around us, we choose a sliver of hope. I was never good at that.

I don't know how long I sat there. I didn't draw myself up when I heard footsteps. If they came for me today then I wouldn't sob or scream or rain a thousand curses on their heads like some I've known, but I wouldn't stand up for them either. It's come to be that that's what they expect, that we stand for them. They'd have us doff our hats as they led us to the gallows, if hats we had.

My jailer appeared as a darker silhouette against the deep gloom of the distant candlelight. He jangled his keys. He wasn't the man I knew when they first brought me here – that man was long gone, probably to the same war that had kept me from home for five long years. The soldier who appeared before me instead was scarcely more than a boy, no older than the son I was certain I'd never see again. He fumbled a jangling ring of keys until he found the one to fit

my lock. A faint smell of gunpowder reached across the air
between us, sharp and sulphurous. A thought flashed across
the backs of my eyes: that I was still strong enough to run
this boy down. The gate to my cell squealed back but I
didn't move. It wouldn't serve any purpose. It just felt good
that that part of me hadn't withered away, no matter how
long they'd kept me alone in the dark.

'Falkland,' the boy said. His voice had barely broken.

I looked up. Nothing more.

'You're to come with me.'

So there it was. My time. When the boy decided I
wouldn't thrash about and grapple him, he strode in –
purposefully, as he must have been taught – and fiddled with
keys again. He left my ankles and wrists manacled but
unlocked me from the grille and bade me stand. I stayed sat
where I was just long enough to make him think he might
have to call for his masters and then did as he asked. I had
no interest in causing trouble. He was just a boy. Nothing I
did was going to change things now. I'd be dead within the
hour and in a way it would be a relief. It's a bitter war whose
purpose is lost to those who fight it. It has a will of its own, I
think. It grinds men to husks and those are the lucky ones.

I walked with the boy behind me along rows of cells just
like mine. Some were open-faced with grilles and I could see
the men lying in scarred heaps inside. I'd shared
conversations with some of these fellows though most were
too deranged to remember. I tried not to look but I couldn't
stop my eyes from being drawn. One man lay stretched
across the cold stones in a horrible paroxysm of grief. He
dead-eyed me, his tongue lolling out. I saw another man lay
underneath him, already dead.

Somebody shrieked from the cell opposite, startling us both. I looked round. Chains rattled against bars. Even if I didn't hear a word, I knew the other prisoners were singing me on my way. There was only one exit to a place like this.

We reached the end of the row of cells and climbed a stone stairway to the next. The steps were old, chipped and uneven, thinly coated in a wet slime of mud and dung, trampled back and forth by the boots of our jailers. A fresh reek of rot and offal rose from them, climbing through the stink of the prison. Even when we came to a passage where cold daylight streamed in to dazzle me, it still felt as if we were six feet underground. The air remained stagnant and rank. I began to think this wasn't Newgate at all as some of my fellow prisoners had said. Perhaps we weren't even in London.

We came to a gate where two turnkeys sat. The boy instructed me to stop. 'I'm sorry, Falkland,' he said.

'Nothing to be sorry for, son. It's not you who'll pull the lever.'

He paused as if he didn't understand.

'I have to, sir . . .'

Sir? I must have misheard. He probably meant cur.

The boy produced a hood stitched out of an old grain sack from a loop on his belt. The sight of it killed any last flickering thoughts I might have had of some miraculous escape. That hood and I had become friends these last long months. I'd been wearing it when they brought me in here and now I'd wear it on my way out too. I managed a smirk. It was the sort of neat pattern by which I once wanted to live my life.

'Do what you've got to do, boy. But I'd rather look my hangman in the eye. That's a mercy the King used to grant every man he condemned, no matter what he'd done.'

The boy mumbled something I didn't hear and dropped the hood over my eyes. It tightened with a drawstring around my neck. I heard the gate lift and we were on our way again. It was difficult enough to move with my ankles still shackled, so the hood didn't make much difference. I felt daylight strike me for the first time in months and, even under the grain sack, it was brighter than any light I'd ever seen in my cell. I knew it was beautiful, as was the wind that touched my skin, the air bitter cold. In my cell I'd judged the month to be November: now I wasn't so sure. This felt more of a January or February chill. However we tried, we all lost track of time in the relentless gloom.

I stepped where I was told. I slowed when I was told and stopped when I was told so that gates might be opened and steps pointed out. The boy tugged me along like a dog on a leash. I didn't resist. Wherever we were, the day was eerily silent. I've seen more than my fair share of public executions and never felt one as miserable and unwatched as this. I began to climb what I supposed must be the gallows steps and didn't hear a single scream, a single cry, the smashing of a single stone thrown by some onlooker in the crowd. Underneath the hood I started to smile. I couldn't suppress it. Had it finally come to this, then? Not even the common-folk could bear it any more? Usually they turn out for any spectacle at all, no matter how grisly, but today the will of the people was being heard and it sounded like nothing I'd ever known: it sounded like silence. Had they had enough at last? Was it coming to an end? I'd heard as much but prison rumours are wild things, whole stories grown from a single misheard word.

'Watch your head, Falkland.'

The boy pressed his palm on the top of my head and bade me stoop down low. I supposed they were fitting me for the rope and I was pleased to find that I wasn't afraid. I was ready for this, as ready as I could be, even as the last regrets and a final memory of my Caroline filled me. A hand pushed me forward. I stumbled and almost fell as the boy pushed me down into a rough wooden seat. I felt him withdraw and heard a door shut close by. A horse whinnied.

Wait. What? This was no scaffold and gallows – was I in a carriage now?

At once my calm was gone and a fear took me in its place. I whipped my head left and then right. I'd been ready to hang, ready to die, but not ready for this. I felt certain that I was not alone, too, but I would have known it if the boy had climbed aboard behind me. Someone was already here then. I tried to lift my hands but now the boy had locked them down. A horrible panic churned deep inside me. I heard a heavy breath and then a stench crept into the air inside my hood, the like of which I've only known from men on starvation rations whose very bodies have started to eat themselves. The sickly smell came through the grain bag hood and wrapped itself around me. I had no choice but to breathe it in.

'Sit still, Falkland.' I didn't know the voice. It sounded deep and musical: a thespian or a minstrel, some courtly fool too cowardly ever to fight. I imagined it might belong to a jester, except the Puritan men who held me would never entertain such a thing.

'Who are you?' I knew then how afraid I was from how desperate I was to know. A condemned man can come to peace with his fate; but a man who doesn't know it might kill himself with worry.

'You might count yourself fortunate, Falkland, that you're even here to ask that question.'

'You didn't answer.'

'It matters little,' the syrupy voice returned. 'I'm an escort. Nothing more.'

'Escorting me where? I was supposed to die today.'

'Were you?' This must have amused the man for he let out a little chortle. 'You were supposed to die every day for the last month. Fortune smiles on you, Falkland. When we heard who you were, we were intrigued.'

Who I was? I was nobody. I wasn't even a commander. A mistake, then, but now some intelligencer wanted to ask his questions before they hanged me, was that it? Damn it but I wasn't even with the King, not really, not through anything other than blasted chance. Hundreds and hundreds of men out there were dying for their ideals but there were thousands more like me, dying just for the sake of dying. I was tired of this war long before it even began. I just wished they'd hurry up and get on with it – let me die for somebody else's crusade and then let me rot in peace.

I sat in silence. The other man didn't make a sound but sometimes you can *hear* a smirk.

'Where are we going?' I asked. I knew my questions must be futile but I felt compelled to break the silence. At least, for a few seconds, it saved me from breathing his hideous breath.

'Settle down, Falkland. You'll find out soon enough.'

The carriage rattled on. I had no idea where we were going but I knew we hadn't left the city. The air was fresher than I remembered of London from five years before, but that was only because the King held Newcastle and so there wasn't any coal. People would freeze on the streets this winter. All the same, I could hear the city sounds and smell the city smells. I fancied we'd come to the river and were following its banks because we stopped threading through narrow streets and I could hear seagulls. Their screeching reminded me of home, of those Cornish beaches where the waves would thunder and crash, and I felt a horrible flurry of joy – horrible because I'd abandoned both hope and joy long ago. To know it could reappear so suddenly, so violently, felt like a betrayal.

I heard bells then, and not the plaintive pealing of bells from a country church – I've heard *that* sound too often, as if the church towers themselves are crying out against the marauders ripping out their altars and setting fire to every icon. No, these bells were more powerful, more strident and they were getting nearer. They were the bells of Parliament, of St Stephen's Chapel.

I heard the man beside me shuffle. He must have known, now, that I had guessed.

'Why?' I asked him.

'Your questions will be answered, Falkland.'

'You'll answer them now!' I was so desperate to understand why they'd bring me all this way, and for what purpose, that against my own will I lashed out, but the chains only snapped me back with a jolt that shuddered right through me. Bones jarred and old wounds started to shriek. My heart pounded in my breast.

'You exert yourself too much for a man who's been shackled to a rail for four months.' There was a sneering disdain to the voice.

'Four months? Is that all it's been?' Four months. Barely November. I wasn't as wrong as I'd first thought, though the chill of the air remained as of the very depths of winter.

The carriage slowed to a halt. I felt it turn and cut a tight circle. The horses whinnied and then we were still. The man beside me stood and bustled past, dropping out of the door on my right. 'It feels longer, doesn't it, Falkland?'

He sounded contrite, as if he too had suffered similar deprivations. Hatred would have angered me less. I wasn't expecting him to feel anything for me at all. 'You have the wrong man,' I told him, though I knew I was wasting my breath. His hand grappled with mine and in that way he steered me to the ground. Somewhere above us the pealing of the bells went on. It was, I had counted, noon. In my cell I had made it midnight.

'It's almost over, Falkland.'

There was a terrible irony in that. I had thought it almost over from the very beginning.

CHAPTER 2

When the hood came off my head I kept my eyes tightly closed. Even then I could still see pillars of light that might have blinded me; but as I slowly squinted out at the world I saw they were only tall, narrow windows throwing columns of winter sunlight up the stone walls, not the fierce torches my inquisitors had once held perilously close to my face. I was in a stone chamber – but apart from the ornate windows and a candelabrum it was as bare as a cavern with only a fireplace and bookshelves to break up the walls.

I heard the footsteps of my syrupy escort patter away behind me. I turned to look but all I saw was the shape of him vanishing through an arch as a door closed behind him. My eyes slowly took a grip on their situation and adjusted to the glare from the windows. I realised the chamber was bigger than I'd first thought, and long. At the end of it a man in black robes sat behind a broad, bare desk. The light gradually faded to the edges of my vision and I saw that on one side of the desk were piles of parchment and on the other a Bible and an ink pot. The man didn't look up and I began to wonder if he even knew I was there. He was sitting in a tall wooden chair – perhaps in other circumstances, if it had only been decorated thus, I might have called it a throne

– and rhythmically lifting the pieces of parchment from one pile, signing his name at the bottom and then placing them in another. He worked with a fierce and studious concentration. Even when I jangled my chains he didn't look up.

'I shall be with you shortly,' he said. He had a deep baritone voice but seemed to be sick; he spoke from the back of his throat, or through his nose. I tried to reason out my circumstances. I'd thought, when they took me from Newgate, that it was to beat information from me – information I'd gladly have given away if I'd had it. I'd not been much looking forward to that, but if they'd brought me here for such purposes then shouldn't there be a guard? I stared at the man behind the desk. He didn't strike me as a torturer.

Abruptly he finished signing his papers. He looked up and we met eye to eye at last. He was about my age, past his fortieth year and perhaps a touch older. He had a big hawk's nose and matching chin; and while I have long lost my hair, his hung wild around his shoulders, though it was not as deep and lustrous as he probably thought. He wore a stiff white collar and a black coat. He had no rings on his fingers, no chain round his neck, and rather gave the impression of a scarecrow.

'Letters of condolence, you understand,' he said. 'For boys we've lost. Their fathers deserve that.'

I wondered if there was anybody doing that on our side. It didn't seem the sort of thing to preoccupy the King, but if there was some loyal minister sending out letters then perhaps one had already been sent for me. It had been years since I last lay with my wife or saw our children, many months since I had last had a chance to write and more than twelve since I had heard any manner of word at all; now the idea that they might have received such a letter haunted me. Perhaps they thought me dead. For my own part, and in spite of everything I'd seen, I couldn't begin to imagine them other than as I remembered them, bright and full of life.

'Come forward,' the man said.

There was still a distance between me and the desk where he sat. I shuffled forward in the tiny baby steps that my shackles would allow.

'I had thought,' he began, 'you would look *different*.'

My eyes flickered but I didn't reply.

'I had thought,' he went on, 'that you would cut a more *dashing* figure. Preen about your appearance a little more, like the rest of you cavaliers.'

Most of us hated it when they called us that. You could tell which of the King's men you wanted to fight alongside by whether or not they enjoyed the name. You were best to stay away from any man who styled himself a cavalier and didn't look on it as an insult: they were the ones who spent their time peering into a looking glass instead of training with swords or priming their muskets. I'd seen friends die because *cavaliers* weren't watching their backs.

'You know who I am?'

I thought by now that I did but I didn't deign to say it.

'Because I know who you are.'

'Perhaps, sir, you might condescend to tell me. I seem to have lost myself these last years. I don't know if I've come out of that hole the same man I went in.'

'Yes,' the man said. 'How droll. I heard you were reputed for it – your sense of humour. But you'd have found precious little to laugh at if I hadn't got word we were holding you. They'd have strung you up like every other traitor.' He stood and came around his desk and then perched on the edge of it like a coquettish maid in a drinking room. 'It's over, you understand.'

'What is?'

'The war. By the time spring comes your King will make terms.'

'Good.' I could see it was possible. It was the deep of winter in 1645 and we'd been at this endless back and forth for years. In all of that time I couldn't tell you what grounds had been won or lost or won again. It was an endless game of catch-me-if-you-can – but even children at play have better tactics for this than we did. It seemed to me sometimes that the armies were like two blind men with clubs blundering around a taproom where chance had the only say as to where and when they might meet. When they met they hit each other until one staggered away and the other couldn't find him again. Though Parliament's blind man had found a new and bigger club of late, and I'd heard that the King had taken a disastrous beating at Naseby. Perhaps he was right. Perhaps it really was done. For my own part I'd weep no tears whoever the victor.

'Mr Falkland . . . William. I'll come to the point, if I may?'

'I was hoping you would. I have a dinner engagement.'

That at least raised his smile.

'My name is Oliver Cromwell. Parliament has charged me with winning this conflict and that is what I intend. The King and Parliament have been at war for three years and in that time the country has been in chaos. Towns have changed hands back and forth in an ever-shifting patchwork between each side, but now we have the means to end it, to bring back peace and force the King to terms.'

He came forward and made as if he was going to hold my hands like a girl pleading with her lover. Instead he merely inspected the manacles and chain and rolled his eyes as if unsurprised. When he saw I was wearing chains around my ankles as well, he strode past me, opened the door a crack and halloed a man standing waiting in the passage. The man scuttled in and unlocked me. I felt suddenly naked. I'd been in chains since the night they rounded us up, and without them I no longer knew what to do. I found that I wanted, *needed*, their chains. If I hated them for anything in that moment, I hated them for that.

Cromwell whispered to a second man who hurried away and returned shortly carrying a plain wooden tray with slices of meat and a hunk of dry bread; then Cromwell poured us both beer. It was as sour as any I've tasted but I felt better all the same. The food settled less well. Moments after I took my first bite I felt my stomach in revolt. I'd eaten precious little while I was in my cell but it had been more than I was used to out on the march. Sometimes it seemed as if there was no food left in the country at all and what little there was we would rather burn than harvest.

Cromwell watched me carefully. 'Tell me, Falkland,' he said, 'what is this war about?'

I opened my mouth to speak and then held my tongue. I realised I no longer knew and wondered if I ever had. I looked away. 'God, I suppose,' I muttered.

'God? Presbyterians and Independents against the Catholics?' Cromwell shook his head. 'Catholicism has been outlawed for over a century. Our Church of England nurtures us now. It is far too late for a turning back of *that* hand. It is about how the people of England wish to be governed, no more and no less.' He turned and faced me square. He had an odd look to him, I thought, a strange kind of almost-pride, the type I'd once had teaching my son to take his first steps. 'What do you know about our New Model?'

So that was it. 'Your army,' I replied. The blind man's new club. 'I've met them once or twice.'

'It was New Model soldiers who shattered your company.'

I didn't doubt it. Once there were dozens of armies, local militias, and they were all stacked up against us. Then, as the last winter came to an end, came the New Model. From the rumours I'd heard since, all the Parliament soldiers were New Model now. They were fit and healthy and, more than anything else, they were *paid*. That was how Parliament made its soldiers fight. *We* were fighting for King and country, but King and country don't fill your stomach at night or stitch you up when a sabre cuts you apart. Money does that. I had heard of prisoners choosing defection rather than torture or execution. I'd never asked myself what I would do if posed the same question but that, I supposed, was for the best. Perhaps I was about to find out.

'I spent last winter in Oxford. After Newbury I was hurt. You might say mortally. I took musket fire to the leg and it turned gangrenous. They said I was going to die. I was at peace with that. Then I came out of it. They said it was God who spared me, to fight the good fight. But I knew different. Maggots got into the wound and ate the putrefied flesh. That's what stopped the infections. *Our* God –' I said it pointedly, for I was certain we shared the same Father – 'did not save me, but the maggots came through.'

If Cromwell felt anything at this he didn't let it show. I scarcely believed that men like him were interested in God. What they were really interested in was power. Even their brutes who tore around the countryside burning altars and stringing up simple folk who just wanted to pray, even *they* must have known it wasn't done for the simple purity of our faith. When you've seen such acts as closely and as many times as I have, you come to understand it isn't about religion at all; it's about children fighting: which boy is bigger, which boy is stronger, which boy has the meatiest fists. No, for all its dressings, God had no part in this bloody war.

'When I was fit I begged leave to go home. I hadn't had word from my wife and children in twelve months, had not seen them in years. But they said I couldn't go. I'd have to journey through Parliament lands to reach them and that couldn't be risked. That's how the King saw things – us and *them*. You see, even then you'd got what you wanted. The King was starting to give up what, by divine right, was his.' I didn't care much for divine right. Not then and not even six years before when I first marched north to face the Scots. The only right I knew was the opposite of wrong. But it did me a service seeing how the words caused Cromwell's face to flicker. I'll admit I took some joy from that.

'The King refused me. I'd served in his armies since before this madness began but he still wouldn't spare me. It wasn't long before I was pressed back into service. We'd been wrestling for that pointless little town of Abingdon for so long it hardly seemed worth getting killed over, but get killed we did. Your New Model men cut us down as we ran. I thought I'd almost got away. I found myself a burned-out farmhouse to hide in. I'd been there three days when those boys turned up. I gave myself up for a mouthful of water.'

Cromwell listened to my story with a patience that belied his natural instinct. He wanted to probe and prod – I've heard it told that he is his army's best inquisitor, a politician, a strategist, deftly flitting from gentry to common man – but I'd been careful not to allow him in.

'You do yourself a disservice, of course, Falkland. You've left out the most intriguing parts of your own tale.'

'Beg pardon, sir, but my tale is my own.'

'You have chosen to omit, for instance, how you escaped our men at Newbury or how you sustained the wound that almost did for you.'

He was toying with me like a cat with a mouse. We'd get to it soon, whatever it was, this intelligence he believed I possessed. I supposed it must be something quite remarkable that he would call me here and so his disappointment not to receive whatever he sought would be equally large. I wished some giant hand would pluck me up, see I was done for and gently squeeze me until my eyes bulged and my heart stopped. Then Cromwell could play with a dead thing and I, at least, would be content.

'You have left out too, though why I can only imagine, the very reason you're not now dangling from a scaffold but are here instead. In the company of gentlemen.'

He said it as a jibe, for Oliver Cromwell was no more a gentleman than I. Like me, he was a man who had clawed his way into significance just as surely as his forebear had a century ago.

'Falkland, I'll put it to you plainly. I created the New Model to end this war and so it shall. It is a different kind of army, a constant arm of Parliament, always there, not like these rabble militias that must be hurriedly raised as the need arises. The New Model does not care where your allegiances once lay. My soldiers are paid and so they take their oaths and fight as they are told. But once again we are back to the matter at the heart of it all: how shall this be governed?' He turned away from me and walked to one of the windows, staring out at the sunlight. For my own part, used as I was to the perpetual dark and gloom of my prison, I dared not venture too close.

'I've heard stories about your . . . *presence* in the King's armies,' he said. 'I've heard it said that you're a man with a conscience.' He said the next wearily and I had the impression that this was the only time I might see a crack in the implacable Cromwell, something to let the light shine in. 'And Falkland, I am in great need of a man with a *conscience.*'

I knew what he was referring to though I couldn't imagine how he'd come to hear of it. But maybe it simply says something about the nature of this wretched war when a simple thing like knowing right from wrong can set you apart from other men. That, I despair to say, is what England has become.

'Is the story true?'

I nodded.

'You disobeyed the King and had a man put to death?'

I didn't need to nod again. My eyes told the story. 'It was a long time ago. He was a rapist. A butcherer.'

'But he was one of your own. One of the King's men.

I would hear the story in your own words, Falkland.'

He was playing games again. I had the feeling I was taking part in an unfamiliar, unforgiving dance, and I was not the lead. 'We were garrisoned in Yorkshire. Most of us went up there in 1639, the King's army, to fight the Scots. I dare say you know better than I how that went. We were in Yorkshire for a little more than a year, licking our wounds from that before the King began his fight with Parliament, but it felt like ten. Just *waiting*. Waiting can do things to a man. Turn him into a monster. There was a woman ravished. Then another, but the second one was murdered too. Then a third, murdered again. The first woman said she didn't properly see the man who attacked her. When it became clear to me that all three were the same villain, I asked her again. She said she wished to drop the matter. I told her that *I* did not but I understood quickly enough from her answers that she'd been paid money for her silence.' I paused as I remembered her face. The fear in it.

'Did that not deter you, Falkland?'

'On the contrary, I would say it spurred me.' I wondered now why I was telling this to Cromwell, why it seemed to matter so much to him. 'So I continued looking. I didn't have much else to do. A few days later I was asked to attend on the King himself. I wouldn't say summoned, for the invitation was polite enough. But one does not decline the King. So I waited on him as was my duty. When my turn came he asked me after the disposition of my company, which I thought odd since I was not its commander. Then he spoke of the murdered women. He was, he told me, quite sure it had been some vagabond now long gone. I understood, then, that this was why he'd called me. It was to tell me to stop my prying.'

Cromwell purred. 'And yet pry you did. You hunted and sought evidence and you saw a man put to death.'

'I did. There were no other murders after my conversation with the King, not at first, and I thought perhaps he was right; but then I heard word of another woman from a village not far away. It was the same thing again. It seemed to me the work of the same brute.'

'How did you find him?'

'It wasn't so hard. On the day before I saw the King, the butcher left his company and moved to another. I suppose he made his transfer to get away from me, but such things are hardly commonplace. When he killed again, this time where his new company was billeted, he might as well have sent me a confession note. I knew I was looking for a man who carried the King's favour but I didn't care. Once I knew his name, it wasn't so hard to expose him. I saw to it that his new commander hanged him before the King heard aught about it.'

'You did this, knowingly against the wish of your King?' All this time Cromwell stood with his back to me, staring out of the window.

'I suppose that's the gist of it.'

'And was he not displeased?'

'If we may suppose a man is displeased when another acts against his wishes then we may suppose he was. He'd as good as told me not to pry but he didn't come right out and tell me to stay my hand. It's not my place to reason with King Charles nor to guess his mind.'

At last Cromwell turned towards me once more. He

crossed back from the window and stood before me. For the first time he smiled, though I saw little kindness in his eyes even so. 'Falkland, you are indeed the man I am looking for. I'll spell it out for you why you're here. I have a bald proposition. Help me and you might yet live. How does that sound?'

'It sounds like something Christopher Marlowe might have written.' I will admit to some confusion now. I'd become so beholden to the notion that I was to be questioned for some piece of intelligence I did not possess that I saw everything else as a trick. It seemed that at last we might be getting there. 'What do you want from me?'

He ignored my question. 'You refer me to Faust?'

'I refer you to his sonnets.'

Cromwell did not appreciate the jest. He took me by the arm and began leading me along the length of the room. 'The New Model,' he said, 'is wintering in a town named Crediton. In the spring will come the final push and this will all be over.' We stood at the tall, ornate windows and for the first time I could see London herself. I looked out across the broad sweep of the Thames. Snow lay piled in drifts and mounds. Not a ripple moved across the water: it was frozen from bank to bank. 'As you say, waiting can do strange things to a man, and so strange things happen to an army in the winter where all there is is the waiting. Too many men with too little to do and so men breed their own sport.'

That was how it had been in Yorkshire too, though rape and butchery were never a sport even in times of war. Of course, neither was storming a man's church and ripping up its altar, but I wasn't about to tell Cromwell that. We'd always been told he was the fiercest of all Puritans but, looking at him now, I fancied he was something more dangerous by far: an outsider looking in. He didn't believe any of it. I knew more than a little about that kind of man.

'The New Model is under the command of Sir Thomas Fairfax. Though he winters with them, you will understand that however strong one man's discipline and morality may be, he cannot be everywhere in an army's winter camp. It has come to my attention that one of the youngest soldiers strung himself from a tree while on watch in the thick of the night. Hanged himself, to be clear. A simple suicide, you might say – some boys are not made of stern enough stuff to be soldiering at all – and, yet,' and here Cromwell's eyes darkened. He took me by the arm again and turned me away from the window. I was momentarily caught off guard because the pure white snow had blinded me and now the room seemed impossibly dark. 'Several days later there was a second suicide. Then, some nights ago, a third. Each was exactly the same. Three boys strung up from the same branch of the same tree.' Again he paused. He was fond of dramatic pauses. My jest about Marlowe had not been so far from the truth. 'The first occurred three weeks ago. Who knows how many have hanged themselves by now? An astute man like you can, of course, see where this is leading me.'

'To wonder why somebody wasn't posted to watch that tree?' I ventured.

This time Cromwell's displeasure was clear. 'I am giving you a chance, Falkland. I am not asking you to beg for your life. I only ask a little decorum.'

We stared at each other for a long time. Over his shoulder I could see the white havens of London stretching out. This was once a proud city. It had had a king. It's commonfolk – and I now counted myself among them – could live their lives in the knowledge that the country had a leader, assured of a future for themselves and their children. This was a dangerous stream of thought because now it turned me to my own family. John was twelve years old when I left for the King's service. He would call himself a man now. His sister had been barely nine but six years had passed since then. Had she already had her first suitors come to call? On the day I left, my darling Caro bade me goodbye from the end of the track but neither my son nor my daughter could bear to see me go. When I tried to imagine them as they were now, I couldn't; or else they were all three changed beyond my recognition and when we rode and ate together, I was in the company of strangers and they beheld me as an interloper from another land.

Yet I thought about them every day. And now all it took was for me to look into Cromwell's eyes and suddenly I saw: to the King, I was dead. To my fellow soldiers I was taken alive and strung up. I was a martyr.

But I had been reprieved.

If what Cromwell said was true – and I had no reason to doubt him here, in this palace that was built for kings in the heart of the city from which kings have always ruled – then the war would soon be over. I'd done enough. Whatever I once believed, for whatever reasons I first took up arms – and those reasons were never my own – I'd played my part. Do this thing, whatever it was, and perhaps I could have exactly what I barely dared to imagine any more: to find my family a corner of the world somewhere that no other man could touch; to grow old with them and die.

The silence had gone on too long.

'Three men lost is one thing.' Cromwell frowned. 'There have been desertions too. My instinct is of something amiss. The New Model is young. Fragile, even, if you will. I would not see it fall apart.'

'What would you have me do?' I asked.

'What you've done before, Falkland. The New Model is nothing without discipline. See this thing finished before it starts. I require a man of conscience who stands outside the New Model and is not a part of it, to whom those whose sympathies are uncertain might turn. If suicides they are, tell me why. If something else . . . Tell me if I should be concerned.'

'I'll need provisions,' I said.

Cromwell had closed his hands. In another man I might have seen the gesture as the clutching and kneading of a rosary. 'You will be well provisioned.'

With those words I was dismissed. I turned on my heel – it was still a novelty to move so freely and I felt I might fall – and I saw that the man with the syrupy voice had reappeared in the doorway, beckoning me closer. He was shorter than I'd thought, thin and wiry with a mean, pinched face and narrow eyes that darted all about between their glares. Before I reached him Cromwell called out.

'One more thing, Falkland.'

I raised an eyebrow and waited.

'Remember who came for you in your hour of need,' he said. I thought he was being deliberately cryptic, as men who love the bluff and counter-bluff of politics often are. 'You will, no doubt, hear murmurs in the New Model, both for me and against me. But when foul words are whispered,

Falkland, remember where your loyalties lie. The King is beaten either way. The New Model will bring him more quickly to terms and end this madness. Think on that.'

Out in the corridor I had chance to pause while the man with the syrupy voice walked on. Cromwell spoke of loyalties as if he knew me. I smiled at that, the first true smile since they saved me from the scaffold. Oliver Cromwell, I had no doubt, was a man who knew a great deal about trading in loyalties. A man does not fall and rise again so spectacularly as he had done without knowing the politics of people. And yet – and here was the cause of my smile – he'd made a terrible error. You can only buy a man's loyalty when he has a loyalty to sell, and I had none. I was not the King's man. I'd promised myself that long ago, that I was not truly in the service of any man at all. Nor was I in the service of God – who, though He has always been there, has never once stooped so low as to lend me His hand.

No. What Cromwell could not know was that I was in the service of only one man. His name was William James Falkland. He had a wife and two beautiful children whose lives he was missing and somehow, come hell or high water, come roundhead or cavalier, he was going to piece his family back together.

My escort paused, waiting for me to catch up. 'Don't fret, Falkland.' He sounded weary. 'I'll be there to keep a watch over you, there and back again. Have no fear on that account.'

CHAPTER 3

M y escort who had brought me from Newgate now led me to where I was to be billeted for the night, above one of the old Inns of Court where Cromwell had once studied.

'Cromwell thinks you're something special, Falkland, but I don't. Make sure your feet still fit in your boots come the morning.' He gave me a curious look then. 'Still, it's no small thing to disobey your King. Were you not afraid?'

I answered him truthfully that no, I hadn't been, that I hadn't given it a thought. I couldn't have told him why, had he asked, only that I did what was right to be done. I might have said something about how a man who follows what he knows to be right walks without fear, thinking perhaps that any man who was a part of Cromwell's coterie might under-stand that; might understand that even kings can be wrong. Afterwards, after I was done and saw the brute swinging dead, then I'd had my doubts. But not before. 'If we're to be companions on the road, sir, might I know your name?'

He hesitated only a moment. 'Warbeck,' he said. 'Henry Warbeck, and I'm no sir or lord. We'll see, Falkland, whether or not you're afraid of Black Tom. A King's man poking around his army? He'll not like you for that, not one bit, and nor that Cromwell sent you neither.' He eyed me closely. 'A King's man might like nothing more than to spread a little discord in our New Model. It won't make a bit of difference. The King's done for.'

He spat the words out in disgust, a sentiment heightened by his rotten breath. Perhaps he meant it as provocation but if so then he sorely missed his mark. 'Good riddance to this war then,' I answered; and then: 'Cromwell and Fairfax? Do they not trust one another?' From our side it had always seemed they were as thick as thieves.

Warbeck glared. For a moment I thought he might raise his fists and after four months in the cells I wasn't sure I could best him. But he slowly mastered himself. 'I would say they do, Falkland,' he said at last. 'As much as any two great men in these times. When this is done they will rule England between them and we'll all be better for it. But the New Model is . . .' He hesitated, searching for the right word, I thought. 'It's *precious* to Cromwell.' He backed away and as he parted I was left in no doubt of my place. The key turned in the lock behind me. Out of my cell or not, I was still a prisoner.

My room was a small chamber with a single bedstead – a menial little room, but it felt a palace after that cell in Newgate. A candle stub guttered on the ledge and the window was so thick with ice that I could hardly look out, but no matter – it *had* these things. For the first time since the summer I might wake in the morning and see daylight. I stood at my window and stared as a man parched might stare at the sea. Through the frost I saw the green grass and skeletal trees of Gray's Inn. A man in long black robes marched purposefully with a small white dog trotting behind and I had a sudden surge of feeling. Prince Rupert, in whose lines I had oftentimes fought, had had a dog just the same until Cromwell and his men had butchered it on Marston Moor. The dog was called Boy and, until that day, seemed impervious to shots. The roundheads had named it a familiar, called it a kind of popery, a kind of witchcraft. I suppose they thought the tide had turned the day they cut that poor dog down.

Beside the bedstead was a simple wooden chair and, draped over it, a murrey gown, breeches and a stiff woollen shirt with a tall, broad collar. Perched on top sat a black hat with a wide brim and steepled crown. There were boots as well – not new but better than the sacking bound around my feet. I supposed I should have been grateful. When I bent down I saw on the floor a bowl of water and rags. I disrobed and slowly and gently lifted away the dirt. Four months of it, and when I was done I was beginning to feel like a man again. I glanced at my feet and decided not to look too closely in order to preserve that feeling. They were falling apart in a way a soldier should never allow and I wasn't ready to witness it yet.

I put on the shirt, the breeches, the murrey gown, the wide-brimmed hat. The rippled reflection of myself in the window glass, I decided, didn't really look like one of the King's traitors, one of Parliament's own. If I ever found them again then my own men would take me for what I was. I wondered if the same could be said for my family. I thought about them then, tried to picture them as I often had back in my cell; but now, at last, I allowed myself that luxury, that joy that I might yet see them again. I'm not ashamed that I wept. Nor that I cannot say for how long.

I had held them away from myself, as far as I could, for so long.

Caro and I were joined in July 1625. It was a swift romance and, if the story is to be told, then I must say it was Caro who did the romancing. She had, she told me later, set her eyes on me from the very first. Her father was a local lord, a man whose faith in the King was only out-matched by his faith in God, and if he was ever dismayed that his firstborn daughter fell for me, a lowly tenant farmer, he was graceful enough not to show it. He took me hunting and told me of his daughter's intent. I did not agree immedi-ately though it was always imagined that I would not refuse. The marriage contract was not only for a wife but for lands and titles. A position. When I shook the old man's hand I knew my life was changing forever.

I was a young man then and had not before considered myself the marrying type. I worked the farm and had no great desire to go beyond it. Yet Caroline Miller claimed she saw something in me that she found lacking in the nearby men of her own standing. Later she would tell me she'd seen me in church and watched me working the land. She took me for a native Cornishman but really I was an interloper, sent here by my father before he died. Caro's own father had had bigger things planned for her – alliances, he confided in me, that might see his family rising higher in political circles, something that might even bring a grandson one day to the King's court – but Caro was her father's little girl and, no matter how he protested, she knew she would get what she wanted. To this day I don't know why it was she wanted me. I'm certain it wasn't rebellion; for Caro, no matter how obstinate, was never one for frippery and nonsense. If there was an explanation other than love then I never knew it. Nor, in truth, did I want to find it out.

If I'd never seen myself being a husband then I'd surely never seen myself a father. As fate would have it we were married three years before we were blessed with our first child. By then Caro feared she was barren – and I dare say her father feared I was as impotent as Essex, that commander of Parliament we were one day bound to meet in battle – but, at last, we were given a son. We named him John after a brother Caro had lost. Three years later there came a daughter. We named her Charlotte; and if that was to be my life then I was happy.

Nor had I ever thought to find myself in London, not a whit of intent to accompany Caro's father into this seditious world of kings and parliaments. But the things you do for love are many and oftentimes unexpected. Caro earnestly desired that I stand alongside her father. So when her father came to London in service of the King, I was at his side. And when the King marshalled an army to go north in the winter of 1639 to meet the treasonous Scots, I too was part of that army. For her. For love.

In that room looking out over the frozen Thames, six years later, when the tears would not go away, I lay back on the bed and closed my eyes, willing sleep to come and rescue me for a few brief hours. How I wished I'd stayed on the farm and not become part of this wretched war.

Warbeck returned in the morning and took me to a kitchen on the other side of the Inns. England was starving but it seemed London was not. It was, though, bitterly cold and they were burning wood in the range. I noticed trees being felled in the courts and a small part of me took pleasure in that. It meant, against all their proud declarations, that Cromwell and his crowd had not returned coal to their capital. Newcastle was still with the King or else under the fist of the dreaded Scots.

Warbeck fed me a breakfast of pottage and cider and we were on our way, yet it seemed to me that our carriage took us further into the city and not away towards the West Country. My suspicion was proved well founded when we stopped and Warbeck snarled at me to get out. We were close to a wooden bridge over a small river that I thought must be the Fleet. The street ran close beside it and an inn stood nearby, though Warbeck paid it no attention. A little way further the cobbles were bridged by a stone arch whose purpose seemed obscure. Warbeck pointed and I saw his meaning. At the far end of the street stood a scaffold and gallows and the sight of them conjured a dagger of fear that struck hard and deep. Yesterday I'd come from my cell ready to die. But much had happened. I'd allowed myself to have hope again.

'Take a good long look, Falkland,' hissed Warbeck. 'Keep this sight in your mind. Stray a foot out of place and that's what awaits you.'

'It appears the same as what awaited me yesterday,' I said with a lightness I certainly didn't feel. Warbeck had made his point well.

'Two men from this very street were found to be plotting against Parliament. They were hanged from those gallows. We find use for them often enough.' I knew it must be true: the gallows were quiet now but surely saw frequent service, otherwise they would have been disassembled and the guardsmen who stood watch to keep them from being pilfered for firewood assigned to other duties. Warbeck turned a cold look on me and then slowly shifted his eyes to the street under my feet. 'Fifty years ago, recusant papists were hanged and quartered on this spot.'

If we were to be given a tour of every part of London in which murder had been dealt to those Parliament considered stood against it then I doubted we'd ever reach our destination. I felt a strong desire to change the subject away from hangings; and what interested me far more was why Cromwell would employ a royalist plucked from a Newgate cell to spy on his own ally Fairfax. Perhaps his intent was honest, but as a spy was certainly how I'd be seen. 'Have you ever met Fairfax?' I asked.

Warbeck favoured me with a thin smile. 'Get in the carriage, Falkland. We have ground to cover.'

The carriage took us out of the barren city and I had the chance to see, first hand, the excavations and fortifications we'd heard about winters before when I was billeted in Oxford with a splint upon my leg. I'll not say they were impressive things but they were better than nothing. The commonfolk had turned out to dig ditches and build tall earthen walls, and while they wouldn't keep Prince Rupert and the King out if they ever gathered a strong enough army, they would certainly hold back any that tried to pass in the face of an organised defence. In the waxing and waning of powers, the King had never come close enough to London for those earthworks to earn their keep. If Cromwell was right then they never would. All the effort of their creation would become wasted, as this war had wasted so many.

Shortly after we passed some common land where a vast

bonfire had been piled high. It frustrated me to see, because I'd spent more than my fair share of nights freezing in army camps, huddled up with my horse for warmth, and I knew that Londoners would freeze in their houses this winter. The river was already covered in ice right across and this fuel would be better used warming their homes. It was only when we came close that I understood: there was no cheap Guy Fawkes on the pyre. There was a crude effigy of the Pope.

I asked Warbeck for the date. He gave me a look that said it was none of my concern but at last he muttered, 'The fifth, Falkland. The fifth of November.'

So tonight they'd watch the Pope burn and cheer as he went up in smoke. There was once a time when the idea would have wounded me deeply, and though that time had passed many years ago, groping through a sea of blood and earth in some Yorkshire field, for some reason I still cringed from the image. I cringed too at the thought that a month from now those cheering, dancing men would be dying from the cold.

'Does it injure you, Falkland, to see what Englishmen really think of your church?'

'It's not my quarrel.'

I meant for him to understand that I was referring him to God but he must have been simpler than I thought. 'Your quarrel?' he gasped. 'Isn't that what you're fighting for?'

I gawped at him. 'You think we take the King's banner because the Queen is a Catholic or some nonsense like that? You think we fight because we wish to reunite our church with that of Rome?' Perhaps some men did, but none that I'd seen, and in truth Cromwell had the right of it – that idea had been dead and buried long before I'd been born. Most of us were fighting because there was no way out, not for King or country or God – notions of God, I had supposed, were reserved for those who fought for Parliament. Cromwell had said otherwise. For my own part, I had long lost any idea of what any of us were fighting for. In the early days, I knew, much of England had tried simply to keep out of it, hiring bands of clubmen to try and hold the armies of both sides at bay, but it hadn't done them any good. The war was a kind of collective mania and it touched us all. It's hard to explain to the true believers. I'd tried before and never found much joy, and I supposed Warbeck would be the same. 'How long will we be on the road?' I asked.

'Seven nights. Perhaps more, perhaps less. It will depend on what we find.' He reached beneath the carriage seat, produced a bundle and handed it to me. I didn't have to unwrap it to know that within it was a musket. Being a cavalryman I wasn't used to the weapon, so I made to hand it back.

'No.' He pressed the musket into my hands. 'You must carry it until we reach the camp. The roads are not safe.' He had more under his seat, I saw. Three or four at least, wrapped to keep them dry. He didn't offer me any powder. I was to bluff, then? And yet it pleased a small part of me – despite myself – to know that, even this close to London, bands of the King's men perhaps travelled the roads. I hoped we didn't find them. I'd sooner have died at the hands of an enemy than a friend.

We passed through Richmond and the long hours drew out in silence. There was no incident that day and we repaired for the night to an inn on the road near the hamlet

of Longcross. It was called the Lantern but no light shone
from within. Indeed, I hadn't known it was there until
Warbeck commanded the carriage to stop and ordered me
out. We were on a desolate stretch of highway where there
had once been farmland but now only wild grasses grew. It
had been dark for hours already and I could see a sweep
of majestic stars. The inn door was locked but Warbeck
made a special knock and, after much fumbling, we were
invited inside. A candle flickered and I could see what had
once been the inn's front room in a state of disarray. Only
a single stool remained. Apart from that the building had
been gutted. Even the floor had been torn apart, the boards
stolen to be burned to keep soldiers warm through a freezing
night. The innkeeper returned from a back room with a
bottle of something dark which he gave to Warbeck without
a word. Then he shuffled away. I watched him go.

'Don't bother yourself with him, Falkland. We keep him
well fed. That's about all he can ask for.'

'Your soldiers gutted this place,' I said.

Warbeck didn't dispute it. He handed me the bottle.
'Drink,' he insisted. 'You'll freeze.'

I supposed there was some wisdom to that and took a
long swallow from the bottle. It was strong, sweet wine and
in seconds I felt light-headed. Starvation and deprivation
do that to a man.

'Time to rest, Falkland. There'll be no carriage for us in
the morning. From here, we ride.'

In the morning there were two horses waiting in the
stable. Both were piebald and difficult to saddle but they
looked better fed than any soldier I'd seen since almost the
start of the war. From the way he took to his horse I

supposed Warbeck had been a cavalryman as well. He
whispered into its ears just the same as I would, knew when
to console and when to cajole. I wondered if we'd once
met in battle.

We rode in silence. By the afternoon the land looked
untouched by the war and I began to think that there was
something worth saving in England after all. I'd been so long
between battlefields and then in a prison cell that I'd
forgotten there was indeed a country worth fighting for.
Even though the fields were brown and the trees out of leaf,
I was reminded of the little farm on which I had imagined
Caro and myself living out our days. I knew I wasn't headed
there but, all the same, with every hour that passed I was an
hour closer. In the evening, Warbeck demanded to know
why I seemed so happy. I told him it was only the fresh
air, the sight of England that had renewed my spirits, but
that was only a part of the truth. I was thinking of my family
and it no longer hurt as it had in that Newgate cell.

Warbeck pushed us on towards Andover. The King's
armies under Hopton had been driven out of this part of
England two years back but that hadn't stopped the fighting
from swinging back and forth until the New Model had
come. I had no notion of how things stood now – back
before I was taken, Winchester and Basing House both
remained for the King, though both had been attacked
several times. Near midday we passed within a few miles of
the latter. It occurred to me then that I had no idea through
whose England we were travelling now, whether any soldiers
we might encounter would most likely be roundheads or
cavaliers or – most likely of all – deserters. Twice Warbeck
hurried us off the road when he saw soldiers. He must have

seen my face the second time, some sparking hope of escape, because he rounded on me after the soldiers were past. 'Don't get up your hopes, Falkland. Winchester surrendered a month ago. Cromwell and the New Model took Basing House by storm shortly after.' He had a look in his eye as though he'd been there himself. A fiery glee. 'After we looted the place, some fool set it alight. It burned for a day and a night and when it was done there was naught left but bare walls and chimneys. Before he left it, Cromwell's orders were to tear them down, demolish the ruin and cart away the bricks and stones. There's nothing left of your King here.'

I said nothing by reply but I saw we still kept away from the road when bands of soldiers hove into view. In truth I had little interest in running, not yet. Warbeck was already taking me towards the places I wanted to be.

With Andover in sight we spent the second night huddled in an abandoned farmhouse and pushed our horses hard through the third day to another, a bleak and lonely place on the top of a hill. We saw almost no one on those days of riding together. I thought perhaps we might be somewhere within a day of Bristol now, a city which, last I'd heard, was still held by the King after Prince Rupert had stormed it in the summer of 1643. When I asked Warbeck he merely grunted.

'Your Prince surrendered the city to Fairfax and the New Model in September, Falkland.' He watched me closely that night, perhaps imagining that I saw my old friends and allies not so far away. If I could escape and keep free of him for a day then perhaps I could be among royalists once more. I could see him thinking it.

'Would you like to bind me?' I asked him, full of disdain.
'Oh I'll catch you quick enough if you run, Falkland.'

And in truth I did lie awake a while, weighing that choice,
but in the end I found it wanting. I might slip away from
Warbeck but what then? I didn't know this land. We'd
ridden through wild and lonely hills these last few hours and
in the night with no sun to guide me I might confuse my
direction. England had become such a patchwork of loyalties,
some conquered, some divided. Yet most of all what stayed
me was the thought of success – what if I reached the King
in Oxford or some other place, what then? If the King's
armies were in retreat as Cromwell had said then I'd be
pressed into service once more. So I slept and in the morning
let Warbeck lead us on. I suppose he thought me weak or
afraid and it never crossed his mind that each step I took
at his side was a step closer to my Caro. Alone, I would
have travelled the same roads. Better to ride them with
Warbeck behind me than as a hunted man.

He pushed us hard that next day and, from what little he
would admit when I questioned him, I gathered we were
approaching Taunton, which I'd last heard was held for
Parliament but under siege. We reached another one of
Warbeck's inns where a secret knock allowed us entry. Once
again every room had been plundered, although this time I
supposed it could have been either army. I wondered why
we had not camped instead but got my answer when
Warbeck led me to the inn's pantry and pushed me inside.
'You sleep in here tonight, Falkland.' From his nervous
disposition I surmised that the siege must continue and
that he didn't trust me not to run. Can't say as I blamed him
for that.

I supposed he would simply lock me inside and leave but instead he squatted in the doorway as I sat down and regarded me with a curious expression. It was cramped in that pantry but not because the shelves were packed. There was only a single jar and even that, when I opened it, was empty. I breathed in the scent of honey and found myself taken back to my boyhood, to summer days and sunshine and flowers and the bees.

'Doesn't it fly against everything you're fighting for, Falkland?' he asked me. 'If your King can be wrong?'

I could hardly see why. 'A king is just a man like any other.' I tried to stretch out but there wasn't enough room, so instead I made myself a pillow of my boots and twisted into a shape I thought might give me a little sleep. 'A man was justly hanged for his crimes and that was all I saw of it. I gave it little thought at all.' I suppose at the time I doubted the King would even notice. Afterwards I'd had my fears for a time but I'd never suffered any consequence. 'How is it that you and Cromwell give it so much more?'

'Oh, you caused quite a stir.' Warbeck gave a sly smile and then shook his head. 'You defy him and yet you continue to fight for him. You confound me, Falkland.' Abruptly he rose. I wondered, then, if that was why the King would never let me go home after I was wounded. Perhaps there had been consequences after all, just too subtle for me to see. 'Good night, Falkland. I dare say you'd give me your word not to run if I asked for it and I dare say you'd run anyway.' He closed the door and I heard the click of the lock.

Taunton. We were close to the country I knew now. Caro had fled to Taunton for a time but she hadn't stayed there

long. Perhaps Warbeck was right. Perhaps I *would* run now if
I could, this close to home; but there was no sense thinking
about it locked in a pantry until morning and so I dozed.
Though I kept waking to the sounds of scurrying in the
walls. The rats would be as sore disappointed as I was,
because there was no food for them here. They'd have done
better out on the road. Sometimes we didn't have time to
bury our dead before beating a retreat.

CHAPTER 4

When I next opened my eyes I thought I heard the rats again. I hammered my fist at the wall for it felt as though they were ferreting away only inches from my head. Then I heard a sound that made me freeze. Seconds later it came again. Footsteps on the other side of the pantry door. Footsteps that weren't Warbeck. It was a heavy tread. That was how I knew it wasn't him – a man with a voice as musical as his walks lightly, graceful as a dancer, but this man was bigger, broader, and he was wearing heavy boots. There was another sound like the clanking of metal tassets. It was an armour I only knew pikemen to wear – but what pikemen were doing roaming this inn at night escaped me.

I had a horrible thought. Locked in this pantry I had no way of telling the hour. My body's clock told me it was still the thick of night but prison had played cruel tricks on my body's clock before. Perhaps it was morning already. Silently I crouched by the door. My legs were cramped and my feet sore but I gritted my teeth and pressed my eye to the keyhole. I had to be careful not to touch the door in case the man outside saw it shift. It was dark in the passage but somebody was carrying a lantern and strange shadows like spiderwebs danced up and down the hall. Then, suddenly, there was blackness. Moments passed and the light returned. A second man had passed by the door, blocking the lamp. Now I was certain it wasn't simply Warbeck prowling about.

And that, of course, begged the question: what exactly *had* become of Warbeck?

The footsteps stopped and I saw a flash of purple as one of the men turned around. I'd seen purple dress only once before. On the battlefield it's notoriously difficult to tell one's enemy from one's allies, especially when the fighting comes to close quarter in the thick of the mud, but in the early years we'd come against a militia with purple sashes on many occasions. Their leader, Lord Brooke, was said to be Exeter's heir – indeed, more of a man than that poor cuckold could ever be – and his purple soldiers were as well drilled a unit as any I've come up against. It was Brooke who took Kineton for Parliament, Brooke who held Lichfield Cathedral to that terrible siege. In the end we couldn't defeat him in open battle. I used to think it a coward's move, but we got him with a musket ball from a hidden hillside. It is a terrible war when you don't even have to look into the eyes of the men you kill.

Brooke's militia had been gone for two years, probably more. Perhaps some soldiers still wore the purple sash but something about it didn't seem right. Cromwell had been clear: his army was the New Model now, not a hundred different militias under a hundred different generals. Now there was only Cromwell and Fairfax, commanders of twelve thousand men. The New Model stripped men down. It took their ranks, their names, their histories and made them anew: fresh, brave, godly and pure. From what I remembered they all dressed the same: Venice red coats, in better or worse states of repair.

Suddenly I knew who had stumbled into the inn tonight. I lifted back my fist and hammered at the door – these weren't Parliament's men, they were from the King's armies, perhaps the ones that laid siege to Taunton, deserting or scattered by a skirmish. They were wearing foraged clothes, hoping to slide under Parliament's nose.

'In here!'

I heard the clanking of armour again as the men turned around, desperate to know who was shouting.

'This door!' I bellowed. 'Quickly!'

A fist grappled at the handle but quickly stopped.

'What if it's a trap?' asked a voice.

'From inside a locked cupboard?' said a second.

They wrestled with the door until I heard something snap. I recoiled. When the door flew open all I saw at first was a ball of fiery light as they pushed their lantern inside. The next was a pointed silhouette – the tip of a sabre that came perilously close to my throat.

'Name yourself!' the first voice growled.

'I'm Falkland,' I said. 'I'm the King's man!'

They lowered the lantern a few degrees, the better to get a look at me. I must have seemed pathetic, scrabbling around in the dirt. At least they didn't run me through.

'What are you doing in there? Explain yourself!'

'There's another man in the inn. He has me captive.'

'One man?'

The way his voice rose at the end of the question made me seem foolish. No true soldier fighting for the King could be taken captive by a single weaselly Puritan.

'Out of there, sir. Be quick now!'

It took me a moment to get to my feet, longer to wrestle them back into my boots. They were still sore and I grimaced as I dressed.

'This man who has you captive, where is he?' one of the men asked.

'I don't know. He said he would come for me in the morning.'

'A Parliament man?'

I nodded. 'You're from the siege of Taunton?' I asked. The way the man in front of me paused told me at once that I was wrong.

'The roundheads routed that siege months ago,' he said. 'There's no place safe for a King's man in these parts now. What garrison are you from?'

'They had me in Newgate.' As soon as I spoke, I regretted it. I was being foolish. There was too much mystery in a man released from prison and at once they took me for a trickster. The man behind me drew up his sabre while the one in front revealed a small dagger in his hand. I could have said I was fleeing from the slaughter at Basing House or the capitulation of Winchester, things I'd garnered from Warbeck on the road. But it was too late for that now.

'Sir,' I said, 'I am unarmed.' I opened my palms to prove it.

'Out,' whispered the man behind me. 'We can't stay here tonight.'

I thought a little before I moved. I'd never supposed myself to have much truck with deserters and their ilk; but I'd made my choice when I rattled that door and called for their help and so I rose, unsteady, to my feet. The men hurried away. There was a door at the end of the passage that opened onto a courtyard. We came to it in single file. There had once been a tree in the centre but it was freshly hacked down. A single bough lay across the stones; apart from that the yard was barren. The night was deathly cold, the sky clear and plastered with stars and I felt, all of a sudden, as small as an ant. I'd been in a prison cell with only stinking stones above my head for too long. A terrible thing to do to a man, make him afraid of the sky.

We kept to the south wall and crossed the courtyard, finding an archway that led to the stables. Our horses were still in the stalls so I knew that Warbeck had not gone far. I allowed myself to hope he still slept but I knew it was a foolish notion; if he'd not heard me hammering at the door, he'd surely heard them wrenching it apart.

The first man reached over the stall door to fumble with the catch.

'Your horses?' he asked.

I nodded. 'What is your name, sir?' I asked him. Years of soldiering had taught me that it becomes harder to simply murder a man once he calls you by your name.

'You ride with the Parliament man?' He looked right through me and I became aware again of the dagger in his hand.

'I told you,' I said. 'He has me captive.'

'Yet you ride with him without a guard?'

I wanted to answer but I had no words. It dawned on me that he was right, that the man I had been before they put me in that prison cell would have run Warbeck down when we passed Bristol. I was a tenant farmer once but William Falkland had become a different man in these last years. I'd been a pikeman first and then a dragoon. At the last I'd been a cavalryman who could soothe the fears of a dozen others with a single look. Surely I'd not lost all of that? Yet I'd followed Warbeck without complaint and told myself it was because he was leading me towards my home. One last thing, they had said, and you can live – but who had decided my life was theirs to make as a gift to me?

'Who are you?' I demanded.

'We were in the New Model,' the man behind me said. His hand was still on his sabre but at least he'd lowered it.

I started. 'Parliament men? But I thought—'

'Shut your mouth,' snapped the first. 'Hardly half the New Model is Parliament. The rest are men they rounded up as surely as a farmer rounds up lost sheep. We were the King's horses but we came to it outside Islip. We didn't know they were pushing that close to Oxford. It was Cromwell himself. He carved us in two and took what was left standing for himself.' He paused. His face was etched in horror at the memory and I thought this was not the first time he had relived it. 'You don't understand. He had hardly a gun in his whole force but he took us apart.'

'They forced you . . . ?'

'He said it was servitude or service. But we knew what servitude meant. It meant a rope around your neck. So we signed on. They gave us pay. They fed us. Then they put pikes in our hands. We were the King's horses and now they wanted us to form a front line against our very kin . . .'

'Your colours . . .'

'They have plenty enough coats of Venice red for their own. But they've taken so many men who once fought for the King that we take whatever we can find.'

'Did you fight?' It occurred to me that their story was not unlike my own. King's men that Cromwell had turned – or thought he had. These soldiers he bribed with money and food. For me it was the promise of growing old with my Caro.

'We marched. When we could, we ran. We're on our way back to Oxford now. We heard tell the King is wintering there.' He stopped. 'Tell me – what news of Prince Rupert?'

'I told you. They had me in Newgate. They took me outside Abingdon. I heard from a Parliament man that Prince Rupert surrendered Bristol two months back. I cannot speak for the truth of his claim.' I doubted Warbeck had lied. It seemed, from what I'd seen, that he had little reason to. Since they'd let me out of my cell I'd heard of nothing but defeat after defeat for the King's armies.

In the blackness an owl hooted. I fancied I could hear its wings beating feverishly. Something darted above. Perhaps it was bats. 'Is it over?' I begged. 'The Parliament man told me it was over.' I didn't dare tell them I'd seen Cromwell himself, spoken with him face to face. I already knew they feared me a traitor. I suppose, if such a thing might be measured, they'd be right in the assertion. I'd stopped taking sides a long time ago. Doubtless they saw their own situation differently.

'Not over,' the first man whispered. 'Not until the King is restored. But this New Model . . . Falkland, they are fifteen thousand men and more. Paid and fed and whored. *Drilled*. Not even Prince Rupert will carve them a . . .'

A sound like concentrated thunder split the air between us. I saw a flash of light from one of the inn's windows. It lasted only a moment but stayed afterwards in my eye. It was

Warbeck I'd seen up there and the flash had been the pan of a musket. 'Quickly!' I screamed.

It would take him an age to prime the musket again but I already knew that he carried three or four and I didn't dare risk the chance that he'd primed a one-man regiment for the night. We hurried through the stall door. Warbeck's horse, spooked by the shot, whinnied and refused to take the halter. I whispered to him but he didn't hear. In the neighbouring stall one of the deserters had already mounted my own horse. He pushed it quickly out and reined it in just outside the stall door.

'Hurry!' he yelled.

I looked over my shoulder. The second man had already abandoned the stall and was scrambling onto the horse behind his companion. They waited for a second before the first man kicked his heels into the horse's rump and forced it forward.

The boom of a musket fired again into the night and I knew I was right about Warbeck and his arsenal. I heard a scream and saw the second man fall from the back of my horse as they vanished into the night. The other didn't so much as pause. A moment and he was gone.

I was alone but all was not lost yet. I turned again to try and calm Warbeck's horse. Its eyes rolled at me in the silvery light. I took a slow step forward and then another. The horse had stopped panicking but it still made low, throaty sounds. At last it allowed me to lay a hand on its mane. I ran my fingers softly in its hair. I teased its ears between my forefinger and thumb. 'Come on, girl,' I said. 'You've been through worse than this. You've charged a row of pikes, I shouldn't wonder. You've . . .'

The horse froze and I knew something was wrong. Its eye, once fixed only on me, shifted and I dared to think I could see a glimmer of a reflection. Somebody was staring at me out of that eye. A man.

I turned very slowly around. In the open stall door Warbeck stared at me down the barrel of his musket, a weapon with a range of a hundred yards. Then again they misfired as often as not. He'd already had his share of luck plucking one of the deserters from the back of my horse. I fancied I should risk it. Three days ago I'd been going to die anyway. But there was no point without his horse. Silently a part of me begged him to fire, to get it over with and see which way the die would fall. Another part prayed that he would not. It felt a cowardly part there in that moment.

'Who were they?' Warbeck asked. He was only slightly breathless, his perfect composure hardly touched.

'I don't know.'

'How did you get word to them?'

There had always been a lot of paranoia about ciphers and codes but surely he wasn't superstitious enough to believe that I'd somehow delivered a message through a locked pantry door. 'They were New Model,' I said.

'New Model soldiers don't desert. They're paid. They're fed.'

Cromwell had spoken otherwise. 'They do if they're King's men. Warbeck,' I said, and here I faltered. Suddenly I was tired. I was hungry. I was cold. 'How did Cromwell do it? Turn royalists to the Parliament?'

Warbeck must have sensed I wasn't going to run and slowly lowered the musket. There was nothing between us now but the ice cold air making mist of our breath.

'Every man has his price, Falkland,' he whispered. 'For most Englishmen it's not much more than a sausage.' He reached to a loop on his belt and threw me a manacle for my ankles. Out in the gloom of night, a ghastly moaning stopped us both short. Warbeck lifted his musket again, pointing it now into the night, perhaps thinking it was some animal, but he must have come to the same answer as I did for the musket turned sharply back on me just as the thought came again that I should run. The sound was from the man he'd shot, not yet dead. That was the horror of these wars. Musket balls rarely offered a gracious end. They tore holes in flesh and bone but more often than not men lingered before they died. I'd seen plenty enough. Some screamed for hours. Others lay glassy-eyed and clammy, panting their way to the last. I'd been lucky after Newbury. Most men weren't.

'The manacles, Falkland,' said Warbeck. As I put them on I told myself I was doing this for Caro. For our future. That there would be other chances and better ones and that I owed it to my children to wait and take them as they came. And as I told myself these things I knew that Newgate had made me into a coward.

The wounded deserter lay on his back. He lay where he'd fallen and barely moved. Once I was chained, Warbeck lowered the musket and turned. I caught a flash of moonlight on steel as he drew out a dagger.

'Warbeck!'

He stopped. The moonlight caught his eye and I knew I'd been wrong about him. His voice might sound syrupy, but Warbeck was no jester. He was a cold killer. 'Falkland?'

'At least give him some words.'

'Words to a King's man and a deserter?' He shook his head and spat, turned away and then paused again as if struck by some second thought. 'God will judge each and every one of us, Falkland, when our time comes. If it troubles you to see a papist pass without his last rites then give them.'

He moved aside and I shuffled out of the stable. I moved so slowly that I feared the man would be dead before I reached him, but as I knelt he was still breathing, moaning his harsh, ragged breaths. Warbeck's ball had hit him in the back and he was lying on the wound. I couldn't see exactly where it had taken him but the steady trickle of bloody foam that issued from the corner of his mouth told me enough. There was never a coming back from a wound like this. I started to search his pockets for a cross or a rosary but all I found was a small pocket Bible. The man lifted his hand and caught a hold of me. I suppose he thought I was looting him.

'What's your name?' I asked him. He croaked something and more frothy blood ran out of his mouth. At the third attempt I thought I understood him. 'Rowland?'

He blinked. Perhaps he nodded a little. Something in his face said yes.

'Do you have a cross, Rowland? A rosary? Something you need?' I'd hoped he might show me but he shook his head and pulled me closer.

'No . . . popery,' he said and reached for the Bible. As I handed it to him he opened it and the moon caught the words across the front. *The Soldier's Pocket Bible*. His quivering fingers turned to the last page and then back and he returned it and pulled me close again. 'I was with . . . Northampton's . . . Regiment of . . . horse at . . . Naseby,' he said, forcing out each part of every word with an effort. 'Read to me.' He stabbed at the book with a bloody finger. I looked at the page to which he pointed.

'"The Lord is a man of war",' I read. '"Jehovah is his name. Thy right hand, O Lord, is become glorious in its power: thy right hand, O Lord, hath dashed in pieces the enemy. And in the greatness of thine excellency thou has overthrown them that rose up against . . ."' I stopped. The soldier had fallen quiet. He wasn't yet gone but somehow his breathing was eased. But I couldn't go on. I had a terrible sense of myself lying in his place, my Caro standing distant over me, black in mourning, her brilliant grey eyes hidden behind a veil of lace. And beside her my son and daughter, John and Charlotte, John all dressed up in a Venice red coat with a pike in his hand, Charlotte weeping into her arm, her long black curls quivering in a harsh, cold wind. I shivered; and then I felt Warbeck behind me.

'Enough, Falkland,' he said. 'Leave him with me.' His voice was oddly gentle as he drew me away and took the Bible from between my fingers. He returned to the dying man and crouched beside him, pulling back the man's collar. Now Warbeck, too, read: '"Seeing that thou, our God, has punished us less than our iniquities deserve, and hast given us such deliverance as this, should we again break thy commandments."' He paused and put the Bible aside. The knife flashed once in the darkness, opening the dying soldier's throat. He read on. '"I will walk before the Lord in the land of the living. I have sworn and I will perform it, that I will keep thy righteous judgements."'

He leaned forward and ran a hand over the dead man's face, closing his eyes. It was a mercy, that killing.

CHAPTER 5

I came to Devon on the back of a pack mule we found wandering in a farmer's razed field. For the first hours of the day I rode with my wrists bound behind Warbeck, but he kept sneaking looks over his shoulder as if he thought I might try to throttle him. I'll admit the thought crossed my mind more than once. The pack mule had been doing well for himself, finding clean shoots among the black stalks, but he wasn't difficult to capture. I supposed he'd been part of a baggage train attacked and scattered. If so, he was fortunate to get away. I'd eaten my own share of horsemeat in the winters I'd spent in camps, and even a scrawny pack mule like this would have been a delight to a company of ravaged soldiers.

The snows had started to fall in earnest. We seemed to be travelling with the clouds following behind – Warbeck fancied London was entrenched in white now, that the Thames might never thaw again – and as we came into Devon they caught up. By midday the sky was thick with it and for much of the afternoon we were obliged to seek shelter and wait out the worst. I could see how this infuriated Warbeck. By evening the land was so white that it seemed almost day. The hills took on the ghostly glow of winter and we rode on until we came to a small hamlet. Here Warbeck found us quarters with an old spinster who, ignoring the prying eyes of her neighbours, found us more food than we'd seen in the whole of our journey so far and beds more comfortable than I'd had since Oxford. In return we listened to the story of her life – for Warbeck a torture but for me a sweet salve. I was glad to know people still wanted to go on living, even if these truly were the end times.

The hamlet sat on the banks of the River Exe, somewhere downstream of Tiverton, a town whose name I knew. In the morning we followed the water down. There were fish in the river and we boiled soup. It's remarkable how good food can restore one's vitals, a lesson every soldier learns but one that still feels like a revelation every time. By the evening Warbeck had changed our course, following a second river, this time against its flow and to my mind very much back the way we'd come. I began to wonder if he was lost, if the snow had confused his bearings. It was a greedy thought and from it grew others – that there might yet be another chance to escape. I was, perhaps for the first time since my imprisonment, daring to think that I was *strong* again. I wondered how long the feeling would last.

The river wound through two steep hills. I might have been in Yorkshire; and now and then, when a rise or a valley struck me as oddly familiar, the terror of those old battles forced itself upon me as surely as a bloodthirsty soldier upon a captured whore. The hills were thick with hawthorn and gorse. The snow had settled deeply on top of the branches, making winter crowns. There might have been men hiding in any one of a thousand different holes. I said nothing but

Warbeck was sensing it too. He kept throwing looks into the forest.

'We should have made camp by now,' I said.

Warbeck nodded. 'We're almost there.'

Where the river twisted it was starting to freeze. By morning, I thought, it would be a ribbon of ice winding to the sea. We rounded another bend and I saw lights for the first time. We were closer to Crediton than I'd thought and it was, in my opinion, a foolish place to winter an army where roving bands could get so near without being seen. As we drew towards it, I saw that fires had been built along a low ridge. Below them, a hundred other lights pierced the darkness. It might have been a fancy but I thought I could hear the sound of men cheering. Warbeck drew his horse to a stand and jumped down, sinking to his shins in the snow. As my own pack mule teetered to a stop, Warbeck approached with surprising caution, considering how tightly I was bound. I managed a smirk.

'You have to ride in a free man, Falkland. If there's a rumour among the common soldiery of what you truly are then you might not come out of here very well. I shan't weep, but Cromwell has a purpose for you and would not be best pleased.'

'I thought half the New Model were royalists you've turned,' I said.

Warbeck didn't answer. He took hold of my hands and teased at the knot. His fingers were numb in the cold and it seemed to take forever to untie me. 'Are you ready?'

I looked over his head at the fires. Now that my eyes were accustomed to the land, I saw the spire of a church and the outline of rooftops standing underneath it. 'I'm ready.'

'Then get off the mule.'

I threw him a curious look.

'You can't ride in there looking like that,' he scoffed. Then, with a certain hint of disdain in his voice, 'Take the horse, Falkland. I'll be right behind.'

The camp began long before we reached the outskirts of Crediton itself. There were tents as I had seen in countless other winter billets – but there were wooden huts as well, things hastily erected and then extended out with annexes of timber and cloth. Snow grew in tall banks around the constructions and it looked as if some were miniature palaces of ice. And the size of it! This was more than a camp. This, I knew long before we reached the border fires, was much more than an army.

A single man was keeping watch over the fires but apart from him I saw nobody. We came through the border like ghostly horsemen. No one noticed us or cried out. No one saw us, yet still I had the terrible feeling we were being watched. It had been with me since we came out of the valley and now it got worse. Sounds came from among the huts and tents, snores here and there, a rattle of laughter, the muffled talk of soldiers that's much the same everywhere and with every army. Except here there *was* a difference. Now and then, though the snow muted everything, I thought I picked out a strident voice reading what could have been a passage from the Bible. There was something missing. Singing. No one was singing.

Abruptly, close enough to startle Warbeck's horse, a door slammed from one of the huts and a man came stumbling out, hurriedly pulling down his breeches and muttering at the cold. He was so intent on the urgency of relieving himself that he didn't see us right away, though we were no more than a dozen paces short. When he did, I've never seen a man's face change so utterly. He stared at us, bewildered at first to see two men riding in in the dark; and then a moment later his jaw dropped and his eyes bulged and his demeanour changed to an expression of an abject fear more profound than any I ever saw, even in the condemned of Newgate. He turned and opened the door and flung himself inside, tugging at his breeches as he did. As we passed I heard him speak in an anguished cry: *He's here*. We passed the hut and I looked back and saw the door ajar once more and pairs of eyes peering through the opening, though they withdrew quickly enough when I met them. The door slammed shut again but they knew I'd seen them.

'What was that about?' I asked Warbeck but he seemed as bemused as I. One thing had been clear to me, though. When that man's face had turned to fear, he'd been looking directly at me. He'd barely noticed Warbeck at all. I wondered if we'd once faced each other in battle. Had I ever been face to face with my enemies and warranted such terror? I found I could not see how. If I'd ever made such an impression on a man, would I not remember? And even if I had, what unlikely twist of fate would cause our paths to cross again in such a way?

Warbeck signalled me to a cluster of huts hunched around what might once have been a farm worker's cottage. I nudged the horse as he directed. Paths had been cleared through the drifting snow but more kept falling and the horse moved slowly. We stopped some distance away and dismounted. The doors of the farmhouse were open and the

light of oil lanterns spilled out. Warbeck led his pack mule
on and saw a young boy appear from a neighbouring tent; he
beckoned and the lad came to take the horses away. He
couldn't have been more than eleven or twelve years old.

'Boy!' Warbeck called after him. 'Where will we find
Black Tom?'

The lad was hesitant.

'Black Tom?'

The boy paused a moment more and then tipped his chin
at the open farmhouse and hurried away. Warbeck smiled
grimly. 'Well, Falkland, here we are. You ask about him
often enough. Now you get to meet him. Good luck.' He
laughed and led the way into a welcome haze of warm,
smoky air and a hubbub of men and talk that stopped
dead as we entered. Officers – men in red coats with hair
cropped close – stared at us. I met their gaze one by one as I
looked about. The farmhouse had been gutted, most of it
opened out into a single room with a great fire smoking in
a hearth. At the head was a single chair and in the centre a
table that, I hazarded to guess, would be fed to the fire
before long. It wasn't hard to deduce which one of them
must be Fairfax. He was younger than I'd imagined, younger
than me by five or ten years. He had hair of jet black and a
swarthy complexion. A scar, not old but not fresh, crossed
his right cheek. It was certainly a new world that would put
this sort of man in charge of an army. I didn't know what I
thought of that. I supposed it must have seemed a delicious
insult to put a man like Black Tom at the head of the New
Model.

'Warbeck,' he said, though his eyes had settled to meet
my own. 'This is him, is it?' Fairfax had the strongest

Yorkshire brogue I could remember. The sort of voice that still strikes ridiculous terror in me, even though it's as dull and simple as most Yorkshiremen are. He didn't wait for an answer but nodded to himself, then turned to his officers and shooed them out with expansive waves of his arms. They filed out past us, one by one, looking us over, most with expressions utterly devoid of interest, a few with a sneer or a shake of the head. That much I'd expected. What I did not expect were the ones who hurried past nervous and too afraid to meet my eye. One flinched away when I moved, and I was left to wonder what struck them so, like the man from the hut who had seemed to know me. I was no officer with some great string of victories to my name, nor the perpetrator of any great mercy or atrocity. Who was I, I wondered, to be so feared?

Apart from Warbeck still sloping around the edges of the room, we were alone. Fairfax moved slowly to the chair and sat, fingers steepled beneath his chin as he regarded me. His look was shrewd and calculating. 'So you're the intelligencer. What did Cromwell tell you?' he asked.

A serving boy appeared with cider and rabbit meat. He placed it on the table and then disappeared. Fairfax nodded to it, indicating that Warbeck and I should eat, though there were no other chairs on which to sit. Warbeck seemed troubled by this but six years of soldiering had taught me to take food when food was to be had. I might have sat on the table itself in other company. As it was I stood, and as I ate and drank I told this Fairfax all that Cromwell had said. I left nothing out. I knew he was testing me.

'It isn't uncommon that an army would have deaths in winter, Master Falkland,' mused Fairfax when I was done.

Master was certainly his way of speaking down to me. To him I was royalist filth. 'In an army of this size I wouldn't care if we lost three hundred men. Soldiers quarrel and fight. They whore with the wrong girl and catch a disease. Accidents occur. And I'll be honest, Falkland. We haven't the food to last out the winter without forage and plunder.'

'Yet here I am.' I'd had the same thoughts, yet somehow Cromwell thought his entire army under threat. There had to be something then, didn't there? And this Fairfax, something about him needled me. 'There was a manner about these deaths,' I said.

'A ritual to it,' said Fairfax. 'That's fair to say. How is it they were drawn to Cromwell's eye?'

I opened my mouth to reply that I didn't know, then saw that no answer was expected. The question was for Warbeck, not for me, and it wasn't a question at all but a rebuke. 'There must be rumours,' I said.

Fairfax snorted, 'Master Falkland, an army without rumours? That's like a dancing girl without the itch.'

'All the same,' I said again, 'here I am. I'm told there have been desertions.'

He nodded. It was a curt nod that said: Cromwell sent you; I did not *ask*. 'Aren't there always? They're nothing Cromwell needs concern himself with. Men who haven't the stomach to fight in my army have no place here.'

I thought of the two men who had rescued me from the pantry. They'd deserted from the New Model. Had they come from here? They'd been seasoned soldiers, not scared raw recruits yet to be bloodied.

All of a sudden Black Tom grinned. I wasn't expecting it and it made a curious picture with the big sabre scar on his face. 'We'll look after you, Master Falkland. We'll provision you and put a roof over you. More than you've been used to. Do as you are required to do. You'll see soon enough that all's well.'

It sounded the same as prison to me. I hoped the food was better.

'There is even entertainment, if it's entertainment you're after.'

'Entertainment?'

'These boys can't be drilled all winter long, Master Falkland. They'll have tournaments. Duels. Contests. Anything to while away the hours.' There was a change in him now. His arms were open and the smile had turned into a beam that took over his entire face. It was like a strange mockery of an innkeeper working his hardest to win trade, and I wasn't sure of the jest. 'Come with me, Master Falkland. I'll see you and Warbeck to your quarters.'

Black Tom pulled the fastenings tight on his leather jerkin and swept past me towards the open door. 'If it's all the same to you, sir, I'd rather see the camp,' I said.

'The camp? Tonight?' In the corner of my eye I saw Warbeck give an imperceptible shake of the head. But I'd been told what to do by that sickly sweet impostor for long enough. The sooner I got out of here the better. I meant to be done with this and return to my Caro. Cromwell was concerned as to the well-being of his army, was he? I wasn't sure why I should care, nor why he thought that I might.

'With respect, sir, I didn't come here for entertainment,' I said. 'I didn't come here for tournaments or contests. I came here because I have a task. As soon as it's done I can be gone.'

Fairfax studied me for a second too long, enough to make me think I'd spoken too forcefully. 'Master Falkland,' he said with a sudden weariness. 'It is dark. It's snowing.'

I looked behind me through the door. 'The snow has stopped, sir.' And yes, it was dark, but the clouds had parted and there was a moon to light our way.

'We can see the camp as we pass through it, Master Falkland. I'll send you a guide in the morning.' He spoke with a finality that would brook no argument. Warbeck gave me a sour look. Fairfax, meanwhile, opened his arms and I was bustled out to wait in the cold while a boy was sent for our mounts. When they were brought I rode on Warbeck's horse, though truth be known I preferred the pack animal; I'd grown accustomed to its disaffected wheeze.

We rode through the makeshift town that had grown up around Crediton and I realised how fortunate we'd been coming at it the way we had, which was as close to Fairfax's farm as could be; or else it wasn't luck at all but Warbeck had known the camp and chosen his approach deliberately. We came down a broad track and crossed a stone bridge over a freezing brook. In the fields on the other side, horses had been corralled. I hadn't expected the cavalry would be wintering here as well. Cromwell was the New Model's cavalry man and I had supposed they had all cantered back to London with him. Some of the animals looked better fed than the men we passed. It wouldn't last long though. A few would be stewed before Christmas, I was sure.

Past the field we came back among tents and shelters. The closer we got to the stone cottages the more complete the camp seemed. Some of the new buildings were made of stone. Some were even thatched. It was a simple kind of thatching, without any art, but now that snow was piled high on top it was as good a roof as any. Outside one of the older cottages a soldier stood watch, shuffling from one foot to the other and blowing on his hands, trying to keep warm through this bitter night.

Crediton itself wasn't as small as I'd reckoned. We approached from the south and part of the town was obscured by a great wall with posts like the turrets of a castle. Cauldrons of fire were stoked along the ramparts. Sometimes I could see the black outline of a man as he passed, walking his watch. Through a gap in the wall I saw the church. It dominated the town. I thought it an old church but I didn't know if it was always with the King or against, or had changed hands back and forth as so many places had done. We passed through the gap and rode among the stone cottages. There were men walking the street here and there, a few busy about some errand or other, others in pairs with pikes over their shoulders, marking out their watches. Some passed in groups but I saw no drunken revellers. Most men simply moved aside to let us pass. Several recognised Fairfax and doffed their hats. I saw two whose eyes glanced nervously back and forth between us and lingered more on me than on their general; as we passed they ran quickly away. Less than a minute later a young soldier – so young he was scarcely more than a boy – came running past on some errand and stopped as he saw us. He looked at me long and hard and smiled as if deeply satisfied. When he ran on I could swear it was with a spring in his step.

We came presently into the shadow of the church. Deep drifts of snow grew up against it and the gravestones of the churchyard were topped with thick white hats. As we passed

I saw a glimpse of movement in a narrow alley almost black with shadow. I turned to look and saw two men stare back at me from beside the graveyard. The moonlight revealed their faces, aghast, before they turned and ran as though I was the devil.

'Stop!' I drew my horse to a halt. One of the men, I was sure, had dropped something. As I dismounted, Warbeck glared at me with impatient disbelief. Fairfax merely frowned. I handed my reins to Warbeck as though he was my servant – I'll admit to taking some pleasure in that – and walked into the alley. It was impenetrably dark and I immediately gave up any thought of pursuing these men. Why, though, had they been so afraid?

Perhaps the answer was in what I found, dropped in the snow. By fortune I had my back to Warbeck and Fairfax when I took it. It was a Catholic's rosary. The New Model not only had the King's men in its ranks, it harboured papists too. I wondered if Fairfax knew. I supposed he must. Perhaps these men had heard that some inquisitor from Cromwell was coming, then – had that been the root of their fear? If so then I would be quite a disappointment, for I'd long since lost any care as to how any man might worship his God.

I pocketed the rosary and determined to say nothing.

CHAPTER 6

A little way past the church we reached the town square. There were more tents here, formed in rings around a pyramid of steps where a market cross used to sit. I'd seen the same thing in my journeys before Newgate. Even a market cross was considered an icon by the most ardent of the Puritans. Wherever they roamed, whether with the New Model or one of the militias before it, they tore them down and smashed them up, revelling in the anguished looks of the people who watched. It had been a long time since I cared for gods and devils and heavens and hells. For me, a cross was just a cross, nothing more, nothing less, but I could never look at young men tearing up objects somebody else thought sacred and think it godly work.

Some of the tents we passed spilled light. There were soldiers inside, lounging or playing the games of stones I used to play. Most were young men. Many would never grow old and I felt a surge of pity for them. I'd shed my youth by the time I first started soldiering and age had better prepared me for its horrors. When they saw us trot past, some came out to watch. A few saw Fairfax and cheered but yet again I saw eyes fixed upon me with strangely mixed expressions: of awe and wonder and now and then of fear.

'It is him?' I heard one of them ask.

'Who do they think I am?' I asked Fairfax. 'What have you told them?'

'Nothing at all. You're an intelligencer. One does not shout the arrival of an intelligencer. Though one can't account for rumour . . .' He seemed less perplexed than vexed. I fancied he knew the answer to my question but rather wished he didn't.

We came around the square and into an older part of town. There was a high street, broad and cobbled, and up and down it lights in the houses. I wondered how many were the folk of Crediton and how many houses had been requisitioned for soldiers. I'd not heard it was a Cromwell tactic to drive people from their homes, but I didn't know about Fairfax and I shuddered to guess. One thing was certain – there would barely be a house in Crediton that wasn't bunking soldiers from floor to ceiling, whether the locals had stayed or not.

At the far end of this street loomed a tall horse chestnut, branches heavy with snow. Underneath was a scaffold. As we closed upon it I saw the shadow of a hanged man dangling from the biggest bough. He looked a wretched sight and I fancied he had been up there for weeks. Half of him was frozen and the birds would have difficulty taking what was left until he thawed, but the other half of him was gone. He had no eyes, and not even his mother would tell who he was.

We slowed as we came around the dead man and I gave him a wider berth than Fairfax, who seemed not even to notice. My fellows used to say it was a curious thing about me, that I'd killed so many men and still cringed from a dead body. In my own mind, the strange part was the killing, not the other.

Fairfax had trotted ahead of me. When he realised we were apart he slowed and looked round. 'Is this it?' I asked. 'One of the boys?' I could see my words as fog in front of my mouth.

'In the middle of town, Master Falkland? I'd reckoned on you being cleverer than that.'

'Then what?'

'You'd be better asking Master Cromwell.' He brought his horse back to mine. Together we peered up at the dangling man. 'He was a pikeman. He ravished the daughter of one of the merchants here soon after we came in for the winter. What you see is the result . . .'

'Cromwell did this?' I asked, a little too brusquely.

'Discipline is important in any army, Master Falkland. I dare say you know that. How does a soldier make his living?'

I cocked my head at him. 'In your New Model he's paid, is he not?'

'So he is; but in any other army he makes his living from the aftermath of battle, from loot and plunder. I've always been of the mind that even in the New Model a little plunder must be overlooked, but Cromwell has other ideas, as is his wont. He makes examples of men.' He tipped his chin up at the cadaver. The snow lit him from beneath and I could see the scar across his face picked out starkly. 'You look faint, Master Falkland. Are you squeamish?'

He'd mistaken my expression in the moonlight. It was the first time I'd understood what Cromwell's New Model could mean. It could mean an end to what came after a battle was done, an end to the sacking of towns and the ravishing of villages. I'd found myself struck by an unexpected moment of admiration, that was all. It bewildered me to think it, but maybe this New Model was worth saving after all. 'Not squeamish, sir,' I said. 'I would have hanged the man myself.'

'Were he one of your soldiers?'

'You mistake me, sir. I've never commanded men, only been commanded by them.'

Fairfax trotted on. 'Yet I have heard, just as we've *all* heard, what you did in Yorkshire.'

I hadn't wanted him to bring it up. I hadn't wanted Cromwell to do so either, but Yorkshire was Black Tom's home. I didn't think we'd clashed on the battlefields up there but the very idea was enough to bring terrible pictures flickering across the backs of my eyes. I could see myself in a ditch, grasping a dead man's dagger. I could see myself drawing a friend over my head to hide my body from advancing dragoons, his entrails slipping out to make a bloody curtain.

'Come now, Falkland, don't be coy. A man doesn't like to be teased! What was it like to stand up to your King like that?'

I dug my heels into my horse and spurred him on. 'Tell me yourself,' I said. 'You've stood up to *yours* for long enough.' I wondered if that might anger him but Fairfax only laughed, loud and long.

We reached the end of the street and there, beyond an inn where no lights were lit, he reined his horse in and bade me stop. When he climbed down, so did I. He marched across the snow and hammered twice at a door. Warbeck followed, silent and simmering. I heard footsteps from within the house and then the door drew back. The woman who stood in the threshold was young and comely. She had black hair cropped as short as a soldier's and sparkling eyes that made her face come alive. She was dressed in a threadbare woollen cloak and, though the winter evening wind wailed, she didn't meekly peep around the door but stood tall and brazen and looked Fairfax up and down.

'I have guests for you, Miss Cain,' said Fairfax.

As he spoke she looked past him. She spied me and Warbeck and her face turned ashen. It was the expression I'd seen on the man who'd just come out of his hut as we entered the camp. Dread, as if I was the devil. She looked back into the house and barked something. Then turned back. 'I've too many already,' she said. Her accent told me she was not a native of Crediton and I wondered if she was a follower. Every army I had marched with had its followers: whores, merchants, hunters and thieves making a living out of the soldiers. They could usually be found at an encampment separate from the rest but, I supposed, the rules of warfare had been changed to create the New Model, so perhaps other things had changed as well.

'You have more than enough room after your family's desertion,' Fairfax began, 'and your other guests can now be gone. This man is here at Master Cromwell's bidding to look into the matter of the suicide tree. I beg you look after him.' He nodded at Warbeck. 'Warbeck here will see to emptying your house for you.'

Miss Cain blinked in surprise and looked me up and down anew. She was afraid but she was hiding it better now. I opened my hands and tried to show her I meant her no harm. 'An intelligencer?' she asked. I was fairly certain it was a London accent.

'Of that ilk.' I peered back at her. Her fear had changed on hearing that. Now I was little more than a nuisance, whereas before . . . before she had taken me for something else.

Fairfax stepped aside. He returned to his horse and looked down at me.

'Falkland, Warbeck, Miss Cain will see your horse and mule stabled at the livery at the inn. There are none of the Model's horses there so they'll be quite safe. In the morning I'll send a man to show you to the . . .' Here he paused. '. . . the place those boys chose for their end. Master Falkland, Warbeck, I bid you goodnight.'

With that he was gone.

The snow started to fall again, big flakes that would smother the camp in another foot of white. Miss Cain only looked at me, frowning. Eventually she stepped back and indicated stiffly that I should enter. I waited in the hallway while she took care of my horse. Warbeck moved on into the house. I heard him rousing men from their cots, poking and kicking at them to gather their things and get out. I wondered where they would go with the sun already set and snow falling from the sky, but Warbeck seemed unconcerned. By the time Miss Cain returned from the stables the other men were mostly gone. The last two had taken it upon themselves to protest at such a sudden eviction. It was a small pleasure listening to Warbeck snarl.

Miss Cain's teeth were chattering when she came inside. I made my apologies but she appeared disinclined to listen, bustling me brusquely out of the hallway and into her front room, where there was a table and chair as well as a cot. There was a hearth but no fire was burning tonight: nor, I guessed, had one burned in the past several months, for it was warmer inside than out but not by much. I could see the litter on the floor where other soldiers had bunked here in recent days. Miss Cain returned shortly with mulled wine spiced with cinnamon and the room suddenly and unexpectedly smelled of the childhood Christmases I'd always cherished. I felt my spirits lift. It didn't matter a bit to me that I was in the heart of a camp that would have eradicated Christmas forever. I would take my pleasures where and when I could.

'I'm sorry, Mr Falkland,' she began. 'I do not mean to appear rude.'

'And I do not mean to intrude, Miss Cain.'

'Nor do you. At least, no more than we have already been intruded upon by your army.' She looked around her. 'I suppose you and your man are a blessing. At least there's only two of you.'

'Miss Cain, you mistake me. This is not my army. I am . . . I am not a soldier.'

This she scoffed at. 'Intelligence is just another sort of soldiering. My father taught me you could wage war with ideas every bit as well as you could wage war with cannons.'

'Your father taught you well,' I said. 'This is a war of ideas as much as it's a war of armies. But I'm not with the New Model, Miss Cain. I'm not here of my own accord.'

Once she understood this she seemed to soften. She took a sip of her drink. 'A prisoner?'

'Until recently. But I imagine no more a prisoner than you.'

'And your man?' Warbeck was still shouting at the two soldiers in the upstairs room.

'Is not my man,' I told her, although I thought she'd already guessed. She didn't reply but rather shuffled her feet and left to get more wine. While she was gone I paced the edge of the room. There was little to look at but I had the feeling that this was a family home, that Miss Cain was not one of the camp followers I'd taken her to be. I recalled what Fairfax had said – that her family were deserters – but I couldn't fathom what it meant, if this truly *was* her home.

From the top of the stairs came a scuffle. A moment after it ended I watched Warbeck march the last two pikemen out of the house at sabre-point. They left but not without a deal of oaths and cursing. Miss Cain looked weary. 'I can't offer much,' she said. 'But I can offer you some hospitality. Black Tom has all his favourites here when they come. A place they can have a proper bed and not some tent in the fields.'

'Yes,' I said, 'Crediton has become like a city of tents for the winter.'

'I never liked the city.'

'I'd thought to see some more of it tonight, Miss Cain, to begin my work. I'm eager to have it finished and be gone.'

Beside me Warbeck sighed and rolled his eyes but Miss Cain chose to ignore him. 'Is it . . .' She handed me more wine but I didn't drink. It was already touching me and I didn't want to sleep, not yet. 'Is it those boys, Mr Falkland?'

It surprised me that she knew about them. I judged the New Model to be ten thousand strong, perhaps more, and though rumours spread through bored soldiers like the pox, as Fairfax had put it, it didn't seem to me that the loss of a few men should stir such stories. I asked her what she'd heard.

'Only that . . .' She gulped at her wine. 'They were sweet boys, Mr Falkland. Young boys. I had a brother their age. It's not right that boys like them should be fighting. They do not choose it, do they, Mr Falkland?'

I certainly had not. I shook my head.

'Would you see where they were hanged?' she ventured.

'I'd wanted to see it from the start but *Black Tom*,' I said with an emphasis that took her into my confidence, 'would have me wait until the morning.' I could feel Warbeck's glare on my back. I'd learned the sense of it these last few days. 'Still, I suppose it doesn't matter. It's already been several weeks.'

Miss Cain furrowed her eyes and took the cup away from her lips. In the gloom her green eyes glimmered.

'Mr Falkland,' she said, 'it has indeed been several weeks since the first boy was discovered. But you're mistaken! A fourth boy died at that tree only three nights ago.'

I was still. 'A fourth?'

She nodded, trying to suppress a shiver.

'I was on the road,' I said. 'The same as the last?'

Here she took a deep breath and straightened her cloak. 'Oh no, Mr Falkland. Not the same at all. This boy . . . This boy blew himself to pieces with a granadoe.'

CHAPTER 7

W hen I was a soldier I was, for a time, a dragoon. Some of the men I rode with thought we were better than the King's pikemen, better even than his horse, because we were the men sent out as sharp and swiftly as a crossbow bolt between the eyes. If we got word of some threat, or if we needed to launch an attack lightning fast, we'd saddle up and gallop out, dismounting to take up positions with muskets and sabres. Myself, I was never of the opinion that we were better than the rest. To me, we dragoons were simply jacks of all trades and masters of none. I would rather have held a pike, vicious, unwieldy weapons that they are. At least there is honesty in a pike.

It didn't suit me well to be back in an army camp. I had, I supposed, grown used to my prison cell. More than that, I'd grown used to the idea that I was never going to see the light of day again. If Cromwell hadn't come for me then I would have been on the gallows by now and all of this would have been over. Even in the comfort of Miss Cain's home, a part of me wished it had gone the other way. As we went out, leaving the fractious Warbeck behind us, as I breathed in the smells – for there were horrible smells clinging like fog, even around the snowy streets of Crediton – I could remember exactly how it had been, my first winter in Yorkshire waiting for the wild Scots to appear across the moors. I did not much like the fear it struck in me, for as Miss Cain and I went into the night, I felt as small as a child crying in his cot to be cuddled by his mother. I'm ashamed to say that I'd cried that way once, a thirty-nine-year-old man with his mother already twenty years in the grave.

The snow had stopped again and the sky was partly clear, the air as sharp as cut glass. There must have been a bell tower in the church because I heard it ring for a change of watch. Ten bells. Later than I'd thought. As a soldier I'd hated the midnight watch. I was never a superstitious man – not even when I still believed in God – but it was during this watch that people believed foul creatures were abroad, the witching hour when diabolical things might happen. I wondered if it had been the midnight watch when those boys took their lives.

Miss Cain and I came on foot past the hanged man and across the northern end of Crediton. Where the streets petered out, another city of tents and wooden shelters rose up. Two watchmen sat on upturned buckets, huddled and rubbing their hands around a small fire. They barely glanced at us as we passed and made no attempt to offer a challenge. I wondered if they knew Miss Cain by sight; although wrapped as we were with our cloaks pulled tight around us I wondered how they might know us at all.

Main Street broadened and then disappeared. The snow at this end of the town was thicker and I felt the bite of the wind. We walked along trails that the soldiers themselves had carved and rolled. It was a thing of monstrous industry, this New Model Army. The bands I'd fought in were of a hundred men, but here the companies must have been a thousand strong and more. The New Model, it seemed, was less an army than it was a city that could move. Even under the blankets of snow I could see the way the tents had been erected as if according to a map of streets. Fires were built at exact intervals between them. A thin trail led to the latrines. Here and there men paced up and down, warding off the chill as they kept watch.

A thought occurred to me. I remembered the man hanging from the chestnut tree. 'Miss Cain, how many women are left in Crediton?'

Her eyes flashed in the darkness. 'You mean whores.'

'No, I do not.'

Miss Cain trudged on through the snow in silence. The further we went the less ordered the camp became, as if even the strict whips of Cromwell and Fairfax could only reach so far. The tents were no longer laid out according to a pattern but grew up haphazardly, a little like weeds sneaking in to take over a perfectly laid bed of flowers. They were sparser too and I fancied that some of the soldiers had struck out here to be as far from the drills and discipline of their commanders as they could. In one field I saw, quite distinct from the rest, a circle of tents standing in the shelter of a ruined barn. An enormous fire had been stoked underneath the stone and still burned bright even in spite of the snow. Although here and there men paced back and forth casting an illusion of watchfulness, we were not challenged once nor, I dare say, even noticed. I wondered what Fairfax would say to that if he knew; but then, what threat could there be to such a vast encampment as this? If I was to believe Warbeck then the King's men were done for in this part of

England, reduced to a few roving bands and skeletal garrisons that would doubtless melt away at the first whisper of the New Model on the march.

'As soon as we knew they were coming, a lot of us left,' said Miss Cain at last. 'If you had relations in Exeter, that's where you went. My neighbours went to a farm in Dorset, though it was a perilous journey. I heard some tried to get to London.'

'Straight into Parliament's hands?'

'The people here don't care for Parliaments or Kings, Mr Falkland. They just want to see the spring.'

'Yet, Miss Cain, *you* stayed.'

'Would that we had not. I begged and I begged but my father was a stubborn fool. He wouldn't leave the town he's known all his life. Until . . .'

She fell silent and stopped. I told her she didn't have to go on but she shook her head.

'No,' she said. 'I'd have you hear it, what monsters you're bound to. When the army moved in, they took every spare room they could find. If they didn't drive people straight from their homes, it was only to displace them by fouler means. When my father and brother would not give up their own shelter for housing soldiers, they had a cruel trick. They pressed them into serving for the New Model and gave them such a lowly rank that they would have to sleep wild in the fields, worse than cattle.'

I remembered how slyly Fairfax had spoken to her. 'That was why they *deserted*.'

'Yes,' she said. Her voice trembled not with fear or cold but with an anger hungry for revenge. 'But never has the word been used with less just cause.'

We reached the very edge of the encampment where the frozen river ran. All around us was stark white and black with nothing in between. All the same, I knew there would be men out there, keeping watch along every trail and track leading from the town. I looked around and tried to see the lie of the land, looking for the points I'd have chosen if this monster was my own to command. I could hardly see a hillside, only the endless rolling white.

Some way out from the centre of Crediton, an acre from the bank of the river, stood an old oak like a giant taloned hand clawing out of the white earth. Its branches were topped with a crown of ice but against the white hills it stood out like a burn. On one side there was an entangled mess of branches large and small. On the other, only a single bough protruded, nearly as thick as the trunk itself. Miss Cain pointed to it. 'There.'

'You do not have to approach,' I said, thinking her superstitious.

'You'd leave me here?'

I looked around at the desolate cold and the scattered camp full of soldiers. 'You have a fair argument.'

We stepped off the trail and at once the snow reached above our boots. We crossed the field and plunged in drifts as high as our knees. I went first so as to blaze a path for Miss Cain to follow. In this way it took us half an hour to cross an acre of ground. The exertion, at least, kept the cold at bay. A hundred yards short of the oak we stopped and the tree seemed as tall as the distance between us. It was a true colossus.

The single bough drew my eye. It was perhaps fifteen feet off the ground, well over twice my height, and the end of a rope still hung from halfway along. These, I decided, had been brave boys. I'd known men take a dagger to their wrists or drink a sleeping draught laced with nightshade, but those were things that could be done in the blink of an eye. These boys had first had to scale the tree – no mean feat in itself, for the first hand-hold was not until two feet above my head – and then crawl out along that branch and tie a rope around their necks before they made the long, lonesome jump.

As we drew close, the snow underfoot grew shallower, much of it caught in the branches above. I circled the tree, though I couldn't say what it was I hoped to find. Miss Cain followed three paces behind. The night was bitter now and she wrapped her arms around herself.

'You'll catch your death,' I said.

'Your jests are in the poorest taste, Master Falkland.'

I'd secretly known all along that I'd find nothing of note. The snow had fallen so deep that I might have been walking on fresh graves and I wouldn't have known it. Still, something compelled me. I wanted to get a closer look. 'Miss Cain,' I said, 'you would do well to stand back.'

I was fortunate that the snow had piled drifts against the trunk. Once compacted underfoot it made for a good stool and, in that way, I was able to reach the first hand-hold in the bark and haul myself onto the lowest branch on the side opposite the one from which the boys had jumped. Miss Cain cried out a warning but I told her to be calm and keep talking; I wanted the comfort of her voice calling out to me in the dark. I didn't like to admit it but I knew, suddenly, that I was not a young man any more. A cramp seized my leg and told me I should retreat but I refused to listen. It was an ungainly scramble, one I was glad nobody else could see, but I climbed higher and shimmied around the trunk to reach the hanging branch. With my legs wrapped around the ice cold bough I inched my way out to the rope. I reeled it in. The end was frayed where the last boy had been cut down. There were no ropes for the two boys before that, so they must have been brought in. Somebody was getting lazy.

I took out my dagger and began to cut, but the rope was frozen solid and I might as well have been trying to drive a darning needle through plate armour. From atop the branch I could see for miles. Crediton was just a little town with an implausible number of fires dotted around. Perhaps Miss Cain's cinnamon-spiced wine still lingered in my memory for I found myself thinking of Christmas once more – if there was ever to be a Christmas again. I imagined Crediton would be a peaceful place to spend it once the army was gone.

I didn't have the heart to scramble back through the branches so I lowered myself to hang under the branch, clinging to the rope. In that way I had a terrible flash of the boys' last moments. Only when I let go, I did not dangle but dropped and rolled in the snow. It was further than it seemed and I landed hard; it knocked the wind out of me and I suppose I was lucky not to do myself an injury. When I didn't immediately rise, Miss Cain rushed over.

'It was further than I reckoned,' I gasped, staggering to my feet with the help of her hand and struggling for breath. My back was jarred but nothing more; nevertheless I made a solemn vow that in future I would act my age.

'I tried to tell you, sir. It's because of the granadoe.'

I stood back and scrutinised the land with eyes half

squinting. It was difficult to tell because of the way the snow had fallen but Miss Cain was correct: there was a depression in the earth. I kicked away some of the snow and could even see where portions of the tree's roots, as thick and gnarled as the branches, had been exposed at the bottom of a shallow crater. Here was where the fourth boy had met his end, right underneath that rope. A granadoe is a terrible thing. I'd seen them deployed on several occasions. They were little more than balls of gunpowder, tightly compacted and encased in a shell of pottery. There wasn't a single soldier I'd known who didn't fear them. More often than not the things would ignite before they could be bowled at the enemy. Half of the crippled beggars haunting London's streets had once been soldiers using these new weapons of war.

'Tell me all you know,' I said.

'It was three nights ago. I didn't know until morning. He was a boy from the store rooms. They're using the crypt underneath the church. They said it didn't matter if there was an accident and the church was demolished because then the village would be more godly. But it was only an excuse – there are no papists in Crediton, Master Falkland. There never have been.'

I thought of the rosary I'd picked up from the snow only hours before. 'And the boy?'

'His name was Thomas. He had hair so blond it was almost white. That's why they called him White Tom, in mockery of Fairfax. He was one of ours, Master Falkland. They pressed him as soon as they came into the village – and he a boy of only sixteen.'

'Came down here and threw himself on a granadoe?'

'Lit it first.'

I looked at the dangling rope. 'Why here?'

'Why anywhere, sir? He was sixteen, a soft boy, a sweet boy. Not a boy to be a soldier. Yet soldier he was. And now . . .'

I stood in the exact spot where four boys had taken their lives and tried to breathe it in. I was too late for clues. I was too late for doing anything but probing and prodding and hazarding my best guess. I told myself I didn't care, that I was only here because – like White Tom – I'd been pressed into service in the New Model Army. But their ghosts were all around me and I knew, suddenly, that I *wanted* to know, that I *needed* to know, that whatever had happened to those boys they deserved their stories to be told. I knew what it was like to be a faceless soul in an engine of war. I owed it to them to lay their ghosts to rest. I owed it to myself.

'Miss Cain?' Another thought had come nagging, something that had troubled me since Warbeck and I first entered the camp. 'When I came to your door, when you saw me, before Fairfax told you who I was, who did you *think* I was?'

Miss Cain shook her head. 'I don't understand you, sir,' she said, but I saw I'd struck a chord.

'You looked at me as though I was the devil himself. And you're not the first.' Though I remembered there had been others whose look had been far different, as though I was a saint.

Miss Cain shuddered and looked away. 'There were whispers,' she said, 'of an inquisitor of some ilk and his assistant come to make this monstrous army clean. To make it pure and godly, whatever that word has come to mean. I thought perhaps that you and your . . .' She shrugged.

'Someone come to hunt after whores and Catholics and witches and any others to whom *godly* men might take offence. I think, sir, you know of what I speak.'

I remembered the bonfire I'd seen as I left London with its effigy of the pope and thought perhaps I did. I turned and was about to take Miss Cain by the arm and begin the journey back into Crediton when I saw something move at the head of the field. It was almost imperceptible, a black flash against the white land, but then it stopped and I was certain. A scrawny stick of a man was watching us from a ridge between here and the edge of the town. I stared back and wondered if he was staring at me. At this distance we could neither of us know the other. I stared all the same. Then he moved again and was gone.

CHAPTER 8

In the morning Miss Cain brought me pottage and dark beer. I ate it on the doorstep with Warbeck. I'd expected him to ask me about my excursion in the night and rain dire warnings over my head – it would have been simple enough to have continued and walked right on out of the camp after all. But he said nothing. Perhaps he understood as I did that in the cold I'd be lucky to find shelter before I froze; or perhaps he'd been the man I saw watching us by the oak. As it was he barely spoke three words, and all of them to Miss Cain, before he was gone about some business of his own.

I had in mind to visit the church and see for myself where this store of powder and pottery was kept, but before I could go, a stout fellow appeared on the step. He wasn't short enough to be considered a dwarf but I imagined he might have heard the insult more than once. His beard was thick and hid a collection of little scars underneath, as of a man pushed head first through glass. One of his ears had had a bite taken out of it, but it was an old injury and long healed. His face was wrinkled and dark from a life out under the sky, his cheeks and nose rosy from cold or wine. His eyebrows struck me most – huge and bushy like great hairy caterpillars. The eyes beneath them held mine and I found I couldn't make anything of him – he could have been a fool or a murderer for all I could tell. He was not, I thought, the most wholesome of men to look at. He begged my pardon and introduced himself as Alfred Purkiss.

'I am sent,' he said, puffing himself up, 'from Black Tom hisself. I'm to take you to the spot.'

'The spot?'

He bent in and I thought for a second that he might bow. The way Cromwell would have the world ordered, lords should bow at commoners, and so it came as no great surprise; but I had misjudged him. He wanted only to take me in his confidence. 'The witching tree, sir.'

He meant the tree where the boys had hanged and the granadoe exploded. 'Please don't trouble,' I said, biting on an end of dry bread. 'I visited the tree last night. There was nothing I could see.'

He nodded knowingly as if I was returning his confidence and telling him secrets. 'Because of the night,' he whispered.

So Fairfax had delivered me a simpleton. 'And the snow,' I said.

I jumped to my feet and retreated into the house, leaving this Purkiss in the street. Inside, Miss Cain busied herself stoking a fire. She had risen earlier than me to collect snow for the pot and a thin, watery soup was already simmering for later in the day. In her presence I felt foolish and awkward. In part I felt an imposition, in part I knew that Warbeck and I saved her from one far greater. I had no doubt, too, that I had received far more amiable company in our walk to and from the tree than I would from Purkiss. 'I thank you for your kind hospitality,' I said.

She gave me a look I couldn't decipher, annoyed and

nervous and weary and hopeful all at once.

'I'm grateful for your assistance, Miss Cain,' I added. I waited a moment but she returned to her pot and I understood that she wished me to leave.

I returned to Purkiss then and took off along the street, marking my way by the shapes I'd seen the night before, passing the warped whitewashed walls of the houses with their little windows and sharply pointed rooftops. Although the air was still icy, the sky was clear and the thin November sun still carried a little warmth. Men sat on the doorsteps in front of open doors or leaning against the walls, some of them with their hands cupped around steaming cups of soup or bowls of pottage. They glanced at us as we passed but with little interest, even in poor Purkiss who plodded after me, dragging his left leg behind him. I had some pity for that; had the King's surgeons been less practised then I too might have been walking with such a gait. Other men gathered and pressed snow into buckets for water or else hurried away with stinking pails of slurry, off to the latrine pits. Without a horse and Fairfax beside me, they paid me no heed. The air wafting from the houses smelled stale and rank, of too many men crushed together and of smoke from warm hearths. I shook my head at that. Winters were long and we were only at the beginning. These men would regret their cosy November mornings in the freezing heart of January. I was glad I would be gone long before then.

Around the desecrated market cross some young soldiers were clearing snow. They watched me as I passed. It couldn't have been because they hadn't seen me before, for the army was so enormous that any fellow soldier might easily seem a stranger and I'd passed a hundred men already who couldn't possibly recognise me and yet hadn't cared a hoot. A little way past them I waited while Purkiss caught up. 'Do you know those men?' I asked him, but he only shrugged and shook his head and then looked up at me, blank and vacant.

A little further down the road I reached Crediton church. In the daylight it appeared less imposing than it had the night before. The steeple seemed to burst out of a great mound of snow into which a great oak door and stained glass windows were set. One of the windows had been smashed but the others remained intact. It was the work of lazy Puritans – a more zealous man would have put out all the windows and made a mockery of the pieces. Truly godly men, I thought, might have left all well alone.

I'd lost track of the days but I knew it wasn't Sunday, and yet I wasn't the first to church that morning. A single pair of boots had already tramped a path through the thick virgin snow. They led from the south end of the town where Fairfax and the other commanders quartered and where the cavalry horses were corralled. I wondered if it was a New Modeller roaming around inside and what that might mean, but there was only one way to find out. Cromwell had promised me my run of the camp and I meant to find out how closely his words would be kept.

I told Purkiss to wait for me outside and went to the door. As I quietly slipped in, I felt that rush of peacefulness that no man, no matter what he is, can deny. It had been a long time since I'd prayed, longer still – you will think me a hypocrite – since I believed there was anybody up there to pray to, but I found myself thinking of old services and I smiled. I'd enjoyed church as a boy. I have no voice but I liked the hymns, how a hundred voices soared together to create an entirely different sound. Here, though, the only sounds were the heavy echoes of my footsteps as I walked between rows of simple wooden pews. There was no altar in the chancel and I imagined that there had been no Mass here since my grandfather's age. If I was right then the stained glass windows were an aberration, an oversight – or perhaps the wistful indulgence of a priest harking back to better times.

At the front of the chancel were two doors. The one on the left led to a smaller chamber that might once have been a confessional – I wasn't sure. The other opened to a stairway going down. I followed it, making certain my steps were loud. Whoever was lurking below, I didn't want them to think me an intruder. I had, after all, been told this place was sitting on a nest of gunpowder.

The stairs turned and turned again and I thought I heard footsteps other than my own. At the second turn I held my foot back but the footsteps continued, and before I could call out a man appeared and almost barrelled into me. Startled, he jumped back and had to hold onto the wall to stop himself from tumbling. He clutched his chest with a theatrical flourish, miming how his heart had raced. He was a scrawny thing, dressed all in black. I judged him about seventy years old. His hair – what was left – was white and stained yellow at the ends. A big nose, broken in two places and never set, was squashed into the middle of a face that had lost so much weight that he made me think of my fellows in Newgate. Cheekbones poked through sallow skin.

'I . . . I'm . . . Sir, I b-beg, forgive me.' I'd expected anger, not apologies, but this old man looked as if, had there been

room on the step, he might have dropped to his knees and
grovelled. 'I only . . . meant to . . . to take a look.'

'A look?' I decided to let the lie unravel. I had, I now
thought, disturbed an intruder in the act and I needed a
stroke of fortune if I was to get anywhere with this investigation. There was always the niggling feeling that if I didn't
get anywhere, then Cromwell would see me back in irons.

'Please, sir. I kn-know what I was told – I should stay
away – but I . . . it was a . . . moment of weakness. Pitiable,
poor human weakness! We are all unworthy creatures, sir.
Ev-every last one of us.' His head was hanging down but he
risked a look up with a single rolling eye, assaying me for
any hint of sympathy.

'Every last one?'

'S-some, sir, are weaker than . . . others.' He was taking
me for a fool. I had, of course, been a flatterer in my lifetime
but I had rarely been flattered myself. It was as well. I didn't
have a taste for it. 'You . . . would not tell?' he asked
hopefully.

He was trying to reel me in. I decided I would let him.
'Who are you?' I asked.

'But sir . . .' he whispered. 'This is my church.' He must
have noted the look of surprise on my face, an involuntary
twitching of the eyebrows, and taken it for anger, for no
sooner had he spoken the words than he threw a hand to his
mouth, cringed and scuttled two steps back down the stairs.
'B-beg pardon,' he squealed. 'This is Black Tom's church,
of . . . of course. I was only its –' he tried desperately to grab
the right word – 'keeper. An . . . honoured . . . keeper.'

I took a step down and then another, slow and firm, and
in that way forced him to the bottom of the stairs ahead of

me. We stood in a narrow hall so low I could not stand straight and had to stoop. The scrawny man was shorter than the ceiling by three or four inches, but he still bowed his head to his chest like a hunchback or a man who has spent his life buried in books. 'You're the priest?' I asked.

He gave me a look like an inquisitive greyhound.

'Save it,' I said. 'I'm not with the New Model. I was sent here because of the suicides.'

'You're the intelligencer!' His relief was palpable. He breathed more easily now and even stood straighter. I'd been right: his cringing had been only an act. I've noticed in my time how you will often find that a man of God is the best actor of all.

'I was told they were using the church as a store.'

The priest nodded. 'They . . . desecrate God's house in this manner. And all for a . . . piece of stained glass! They called it a devil's chapel, me a whoreson. They . . . do it out of mockery.'

'Did you give the Mass?'

The priest opened his lips but quickly shut them again. 'It has not been allowed in my lifetime, sir.'

That was answer enough. I thought again of the rosary I still carried in my pocket, plucked last night from the snow. 'I would see the stores, if you would,' I said. 'The gunpowder. The granadoes.'

The old priest beckoned me along the passage. Now that he was sure I was not here to scold him, he didn't walk like the wizened old man who'd met me on the stair. It took twenty years off his age and I saw him suddenly for just another victim of these wars, no matter how foolish his notions of godliness. At the end of the passage we passed through a door into what had once been wine cellars. There were no racks or bottles on display but the smell was unmistakable. I wondered when they had been raided and fancied it had been before the New Model arrived. There was probably a stash somewhere. Perhaps that – and not love for his forsaken church – was why the priest had sneaked back in; but now the walls were stacked high with wooden barrels. I knew what they were without having to look. Once you've manned artillery or held a musket you don't forget the smell of powder. I made a show of inspecting them.

'Who looks over it?' I asked.

'There is a storekeeper.'

'Who is he?'

The priest shook his head sadly. 'I am not with . . . the New Model, sir.'

I walked the length of the cellar. At the end was a trapdoor. I knelt and fingered the latch. There was a thin coating of powder everywhere and, beneath that, dust. The dust had been disturbed, but long before the powder had had a chance to settle. 'The crypts?' I asked.

'It is . . . only . . . the dead,' he replied. That stutter must not have been part of the act.

'You're in charge of the dead?'

Again the priest shook his head. 'The army looks . . . after its own.'

'What about the dead boys? The ones who hung themselves? And the other . . .'

The priest shuddered. 'You would not want to see *him*, sir. He was in . . . pieces.'

'I've seen it before.'

'Are you a soldier, sir, as well as a . . . a . . . an intelligencer?'

I brushed past him on the way back to the stairway. The stench of powder and wine was too much and I wanted to retch. It was best that I did not, as the pottage I'd had for breakfast was likely my only meal of the day. 'Would you take me to the bodies?' I asked.

He scuttled after me and up the stairs. 'They are army graves, sir.'

'What does that mean?'

'There is . . . only one. One grave. And . . . it has many bodies.'

I was glad he was behind me then so he couldn't see my face. Even on the road with the King we gave our boys proper burials. Had the New Model been marching and taking casualties along the way then perhaps I could have understood. But this was less a winter camp than it was a winter city. They'd built their own roads, their own houses, latrines, stores, grounds for drilling. Why, in all this industry, could they not build their own graveyards as well, something to honour their dead? The only reason I could find was that it wasn't practical: that a man's hours could be put to better use than in digging individual graves. This New Model was indeed a calculating monster. I'd seen how efficient they were on the battlefield at Naseby, how Cromwell's cavalry were so disciplined they didn't chase retreating men but turned and took formation and charged again. Now I was seeing how efficient they were off the battlefield as well. But this was a cold thing, unworthy of an army forged in the name of even a puritan God.

'Take me there,' I said. We were standing in the chancel

again. A bitter wind came in through the shattered glass. As I walked to the door I stopped: Purkiss was where I'd left him but now he had three men clustered around him. I thought at first they were threatening him but it was only his diminutive stature that had them looming over. He was talking with quite some animation. I squinted and thought perhaps the three men were the ones who had watched us so intently in the market square. I crept forward to look closer before they saw me in their turn but as I did the priest caught my arm.

'Sir,' he whispered. 'I should . . . not. I should not e-even be here.' Here his stutter returned in force and it took some moments for him to calm. One of the men around Purkiss threw a sharp look my way and a moment later the three of them hurried off.

'All the same,' I said, 'I need a guide, so lead on.' I paused. 'Or would you like the New Model to know you were sniffing around their stores?' I hurried to Purkiss and tried to see who these three men were and where they'd gone, but they were already out of sight. They must have been swift on their legs, then. I took Purkiss by the shoulder. 'Those men. They were from the market square, were they not?'

He shrugged, but this time I thought I saw through him. 'Perhaps,' he admitted when I wouldn't let him go.

'What did they want?'

He shrugged again. 'They wanted to know who you was. I told them you was Cromwell's man come about them boys who hanged theirselves.'

'And?'

He looked at me blankly.

'You were talking too long for just that,' I said. And if these men hadn't known who I was then why had they stared so when they saw me in the market square? But Purkiss only gawped back in slack-jawed silence until my patience gave up.

Fairfax had sent me an idiot. I had no use for him and told him so, but Purkiss followed along anyway as the priest led me through the town. We passed back through the market square where a crowd was beginning to form, jostling us even as we made our way around the edges. I looked hard at all the faces in case I saw the men who'd questioned Purkiss, but all I noted was how a space had been cleared and marked near the centre of the square. I couldn't tell whether the space was meant for a duel of some sort, or for some pre-arranged sport, but I saw no officers.

'What is it?' I asked the priest. I could see he was anxious to be gone.

'They will . . . have their sport, these boys.' He tugged at my arm. Purkiss, when I asked him the same thing, gave his usual shrug.

The old priest led us to a field on the western edge of Crediton set aside for the men whom God – or luck or fate – had deemed fit to spare the coming winter. It wasn't yet December and I could already see several mounds, places where the snow lay heaped even higher. There were no soldiers camped this far out but we could hear their cheers getting louder in the square. From the sound of it some sort of a contest was going on, not a duel. Jousting without horses, perhaps, and from the wildness of the cheers the competition was growing severe. It would, I suspected, take blood to be spilled before some commander waded in and stopped it. A soldier must not get bored or his mind will wander to darker things.

The graves, such as they were, were simple and unadorned. Some way across the field a pair of men as old as I were standing before a mound of snow. The ground was open at their feet. I wondered if they were looking grimly into their future – it would have been the sort of joke a certain kind of soldier might have made. Apart from them the only other person stalking this white pasture was a slight figure. It was the first time I'd seen a woman in the camp apart from Miss Cain, and this one was of a similar age – young. She loitered on the edge of the field and didn't seem to be coming or going. Her hair had once been blond but it had been cropped so fiercely that she was almost bald. I thought perhaps she'd had lice – I have seen men strip their skin raw rather than stay in that condition. I walked towards her but as soon as she saw me she spooked like a deer being hunted. Her hand flew to her face and she let out a squeal of fright then took off. I was in no condition to go chasing her, but I thought I might recognise her face if I saw it again.

The priest watched her go and then met my eyes. 'A camp whore,' he said.

'Come to forage in the graves?'

'God made women to take from men.'

We waited until the two old soldiers limped away and then the priest took me to the mound where the suicides lay. I'd been standing there for some minutes, picturing those strangled boys holding each other six feet below, when I saw a stick poking through the snow like the shoot of a plant already grown brittle and dead. I approached with caution, not sure where the field ended and the graves started. When

I pulled on the shoot it resisted. I tugged again and lifted it free. Once the snow had shaken loose I could see what it was: a simple cross made of two twigs, tied at the centre with a knot of horse's hair.

I turned with it in my hand. When I held it up to the priest he cringed away from it as though he was Satan-spawned and not a brother of Christ. 'Yours?' I asked him.

He shook his head fervently, bobbing it back and forth like a demented buzzard. 'I . . . Sir, I . . . wouldn't.'

'But who could blame you?' I went on. The priest was an old man and frightened, terrified even, but I felt a crystallising dislike for him. There's only one type of man I despise indiscriminately – not a godly man, not an ungodly man, not a soldier, not a thief, not a roundhead or a cavalier, nor Catholic nor Puritan – each may have his own in that regard; but I have never been able to like a coward, especially not in a man of God. 'You've seen it yourself,' I snapped. 'There are as many Catholics in this army as there are . . .'

'Of the true Church!' he squealed.

I rounded on him. 'But it must be an affront, mustn't it, to watch boys who'd gladly take your Mass be buried with that *other* sort of boy? Good Christian men deserve a good Christian burial, don't they? It's not as if you can sneak out at night and start digging up bodies – but perhaps a little cross might help them into God's Heaven?'

I was taunting him but he was too taken by his own fears to see it. 'You . . . have me wrong, kind sir. I . . . icons like this only . . . draw the eye. They cannot draw the spirit. You must . . . believe, sir, if you work for Black Tom.' He was shaking his head so violently I thought he might be having a fit. 'But sir . . . they would not . . . put others in with those boys.'

I put the cross back in the snow. This time I made sure its tip did not protrude. Somebody had planted it here but I was certain it wasn't the priest. Whoever it was had cared enough for those hanged boys to try, in whatever small way, to appease God; for God – no matter to whom you spoke – did not look kindly on suicides. 'Did you know them?'

The priest took it as a welcome question. His body straightened and his face didn't look so tightly false. 'Not . . . closely, sir. The New Model had only been in . . . Crediton two weeks when they . . .' He floundered for words and this time I felt certain he was genuine. He choked. 'I had . . . met them, sir . . . They came to me for . . .'

'It is as well that you say it. I won't let them beat you for it.'

'We . . . we don't have a confessional.'

'But it was confession they wanted?'

He nodded meekly. I could see he thought he had already said too much, but we were in the middle of nowhere with only the snow and skeletons to hear. 'I might come to you for the same,' I told him. I certainly would not but I thought it might ease his fears. 'Have many soldiers come for confession?'

'It is difficult. When the New Model . . . came they sacked my church. But it has been a . . . godly church since King Henry –' he crossed himself at the mere mention of the long-dead King – 'saw the light. They sacked it because of the . . . windows.'

'The stained glass.'

'They call it . . . idol . . . idolatry. They think we worship the glass.' He whispered the next words. 'But we only worship God. We worship the same God. We are not heathens.'

'Soldiers came and smashed it apart?'

'They were just boys. They had the wine from the cellar that we keep for . . . the sacrament.'

'Drunk on Christ's blood and they staved in his windows?' Yes, this sounded like Cromwell's army.

'I wasn't to . . . g-go back. But some of the . . . soldiers s-sought me out . . . Even the ones who . . .'

He began to cry, big sniffling tears like a child, and I couldn't hate him now, no matter how much of a coward he was. He was a wretch, but some people are born to be wretches. It's no more their fault than when a man is born with six fingers or webbed toes. 'You gave them confessions,' I said, 'in a secret place. Where?'

'By the tree . . .' he stuttered.

'Which tree?'

'The tree,' he said between gasps for breath, 'where they hanged.'

I could get no more out of him for minutes on end after that. He seemed to reach out for me like my son used to do. If he *were* my son then I would have taken him in my arms, no matter how old he was. I would have smothered him in an embrace and never let go. Instead I just let him cry. When he had swallowed all his sobbing I looked him in the eye. 'What were they called?' I asked.

'I . . . can't tell you what they said!' he shrieked. 'The confessional is sacrosanct!'

'Their names,' I insisted. 'The dead boys – I'm not interested in their sins.'

He sniffed. 'The first was Richard . . . Richard Wildman,' he whispered. 'And Samuel. Samuel Whitelock.'

I let the names sink in. I thought I could picture them, two unknowing Catholic boys swept up in the colossus that was the New Model Army, plundered from their homes like any old pair of boots or piece of jewellery. They must have been relieved to find this weakly priest when they came to Crediton. It must have been a chance to unburden themselves of everything they'd seen and done. I wondered if I'd seen these boys, if our eyes had locked outside Oxford or Abingdon. Six months ago I would have put a sabre through either of them and not given it a second thought. I could have killed them and been content; yet that they had killed themselves left me chilled and eager to know more. In that moment I didn't understand myself at all.

'And the third boy?' I asked.

'The boy with the . . . the granadoe? His name was Thomas Fletcher. He was one of our own. A shy boy.'

'No,' I said, 'not him. The other. The third boy who hanged himself. The third boy in this grave.'

The priest suddenly straightened and rubbed his eyes with the heels of his hands.

'Sir, he is-isn't in that grave.'

I look at the mounds. 'Then which?' Tiny flakes of snow started to fall and I felt a dull hunger aching in my gut.

'He isn't . . . in a grave a-at all, sir. He's in the . . . surgeon's quarters.'

'Not buried yet?'

The priest shook his head and put his hands together in what seemed a mockery of rapturous praise. 'Not buried, sir,' he whispered, 'and not dead.'

CHAPTER 9

The New Model had taken over the town's biggest house – a place close to the church where a local lord might have lived before raising a militia and going off to war – for its wounded. In an army of this size I supposed there would be an unending parade of the injured and sick. The surgeons would be desperate this winter. Plague would destroy this New Model with more ease than a hundred thousand men fighting for the King.

By the time we got back to the square, the cheering had ended and the soldiers were dispersing back to their tents and their bunks. I pushed against the flow of them, left the priest to scuttle back to whatever hole he was living in and came to the surgeon's quarters on foot, Purkiss still trailing in my wake. I wondered if Cromwell had known that one of the boys still lived all along – and if he had, why he hadn't cared to tell me. There was a chance the message hadn't reached him. If Warbeck was right, he hadn't been long back from storming Basing House and finally bringing down the Marquis of Winchester, that constant thorn in Parliament's side. Cromwell was quickly climbing to the highest level of Parliament at the same time as controlling the biggest army the kingdom had ever known. He'd had to bend rules to get that far, somehow sneaking through the particulars of the Self-Denying Ordinance, and a peculiarity of the man was that he seemed to be everywhere, all at once, rushing hither and yon to watch over everything. Perhaps it wasn't too fanciful to imagine a detail like this escaping him.

The boy's name was Jacob Hotham. He hadn't been to confessional like the first two, was some years older and, so the priest had heard, devoutly Puritan. Nonetheless he'd abandoned his watch and gone to the same tree in the dead of night, slipped the noose around his neck and taken the lonesome plunge from the branch. I'd begun to devise an idea when the priest had told me about their confessions, that these suicides had not been suicides at all. Two Catholic boys hanging from the tree where they secretly took confession? An army full of Puritans around them? And secrets don't keep well in armies where men are packed so close about. I could see it done by the sort of boys who'd smashed the priest's stained glass and torn down the market cross, a gruesome warning to any others of the old faith; but if Hotham was a Puritan then he didn't fit my notion. That he still lived seemed a miracle, but a miracle I was willing to believe. Some men are reprieved. I once saw musket fire take a man's face clean off. He lived to fight on. Indeed he fought more fiercely, more proudly than ever, striking fear into the hearts of all those who stood against him.

I stopped at a distance to watch the surgeon's house. It was wide and double-fronted, not as big as a lord's country estate but a good imitation. Probably it had been the home of some minor gentry, perhaps even the same sort of man that my darling Caro's father had been. Perhaps, like Caro's father, he'd ridden out in service of his King, taking a loyal band with him and never coming back. Caro's father was dead four years now. Many of the men who'd marched with him from London we'd put in the ground in the first two years fighting against the Scots. The rest of us were scattered. Some had gone back to their families. I wished I had too; and I caught myself wondering for the thousandth time what had become of that little place I used to call home. Its name was Launcells, two days' journey on a horse from Taunton – Taunton whose walls I knew had been besieged and then besieged again. I knew, too, from the letters that had finally reached me in Oxford that Caro had considered going there once the farms in this part of the kingdom started to be ravaged. Caro was made of stern stuff and I fancied she could have outlasted any siege, but the town had been with the King and then with Parliament so many different times that sheltering there would have been folly.

Men came in and out of the surgeon's house with alarming regularity. I supposed there must have been war wounds still festering, and there must have been disease as well, because here I saw camp whores for the first time. They didn't go into the surgeon's house – the New Model was an army and its whores were, as with all armies, casualties that no general would lament – but some lingered in nooks and crannies thereabouts. I watched one man, as old as I and with a tender face, come out and call for one of them. He was carrying a wineskin and he passed it to her. I fancied it was filled with some doctor's brew to stop the dreaded itch.

Home. I couldn't stop thinking of it. I knew I must go

further west and I fancied a little north, but it couldn't be far. If I stole my horse and some food, if I was lucky, if the horse lived the first few days out there in the snow, if I was not waylaid, if I followed the right road . . . But it would be madness in this cold. For all I knew, Warbeck and Fairfax would send a hundred dragoons to bring me back and return me to Newgate and Cromwell for the noose they both thought I so richly deserved.

The steps up to the door of the surgeon's house were covered in a thick sheen of ice. I navigated them with care and went in to find a wide hall with stairs on either side leading to a balcony above. I watched two men walk past up there on the other side of the balustrade. There was a low murmur of noise from upstairs.

Nobody looked at me askance as I went up. In the first room there were empty beds and no surgeon to be found. I took this for a good sign until I saw the way the walls were marbled with dark black stains where blood had been wiped away and the job poorly done. In the next were three pallets with three men stretched out. These, I saw, had been amputations. I'd been present at an amputation once, a man whose leg was blown off beneath the knee. Gangrene had set in and would have taken his life if the surgeons had not intervened. I held him as he thrashed, drunk beyond pain but terribly aware of what we were about to do. The most horrible thing was when he just stopped screaming.

While I stood there, lost in my own bleak memory, I sensed a presence behind me. I turned to see a young man who must have been no older than twenty-five. Still, I supposed that made him a veteran of these wars and certainly a veteran of the New Model Army. He had mousy hair shorn close to the scalp and soft features almost like a girl, all apart from the nose which seemed an aberrant protrusion from his face.

'Are you a friend?' he asked me. He meant of the men lying in their cots.

'I was looking for someone,' I said. 'Name of Hotham. Jacob Hotham.'

'The pikeman,' the boy said. He kneaded his hands and I saw they were stained a rose colour, darker where there were creases in his knuckles. I could scarcely believe a boy this young was one of the army's surgeons but this war had already thrown up so many strange things.

'Where might I find him?'

'I'll look after this,' came a second voice, somewhere along the passage. 'Lucas, I think the artillery man needs your attention. The wound is open again.'

The surgeon whose name was Lucas caught my eye unaware. I saw that his resolve was almost gone and wondered how long he'd been treating such hopeless cases. As if in sympathy, my own leg twinged. I pictured myself hobbling around my quarters in Oxford last winter. Lucas turned to leave and I saw the man who had been standing behind him, as young as the surgeon but with a less harrowed look. He must have avoided the lice going around because his hair wasn't shorn. It was thick, black and shaggy. His eyes were green and he had high cheekbones, cresting through his narrow face to give him the appearance of a little lord. It struck me as odd that the tunic he wore was clean; and his breeches too seemed hardly worn. I wondered which dead man they had come from. I'd seen him before, I was sure. He was one of the men from the market square who'd accosted Purkiss while I was in the church. 'You said you could help,' I began.

He extended his hand and clasped mine. His fingers were long and etched with dark stains in the creases of the knuckles which seemed at odds with his pristine clothes. Blood, I supposed, from working with the surgeon. His arms were thin like the rest of him but his grip was strong and sure. Then he put his other hand on top of mine and smiled, and I felt fortunate he didn't bend down to kiss me as if I was a maid he was intent on courting. 'My name,' he said, 'is Carew. Edmund Carew. Might I have the pleasure?'

'Falkland,' I said.

'With which troop?' He smiled as he asked it.

'I'm not with any troop,' I said. 'I'm here on Cromwell's account to look into the killings.' I felt quite sure I was telling him something he already knew.

'Killings?'

'The boys who hanged themselves,' I corrected. 'It creates a bad atmosphere in an army when you don't even need an enemy and your boys end up dying. So I'm here to settle his stomach.'

This Carew had a careful air about him quite unlike the other boys I'd seen thus far in the camp. He was thoughtful and quiet. I imagined he'd been the son of a lord but as I followed him along the balcony he told me he was only a soldier. I knew that the New Model was a different kind of beast but the idea that the sons of lords and the sons of commonfolk could fight alongside each other was preposterous. I followed him to the end of a passage and he opened a door into a room that had once been a lady's bedchamber.

There was still a tall mirror on the wall. There was only one bed here, a broad cot with a real mattress instead of a straw pallet. I'll admit I stared – I'd forgotten what it was to sleep in a bed like that. Unlike the chamber with the amputees there was no fetid smell in the air. The place had been perfumed. He was being treated well, this boy, better than the others here. It struck me as strange for an attempted suicide.

Two other boys sat by the bed beside him. At first I thought they looked remarkably similar to Carew but then I realised it was nothing physical, only the way they held themselves with the same easy pride. The first had thin blond hair and a complexion to match, with piercing blue eyes. The second was shorter and rounder and his hair was cropped close to his head. Like Carew they were wearing the cleanest clothes of any soldier I'd seen in camp, perhaps even cleaner than Fairfax himself. They did not wear the usual soldier's uniform: instead of the red coats they wore black.

I recognised the smell now. It was soap.

Carew took me to the bed where, in real woollen sheets, lay Jacob Hotham. At first I thought him asleep but he stirred when I stood above him and I saw the flagon at his bedside. He'd taken some sort of draught. He'd been a handsome lad once but now he wore a necklace of black and blue bruises and his face was swollen besides. I thought he might once have had the same way about him as Carew and the others in the room, the sense of oneself that can only come with a proper ancestry. Now his eyes were grey and bloodshot. They rolled, locked with mine, and he tried to draw himself up. There was a fear in his face as though he'd seen a ghost. The sheets were wrapped tight around him and he struggled to get his hands free, and it was only then that I saw they were bandaged up, both of them, so he looked to have two hoofs instead of hands; and what I'd taken for a tunic was another kind of bandage, designed to keep his back braced. I wondered what damage he'd done to himself when he fell out of the tree.

A thought hit me. The rope around the branch had not unravelled. I could still see it as clear as day. Somebody had taken a knife to it. Somebody had cut Jacob Hotham down. I thought I would like to meet this someone and ask them what had brought them to be watching that tree so they were there to save him; and to ask what else they might have seen.

The boys at his bedside took alarm at seeing him put himself to such exertion and quickly stood to help him back down. In seconds he was back in the bedsheets. He made a feeble motion for the flagon at the bedside and Carew went to put it to his lips.

'Please,' I said, holding it back. 'I would speak to him first.'

'I'm afraid you can speak all you wish,' Carew began, shaking my hand away and helping Hotham take a drink. 'He can hear you but he won't be able to answer. The ropes hurt him more than we thought. The surgeon doesn't know if he'll ever speak again.'

At this Hotham's grey eyes found mine again. I could have been wrong but I thought he was screaming out.

'Which one of you was it?'

Carew turned so suddenly that he spilled some of the herbal draught onto the bed.

'Which one of you cut him down?' I went on. 'It was one of you, I presume?'

Carew nodded. His expression eased and I wondered what he'd first thought I'd meant. 'We are old friends,' he said. 'We grew up together. It was only natural we should fight for the good cause together too. He was fortunate I was there for him.' Carew made certain his friend was not wet from the spill and brushed back his hair. 'Still, I have no doubt he would have done the same for me. We are, all of us, praying for his recovery.'

'Do you want to tell me what happened?' I said it as much to Hotham as I did to Carew. Again his grey eyes rolled. This time he didn't try and drag himself up. The draught was working on him and his eyelids looked heavy. I could not quite be sure whether his friends here were caring for him or keeping him quiet.

'We were part of the watch that night,' said Carew. 'We walk circuits around certain parts of the camp and the countryside all around. It isn't the King's army you have to watch out for. Those womanly cavaliers are wintering in Oxford, getting lazy and fat. They know the war's as good as over so they might as well enjoy their freedom while they can.' He sounded scornful, of course, but he also betrayed a vicious glee.

I didn't rise to his bait. I too was young and foolish once.

'We'd known about those other boys, of course,' he said. 'I won't say we knew them. We don't fraternise with *that* sort.'

'Catholics?'

'*Royalists*,' Carew replied. 'It's insult enough we have to stand alongside them when the battles come. To spend a winter fraternising is more than a godly man can bear. All the same, what happened . . .' He shook his head solemnly. 'Jacob wanted to see the place. We'd been calling it the witching tree. Not our name, you understand, only a name that's been going around camp. The rest of us had no interest in seeing that sinful place and I suppose he must have been counting on it.' Carew looked up at me. His eyes were shimmering as if he was on the verge of tears. Godly tears for a good friend. 'When he didn't come back, God sent me the truth of what he'd done. Have you had a vision like that before, Master Falkland?'

'I have not.'

'Are you a godly man?'

'I am not god*less*.'

He knew I was evading the question; but how do you tell a young man who believes that God helped him rescue his dear friend that, to you, God is as much a story as fairies at the bottom of the garden? It hardened him, though. If there had been a chance we might be friends, it had gone. 'I started running,' he told me. 'I got there in time. God had already intervened. He was dangling but not dead. I climbed to the branch and cut him down.' Here he looked more sad than ever. 'I knew the fall might kill him just as easily as the rope. But I had to cut. The surgeon has put a splint on his leg and both his wrists are shattered. Jacob's war is finished, Master Falkland. He will return home as soon as he is able. That the rope has taken away his voice might even be a blessing. At least now his dear mother will not have to hear the story.'

Carew had his hands together as if to pray. Against my will I found myself doing the same. 'I would like to ask him some questions,' I said. It seemed strange that he had hurt himself so. I had dropped from the same branch but the night before and survived with nothing more than a twinge in my knees and bruises to my pride. The snow had cushioned my fall, true, but to such an extent?

'Have you listened, Master Falkland?' Carew's voice was level, each word enunciated perfectly as if he was an actor. He was definitely a boy trained for a lordly life. 'He cannot speak.'

'There are ways,' I began.

'Oh yes?'

'Things I might ask. I might need only a nod of the head.'

'He needs his rest.'

'Can he write?'

Carew snorted with derision. 'Did you *see* his hands, Master Falkland? Broken so that the surgeon believes they will be little more use than stumps.'

'But he knows *how* to write?'

I heard footsteps behind me. I turned to see Lucas, the surgeon, and had the sudden feeling that I was surrounded, trapped in a classic bluff by two small bands of soldiers. 'Master Carew,' I said, 'I'm grateful for what you could tell me. I take it you know nothing of the other two boys who hanged themselves?'

'Only their names, sir, and that they had no place in this army.'

I walked past the surgeon. At the door I turned around. 'There was one other thing,' I said. 'There was another boy. Thomas Fletcher. You might know him as White Tom.'

'The boy who stole the granadoe. Yes?'

'You knew him?'

'Only his story. You are right, sir – it is intriguing to

wonder why White Tom and Jacob both went down to the tree where those boys died. I am afraid, though, that we have stopped thinking about it. There will be many more die before the winter is out. More if the King does not quickly come to terms as he must. These unfortunate incidents are best forgotten. We just want our friend back.'

CHAPTER 10

I'd spent much of the morning by now walking from
one place to another, asking my questions and finding
little by way of answers. I still couldn't say whether the first
two boys had hanged themselves or whether they had
received some considerable help. They had been Catholics,
and Catholics clearly lived in fear and perhaps some
considerable peril. Edmund Carew knew more than he'd
chosen to tell me but I doubted even a skilled torturer would
coerce the truth from him. I suspected the same was true of
the other boys who surrounded Jacob Hotham. Hotham
himself would tell me a far more interesting story, I felt sure,
but only if God saw fit to return his voice. I began to muse
on ways to speak with Hotham alone and then stopped
myself. Why? To what end? The answer I should give to
Cromwell was simple enough: *you've pressed Catholic boys into
service in your army of Puritans. There's simply nothing more to
say.* I doubted he'd be much pleased with such an answer
but I felt sure that, at its core, here was the truth of this
mystery. What did it matter whether they'd hanged
themselves or whether Edmund Carew or some other boy
like him had seen to their murder? It would happen again
with some other boys in some other way, and again and

again, and the cause would remain the same. Was not my task here as good as done? Was it not done before it even started?

I rose from where I sat, watching the surgeon's house, and made my way towards Miss Cain's, resolved to propose to Warbeck that I'd as good as completed my work. I doubted he'd be pleased but I thought perhaps he might see the reason of my argument, and, too, I knew he'd find the notion of an early return to London entirely agreeable. And yet as I walked I felt my resolve wither with each step. I didn't know whether those two boys had died by their own hands or by others. I suspected they had been murdered, but I found that merely thinking it wasn't good enough. They deserved better. Their mothers deserved better. They deserved not to live with the shame of a suicide. For the first time since we'd left London, I found myself cursing the conscience that had hounded me to hang that rapist and murderer in York. I'd confounded the King then. Now it seemed I would confound myself.

It was still possible, I supposed, that Warbeck might see matters otherwise, but when I got back to the house I found him in a foul temper. He didn't speak to me or ask me where I'd been, only where Purkiss was.

'I don't know,' I told him. 'I ordered him to wait outside while I went to see the third boy who tried to hang himself. I learned last night that he didn't die and was cut down before he could strangle. Sadly he's in no condition to speak. When I came out, Purkiss was gone.' Or perhaps he wasn't. For all I knew the little man had been watching me ever since. The simple truth was that I'd been too distracted thinking on ways to get Hotham to tell me what had happened, and Alfred Purkiss had slipped my mind. I wondered why Warbeck had any interest in him. 'I dare say he'll return tomorrow. Or perhaps not. He seems to be a simpleton.'

Warbeck snorted. 'Purkiss? Fooled you so easily, did he, Falkland?' He shook his head and grunted; and when I asked him whether his morning had been in any way productive, thinking I might lead on to the suggestion that I'd already found as good an answer to Cromwell's mystery as any, he snarled more like a roused dog than a man. 'What about Miss Cain? Have you seen Miss Cain?'

I had not, I realised, not since I'd left that morning. Something in Warbeck's tone gave me to think that all might not be well and it troubled me how anxious I became at the notion. 'No,' I said. 'I have not.'

I thought perhaps he relaxed a little, which seemed a trifle odd. He glowered and appeared in no mood for further conversation, though, and so I left him there and went back into the street, leaning beside the doorstep, blowing on my hands. Now and then groups of soldiers walked by, some looking up with a dull curiosity as they passed, others deep in their own thoughts. I tried to set my mind back to thinking about Hotham and how I'd get his story out of him but I found myself constantly distracted. It had not occurred to me until Warbeck had planted the suggestion that Miss Cain might be in any danger; now, though, I saw only too clearly the perils for a young woman alone in this army of men. I wondered what made her stay.

I resolved to take myself to the edge of the camp and see if I could trace our path back to that first hut Warbeck and I had passed as we entered the camp last night; but before I could take a step I spied Miss Cain herself walking quickly along the street from the square. A wave of relief swept over me. It vexed me, the force of it. She had what I took at first to be a black basket swinging from her hand. As she came closer I saw it was a pair of dead crows. She didn't smile as she reached the door but I sensed she was pleased with herself.

'There'll be meat in the morning,' she said brusquely, and stepped past me into the house; then, with the door barely closed behind her, I heard a thud and a squeal of fear. I moved with a speed I thought I no longer possessed, tearing open the door and reaching for a sabre I didn't have and hadn't worn for almost half a year. In the hall, Warbeck had Miss Cain pressed against the wall, one arm almost across her throat. In the other hand he held a dagger almost touching her neck. 'Papist whore!' he spat, then saw me in the door. Something in my face must have seemed terrible indeed for he let Miss Cain go and took a pace back, and for a moment his look became uncertain. I suppose he'd thought I was gone and that they were alone. As I advanced, he took another step away, keeping a distance between us. I had no weapon, yet this time he was the one more afraid. In one hand he held his dagger. In the other he had something small and loose like a bracelet. He threw it to the floor at Miss Cain's feet and I saw it was a rosary. He stared at me and then at Miss Cain, eyes full of accusation. 'It was in her room,' he said. 'I'll not shelter under the roof of a Catholic whore!'

I was of a mind to run him down, dagger and all, for words like that and see who would come out the best of it. Despite my months in prison I fancied I was the stronger man, and the odds lie with the knife only if the man who holds it won't blink from striking. I supposed Warbeck wouldn't flinch if he had to. I supposed, too, that if I were to get the best of him, I might go as far as to murder him, with all the consequences that would bring. With some difficulty, then, I reined in my temper and bent and picked up the rosary. I held it up and made a show of patting down my pockets and studying it. Then I looked Warbeck in the eye. 'Where did you find it?'

His lips peeled back from his teeth in a parody of a laugh. 'Yours, is it, Falkland? I don't think so. I told you – I found it in her room.'

'No,' I said, continuing my appraisal. It was old, I thought. A few wooden beads and a crude wooden cross on a piece of twine. 'Not mine.' I held his eye. 'Cast your mind back: when Fairfax led us past the church last night I saw two men watching us. They turned and ran when I looked back and called out to them to stop. I told you one of them had dropped something.' I had said no such thing but hoped the lie might confound him.

Warbeck shook his head but I could see he wasn't certain. 'You did not.'

'Why else do you suppose I stopped?' I scoffed at him and tossed the rosary back. 'That's what I found, lying there in the snow.'

His laughter was forced. 'You expect me to believe that, Falkland? This is the New Model Army. There are no Catholics hereabouts! None!'

I knew I had him now. I saw even Miss Cain, recovering from her shock, look at him with scorn and pity. 'You have the evidence in front of you, Warbeck, but if that won't do for you then shall I tell you what I've found today? The two boys who hung themselves? Pressed royalists. Catholics. They gave their confessions to a priest. They used to do it by that tree – I suppose that's why it was chosen. Half your army here once fought for the King and a quarter of them were once Catholic, but if you don't believe me then go and ask Fairfax, or ask Cromwell himself – they cannot either of them fail to know the truth of it!'

I think he hated me then more than ever he did on our way from London. He knew, however hard he fought against it, that a man cannot easily lie with such conviction. But I didn't dare give him time to even breathe – instead I rounded at once on Miss Cain. 'But how, Miss Cain, did this come to be in your room? I can only imagine it slipped from my coat pocket as I slept. What did you mean by taking it?' I glared at her. I hoped she understood my pantomime and why it must be done.

'I . . .' She looked abashed and her eyes fell to the floor. 'I didn't know what to do, sir.' She shuddered.

'You should have returned it to me or given it to Warbeck here and told him how you came upon it.' My glare returned to Warbeck. 'And what sort of gentleman do you call yourself, prowling in a lady's room?'

Warbeck hissed at me like an angry cat. He took his knife to the rosary and sliced the twine, then stormed past to the door and hurled the beads out into the street. He rounded on me then. 'I do not call myself a gentleman at all, Falkland, and Miss Cain is no lady!' He slammed the door as he left. Miss Cain and I stared at one another. Her green eyes glistened with tears, I supposed from the fright. Even men may fight as fierce as a bear in battle and then fall to weeping afterwards. Some scoff and say that tears are for cowards but I've seen it's not so.

Miss Cain picked up the two dead crows from the floor. She started to turn away and then stopped. 'Thank you, Master Falkland, but you didn't need to lie for me.'

'Beg pardon, Miss Cain, but I did not lie.' I reached into my pocket and took the rosary I'd picked from the snow beside the church. 'I did not say yours was the one I found.' I offered it to her. 'Do you have a better place to hide it?' But she pushed my hand and the rosary away and took her crows to her kitchen.

The afternoon was bitterly cold though no more snow fell. The night would be worse. I walked the camp, trying to gauge the feel of it, but found nothing that seemed out of place save for the sheer size of it. When I came back, Warbeck hadn't returned. I didn't ask Miss Cain if she knew where he was or whether to expect his return, and she didn't venture to say; all the same, I noticed that she seemed brighter, less cautious, now that he wasn't around. As the evening drew in, she called me to the scullery and we ate crow soup. A lot of the soldiers, I'd seen, ate at camp fires or in the crude dining halls that had sprung up. As well as crows there were rabbits and whatever else could be snared, but the snows were going to make foraging worse. I'd heard there would be horsemeat tomorrow – it had been decided to butcher those animals too weak to make it through the winter before they grew too lean. Miss Cain told me she thought it was a good thing. There would be fewer fights tonight, she said, with all the soldiers filled up on thoughts of tomorrow's bounty.

We emptied our bowls. 'I wish there was more,' she

said, producing a rock of hard bread.

I wished there was more as well, but it was enough. 'It's a bounty to what I might have had.'

'When they came we were told there would be no plunder. Mr Cromwell instructed us. They said the New Model wasn't about plunder, that every one of its soldiers has his pay, plenty enough to feed himself and more besides. I've never heard of soldiers being paid before.'

I broke the bread and passed half back because I'd seen her plate was empty. 'I've never been paid,' I said.

'And now?'

It was a good question. Carew, Hotham, Whitelock and Wildman – all of the soldiers I'd met were taking their coin from Parliament's purses, but all I'd been paid was my freedom. Cromwell would have called it a fair and decent exchange. I could hardly disagree.

'Miss Cain . . .'

'Please,' she said. 'Call me Kate.'

'Kate. Katherine. Have they . . .' I stopped, not much liking where that question was leading. I knew they had plundered from her home. I knew her rooms had been given over to intruders. What else they had done I hardly wanted to know. It troubled me that I felt the desire to pry. 'Forgive me. I should not ask.'

'Mr Cromwell hung men for it in the beginning,' she said, after a silence that drew out too long between us. 'Like that man still hanging in the chestnut square. Now that Mr Cromwell is gone, now the winter is here, things are a little different.' She took away my plate and brought me beer. It was light and weak. She'd watered it down. 'Don't think me ungrateful, Master Falkland, but I didn't need your help with Master Warbeck. I think it would have been better had you not intervened.'

I remembered how fearful she'd appeared and found this hard to believe. 'He's a soldier of the worst kind,' I said darkly. 'A true believer. I fear he'd whip you out of town.'

'That . . . thing that he found. It was not mine. It belonged to my grandmother. I should have thrown it away when the army came but I couldn't bring myself to. It's all I have of her. But it's not mine, it was hers.'

I scoffed at this. 'True or not, I doubt Warbeck would care to see the difference.'

Miss Cain levelled me a long look. 'Again, Master Falkland, I thank you for your concern. You are a soldier and prone to fight battles, but I must fight my own. You'll be gone before long and I will still be here with this army around me all through winter. I mean to still be here after they leave.'

It seemed I was being chastised and yet I will admit I struggled to see why. 'He had a dagger drawn, Kate!'

She smiled at me for the first time since. 'He would not have used it.' Her smile fell. 'Do you think . . . Beg my pardon, Master Falkland, but those boys – do you think they suffered?'

Suffered? No hanging is a clean death. Jumping on a granadoe even worse. But I had an inkling this was not the kind of suffering Miss Katherine Cain meant. The rosary might not have been hers – in that I believed her – but I took her for a secret Catholic nonetheless. There were no crosses in her home, no other icons, but something gleamed in her eyes. She was drawn to those horrible moments the boys must have had before they took their lives, the twisted, terrible questions they must have asked themselves.

I thought of Hotham. 'I think, Miss Cain, that they suffered a great deal.'

CHAPTER 11

I'd seen nothing more of Purkiss since I'd entered the surgeon's house and now I saw nothing of Warbeck after he'd flung his accusations at Kate. I hoped he'd set off to fight through the snow back to London and the warmth of Cromwell's court. However, I'd promised to report to Fairfax as my investigation progressed and at least half of me expected to see Warbeck there, dining at Black Tom's table.

I left behind my empty bowl of Miss Cain's crow soup and took with me a stomach eager for more. Hunger is something every soldier knows, but there's nothing like a small meal to set a man's belly rumbling for something more substantial. In the November twilight I passed the silent inn towards the middle of the town. A small crowd of soldiers had gathered in the square where the dead man hung, his corpse now covered with frost so that he looked like a devil. Some were wearing their red coats but some were wearing black. A smaller group were wearing mismatched bits of armour and clothing, obviously scavenged off royalists they had killed or the bodies of their fallen friends. Most armies I'd seen were as ragtag as this so it didn't bother me in the slightest. Seeing the men in red coats, though, that *did* trouble me. It had been men in red coats who had cornered me in the farmhouse on the night I was captured.

I meant to avoid the gathering but as I entered the square the crowd grew so great that I could hardly get past without being swallowed whole. It seemed that two sides were quickly developing. One side had most of the red coats and the men wearing all black. The other, though there were red coats there too, was composed of those soldiers in ragtag, scavenged dress. I'd seen an alley a little short of the square between the inn and what I took to be a hanging shed and turned back towards it. I had no desire to be caught in a soldiers' brawl. When I reached it there were already men clambering onto the roof of the shed to watch.

The alley took me around the back of the inn past the stables and out to the southern side of the crowd. I came to the other end and was about to head to the market square and its tents and lean-tos when, all at once, the crowd became silent. Over my shoulder I saw a bonfire had been lit and now it spilled a fiery light onto them. I couldn't fathom why they might have made such a pyre in the middle of the square, not when all the houses in Crediton went cold for lack of kindling. A curiosity got the better of me then; I inched my way back to the edge of the crowd where a thin, reedy voice was making a proclamation. I couldn't hear the words but I saw the flash of coins being passed from hand to hand. This wasn't a common soldiers' brawl then. This was a duel, and the soldiers were betting on it.

I found a likely subject, a slight boy in an oversized red coat. He stood with the ragtag soldiers but could see nothing of what was going on himself because he was so small.

'What is it?' I asked.

'Who's asking?' he piped up.

'Falkland,' I said. 'I'm cavalry.'

'Cavalry and you've come *here* to see *this*?'

'What do you think?' I said. 'I'm starved of entertainments up there.'

The boy took to this line of reasoning with aplomb. 'You'd never get me on a horse,' he said. 'When I go into battle I want to be on my own two feet.' He stood tall to try and peer into the middle of the crowd. I could see an arena had developed there with jostling men all around. 'It's one of the newly pressed boys. Said the wrong thing and now he's got to fight for it. My money's on David. He tore chunks out of men at Naseby with only his hands. I should know. I saw it. He won't leave that cavalier whoreson standing.'

'The pressed boy,' I began. 'You mean to say he's a royalist?'

'Place is crawling with them and it's only getting worse. I've seen them give a good show every now and then. But a cavalier isn't born to fight, is he? He's born to strut around his estate and preen in front of his mirror.'

'What will happen if he loses?'

'It's *when* he loses. They'll give him a good hiding and take his clothes, I should think. He won't be so proud about being a cavalier when they've all seen his pizzle shrunken up from the cold! Look, get out of my way, would you? This thing's about to start.'

I decided not to stay for the fighting and walked away without looking back. Over my shoulder I could chart the course of it by the way the crowd groaned and roared. As best I could tell, the loser barely landed a blow and it was over before I reached the end of the lane. The raucous aftermath of the contest faded behind me.

I crossed the market square and headed east. As I passed the church I saw there were guards outside tonight and wondered why they had not been there in the morning. Perhaps the priest and I had been seen sneaking around and somebody had decided to double the watch? Beyond it, the easternmost parts of Crediton were as silent as a winter night should be. I saw lights behind windows, and fires burning in the mouths of the tents and the lean-tos built between the cottages, but I rarely saw a person. Too cold for snow, my breath turned into crystals of ice. On the outskirts of the town, towards the end of the cottages, I again saw a sorrowful lonely watchman standing guard by the road. I pitied him. His feet must be near frozen. I hurried on and turned down the track past the fields where the horses were kept, feeling a strange pang of pity for them, too, remembering what Miss Cain had told me and wondering if the unfortunate chosen ones had already been taken.

I crossed the little bridge over the river. There were fires inside Fairfax's farmhouse but there were border fires lit outside too, circles of stones with fires built low within. As I approached I saw that guards had been placed around the farmyard's edges. I wondered if Fairfax fancied himself some sort of prince now. There had once been a time, I knew, when he was one of the King's bannermen; but we were all loyal once, I suppose. I felt the sprawling camp on my shoulder and something forced me to look around. There was nothing to see but all the same I felt eyes on me. Not the eyes of some secret watcher lurking in the dark but of the army as a thing, as a monster, a living creature beyond the men it claimed. It was a thought I'd had before, lined up

in ranks with a thousand other men, but I'd never felt it as
keenly as I did now.

The guards didn't stir until I was close. I thought them
particularly useless. When I was in Yorkshire with the King,
few men could get this near to him without a horn being
sounded or the clash of steel upon steel. Prince Rupert was
easier with his men but even he would have shuddered at
the thought that a stranger might get this close. I wondered
if these guards already knew who I was but it seemed not:
the first to meet me, a scrawny youth surely too young
to have left his mother's teat, listened without any hint of
recognition as I told him. He turned on his heel and
beckoned me to follow. At the door a second guard – a burly
simpleton but at least he was more frightening than the
first whelp – made a show of searching me for weapons.
He didn't do a very good job and I might easily have
concealed a dagger in each boot. He didn't take me in,
though, but led me around to the back of the farmhouse and
bade me enter.

Inside, Black Tom received me. This little back room
wasn't as stark as the hall where we'd first been introduced
but there was still something austere about the bare stone
walls, unadorned with any weaving or painting, and a floor
as open as the earth. There was a small table and chair.
Writing implements were stacked neatly in one corner but I
didn't suppose that Fairfax, like Cromwell, spent his nights
writing letters to the mothers of soldiers who had died – I
don't mean to say that Cromwell regretted the loss of life
any the more; only that he knew better how to turn it to his
advantage.

Fairfax wasn't alone. The room was lit in each corner by

tall candelabras, and in its hearth by a small fire where I was surprised to see coals. In each of the pools of light stood another man. The first I recognised as Purkiss. I stared at him and he returned my gaze with a cold, flat look. I understood Warbeck's derision now: Purkiss had played at being a fool and played me for one too. He'd been good enough that I'd fallen for it.

The second man was Warbeck himself. He tipped me a curious, knowing look as I entered, as if we two were secret lovers arranging a tryst. There was no sign now of that hatred I'd seen in him in front of Kate. The final man I hadn't met before. He was tall with red hair and a fuzzy, Irish look about him. If he really were an Irishman then he was in the wrong place. Cromwell would have told him: all Irishmen go to Hell.

Fairfax was the last to look up. He did so as if he'd been pondering it some time. 'Gentlemen,' he began. 'I believe we have all met Master William James Falkland.'

The red-haired gentleman shook his head, 'I have yet to have the pleasure.' We shook hands – it was more than any of the others had done – and the gentleman introduced himself as Richard Baxter. When he told me he was the army's chaplain, I wasn't surprised; he had the same methodical, considered way about him as did the scalded priest from the church.

'I've not known an army to have its own chaplain before,' I began.

'You've been away from the world some time, Falkland,' Fairfax said. 'An army without God is a rabble. A general can lead his men onto the field but that is not the only kind of leadership this New Model of ours calls for. The men who fight for our cause shall have leadership for their spirits as well.'

He spoke as if he was waging a war on behalf of Heaven itself. Half of me wanted to pour derision on it, the idea of a godly host marching across the kingdom, rallying up its people and putting them to war. But a spark somewhere deep inside made me stay my tongue. The idea, preposterous as it might be, was like a seed of monstrous dread, the kind a young child has when his mother puts him to bed that sprouts from nothing and grows at frightful speed and never lets him go to sleep. Ideas can be terrible things when brought to men with the means of making them happen.

'The rest,' Black Tom began, 'you have already met: Mr Warbeck must return shortly to take our news back to London. And Alfred –' here he gestured to the imp in the corner of the room who grumbled behind his beard – 'was most affronted that you spurned his attention this morning. He was instructed to help.'

I didn't doubt it, but it was clear to me now that this 'help' mainly entailed keeping Fairfax appraised of my movements.

'I don't like disobeying instructions,' grunted Purkiss.

There was silence.

'I have come to make my report, as I swore,' I said.

Fairfax waved me away. 'Over supper, Falkland,' he smiled. 'You would *like* supper, would you not?'

I couldn't say that I would not, although it would make this day the first in more years than I cared to count when I'd eaten three warm meals between dawn and midnight. I said nothing; Fairfax took my silence for acquiescence and led us to the stark hall where I'd first been received on my arrival with Warbeck. The hall had been decked out since the previous day. I do not mean to say it was like a courtly Christmas, but it was vastly different from the grim hostelries and camps below. In the middle of the room a huge dining table had been erected and on its top there were platters and bowls and flagons of wine, dark and hot. We took our seats, mine between Warbeck and the chaplain Baxter so that I faced Fairfax himself. Two waiting girls appeared with a goose, roasted to a golden brown and around it potatoes heaped high, and placed it in the middle of the table. I took the girls for camp whores dolled up for the occasion. Their skins – no doubt scrubbed in the snow – were red raw. Even so, they were the most delighted among us to be here; there were surely more opportunities for foraging and plundering from our plates than in the whole of Crediton combined. One of the girls caught my eye over the table. I was glad she would not starve tonight.

With that goose sitting right between us all, the chaplain Baxter led us in prayer. I hate to admit how it riled me to wait: the smells – the spices, the good honest grease, the idea of goose flesh dissolving in my mouth – tormented me. I felt like a mariner lost at sea: water everywhere and yet his mouth swollen with thirst. I'd not seen food like this for years. Through eyes only half closed I saw that Baxter was quoting from a pocket book very much like the one I'd found on the deserter Warbeck had shot near Taunton. I'm not a man who sits by his fireside reading pamphlets or treatises and have very rarely cared to indulge in the printed word at all, but there was something unsettling about seeing this book again.

'"A soldier must not do wickedly",' Baxter quoted. His

voice was light and feathery but, nevertheless, trembled with the authority of God. '"A soldier must be valiant for God's cause. A soldier must not rely on his own wisdom or strength nor any provision for war. A soldier must put his confidence in God's wisdom and strength."' He paused and closed the book. '"We who sit above the fighting man give thanks for his bravery and for this bounty."'

It seemed an odd grace to me. We who feast tonight give thanks for those who starve. I tried not to let it bother me unduly. I *was* ravenous.

As we began, the food had me equally in paroxysms of delight and terrible convulsing cramps. I battled through and wolfed it down. As plates were piled up and then emptied again, hardly one of us spoke. They were better practised at disguising it, but all of these men were, to some degree, starving. It was hardly unexpected – I think by then that the same might have been said about the whole of England and I didn't pause to wonder at the sense of keeping chaplains to eat up provisions that would have been better served to the soldiers. Of all of us, Baxter was the one who ate most slowly. He even took time to wipe his lips clean.

'What is your book?' I finally asked.

The men I was dining with conspired with a grin but Baxter's faded first. He seemed troubled. 'Have you not received your *Soldier's Pocket Bible*?' he asked.

I had not. 'Was I supposed to?'

Richard Baxter shared a look with Fairfax. Fairfax nodded. 'He is a New Modeller now. You're right. He should have his Bible.'

Baxter took great care in explaining that every single

soldier in this mongrel army had his own copy of this pocket book. It was full of scripture to aid a soldier's spirit and, so Baxter said, nourished him more than any meal. I wondered what the pikemen in the encampment would make of that assertion if they could see us feasting now. 'I saw you tore apart their church,' I said when he was done. 'Was that instruction in the pocket book as well?'

The priest shook his head solemnly. 'I am aware of the transgression. But, Master Falkland, you must understand: this is a godly army. If sometimes the boys take their godliness to an extreme, it is through fervour and righteousness, not through malice. Some boys saw the glass in those windows and could not stand for it.'

'For a piece of painted glass?'

At this, Fairfax interjected. 'I'd ask you to mind your manners, Falkland. You would do well to remember in whose house you eat.'

'My trouble is,' I went on, 'that barely half this army is as *godly* as you would have it. Oh, I dare say, there are many Puritan boys out there. I've seen some of them myself, scrapping in the streets. But here is my report: I'm of the opinion that those boys died because they were Catholics.'

Black Tom fixed me with a look. Suddenly the sabre scar across his face seemed more prominent, as if, like his eyebrows, it was arching to make a point.

'They were taking confessions out by that tree,' I said.

'The churchman,' whispered Baxter.

'He didn't solicit it. He had boys going to him. And not just the dead boys, I shouldn't wonder. This place is crawling with Catholics.'

Black Tom linked his fingers together to make a steeple

on which he rested his chin. He smirked. 'You say it as if it disgusts you. And you a cavalier.'

He was taunting me. Fairfax wasn't foolish enough to say that all cavaliers were Catholics. It was a fallacy that the rank and file liked to perpetuate: that the New Model was fighting a godly war and hence their enemies had to be *un*godly. It was remarkable how many different ways a sentiment like that could be twisted.

'Is that the extent of your progress, Falkland? That the New Model is not yet complete?' Warbeck's voice was as buttery as it had been the first time we met in the carriage to Cromwell's chambers; but, while then he had seemed a servant, now he was more certain of his stature. He shifted slightly and I fancied he was trying to make himself seem level with Black Tom.

'I wasn't told the third boy survived,' I began. 'I thought I was here to poke around a run of suicides and desertions but—'

'You do not believe them suicides?' Warbeck purred.

'I'm yet to form an opinion.'

'A messenger is leaving for London in the morning,' Warbeck went on. 'It would serve you well if I had a report to make.'

'You can tell your master that he sent me into a nest of vipers. But that's nothing he didn't already know, is it? So you see, gentlemen, I begin to ask myself questions. I begin to ask myself why in *God's* name –' I took the opportunity to invoke the Lord's name in vain just to see if it might make them shudder – 'a man like Oliver Cromwell, who is certainly not squeamish about death and who might hang boys himself and glory in them dangling there, would worry about a few deaths in this monster he's created? I reckon him for a statistician. A tactician. A man who writes letters to the mothers of fallen soldiers not because their deaths burden him but because it adds to his ledger. A man who can stack good against bad and not trouble himself at night so long as the scales balance. And I wonder – why?'

Before anyone could respond, the serving girls reappeared. We were to be served stewed apples and the sweet smell filled the air. It was enough to make me forget.

'Well,' Black Tom smiled. 'We are at least agreed on one matter: the death of three lads makes not one whit of difference. Cromwell has indeed lost control of his senses.' He looked at me intently, as if happy at last. 'Eat,' he instructed. 'Yours is a soul that needs nourishing,' he added, 'in every way there is.'

The tone of dismissal, the sense that he was almost glad these boys were dead, riled me; but once I'd taken my first spoonful I couldn't stop. Black Tom took it to his advantage and caught me off guard while I was savouring the taste. 'What you must appreciate,' he said, 'is that Mr Cromwell, above all else, is interested in the *detail*. He is like an embroiderer in that respect. He is like a tailor. But his trade is in people, not in clothes and thread. Mr Cromwell is an exemplary tactician, and not only when he is leading a hundred horse into your screaming royalist ranks.' Fairfax grinned over his steepled hands. When his face creased the scar shifted. Though it was old it made the impression that it was perilously close to opening again. 'You and I, Falkland, have fought this war for years. On opposite sides, perhaps, but I'll fancy the differences are small ones. So we are of one mind. Three boys died. We lose more than that every week through cold and disease. There are rumours in camp – but I've already told you, a camp without rumours is like a dancing girl without the itch. I'd be more worried if there were no rumours at all.' He paused. 'But,' he went on, 'now that *you* appear, now that Cromwell sends his *man* into my camp, well, you'll appreciate, it isn't exactly the hangings that are stirring up trouble.'

I listened but could not look him in the eye for I was too busy scraping out my bowl and, besides, I didn't want to see the way he could look deep into me. 'And the desertions?' I asked him when I was done. 'How many have there been?'

Fairfax fixed me with a fiery look. 'More than a hundred. But what does Cromwell expect when he insists on pressing royalists and Catholics?' He banged the table, the sudden violence enough to make all four of us jump. At his side, Purkiss leapt up as if he might be about to swoon. 'There is only one thing that can stop us from winning this war, Falkland,' he said. 'Do you know what that is?'

'The King?' I began, though the King could hardly win the favour of his own Court these days.

'Disunity!' Fairfax barked back. He brought his fist down to rattle the table a second time. 'How can a good Puritan pikeman lad fight with the full might of God in his heart when all around his own company are papists and cavaliers?'

'You can press men's bodies, sir, but you cannot press their minds. You cannot press their souls.' As I said the words I realised I believed them. Cromwell had pressed me into his service but he had not turned me to his cause. Perhaps it was only the stewed apples, but I felt warmer inside. Warbeck glowered and twitched his eye to show that

I was chancing my arm, but I thought they would not have brought me to dinner to do me any harm.

Fairfax grinned, showing off his rotten teeth. 'Exactly so. *Exactly* so. And so we have what I believe to be a perfect solution to this whole matter. There is something I would like to show you.'

He rose without a further word and strode for the door. Warbeck, still glowering, was quick to follow. I rose more sedately, my stomach bloated and unsettled by this unaccustomed feast. Purkiss and Baxter showed every sign of staying exactly as they sat. I understood, then, that whatever was to come, all here had known of it before I ever set foot through the door. They'd been waiting for me. Perhaps even this feast had been set to soften my mind.

Outside, Fairfax led us along a path going round to the back of the farm. You could not tell if you approached from the town, but the farmhouse masked a sprawl of outbuildings in its yards. There was a stable where a white stallion was kept, a house for chickens that had long been picked clean and a feed house where cavalrymen were bedding down. Beyond these was a small stone building, no bigger than the room in which we'd dined, with no windows and only a single narrow door. Three guardsmen stood beside it. One of them tended a fire but it didn't seem to be warming them much. As we approached – Fairfax, Warbeck and I – I could hear their teeth chattering from a furlong away. They gathered themselves when they saw us and stood up straight. Warbeck took a lantern from one of the men and led us to the door and opened it. The stench inside was terrible, a mixture of slurry and rot I'd not known since my brief time as warden of the condemned in Yorkshire. The lantern threw our shadows against the stone. There was a deep squelching underfoot and I took it that we were treading in frost-crusted manure.

The lantern swept around and I saw, in the corner, a man scrabbling like a rat. He'd been asleep but he dragged himself up when we loomed above him, shielding his eyes from the light with an arm drenched in muck. In the crook of his elbow I saw his face, all bunched up and beaten.

'Give me that,' I said and took the lantern from Warbeck. I crouched down and held the light near. The man thought I was coming to deliver more blows and shrank as closely as he could to the wall. He tried to say something but his lips were swollen and I couldn't make out the words. 'What did you do to him?' I demanded, looking back over my shoulder.

'It was nothing he didn't deserve,' said Fairfax. 'Nothing Cromwell would not have done himself had he known what this wretch did.'

'Who is he?'

'A deserter,' hissed Warbeck. He was flushed with pride, his simpering baritone voice even more sickly sweet, and I wondered if he'd been the man to administer this justice. More likely he had been a spectator. He didn't have the fists for fighting.

'Worse, I'm afraid,' said Fairfax coolly. 'He was part of the camp guard. When the wintering began, men were appointed to set patrols, keep discipline. The godliest men we could find.'

If this was what came of being godly then I would rather be a devil's whoreson.

'He betrayed his post,' Fairfax went on. 'He was one of those who ravished a local merchant's daughter. It was after

Cromwell returned to London when we rooted him out or else he might already be hanging in the chestnut square. You remember the man hanging there?'

I stood. A part of me still ached for this man – I supposed I would always now have a tender spot for men locked in chains – but another part thought of my own daughter, Charlotte. Wherever she was now, I hoped she was far away from any man, any soldier, any politician. I'd rather lock her in a tower for her whole life than subject her to this. No, if Fairfax spoke the truth then any pity I had for this man was scant, chains or no.

'He has entered into an agreement,' Fairfax said. 'In return for a swift end he will swear an oath to the fact that he goaded those boys to suicide. He will make his confession –' Fairfax smiled – 'but not to that loitering priest. He will make his confession to you, Falkland, and you may deliver a report to your master and be gone. You are, after all, a man with a reputation for an irredeemable conscience. I would not have you lie.'

'This man is innocent?'

'Innocent?' Warbeck gasped. 'Cromwell would have had him drawn and quartered already.'

Fairfax was shaking his head. 'Falkland, now is not the time to be noble. Nobility is dying. And I say that as a man of noble birth myself. You were sent to this camp to stop the rumours of those boys' deaths spiralling into something that could not be controlled. I am asking you to control it. You say they died because they were Catholic. Very well. But do you now mean to question every Puritan lad who joined Parliament to guard our souls against the sins of popery?'

The man in front of me was dead anyway. It was better

that he died quickly rather than agonise in this place the whole winter long, no matter what he'd done.

'You will have a report to make to Cromwell. You must make it knowing it's God's truth as you have heard it. You'll be free to leave the encampment and I will be free of an intelligencer rummaging around, conjuring consternation out of a simple unfortunate occurrence.'

He paused. On the ground, the man scrabbled. But this time he dropped his arm and I could see his face. His eyes, though black and half sealed shut, seemed to speak to me. It did not matter to him, he was saying. Either way, it was not going to be his problem.

'What do you say, Falkland?'

I stepped back. I wanted nothing more than to nod, to press my hands together and leave this place. If I rode swiftly, if luck was on my side, I could be at my old home in Launcells within two days. I could begin my search for what was left of my family. My Caro, my son, my little girl . . . But as I looked at Fairfax something bit me deep inside. It was the same thing that had bitten me all those years ago in Yorkshire when the King had told me to leave it alone, that the rapist might go ignored. I did not like the way Fairfax tossed the deaths of those boys aside as though they were nothing. He reminded me, then and there, a little of the King in that regard.

'There is a boy in the surgeon's quarters,' I said. 'Name of Hotham. The third boy to hang. I'm going to need to speak to him without the presence of his surgeon and without the presence of his friends.' I turned on my heel and flinched as I stepped back into the biting cold of the camp. 'Sirs, I don't know what you have created here. I'm not sure

I *want* to know. But I do know this: those boys didn't have to die. Not here. Kill them on a battlefield if you must, but not like this.'

I turned my back and marched alone down the incline to the bridge across the frozen brook, between the fields of horses, past the lonely watchman at the edge of the town and back towards the market square. All the way I thought I felt Black Tom's eyes following me; and when outside the church I heard footsteps moving quickly behind me, catching up, I turned, my fists clenched and raised and my heart pounding as if ready for battle. I didn't fancy Fairfax had taken well to my refusal and there were much simpler ways to rid himself of Cromwell's unwanted intelligencer.

The footsteps were Warbeck. I relaxed a little, but he must have seen I was ready to fight for he raised his hands to show they were empty and shook his head. He laughed his mocking laugh. 'I'd find a way to make some friends if I were you,' he said and walked with me the rest of the way, whether I wished it or not, back into Crediton and Miss Cain's house.

My stomach groaned. Those stewed apples were not going down well.

CHAPTER 12

I woke on the next morning with a dirty feeling at the back of my throat and a terrible cramping in my gut. Such are the perils of fine dining. I took myself to my chamber pot but heaved only dry flecks and phlegm. My body couldn't tolerate what was inside it but it wasn't done with it yet.

As I sat there, pot between my knees, there was a knocking at the door. I begged a moment to make myself decent but Miss Cain entered nonetheless. She didn't cry out to see me half-dressed and white as a ghost. She had brought beer and bread and I didn't have the heart to tell her I might not keep it down. 'You'd better be swift,' she said. 'The camp guard won't take kindly if you miss it, no matter if you're an interloper or not.'

'Miss what?' I did not follow.

'Do you know what day it is?'

I wheeled through the days in my head. I'd tried to keep track of them when I was imprisoned but it proved impossible. 'Sunday,' I began. 'The Sabbath?'

She nodded. 'You must be quick.'

Warbeck was already gone and, as we set out, the streets were eerily empty. Miss Cain hurried in front of me, urging me along. 'I kept myself to myself at first,' she told me, 'but

I soon wished I hadn't. Camp guards came clattering at the door. They took me to the square and made me a part of it. They would have dragged me had I refused.'

'I'd thought to find the friends of the dead boys today,' I said. 'Whitelock and Wildman. Somebody must have grieved for them. Somebody planted that cross in their grave. The boy Fletcher as well. If he was a local then he must have family . . .'

Miss Cain stopped some yards ahead of me, demanding me to hurry with her eyes. 'It would do you no good,' she sighed. I sensed that she found something to amuse herself in the way I plodded along, still suffering from the night before. 'If they had friends, this is where they'll be.'

We crossed the small square where the dead man hung and heard the low rumble of voices assembled in a large group at the end of the street. Before we got there, the hum became magnificent. There was certainly something godly about it. We took one of the narrow lanes and I saw, at its end, men crowded into the market square, completely filling it. I do not think I had ever seen so many men in one place before, not even on the eve of a battle. They thronged and choked the square and every tributary leading into it. The army had filled half the town, packed tight with men.

'What is it?' I whispered, for my breath was taken quite away.

'Sundays are the army Days of Admonishment,' Miss Cain answered. She too had lowered her voice, though we could scarcely have been overheard beneath the rumble of ten thousand restless tongues. 'They bring their pocket book Bibles and listen to the Admonishments. The chaplain leads them.'

I supposed she meant Baxter, the red-headed ogre I'd met at Fairfax's quarters the night before. 'Everyone is here? The whole camp?'

'Every Sunday since they came into Crediton. They purge themselves. They say it makes them closer to God.'

'It sounds like the confessional to me. Yet they hunt boys who want to make a confession.'

Miss Cain's green eyes flashed and she gave me a look I couldn't mistake. She was of the same mind. She moved so that I thought she was putting her arm through mine but instead she simply took hold of my elbow and urged me forward to join the throng. We found a place against one of the houses that bordered the square where we wouldn't be jostled by soldiers behind us, but we could not escape their stink. It was a peculiar scent: the purity of snow and the fetid musk of man. I looked at Miss Cain but she didn't seem to notice it in the same way as I.

The ranks were arranged around the steps where the defiled cross once stood. In the centre I saw a string of men standing sentry with their arms linked, holding back the soldiers at the front while the men behind jostled to get closer. This was less an army than a rabble. I could scarcely compare the pikemen and cavalry who operated so mercilessly on the battlefield to the horde of which I was now a part.

'Is Fairfax here?' I asked.

'I saw him observe an Admonishment once,' Miss Cain said, pressing her lips close to my ear so I could hear. 'The same way he comes to observe drills. There'll be a hundred pikemen ranked up in one of the fields, dropping and turning and thrusting and wheeling, and Black Tom just watches from his horse, as if he's *studying*. It was the same when he came to the Day of Admonishment.'

'As though the soldiers were being drilled here as well,' I surmised.

'It's as much a drill as any. Their chaplain says the spirit has to be drilled more fiercely than the body.'

That I could believe but I'd never seen it done like this. In the King's army we often shared prayers or else we told stories – which, as any veteran soldier will tell you, are themselves a kind of prayer. I realised, as I thought, that Miss Cain had said *their* chaplain. Not *your* chaplain. It pleased me that she recognised I was not a part of this bastard New Model.

A window ledge pressed uncomfortably into my back. I found that I was able to hoist myself onto it and raise myself a foot above the men ahead of me. From this vantage I tried to survey the crowd, looking for the few figures I'd met since I first came to camp, and at last saw the priest I'd cornered in Crediton church. If I'd imagined he would be a part of this service – was service the right word, or was this something more sinister? – I was wrong. He lurked at the head of one of the lanes that fed into the main square, among a group of boys much younger than himself. They must have been sixteen or seventeen years old, not much older than my own son John would be by now. They were wearing the same Venice red dress as the rest of the soldiers who made up the throng.

The priest crooked his head and whispered something to one of the boys. At that the boy scuttled away out of my sight. I stared at the others, trying to learn their faces. I had no chance to reach them across this crowd but I fancied I might want to speak with them. 'Do you know him?' I asked Miss Cain, cocking my head in the priest's direction.

She levered her way up beside me to see. It took her only a moment to understand who I meant. 'Of course I know him,' she said. 'What they did to him was a blasphemy.'

'They took him for a Catholic,' I said, meaning the New Model.

'They should have taken him for a good man. A devoted man. However you worshipped, he cared for everyone who came to him.'

A sudden hush spread through the crowd as surely as a rumour. By the time it reached us I could already see the rugged red-headed Baxter emerging from a house on the square's edge. He was some distance away but he did not look diminutive. Indeed, he looked more statuesque than when I'd last seen him, shovelling stewed apples into his mouth. It would not have been this man who enacted justice on the camp guard locked up in Fairfax's cell, but perhaps he'd taken part in another sort of justice. I imagined the New Model looked on justice in the same way as they looked on drills: there was physical justice and spiritual justice too. Of the four with whom I had dined last night he had certainly been the most civil; and yet I found in myself a profound dislike for the man and his exclusive notions of God.

'What now?' I whispered.

'Watch.'

With the help of a handful of soldiers, the chaplain forced himself through the mob and onto the steps where the cross had once stood, rising above the crowd around him. When he began to speak the murmuring fell away and all eyes watched him. He had with him the same *Soldier's Pocket Bible* he'd shown me the night before and he began to read a verse. He had a good voice, I was forced to admit, one that carried right across the square. I could see some of the soldiers held their own books too, following his words, tracing them with their fingers. I saw there were great swathes of men in this crowd who took no more interest in this than they did in any other drill. They shuffled from foot to foot, mouthing the *Amens* whenever Baxter exclaimed it, following the prayers without the flourishes that I saw in other parts of the crowd. I'd known men like this in the King's army, plenty of them who did just enough that they would not get punished and yet took care not to stand out from their companions. I wondered how many men were here alongside whom I had once fought.

And then there were the others. I could easily enough pick out the soldiers who were engrossed by every word the chaplain said. They seemed to me to be the better fed, the men with more life to them, but perhaps that was just an illusion; for these soldiers were more animated, more eager to bellow out their *Amens* and even recite the verses along-side the chaplain. It was, I decided, not so very different to the Mass. My eyes wandered instinctively back to the lane where I'd seen the priest but he was gone. I supposed he couldn't stand to hear it.

'Prince Rupert used to lead us in prayers too,' I whispered, 'on the eve of every battle. I think he thought it brought us together.'

Miss Cain's eyes glimmered again and I saw she was confused. In that second I hated myself. I'd not meant to pour scorn on such a simple thing as a prayer. Miss Cain must have had prayers of her own and I did not mean to take that from her.

'It served the younger boys well enough,' I said. I did not add that I'd seen a thousand men utter a prayer before a battle only for it to be their last. In my experience, prayers went unanswered. The last three times I rode out to the horns of war I'd not made a single petition. It was just screaming into the void. I still remembered very starkly the first night I'd not prayed before going out to fight. I'd sat long into the midnight watch with a stupid pup of a lad, the son of some nobleman who was eager to prove himself a swordsman and serve his King. 'There is but one God,' I'd told him, 'and his name is Death.' All the same the boy put his hands together, certain in the knowledge that he would be looked after throughout the fight if only he could draw God's eye with his devotion.

'Do you think that all the men who fought before you, who died screaming for their mothers, overlooked their prayers?' I asked him. 'Do you think the men on the other side don't pray too?' He took it as a jest, as I knew he would, and told me he would say a prayer for me too. We both of us came through the battle and when he saw me after he was wearing the sort of grin that made me certain he should be sent home to suckle on his mother a year or two longer.

'My prayer was answered, Falkland,' he said. He rejoiced long into the night but I was long past any rejoicing after any battle, no matter the outcome. I never knew what became of him after that.

I felt Miss Cain's hand tug my arm and looked up to see a procession of men being led from the same house on the edge of the square. They came with an escort who once more pushed and shoved through the crowd until they reached Baxter's makeshift pulpit – I could not see it as anything else. There were seven of them and they lined up on the steps in front of him only yards from where the mass of soldiers began. Each was wearing a white sheet wrapped around him like a funeral shroud and on the front of each was pinned a leaf of paper. I could see they were printed, but with what words I couldn't tell.

Miss Cain saw my lips part to ask a question but she hushed me. 'The Admonishments,' she explained.

If I'd not understood, all was quickly made clear. On each of the papers were printed the wrongs the soldier was said to have committed. He was to wear them today, for all to see, while Baxter spoke out the things they had done, and then the baying began. 'Plunder,' he recited. 'Blasphemy. Deceit.' Each word sounded like a knell and each time the crowd grew more fervent. It seemed to me likely there was not a single man in the crowd who had not committed the same sins, but all the same they added their voices to the choir.

I looked out over the sea of faces, searching for boys who didn't join in the jeering – to my stark relief I even found some, too contrite or cowed to shout out – when a face leapt out at me. He had high cheekbones and wild, shaggy hair and stood a half foot taller than the boys who crowded him on either side.

'What is it?' asked Miss Cain, sensing me tense.

'Carew,' I said.

If Kate knew who he was then she didn't say. Carew wasn't jeering like the rest. Something in me had suspected he would be jeering more fiercely but it wasn't so. He stood

there with an air of calmness around him, like the minute of
pure silence you sometimes see in the heart of a storm. I
watched his gaze revolve. Clusters of other boys closer to
Miss Cain and myself were not jeering either. They hunched
together, heads bowed down meekly as if to even look at
the catcalls was to become a part of them. My eyes darted
between them and Carew, quickly lest I lose him in the
crowd. I knew suddenly what bothered me about seeing him
there, standing so aloof. Though he was not a part of the
chorus, he was revelling in it. That he did not lend his own
voice set him apart but it did not distance him from the
madness as it did the terrified boys scattered around. They
saw it and cringed. He saw it and *studied*.

'Come,' I said. 'Don't lose me.'

I made certain I had tight hold of Kate's hand as I
dropped back to the stone flags of the square and pushed
forward towards Carew. For a moment she resisted. I looked
back. I was suddenly aware of what she was: the only woman
I could see in a vast sea of men.

'Wait!' she hissed. Somebody beside us had noticed her
consternation and fixed his grubby eyes on her. He was a
low, brawny figure, the perfect sort to wield a pike. His
Venice red coat was mired in filth. My eyes wandered back
and found Carew again. Around us the jeering was dying
away as Baxter turned back to his pocket Bible. Carew
turned my way and I feared our eyes would lock but he
simply looked straight through me. I released my grip on
Miss Cain. She massaged her wrist and I realised how
viciously I'd been holding her, though it was only because I
didn't like the thought of losing her in this sea of soldiers.
'Miss Cain, Kate . . .' I said. 'I beg your forgiveness.'

'Begging forgiveness is too late. That's what I tell every whimpering bastard in this camp.'

'I didn't want to lose you.'

'Black Tom didn't name you my champion, Falkland. He named you my tenant.'

I didn't have time to answer. The silence had returned. The Admonished men and their escort pushed their way through the crowd back whence they came, and then the doors opened again and another procession began, women this time, though I had to squint to be certain, for every one of them was bald. Some of their scalps were bloody and pitted with scabs so that I could tell their hair had only just been sheared. Like the men who came before them, they were wrapped in white sheets with pieces of printed parchment pinned to their breasts. This time there was only one word on each leaf, the same for all of the women.

It read WHORE and was printed big and bold.

Miss Cain, despite her protestations, was still at my side. 'Camp followers?' I asked.

Her eyes met mine. I wasn't certain but something seemed to have soothed in her, though she still held her wrist and I could not see if I'd bruised her. 'I don't know,' she said. 'I haven't seen them before.'

I looked more closely. Miss Cain might not have recognised the women Baxter was parading but I thought that I did. More accurately, I thought I recognised just one of them. She stood on the far right of the procession, her head kept down so that I could not see her eyes, but I still had little doubt. 'I'm sorry,' I said. 'I need to get closer.'

'Falkland – what is it?'

'Please,' I answered. I realised I was begging. 'Come with me.'

She nodded. 'I'll stay close, Falkland. Just don't man-handle me again.'

Aware of the brawny pikeman's eyes still fixed on Miss Cain, I made sure that she went first. We skirted the edge of the square, bustling through the men less eager to be part of the throng, the ones who lingered on the outskirts with their pocket Bibles in hand, and reached the mouth of one of the broader lanes. It was here that I'd seen the priest but now he was gone. Miss Cain and I stopped. We reached the road towards the church but the angle wasn't yet right to see the camp whore's face. I began to weave a way forward, careful not to tread on the toes of any soldier who might have taken it badly. I'm not a small man but I was withered by my time in Newgate and this was not the place to pick a fight.

Halfway into the crowd the men were packed so tightly that we could not have gone further without drawing a sabre and cutting them down. They were like trees in a forest but it didn't matter. We were close enough. I didn't draw Miss Cain beside me for fear she would take it un-kindly, but nevertheless we were thrust together by bodies jostling on either side. We were perhaps twenty yards from the steps to the severed cross where the camp whores were being admonished. Now I was certain I was right. The girl at the far end of the procession with the word WHORE printed across her breast, she was the same girl I'd seen loitering when I'd gone to the graves yesterday morning with the priest. She had the same thin lips, the same freckled complexion. Her hair, already viciously cropped yesterday, was now gone entirely but her eyes were familiar.

In front of the women, Baxter was speaking. This close I could hear him more clearly, his voice cutting through the whispering of the crowd.

'. . . to sustain us in this winter, to see us to the first months of spring and the glory that will be God's when the King will make terms. But a war fought unjustly is not a war that can ever be won. We would be as much defeated by winning this war if we were to turn our back on Christ our Lord as we would were the King to thrash us in the field. But take heart, my brave lads, for neither of these things will come to pass.'

There were soldiers around me who were rapt. I tried to crane back and see Carew – I had a picture in my head of the way he would be observing this and *approving*, as though he was something more than a foot soldier in a fiery mob – but I'd lost him in the sea of faces.

'We are an army of God!' Baxter proclaimed. 'But we are not untouched by the devil's temptations. We are but men. This we admit, because this we *must* admit.' He opened his pocket Bible again and read a line. ' *"We are soldiers in Christ and must strain to hear his wisdom."* ' It was oblique enough that the mob might lend it their own interpretation; but for the more stupid soldiers about, Baxter had one already prepared. 'We want things, do we not? As simple, poor men, we *want*. But it is up to us whether we should *take*.' He stepped around and made as if to reveal the women although they had been there all along. 'War, my dear friends, is a dirty business. It attracts the holy but it attracts the fallen as well. And it comes to us, as godly men, to cast out those who would wilfully embrace the darkness. Those who sell false trinkets. Those who see God in a pane of glass. Those who, like Eve, sell the promise of the flesh.'

There rose a great tide of jeering. For the first time, the girl at the end of the procession let her eyes flicker up, as if she had been daring herself to look into this ocean of men who at night might want her but in the cold light of day would gladly hurl stones. Her gaze did not last long. Just as quickly she dropped her head and shielded herself from their cries.

'These mother's daughters,' Baxter went on, 'will march from the camp today and will not return. Should they seek a way back in then I – by the power invested in me by Thomas Fairfax, rightful and godly commander of this army – pronounce their lives to be forfeit. The camp guard will move through Crediton and root out all other camp followers profiting from sins of the flesh. They too will be expelled. My sons, I say to you again that it will be no victory if come the spring we have fallen from God's grace. This is God's army. We do God's work!'

Four guardsmen, wearing full armour instead of the Venice red coats of the rank and file, emerged from the crowd, two from one side and two from the other. The women must have been instructed as to how it would happen for not one of them protested. It seemed they were to be allowed to keep the white sheets they were wrapped in, though mere sheets would not be much comfort to anyone forced to spend the night in the wild; it was not even midday and the smell of frost was in the air.

The guards led the women away. I thought they were going to carve a path through the horde itself but the crowd opened for them with a surprising grace. They passed us close by, heading along the road that led towards the church. The restless murmuring began again until Baxter opened his book of prayers and began another reading.

I watched as they passed and then leaned and whispered into Miss Cain's ear. 'I can't let them take those girls . . .'

'Why? Itching for one of them, are you?'

It was not the sort of jest I'd imagined Miss Cain would make. Momentarily, I drew back.

'I'm sorry,' she said.

'It isn't that.'

'You can't stop it, Falkland. They'll say you're ungodly.'

'I can't stop it and nor do I want to, but I must speak with one of those girls before she leaves.' I realised I had hold of Miss Cain's wrist again. I let go, urged her to follow me and we pushed again through the crowd, hearing the guttural disapproval of more than one stinking pikeman as we came. Miss Cain led me through an alley where the snow had been trampled but not cleared. The banks were as high as my knees and we kicked our way along, emerging at a narrow lane that ran along the church's rear wall. I could see the Admonished girls now as they were led further off into the camp. From the way they moved I thought they had been roped together: we'd done that to Parliament prisoners we'd taken once, somewhere outside Islip, and they had marched much the same.

We set to following. The girls and their escort passed around the back of the surgeon's house and into the fields where the barns and tents had been erected, along trails through the snow already trampled by a thousand men. I'd become disorientated after we left the church but I realised with a start that I knew this part of the encampment. We were at the track that led to the hanging tree.

Miss Cain and I stopped. We could see the women ahead, the only things moving in that empty expanse. They paused as the soldiers freed them from their ropes. The sheets were still wrapped tightly around them, constricting them so that they had an odd shuffling gait like amputees. Shortly after, a man on horseback rode out from the camp to accompany them.

'Where did you stable my horse?' I asked. I meant Warbeck's horse, the one I'd been given, but it would not pay to quibble.

'At the livery behind the inn like Black Tom said.' She spoke hesitantly and when I turned to see her, had a distressed look about her. 'You don't mean to ride after them?'

'I would speak to her alone where others do not watch and listen. I would have her words come freely.'

'Falkland, you're not supposed to leave camp . . .'

I stopped. 'What did you say?'

Kate screwed her eyes as if regretting some spilled secret. 'You're not meant to leave camp,' she admitted. 'Master Warbeck thinks you want to desert. You're being watched.'

'Warbeck?' I don't know why it felt like such a betrayal to know she spoke with Warbeck behind my back. I'd only known her two days and she'd already proved herself wilful and independent. 'Who does the watching?' I asked.

Her silence told me. She looked away and could not meet my eye.

'He pays you for it, does he?' I demanded.

'Falkland, it's not like that! You make it sound a terrible thing. I'm alive, aren't I? And I have a roof, and food and –' she looked out into the fields – 'and I haven't had to be like them.' She stopped. Her defensiveness turned to anger, as if in my silence I was accusing her. 'Nobody has died on my account, Falkland. If it makes a difference, Black Tom has me keeping a watch over both of you.'

'I'll need my horse,' I said calmly. Silence twisted and turned between us and I felt as if we were having a bitter argument without a single word being said. At last she nodded and turned and disappeared back through the tents into the town. While she was gone I kept watch on the shambling girls as they followed the road away from Crediton and crossed the bridge over the river. It wasn't long before they disappeared – whether into the shadow of a hill or only into the endless white, I could not tell. The cavalry man disappeared with them but it wasn't long before he appeared once more. I watched him slowly get nearer to the camp, the tiny speck of his horse getting gradually bigger. My eyes are not what they were but before he reached camp I recognised him: Purkiss, Fairfax's man. Another pair of eyes sent to watch and spy on me. Purkiss for Fairfax, Warbeck for Cromwell, Kate for Warbeck and Fairfax both? I watched hard. I had a sudden fancy to know exactly who Purkiss was and his role in this camp. I was of a mind to beat it out of him.

He was trotting peacefully through the encampment border fires, still heading towards us but out of sight behind a rise and the rows of tents, when Miss Cain returned astride my horse. She swung herself down and ran a hand across the animal's flank. His eyeballs rolled madly.

'Thank you, Miss Cain.'

'I will be in sore trouble if I don't report you leaving,' she said.

y boot in the stirrup and launched myself into
It was not a comfortable feeling. My inner thighs
felt tender and my joints ached. 'I'll be coming back,' I said.
'You have my word on it.'

'Nevertheless, Master Falkland. The trouble will be the
same either way.'

I wheeled the horse around, eager to be out of there
before Purkiss reappeared. 'Fairfax's man. The one he sent
to show me the tree. Do you know who he is?' I asked.

Kate nodded. 'I heard he was an under-commander to
Nathaniel Rich,' she said.

It was a name I'd learned when fighting under Prince
Rupert's banner. Nathaniel Rich was a colonel in the
Parliament cavalry. We called them the Ironsides for the way
they could smash through our lines no matter how deter-
mined we were to hold position. Rich had been a prominent
Ironside in the stories we told, but I'd not heard of an Alfred
Purkiss. 'Why would Fairfax have an interest in those girls?'

Miss Cain seemed to think me a fool. 'He has an interest
in everything that's happening in camp, Falkland. It was
worse when Cromwell was here. There wasn't a thing that
happened that one of them didn't know.'

'Miss Cain,' I said, 'you must do what you must do. I beg
you give me an hour before you tell them I'm gone. That's
all I ask.'

Kate peered into the whiteness. The black mark that was
Purkiss's horse was getting bigger, more recognisable. I
could see every kick of its legs. 'One hour,' she whispered.
'After that, Falkland, I'll tell them. I'm sorry, but I must.'

I nodded. An hour was enough and I did not wish to see
her punished for anything I had done.

CHAPTER 13

I pushed the horse quickly into the sprawl of tents and lean-tos, losing myself in the labyrinth so Purkiss wouldn't know anyone was there. A lane between two banks of tents broadened into a space where a fire still smouldered from the night before. I found myself a vantage there so that when Purkiss passed by, I would be able to see. He might have seen me and Kate when she brought me Warbeck's horse but I wanted to be sure he didn't see me following the women. I needed to be certain I would reach them before anyone could stop me. Or, as they would say, come to 'escort' me.

The place was eerily silent. I tried to picture what it would be like when the soldiers returned to their camps from the spectacle at the square. Wintering had not been like this for the King's army – nor, I suspected, any army in the history of the kingdom. Not since the Romans held sway over these isles had there been an army like it. While I waited, I peered into the tents. They were big enough to sleep six men, with mattresses of straw and cloth raised from the floor and a variety of different packs. On one of the beds I saw a copy of *The Soldier's Pocket Bible* and decided to take it for my own. Perhaps there was something pertinent here, something that would be of use. I had learned a little about how the New Model nourished its soldiers' spirits but I was keen to know more.

I heard the soft clatter of a horse kicking through the snow and knew that Purkiss was drawing near. I crept between the tents and watched as he trotted past. He was wheezing heavily and his face was purple with cold. This man was, I thought, more at home stuffing his face with stewed apples than fighting a war, although one could never be sure. I'd thought the same of Warbeck at the start. I knew better now; there was a cold killer in him.

When I was certain Purkiss had passed on as far as the borders of Crediton, I hauled myself back into the saddle and, whispering kind words into the horse's ear, climbed up the bank and followed the trail. It had once been farmland in these parts but the fields quickly gave way to a sharp bank and low hills began to rise. It was difficult to tell where sky started and the snowy hills stopped but at least I had Purkiss's tracks to guide me. The trail crossed a bridge over the frozen river. To my left I could plainly see the hanging tree, not far away. Beyond the bridge the track followed a shallow valley and I soon saw the first thickets of skeletal trees. The hills quickly became wooded, a mongrel mix of conifers and ancient forest. I was glad to see it because it meant the banished whores might not freeze to death tonight. There would be shelter and, if they were canny, there could even be a fire. I didn't think much of their chances for finding or snaring a good dinner but perhaps there was some plundering to be done.

In time I came to a sharp bend where the trail suddenly plummeted down a steep bank. At the bottom of the bank the snow had been kicked up in circles. In some places I could even make out bare earth. After that, the tracks changed, became less deep. This was where Purkiss had left the women and turned back to the camp. I went on carefully now, not so slowly that I would risk getting back to the encampment too late, but slow enough that I could spy the wooded banks and find the place where the women had gone to ground. I was certain they would have sought out shelter just as soon as they knew Purkiss wasn't coming back. If I were a camp whore, I'd have judged it my only chance: wait for the fervour of the Day of Admonishment to die away and somehow sneak back. Surely every one of them had somebody in camp who didn't want to see them go, no matter how fervently they lent their voices to the jeering today. Few men are proud of their whores in public but even fewer do not dream of them at night.

I found the spot with surprising ease. The footprints stopped and the snow was kicked up and I judged the women had gathered there, arguing over which way to go. I got down from my horse, roped him to a tree with his rein and followed the footprints up the bank and between the first trees. As I entered the woodland there came a feverish beating of wings. Two wood pigeons hurtled up through the bare branches. I was sorry to have panicked them so; they would have made someone a good dinner tonight.

Inside the wood the air was still and almost silent. With only a few strides I could have imagined I was anywhere in the world. The borders of the Crediton camp were a scant mile away but I might have been in any corner of the kingdom, away from the wars, away from roundheads and cavaliers and godly men and secret Catholics. I allowed myself a brief pause, braced against the trunk of a tree, and closed my eyes. This was what I wanted. I'd not felt peace so intensely as I did then since I had marched from London with the King to face the Scots.

The trail led on into the trees. I followed it a while until I could no longer tell how far I'd come. The forest grew wild and it was dark as dusk among the boughs; it was a ghostly, unearthly world. I looked up, trying to get my bearings. There was no sun to mark the passage of time but I fancied I'd been gone from camp longer than half an hour already. I'd have to turn back soon or risk breaking my promise. I pressed on, making sure to mark my way by snapping dead branches or peeling bark from the trunks of the trees, although in truth I need not have bothered – the trail the camp whores had left was clear enough. The ground here had only a dusting of snow, the rest trapped in the branches so that it felt as if I was walking through a dank cavern of ice, but I could make out the tread of the women. I could even distinguish who were the heaviest and who walked with the lightest feet.

I came to a clearing. The women had stopped here to get their bearings. Perhaps they had thought it a good place for a camp: if so then I was glad they'd moved on for they were surely wrong. A clearing would be too exposed to whatever blizzards the night threw down. I crossed, following their tracks, and had hardly gone another hundred yards through fir trees and air heavy with scent when I heard their voices. Somebody was crying; and somebody else was telling them to be still in words that could not have been less kind. The voice was shrill but commanding, as authoritative as Fairfax or any of the other commanders I'd seen in Crediton camp.

I used to like it when my wife Caro bossed me that way. It made me know I'd been a fool but that it did not matter.

I crept on, careful with where I placed my feet lest I scare them before I announced myself. Twenty yards further on I saw three figures propped against trees, another sitting on a high boulder where moss grew thick. Two others held onto each other while the last stood at a distance. I began to hear their words.

'We must go further,' the authoritative voice insisted.

'There isn't anything further,' a second voice returned. 'You don't really believe a handsome woodcutter is going to take us in, do you?'

'I hardly think a man would devote his life to wandering in the woods if he *were* handsome,' the first voice said, 'but we have to get as far away from camp as we can. I dread to think what will happen if we're followed.'

'Followed?'

'Are you really so foolish, girl? It's time you started using that pretty head of yours for more than pleasing a lad who knows nought else. It was fine in camp. They were good to us there. In camp we were one thing but out here we aren't their whores, we're just a rag of girls. Fugitives. You've seen what those soldiers can do to a refugee girl when the fancy takes them. They'd look after us when we were their whores, but now . . .'

'You don't mean to say they'd come out here after us just to . . .' It was a third voice, warm and frightened. I shifted for a better view and caught a fleeting glance through the trees of the girl to whom it belonged. It was the girl I'd come for, the one I'd seen tending to Whitelock and Wildman's grave.

'Mary,' the lead voice snapped, 'what I mean to say is that we shouldn't take anything for granted. Not any more.'

'But . . . what if we're tired?' the second girl chipped in. 'What if we're cold and we're tired and it's getting dark and . . . we want to make this camp.'

'Yes!' the girl called Mary exclaimed, rising to the challenge. 'If we're not whores any more then that means we don't need whoring. We're not soldiers with you as our officer so who—'

The sound was as loud as musket fire. Mary reeled, clutching her cheek where she'd felt the back of the first woman's hand. Beyond her, somewhere I couldn't see, a fourth voice barked out. Then a fifth joined the din. If there really were soldiers hereabouts then these women were doing a grand job of announcing themselves. They might as well have lit a signal fire. It was, I thought, time to make an entrance. Perhaps in exchange for the information I sought, I might help them with their camp. I doubted they had much practice at such things and a poor choice of shelter through a winter night can be the last mistake any soldier makes. I took a step, then another, careful this time that my tread should be heavy. A fallen branch, iced with thick snow, blocked my path and I stepped on it hard. The snap reverberated through the ghostly woodland and the bickering suddenly stopped.

'Quick!' the lead woman barked. 'Into the trees! Come on, girls!'

I didn't mean for them to scatter. I hurried forward, snagging myself on winter briars. The girl Mary's eyes locked with mine as she turned to flee and I could see the red mark of her mistress's hand on her face. 'Mary,' I said.

She froze at her name. I lifted my hands to show her I held no weapon. 'I came only to . . .'

I was denied the chance to say anything more for suddenly the world shook and a pain such as I'd not felt in years exploded across the back of my head. I lurched forward towards her, instinctively holding my arms up as if she might catch me. Terrified, she stepped back and let me sink to the ground. For a moment I was kneeling. My hearing was suddenly gone and the world whirled in front of me as though I'd lost myself in a dozen skins of wine.

Then the pain came again, a fresh blow as hard as the last. I cried out. All the woodland around me reduced to a single speck of light; and after that there was only the dark.

When I awoke it was night. I knew this from the cold in the air before I even opened my eyes. I kept them closed for as long as I could stand it for there was a fresh Hell opened at the back of my head. Vivid images forced themselves on me but they were not of the winter woodland where surely I still lay. In my head I was back in my prison cell, awaiting a hangman's noose. I'd been so eager for the end then but now the idea brought sticky bile to the back of my throat.

Choking, I wrenched myself upright, heaving whatever morsels were left in my stomach into the dirty trodden snow. My limbs were so stiffened with cold that they would barely move. Once I opened my eyes it took me a moment to accustom them to the night. I dared not think how many hours had passed. There were patches between the branches, laden with snow, where I could make out the sky. Clouds shifted and came apart, and now and then I saw stars. It had been midday, thereabouts, when I had left the camp.

The pain in my head was blinding. One becomes, as a soldier, accustomed to pain, but not such as this. I've been shot, which I'll admit was worse, but it took all the will I could muster not to close my eyes once more and pray for the bliss of unconsciousness. My hands were tied behind my back. They'd not used rope and I strained to get myself free. I was bound in lengths of white sheet, the same sheets with which the women had been wrapped for their Admonishment. I slowly turned myself around, my delicate caution more for fear of a fresh explosion inside my head than of being seen or heard. In a cauldron of stones between the trees a low fire smouldered. One of the women had been wise to the ways of the wild after all: they'd built up walls with the snow, protecting us all from the chill of the wind, and the women slept sitting up on a platform of dead branches, huddled together for warmth. Two sat removed from the others, closer to the fire. They'd been keeping watch, I supposed, but had not been up to the task. That was why the fire burned so low. They'd been taken by sleep and had not been feeding it.

I was too far from the embers. Perhaps that was what had kicked me into wakefulness – my body's last attempt not to freeze. I made as if to stand and it was only then that I realised my ankles were bound in the same way as my wrists. Like a grub I wriggled my way towards the fire, sending waves of shock coursing through my skull and from there throughout my body.

Damn Cromwell, I thought. Damn Fairfax. Damn Whitelock and Wildman and the boy who'd flung himself on the granadoe. I'd been set on dying. I'd made my peace with it. Now here I was, hog-tied by a society of whores, driven to these paltry embers in case they could keep me away from death just a few hours longer. It's not fair the way the body wants to live even if the mind says not.

By the time I reached the fire my breathing was as heavy as a man whose chest has been torn apart by musket fire. I lay there for some time and, when the spasms had subsided, sat up. One of the women who had been supposed to be keeping watch was suddenly awake, her vivid eyes fixed on me. I must have woken her by thrashing across the clearing. I could see she was terrified – terrified of me, bound hand and foot, who had only come to talk. She started back and clenched her partner's shoulders with each hand. She was about to shake her awake when I realised this was the very woman I'd come to question. I fixed her with a look. 'Mary . . . It is Mary, is it not?'

Hearing her name quieted her. She withdrew her hands from her sleeping partner and wrapped her arms about herself.

'Please,' I began. 'I did not come to—'

'I know why you came,' the girl named Mary shivered. 'I know who you are.'

'Then you know I mean you no harm. You needn't have ambushed and bound me.'

'It wasn't me,' Mary began. Her voice was hoarse, her throat constricted by the cold. 'Helena was the one who struck you. She said you'd come to rob us. We don't have anything to rob but she said it didn't matter. You could still take things.'

'How long has it been?'

There came a low grumbling from the huddled girls. Somebody tried to turn in their sleep but was hemmed in and could not move. 'I don't know,' Mary peered at the black patches of sky I'd seen for myself. At least there was no blizzard tonight. 'I wish it were dawn,' she began. 'I wish I were—'

'Would you untie me, Mary?'

'Helena would be mad.'

'I promise not to lay a hand on any of you.'

'You shouldn't have come.'

'I had to talk to you while I still had a chance. They'll be missing me in camp by now. I'm not supposed to leave. I swore I'd be back in no more than an hour. If they come looking . . .' I waited for her to understand. 'You don't want them to find me here, do you?'

She did not.

'It would be best if I could get back so they might call off the search.' I knew they certainly wouldn't be searching *now*, not in the thick of night, but I fancied this Mary was too afraid to consider this. I did not like to think of the promise I'd made to Kate. She'd have reported me gone long ago. I wondered – *would* they come looking? Would Fairfax bother with me when he was so keen for me to be gone? What if he didn't?

Mary eased gently away from her partner and laid her down by the fire. Silently she crossed and knelt to tease out my bonds. I felt her icy fingers on mine. Her hands were tiny and trembling. She knelt over me and her breath, misting the moment it escaped her lips, enveloped me.

'There,' she said after some minutes, 'I'm sorry.' She went to untie my shins as well but I made her go and warm her fingers over the fire and set about doing them myself, pausing now and then to screw up my eyes against the fresh needles of pain that stabbed through my head. When I was done, I foraged for kindling. A dead branch lay in the roots of a tree and, though it was frozen on the outside, inside the wood was dry and flaked easily. I conjured up some more flames and built up the fire. I would like to say I did it for the women to keep them from freezing before dawn, but in truth I was concerned largely for myself. Still, it did no harm. In the rekindled fire, Mary glowed.

'I saw you,' she finally said. 'At the grave mounds. You were with our father from the church.'

'Yes,' I said, 'though the church is no longer his.'

'He used to take my confession when I was a girl. That church will always be his to me.' She was holding her hands too close to the growing flames and snatched them back.

'You're a Crediton girl?' I asked. It seemed preposterous that she should have lived in the town all her life and yet still found herself an exiled whore among the camp followers.

'Oh yes,' she answered. 'So you see, they've driven me out at last. They drove out my mother when they came to town because they needed rooms to house their officers. She went to relatives in Exeter but I refused to go. I wouldn't be thrown out. I had a sweetheart and I wanted to stay. But he was sore injured in one of their contests and—'

'A contest?' I asked. 'I saw them fighting the other night. What manner of contest?'

'Some fusiliers found he tried to join one of the King's militias back when the battling began. They said he had to denounce his own King or pay for it, but he was too proud.'

I didn't ask her more. I saw already how this contest must have ended: death for one and whoredom for the other.

'I knew you were a good man,' Mary whispered, 'when I

saw you at the mounds. Our father doesn't fraternise with bad men. He would have run away long ago but he still thinks that God is looking over us, that we'll be free of the army soon. It isn't a *godly* army, sir. They say it but they don't know what it means.'

'Why were *you* at the grave mounds, Mary?'

'I was . . .' She hesitated as if she did not want to say, yet I sensed this was not some secret she was trying to preserve but that she was merely embarrassed; as if to say the thing might make her blush. 'I was looking over a friend.' She looked at me imploringly. 'We have the same friend, do we not?'

She thought me a friend to one of the boys? Perhaps it was better this way. 'How well did you know him, Mary?'

She couldn't look me in the eye. When she said, 'I was his whore', with a mild shrug, I knew instantly it was more than that.

'You were his only one,' I surmised.

'Lots of men have favourites,' she answered. 'I was his.'

'No,' I said, 'it was more than that. A favourite whore might be aggrieved if her suitor stops coming but she doesn't go sniffing around his grave. She doesn't plant a cross where he lies, especially with all those Puritan boys marching around looking for stained glass windows to smash and market crosses to unearth. No, he was more, wasn't he?'

Mary looked up. Her eyes were shining wet and I saw that she was struggling to hold back tears. 'Helena says a whore doesn't fall in love.' Her whisper was hoarse.

'Is that how it was? You fell in love?'

'Richard,' she said, breathing the name carefully as if to honour his memory. Then she screwed up her eyes. 'I lay with his brother once, but only once. It hurt Richard too much.'

'His brother?'

'Why, the other boy,' Mary said, bemused now. 'The one who hung himself after. Samuel.'

For a moment I was taken aback with enough surprise to forget the pain in my head. 'I'd been told his name was Whitelock.'

'They had different fathers but they grew up together. They counted themselves brothers, sir, that's what matters.' She paused for a while and then went on. 'I think I was Richard's first,' she said quietly. 'Certainly his first whore. He barely knew where to put it. His brother was better but not like a lot of the men in camp. Still, sir, I would rather lie with a royalist boy than a Puritan, no matter how skilful he is with his hands.'

'How long?' The pain threatened to overwhelm me again. I tried to think, forcing myself against the pressure of it. Wildman and Whitelock, brothers?

'Ever since the army came to camp, sir. I fell in with Helena and some of the others soon after my sweetheart died. They're the real camp followers. They latched on to the New Model at Naseby.'

She told me more, our voices hushed so we didn't wake the other girls. I did not want to know how they would react to see me untied and nor did I want Mary to suffer for it. Now and then we paused and braved the cold for more firewood. Wildman had been nervous when he first came to her but she knew the things to say to soothe him and soon he was brave enough. He came every week – the New Model, as I'd discovered, were paid soldiers and could afford to waste their coins on sins of the flesh, no matter how godly they claimed to be. Wildman had grown up with Samuel Whitelock on a farm outside Exeter, the very same country from which Mary's family had once sprung, and he talked of it ceaselessly: the rolling dells and fields of wheat that he hoped, one day, he and his brother might harvest together with a flock of squabbling children of their own. Exeter had been a parliamentary outpost in the kingdom's royalist south-west but we'd put it to siege and wrested it away almost three years ago. I'd been there myself, in charge of the men who turned the Parliament's artillery back against the city and forced them to make terms. After the siege we considered Exeter a safe haven. The King's daughter was even born there, in the eye of the quickening storm. Since then the city had remained loyal to the King but was now under a different kind of siege, a winter siege where sickness and starvation were more potent weapons than any kind of artillery or guns. The presence of the New Model in Crediton was, itself, a part of that siege. They were quartered close enough that they could take up arms at only a few days' warning should Fairfax have been foolish enough to risk a winter march.

'They ran away together two years ago when the war came down. Taunton and Bristol and . . .' She said it as though it was the end of the world. 'They meant to fight for one of the King's militias, and joined up with some men who were on their way to find a relief regiment harrying Parliament when they tried to take Exeter back. But then . . . then came the New Model. It just ate everything up. After Naseby Richard and Samuel were swallowed, just like all the hundreds of other good boys in that camp. They hadn't even had the chance to fight for their King.'

'Perhaps some in the camp knew their true allegiance?'

Mary blanched. 'Sir, it was *never* a secret. How long have you been with the New Model?'

'Long enough to see it for the chimera that it is.'

'They had friends. Enough to make them feel safe even with all those fiery Puritan boys marching around. I won't say there weren't times when being for the King was a bad idea, but it was never a death sentence – if it were then half the New Model would be hanging from that witching tree and Black Tom wouldn't have an army left to fight with, and the King would be back on his throne and . . .'

And I would be with my dear wife and children, catching up on the years that had been stolen from me, trying to be the father I once dreamt of being, had chance not denied me. I blinked back tears of my own. 'Did you see him the day . . . ?' I paused, tried to gauge her reaction. 'The day they found Richard, had you seen him?'

She hesitated and began chewing on her bottom lip. I wondered whether it was to hide a secret or to swallow a truth. 'I hadn't seen him for some days,' she said. 'There had been a . . .' She fumbled to find the right word. From somewhere in the trees came a sudden rustling and her eyes darted to find it – some woodland rat drawn to the fire, drawn to people. 'You see, I loved him. I did love him. But there are things I had to do. Love doesn't feed you in the morning or keep you warm at night. I thought Richard understood that. He must have known I lay with other men because of Samuel. That was only once and I promised him never again. I'd not known then that they were brothers. Once I knew then I made an oath I wouldn't go near Samuel again – even if that meant an idle night, even if it meant Helena's . . .' Her eyes flitted to the huddle of sleeping women. Somewhere there was her mistress, though I did not know which. 'But I could not forsake all others, sir. Even if I'd wanted to, I couldn't do it.'

I thought I knew how it had been. 'He caught you with a man.'

'He was upset about something. He came to find me on a night when he wasn't expected. I was in the tent. I wasn't yet finished.' She paused. 'Do you think me sinful, sir?'

'It doesn't matter what I think.' The sins or otherwise of soldiers and their whores seem to me to be beyond any man, god-fearing or otherwise.

'Have you lain with whores?'

I had not. Caro was the only woman I'd ever lain with. Even on the road with the King's armies I didn't care for whoring and siring bastards like many of the men with whom I marched, Caro's own father included. 'Once or twice,' I lied, seeking to spare the girl her blushes. 'It upset him, did it?'

'He ran away. I feared I wouldn't see him again. For nights he didn't come and I was convinced he'd forsaken me. I knew he'd not found another. I asked but nobody had seen him, nor his brother. When he did come again it was as if he was fevered, though he had no sickness that I could tell. He had a . . . *power* about him. He had an energy.' She paused. 'It was terror.'

'Terror of what?'

She was silent, unable to put it in words, and I understood it wasn't the common sort of terror a boy might have, the terror of living or the terror of holding a musket or a pike, of looking into another man's eyes and then seeing the light in them dim. 'He brought with him that book they all carry,' she said at last. '*The Soldier's Pocket Bible*. Do you know it?'

'I've seen it.'

'He kept fingering the pages. He asked me to read to him. Only it wasn't that he couldn't read. He was a bright boy, his mother a clever woman who kept the ledgers for his step-father's farm. He just wanted to hear me saying it. There was a passage he liked.' Her voice adopted a low whisper as she quoted, '"A Soldier is a Good Man who serves a just Cause. A Soldier must be dutiful in his observance of God." He'd paid it no mind before. I told you already, sir, he went to confession and he had his own book. It didn't matter what verses the New Model wanted to quote at him. He knew his Bible well.'

It was dawning on me, just as she wanted it to. 'But that pocket book – it's not really a Bible. Not for boys like Whitelock and Wildman. Not for royalists. Not for Catholics.'

'He was a good boy, sir. You mustn't think ill of him.'

'It doesn't matter a thing to me how he wanted to worship.'

'Are you a godly man?'

'That word has a hundred different meanings. I don't care to think about it.'

'I tried to tell him he was sick, that he didn't know what he was saying, that he was a good man and God knew good men. But now here he was, fingering that pocket book, his head full of torments. He said he'd finally seen the truth as if his eyes had been opened. He was going to burn in Hell, he said. He'd been worshipping devils all his life and he hadn't even known. He said there were things he had to do, that there was a way he could make things better. He'd been with some of the other boys in camp and smashed the stained glass windows in the church . . .'

I started. 'Wildman did that?' The revelation dashed me from my thoughts and for a second time from the pain throbbing in my skull.

Mary bowed her head and now the tears wouldn't be held back. She wept. I put an arm around her and she didn't resist. I couldn't think what else to do. 'You can't buy your way back into God's favour,' she sobbed. 'He gave me his rosary and a little wooden cross he kept in his pocket. He told me to keep them for him. I begged for him to take them back, that he should stay the night . . .' She paused. 'But that was the last I ever saw of him.'

Her tears returned and we huddled together. The warmth of another soul on a night like this filled me with sadness and a loathing for this useless war. 'What happened,' I began, when her sobbing subsided, 'to terrify him like that?'

She had no reply. 'I've turned it over and over in my head, sir. I've looked at it every way there is. He was a good boy. He had friends in camp. He had me. He had a brother . . .'

'A brother who hung himself from the very same tree.'

She nodded.

I drew away. I'd delayed the question I most wanted to ask, in part to hear her story and in part while the fire warmed my frozen bones. I could put it off no longer. 'Mary, *did* Richard Wildman hang himself from that tree?' I asked, standing at last and feeling the cold of night leech at my skin. 'Or did somebody take him there and put that rope around his neck? And if they did, do you know who?'

For the first time that night Mary's eyes didn't wander. She fixed me with a glare like no other and spoke without any quiver in her throat. 'He did it himself, sir. I know it. Whatever terror had struck him so, he could not run from it. Hanging from that tree was the only way he could escape.' She filled her breast with the cold night air and breathed out steadily as if barely able to contain herself. I'd not seen this in her until now: not fear or sorrow but a sheer, blind rage. 'Would you like to know the very last words my Richard spoke to me, sir? Perhaps the very last things he said to anybody in this whole world?'

I gazed at her across the fire. 'I think I would.'

'He said there was a man coming who would expose all those who worshipped the devil, and then he said, "I would rather die by my own hand than burn on somebody else's pyre."' She exhaled and the air around her became a cloud. 'Do you know what he meant by that, sir?'

I heard a grunting from the huddle of women. A pair of eyes opened and blinked in astonishment to see me standing. 'I do not,' I said, 'but I mean to find out.'

CHAPTER 14

I came back to camp at a slow trot. It was still the black of night as I crossed the border fires. A dark silhouette hallooed me as I rode in but I spurred the horse on and made for the black spire of the church. The only figures abroad in the town so late at night were the camp guards, idly patrolling the lanes. My head throbbed and I struggled to hold my eyes open as I came slowly past the swinging dead man in the chestnut square. I paused underneath him. There was nobody to investigate this man's death. I wondered if, even after the wickedness he'd committed, that was right. I'd had no such hesitation in Yorkshire when, against the King's command, I sent the ravisher to the gallows. Surely I did not regret it? The exertions of this night had sapped me of my strength, that was all. I was in my fortieth year and I felt immeasurably old. I wanted to go home.

I roped my horse to a post in the livery stables behind the inn and approached Miss Cain's house with caution. There were no lights within and only the weakest tendril of smoke curled from the chimney. As I'd returned the sky had grown overcast, readying itself for fresh snow, and it was difficult to judge the time. I reckoned it past midnight. The blackest hour.

The door gave with no resistance. No latch had been dropped. I stole inside: embers still glowed in the range in the scullery and I was drawn to their warmth like a moth to a lantern; yet I had not crossed half the chamber when I heard her voice. I turned and saw her sitting in the darkness, her arms wrapped around herself. She was cast in dark shadows so I couldn't see her face. Sharply, I turned. 'Miss Cain,' I began. 'Forgive me. You gave me a fright.'

I stepped around so the fire might throw more light on her delicate features. Only after a long silence had passed did I know for sure what I was looking at. It took me too long to accustom my eyes to the light; but, when I did, I saw that her face was dark and swollen on one side, one of her eyes half shut. I went to her and dropped to my knees but she flung her hands up and refused to let me near.

'Who did this?' I asked.

'You know.' She said it flatly. It wasn't an accusation, only two simple words. All the same, they stung me exactly as she'd intended.

'Warbeck?' She shook her head. 'Purkiss?'

'Not *his* fists. *His* fists couldn't do this to me.'

She loosened her body. Where she had been holding up her legs, hugging them to her chest, now she sat bolt upright so that I might see her fearsomeness in all its ugly glory. She wanted to look me in the eye but something kept drawing her away. Instead she gazed into the last vestiges of the fire.

'Purkiss,' I said. 'He brought men with him. Camp guards.'

She nodded. 'You promised to come back.'

'I meant to, Miss Cain. It was an oath and I didn't mean to break it. I was . . . waylaid.'

'By a group of whores?' Her voice broke from a whisper to a cry of sorts, but on the last word she strangled it and looked at the ceiling above us, worried she might wake Warbeck in the bedroom above.

'Miss Cain,' I said, 'I don't expect you to believe me, but I'll tell you the truth. They ambushed me. I meant only to speak to them but they took me for some ravisher sneaked out of camp.' I took her hand. She didn't resist so I turned and placed her fingers over the lump on the back of my head. My hair, I realised as I did, was still matted with blood. As she touched the wound fresh knives of pain jabbed through my skull. I flinched from her.

A lingering silence told me that she had not, at least, dismissed the story out of hand. 'A big man like you,' she snorted, 'overcome by a string of camp girls?'

The mockery pleased me. I reckoned it meant I was . . . if not forgiven then at least not blamed. 'I'm truly sorry,' I said. 'You should have told them where I went.'

'I did,' Miss Cain replied. She lifted a cup to her lips and drank slowly. 'I told them even before they began. I told you before you left, I'm not a fool. I do what I have to do to get by, so that one day . . .'

'One day,' I said, kneeling again, 'when the war is over . . .'

She looked away. 'I didn't wait an hour before I went to tell them. I waited four, until I could wait no longer. I knew by then it was too long. Did you at least find what you were looking for, Falkland? Or is all this –' she tilted her head, exposing the worst swelling to the dim orange light – 'for nothing?'

'She was called Mary,' I said. 'Whore to the first boy

that died. Whore to his brother too.'

'Happy families.' She snorted then immediately seemed to regret the jibe and lifted a hand as if it was my own daughter she'd wronged.

'She had a story to tell. She's convinced Richard Wildman hanged himself, that he wasn't murdered.' I frowned then, for I'd expected the opposite. No person cares to believe that the one they love would damn themselves by taking their own life. 'She said that something got to him and made him believe he'd been taking part in devilry all his life just because he was raised to hear Mass and go to confession. Whatever it was, it turned him to that pocket book they all keep. He started devouring it.'

'There are plenty of boys in camp who take pleasure from baiting any cavalier sorts they can find. Catholic cavaliers must have it worse than most.'

'Schoolboy stuff. Two boys picking on another because he can't swim or ride as fast . . . But I've never known a schoolboy start dreading the devil. I've never known a schoolboy take himself to a tree and put a rope round his neck and hurl himself off.'

'Or steal a granadoe.'

I looked up. 'He said a man would come. There was another thing she said. His last words. She told them exactly as he said them. *I would rather die by my own hand than burn on somebody else's pyre.*'

The words floated around us, settling like snow. 'It makes me think of witchcraft,' Miss Cain said slowly.

'Witchcraft?'

'They say to kill a witch you must burn her alive. It forces the spirit out of her and chokes it before it can escape.

Falkland . . .' As I waited, I noticed that I still held her hand.
I had not dropped it and she had not pulled it away. It
seemed very . . . natural.

'Kate?'

'When I took you to the tree two nights back, you asked
me who I thought you'd been when I first saw you standing
at my door. You said I'd mistaken you for someone else,
and I told you it was true and I'd heard whispers of a
man coming who would make this army godly. Do you
remember?'

I nodded.

'I didn't say more because it seemed foolish, but those
whispers were not of priests. They were of two witch-finders
who would cleanse this army, who would find the ones who
secretly worshipped the devil and burn them alive.' She
shuddered. 'That was my first thought when I saw you at my
door with Black Tom, that you'd come to burn ungodly
men alive.'

I thought of the man Warbeck and I had seen, come out
of his hut in the darkness to stare at us with abject terror,
and then of the two Catholics in the alley beside the church
where one had dropped his rosary as he fled. I understood
now: he hadn't dropped it in his panic, he'd thrown it away.
'You weren't the only one,' I said.

I pulled away and took up a bare wooden stool and sat
beside her. This time she turned to me. My legs parted and
enveloped hers. I could feel she was trembling. It rippled
through me until I was trembling in chorus. I tensed, held
myself fast, forced her to do the same. When I reached out, I
meant only to hold her arms, to knead some warmth back
into her body, for she was devilishly cold. When I took her,

however, her whole being seemed to crumble. She flopped forward, her battered face pressed against my chest, and began to heave big, hard, ugly tears. I felt them, warm and wet against my skin.

'I am sorry,' I whispered. 'Truly, I am.'

She drew back, looked up with those vivid green eyes, her face hanging just underneath mine. She gave an almost imperceptible nod, enough for me to know that she believed me, that I might even have been forgiven, and then dropped again, holding me tight. This time, at least, she did not cry.

CHAPTER 15

'Y ou were under the strictest instructions not to leave camp,' Black Tom spoke sluggishly as if he didn't really want to be here. We stood together in the dirty snow between his farmhouse and the little oubliette where the ravisher was detained, his execution stayed indefinitely in case I ever changed my mind. After I left Miss Cain and returned to my bed, I'd slept through most of the day and awoken with a foul temper, a splitting head and an empty stomach. By the time Miss Cain had seen to the last of those the light was already fading. I'd lost almost the entire day and now here I was wasting what remained. I didn't want to be here any more than Fairfax wanted to see me but I owed him an explanation of my actions, if only for Kate's sake.

Fairfax shook his head. 'Do I have to remind you, Falkland, that you are still a prisoner?'

'I wasn't thinking of myself as a prisoner, sir. I've been considering myself a pressed man. Part of the New Model. Like any other soldier you've rounded up and dressed in red.'

'Stop thinking it,' Black Tom said. 'You're not a man who enjoys deluding himself and don't pretend that you are. You're a prisoner here.'

'You didn't have to go after Miss Cain.'

Fairfax nodded. 'She had instructions, as you had yours. And likewise disobeyed them.'

'You'd have done better putting a man to watch me. Men make better guards.'

'Women make better spies.'

'You know why I went?'

Black Tom nodded and waved his hand dismissively. 'Those camp girls were sent away for a reason. You won't have the faintest idea what it takes to drill a beast like this army, Falkland. You should have come and asked permission. I would have sent Purkiss with you.'

'I feared I would lose their trail.'

He laughed at me. 'You feared you would be refused.'

'Then prove my fears wrong, sir. I need your permission to leave camp again.' This was too much. Black Tom turned on his heel and began to plod back towards the farmhouse, shaking his head and muttering under his breath. I marched alongside. 'The two boys who died first were brothers. I have the location of their family farm near Exeter. I wish to go there.'

He stopped and gazed at me, full of derision. 'And what do you hope to find, Falkland?'

In the grounds in front of the farmhouse a troop of pikemen were practising drills: turning and sweeping and adopting each position after the next. I found them an unruly mob and thought any cavalryman worth his horse could have ridden them down and divided them. 'There may be something in their past, sir, to suggest why . . .'

'Falkland, you were sent here to complete a task and I expect you to do it. If those two boys were truly murdered then you'll not find whoever did it lurking in a farmhouse near Exeter, you'll find them here; so go and look and bring me the evidence. Otherwise go back to London and tell Cromwell that it's the price he pays for pressing royalist papists into the New Model instead of hanging them in the first place. All you'll find at that farm is some old dear shivering in her shawl and hiding her Christmas goose.' He paused. 'Or is that it? Are you a Christ-tide kind of man, Falkland?'

'I remember Christmases fondly,' I replied. I refused to call it Christ-tide like any snivelling Puritan, terrified of the Mass. Fairfax's words rankled. He spoke in such an offhand sort of way, as though my discovery that the boys had been brothers came as no surprise at all.

'And your children? Did you have Christmases with them?' he asked.

'I did, sir.'

Black Tom grunted. 'I had Christmases too, of course. I remember them fondly as well.' We'd reached the farmhouse now. Two camp guards stepped aside as we prepared to enter. 'Falkland, finish your task and finish it swiftly and you might have a Christmas with your own family rather than mine.' He rolled his eyes toward the oubliette, where the ravisher was still rotting. 'Of course, it *could* be finished any time you want it. All you have to do is say the word.'

I stopped at the door as Fairfax passed inside. 'Sir,' I called after him, 'are you expecting someone to arrive at your camp who calls himself a witch-finder?'

A flicker of hesitation broke his stride. He paused and then turned back to me and looked me straight in the eye. 'So you've heard these rumours too, have you? In my

opinion, witches are superstitious nonsense.' He paused
again, then sighed. 'Falkland, I'm about to dine. You may
join me again if you wish. I'm afraid you'll find my table
more sparse than two nights ago but I dare say it's better
provisioned than Miss Cain's pantry.' He said no more but
turned from me and walked briskly away. This time the
guards let me pass and so I followed into the farm hall,
where a table had already been set. A moment after he came
in, the same serving girls I'd seen two nights earlier entered
with a plate of cold mutton and a bowl of steaming boiled
potatoes. Fairfax gestured for me to sit at a vacant place and a
plate and knife were quickly found. Neither Warbeck nor
Baxter were present tonight but instead several other men
waited around the table, some of them faces I recognised
from the night we arrived. These, I reasoned, must be
Fairfax's commanders. Purkiss too was here. Fairfax beckoned him over and whispered something while they stood at
the door, and I saw Purkiss turn and scowl in my direction
and then stomp away into the twilight. I wondered if I'd
stolen his place at the table.

The other men waited until Fairfax took his seat. As soon
as he did the girls brought in an artichoke pie. Fairfax took a
slice and passed it to the man on his left, then helped himself
to mutton and potatoes as he waved his knife at me.
'Falkland here has been asking about witches.' The other
men around the table exchanged looks. A few of them
laughed. A few, I saw, did not. 'See, Falkland, I've shared my
opinion with you twice already when it comes to armies and
rumours. This one's merely another. Before Christ-tide I
dare say it will be forgotten, replaced by some nonsense
about the French coming to the aid of the King, or maybe it

will be the Spanish, or perhaps it will be that Prince Rupert has made yet another pact with the devil who now masquerades as his horse instead of his dog. Frankly, Falkland, I have no idea who to expect at my camp from one day to the next. If Cromwell chooses to send a man who calls himself witch-finder, I will tolerate him at my table with no more or less ease than a man who stands for the King and begs for a papist priest to take his confession.' He looked at me hard. 'And I will hang witches as I hang murderers, ravishers and plunderers, with firm evidence and a confession, nothing less.'

He gave no time for me to voice an opinion of my own, should I have one, but launched at once into a series of questions directed at his commanders. One, I deduced, was Henry Ireton who had commanded under him at Naseby. They spoke of drills and numbers of men, and as they talked I saw glances thrown my way full of mistrust and suspicion. I was, in their eyes, a King's man sitting at table with the commanders of the New Model as they discussed their disposition. I made sure to eat well and then rose and begged Fairfax's leave as quickly as I could. I was sure my presence was far from welcome and I fancied that I might prefer the company of Miss Cain over these dour gentlemen, though I had to admit that I preferred Black Tom's larder. Fairfax waved me away without a glance; as I left I wondered why he'd kept me here at all.

Twilight had fallen to night and I hurried back across the bridge and through the fields to the outskirts of Crediton. The watchman was still there at the end of his row of cottages. I walked briskly past and into the town. Along the narrow lanes around the church I passed soldiers going about their business who scarcely spared me a glance; but as I crossed the square where the dead man hung I became aware of two men who pulled away from the shadows and took to following me, matching my stride. They kept their distance but they stayed at my back and I found their presence oddly disconcerting. As I passed the inn they quickened their step.

I never saw the third man until he was upon me – I suppose he must have been waiting in the shadows of the alley beside Miss Cain's house. The first I knew of him, his hands grabbed me and pulled me into the darkness, dragging me off the street. I heard the footsteps behind break into a run and I cried out, knowing I'd been ambushed. The hands in the alley pushed me hard against the wall and let go – I sensed them draw back ready to strike and so dodged sideways, further still from the street, and raised my fists to defend myself. I had to get around this man fast before his two friends came on me from behind. If I could do that then it would be a chase. I didn't fancy I'd win it but I might last long enough to find help.

I felt a glancing blow against my arm. Here in the alley I couldn't see anything of my assailant but that he kept himself positioned so I'd have to run him down to get past. I roared and launched myself and crashed into him. I tried to push past but he caught my coat and twisted me around. My legs tangled with his and we both slammed into the trampled snow together and I heard him cry out. He was big, this man, taller and stronger than I, perhaps more so even than I'd been before my four months wasting away in Newgate. I tore myself free and managed almost to rise but he caught my foot and pulled me down again. I knew the two men

who'd followed me from the square were surely upon me
and that I was lost. Three men against one is never a fair
fight. I kicked and caught my assailant a good blow; whether
against his face or his shoulder I couldn't say, but he
bellowed an oath and let go of my foot, and for a moment I
was free. I twisted my head as I scrambled away but much to
my surprise the other two men were gone; nevertheless, I
needed no encouragement. I pelted along the alley, bouncing
from wall to wall until I tumbled through the tiny ungated
arch into the little yard behind Miss Cain's house and
hammered on the back door. 'Kate! Kate! Open up! It's
Falkland.'

I heard no answer, nor any footsteps. I turned my face to
the arch. As I stood there, waiting, breathing hard, I knew
I'd made a fatal mistake. The yard was walled and there was
no other way out. I'd made a trap for myself. I raised my
fists, ready to make as good a fight of it as a man could,
wishing I had a pistol or a sabre, or at least a dagger that
might make my attackers pause. I wished the alley wasn't so
dark. I would have preferred to at least see the faces of the
men who would murder me.

A shape blundered past the arch, muttering and cursing
under his breath. I swear he cast me a glance right in the
eye but he didn't stop or even pause. I heard his footsteps
a few moments longer and then silence. I waited, counting
out my heartbeats as they gradually slowed, then returned
with caution into the alley, eyes alert for the other men. It
was empty. When I returned to the road, that too was
deserted as though the two who had followed me from the
square had simply vanished away like bats into the night.
I found myself thinking that Helena and Mary and the other

camp follower girls had done a far better job when it came to ambushes.

Then I saw Miss Cain's door ajar and the sight set my heart to pounding again. Was that where they'd gone, those two other men? A moment ago I'd been set on running for my life but now I didn't hesitate. I pushed the door wide open and crept inside.

It was silent in the house. I moved quickly from the threshold into the shadows of the front room, where I stood still and strained my ears. As I did I thought I saw a shape at the back door; I heard the creak of it opening, felt a cold breath of air, and then heard it close again. Footsteps came closer. They were light and slow and cautious. They passed where I lurked in the dark.

'Kate?'

It was her. She gasped in alarm and jumped and almost fell. I stepped out of the shadows and into the moonlit hall.

'Falkland?' She sounded breathless. 'By the Lord you gave me a fright!'

'I'm sorry.' I reached out and took her arm to steady her but she shook me away.

'What was all that?' she asked. 'I heard you cry out. Then I heard someone at the back. What happened?'

'An ambush.'

'I came out to see when I heard your shout. There were three men brawling and shouting in the road.'

'Three?' I remembered only two.

'They were not together. One was on his hands and knees, clutching at the back of his head. A second was dragging him up. I heard a banging at the back of the house and then the third drew a sabre on the other two and they all ran off as fast as they could, the one with the sabre giving chase. I thought I heard you call from the back.'

'I did. There was a third man in the alley. We scuffled. He was meant to hold me there until his friends could join him, but when they didn't he ran away. I suppose he saw your man with the sabre. When I saw the door ajar, I feared . . .' I could not say exactly what I feared. 'I feared they meant some mischief.'

Kate shook her head. 'They ran away. Are you hurt?'

I laughed, echoing the thought I'd had outside. 'The whores did worse.' I touched her arm again. In the dark it was hard to see her face. 'Kate? Did you recognise any of them?'

I thought I saw her shake her head. I could feel how close she was. I could almost feel her trembling. 'No, Falkland, I didn't. It was too dark and the voices when they shouted weren't familiar.'

'A pity. I should like to know who the man with the sabre was most of all. I'm sure he saved me a beating or worse.'

'Oh.' She sounded surprised. 'I thought you meant the others, Falkland. I'm quite sure it was Master Warbeck with the sabre. I thought . . . I thought he was with you.'

CHAPTER 16

W arbeck didn't return that night so I had no opportunity to quiz him. I spent the next morning hunting
down boys who had known Whitelock and Wildman,
worrying them with questions about what had happened in
those last few days to raise such torment in Wildman's heart.
The boys had been camped together on the western edge of
Crediton where the fields were less even and thus their tents
more sparsely set out. A string of derelict farm buildings
lined the fields and, though they were disused, provided
something of a windbreak for snow storms coming in from
the east. It looked almost as if a great white wall had grown
up out of the earth, hiding Crediton from the rest of the
world.

Perhaps because of those drifts and the sense of separation
they brought, this part of the encampment seemed more
settled than the rest. There were no tourneys here, no bored
boys picking up sabres and harrying their companions. On
the edge of the field nearest the town, timber shelters had
been built – and against the old farmhouses too, where some
of the constructions looked almost like fairy-tale cottages
with their crowns of snow. Forming a circle nestled inside
the timber constructions, were more tents like those I'd seen

in the rest of Crediton. If this was how towns grew and spread then I wondered what would be left of the New Model once winter was finished.

The middle expanse of the field was broad and empty, a battlefield where I suspected drills were run and, if my past experience of camp was anything to go by, prayer meetings held. Indeed, as I wandered among them, I saw more than one boy with his face buried in his *Soldier's Pocket Bible*. I was surprised they'd not had enough of it at Baxter's gathering.

The boys here were meeker and, perhaps because of that, more willing to take me into their tents and let me ask my questions. I had nothing to offer in return, not even the coin an informer might usually expect of his intelligencer, but they didn't cast me out and for that I was thankful. By asking only a few probing questions I learned that Richard Wildman and Samuel Whitelock, though brothers, had camped in separate parts of this field. This wasn't to say, I was told, that they weren't close. Indeed, they were as close as brothers ought to be – by which was meant that they bickered and fought and then thought nothing of it. All the same, they had their own friends, own camps, own fraternities.

By chance I spoke to Whitelock's friends first. They were as ugly a bunch as I'd seen in camp, most of them boys no older than my own son John with the pocked faces of youth. They sat me down and offered me a hunk of bread, for which I thanked them but declined to take. I'd eaten at Fairfax's table last night while some of these boys looked starving.

'Did you notice anything untoward,' I asked, 'in the days before his death?'

Each time I asked it the answer came back the same: Samuel had not seemed unusually perturbed until the night Richard could not be found in camp. Come the morning, when the hallo went up that he'd been found hanging from the tree, Whitelock, naturally, changed.

'He said it was his fault,' one boy told me. 'But that's the way of it, isn't it? You always believe there's something you could have done.'

After I'd finished with Whitelock's friends I found my way to the tents where Wildman had camped. The boys here were much like the ones I had just spoken to and I wondered why they had kept their distance. Perhaps it was only the natural nonsense that flows between brothers. I introduced myself to a rangy lad with dark red hair, the progeny of an Irishman if ever I knew one. This army was no place for him, especially if, like Whitelock and Wildman, he'd secretly been seeking confession. Cromwell had a reputation in this camp for hanging ravishers, but his longer reputation across the whole of England was for hanging Irish Catholics by the drove. I fancied he'd see them wiped off the face of the Earth if he could. The thought left me all the more perplexed that Cromwell tolerated this mongrel army – that he, indeed, had pieced it together. Sometimes there's no accounting for the ways a man can compromise with his own ideals.

The rangy boy led me inside the tent where two other lads were sitting, gambling with sticks. This would probably have been a sin and seen them Admonished just like the camp whores, if only they had any coins to be gambling with.

'This is Master Falkland,' the red-headed boy said. 'He's come asking after Richard.'

The boys shifted to their pallets. Their game, it seemed, was now over. A mousy boy a full head smaller than the rest looked me up and down. 'Who sent you?' he asked.

'I won't tell a lie,' I replied. 'I'm here at Oliver Cromwell's request.'

The little boy sat bolt upright, his eyebrows raised. If I was not mistaken, he was impressed. 'Cromwell?'

'Aye.'

'Cromwell hisself knows about Richard?'

'None other.' Perhaps I shouldn't have been surprised but I'd expected associates of Wildman and Whitelock to be dismissive of Cromwell, not in awe. I wondered if they'd seen him leading his cavalry in battle. *That* would be enough to strike awe into any man, no matter his allegiance. I will admit it: having come up against them once before, it had struck awe into me.

'Sit down, sir,' the boy said. 'We haven't got much, but if it's Richard you're here for, you're welcome to it.'

'I see he was liked well enough.'

The boys muttered their agreement. Richard Wildman, it seemed, was not without his admirers. 'He was the sort who cares for things, sir. Sometimes it didn't matter what it was. He'd feel something when you cut down a tree. Found things like that everywhere he turned.'

It wasn't quite the picture Mary had painted of him but perhaps it was closer to the truth. The Richard Wildman they described was a sensitive boy but not without toughness. He was, they said, a natural pikeman – perhaps not as stocky as most, but he took to drills well and his body seemed to remember each motion perfectly without the months of training that others often took. His superiors liked him for that. It might have inspired envy in his companions but Wildman was too ordinary a fellow to inspire much at all. Better than most with a pike perhaps, but he was still a novice in life. Of women and the world, Richard Wildman knew little – and his brother Samuel even less.

'In his last days,' I said, 'he took to *The Soldier's Pocket Bible*.' I watched them to see how they'd react. They were measured. Still. 'He hadn't been a boy for it before, had he?'

This time they shared a secretive look.

'You can speak freely,' I said. 'I know he went to confession. I know he grew up listening to the Mass. He'd have been celebrating Christmas as well, wouldn't he? If he had lived?'

'You mean Christ-tide,' the smallest boy muttered.

'Do I take it you shared this with him?' Not one of them wanted to say it but I could see it on their faces. These were boys who had grown up with communion and confession, red wine and wafers. 'Were you from royalist militias as well?'

'You did say Cromwell sent you?'

This time it was the rangy red-haired boy. He remained seated but he drew himself up and, for the first time, I pictured what it would be like to face him in battle. He wasn't brawny like some soldiers but his arms were heavy and he looked as if he could stand for a long fight. I looked them all over, one by one, and felt a great sympathy for them. I could understand their wariness, how I must seem to them. 'I was a King's man,' I told them. 'I was in Yorkshire before it began, with the King. Afterwards I fought with Prince Rupert. I was at Edgehill and Newbury.'

Edgehill had been the most fearsome battle of my life. I mentioned it now so they might take me for a true King's man. They didn't have to know that I'd long ago given up choosing sides. Edgehill was still a byword for desperation, even for boys too young to have known it. Three years had gone by since we grappled for that Oxfordshire ridge and still no man on either side could say who won or lost.

'You were pressed?'

'Something of the kind. I'm here to learn what happened to Richard and his brothers. Doesn't matter to me if he was a royalist. Doesn't mean a thing to me if he drank the blood of Christ or kept a rosary or . . .' I paused. 'I know he kept a rosary,' I said. 'I spoke to his whore.'

'You must be mistaken,' the red-haired boy said. 'Richard didn't take whores.'

A boy who didn't brag about his whoring? Wildman continued to vex my expectations. 'She was one of those sent away at the Admonishment. She saw him the night before he died. Only it was the first time in days they'd been together. He came carrying that book, talking about Hell and damnation. Something had started eating at him. Something or somebody.'

I said it as pointedly as I could but not one of the boys reacted. They'd been with Richard through those days, they said, but they had noticed nothing unusual. If anything he'd been more dutiful, spending endless hours cleaning his weapons, practising the sweep and parry of a pike even without anyone to bark out orders.

'And his brother Samuel?'

'We went to see him on the day Richard was found. He wouldn't speak to us. After that we didn't know a thing about where he went. Somebody saw him at the church in the village . . .'

'Looking at the glass Richard had smashed?'

The red-haired boy's eyes opened fractionally. 'You know?'

'What made him do it?' I asked. 'A good Catholic boy like Richard Wildman taking a stone to the church? You boys aren't like the ones I saw yesterday. Ripping up market crosses. Pouring church wine into ditches. Wildman wasn't like that either – not until the days before he hanged himself. As best I can make of it he was a decent country lad, the sort who might easily have been forgotten. I've been thinking too much about that long, lonely walk he made. Knowing he was leaving his brother behind, knowing he was leaving his friends and his whore, his mother . . . I don't think he deserved any of it. I simply cannot fathom what would make him do that. Or should I ask who?'

They didn't reply. I stood up as if to leave. When I turned back they were staring at me with blank expressions. For all their courtesy they seemed eager that I should be gone. 'There was another boy,' I said. 'Fletcher. He threw himself on a granadoe underneath the same tree.'

The red-haired boy nodded. 'We heard the story but we didn't know him.'

'It strikes me as strange that he should choose the tree where Richard and his brother died. Perhaps he thought it fitting? He'd have heard, just like the rest of you, about the suicide tree. But you say you don't know him.' I took a step away. Then I paused, slowly and deliberately. 'What do you know,' I asked, 'of a boy named Jacob Hotham?'

The red-haired boy rose. 'Now, you look here!' he

exclaimed. 'We're as sorry as any that Richard isn't here. We grieve for him just like we grieved for the rest of our friends at Naseby and . . .' He must have realised in saying the words that we had perhaps both been at the same battle. Had the day been different then one of us might have died at the other's hands. No matter that we had both started out royalists, this war pitted Englishman against Englishman whoever they were. 'Sir, we'd help you if we could.'

'Hotham still lives,' I said. I'd wanted it to be a revelation but I couldn't tell if I was right. 'You know him, don't you? And Richard – he knew him too?'

'Know and want to know are two separate matters, sir!'

'Is Hotham like you? Seeking the confessional, carrying a rosary, Christmas instead of Christ-tide? Was he royalist as well as Catholic? Is that how Richard Wildman knew him?'

The red-haired boy seemed suddenly to calm. He must have risen to his tiptoes like a man making himself large to face down a wolf or a bear, because now he seemed to shrink. All the tension and anger evaporated from his body. His and the diminutive lad's faces creased in quickly stifled laughter. 'Jacob Hotham isn't a boy who'd care to fraternise with us, sir.' He gestured for me to sit back down. Cautiously, I did so. 'Jacob Hotham was never in the King's army like lots of boys round here. He was a Parliament man from the very beginning. A rabid pamphleteer from London. They say his uncle served in Whitehall. Oh, he's not as vicious as some – he wouldn't drag a boy out of his camp and goad him into a contest or a tourney, or whip him up into swearing an oath to the New Model or quoting from the *Pocket Bible* until his throat is hoarse. But . . .' He paused. 'Boys like Jacob Hotham can be worse than that. They're quiet and they're thoughtful and they'll wait and . . . It's like a spider with a fly, sir. He spins his web first so the fly can never get away. Hotham is too clever to be a bully. He and those friends of his, they're everything Richard and Samuel weren't. Sir, they'd hang every Catholic, every royalist . . .' He took a deep breath and looked me in the eye. 'Sir, Jacob Hotham would see the King dead and start marching in the street for joy.'

'You know him well for a lad you wouldn't call a friend,' I said. 'And yet he was found hanging from that very same tree as Samuel Whitelock and Richard Wildman, above the very same spot where Tom Fletcher blew himself to shreds.'

The red-haired boy nodded. 'But we don't count the scales balanced yet, sir. Three of us for one of them. That hardly seems just, now does it?'

CHAPTER 17

I pondered those last words long into the afternoon as I made my circuit around the camp, watching and waiting. *We don't count the scales balanced yet.* There might have been a confession in those words, more in the way the red-haired boy looked at me as he said them, as if he'd decided he could confide in me. Yet . . . I found I didn't want to believe it.

I thought I was beginning to see. The war between King and Parliament didn't just take place on battlefields and in city sieges. It took place here, too, in miniature – royalist boys and roundheads brawling along the lanes of their shared encampment, seeking whatever petty victories they might. Somehow it had led to the deaths of two naïve brothers and one local lad who'd seen his home town turned into a sprawling garrison and could not stand to watch the horror unfold.

Hotham didn't fit. If I'd ever fancied him a royalist or secret Catholic – and I have to admit that a part of me had so, even though I'd seen the nature of his friend Carew, smiling with a sanguine curiosity as he watched the crowds on the Day of Admonishment – that part of me was now thoroughly vexed. Jacob Hotham, spirited Puritan, ardent London pamphleteer – a boy who might spend his evenings at heated coffee house debates or setting in print the latest outpourings of some scholar disgusted with the state of the Crown – dangling from the same tree as two harried, tormented royalist boys? The matter didn't make sense. Two Catholic royalists murdered and one of the murderers strung up for revenge, *that* made sense, although even there I couldn't help wondering about the last boy with the granadoe. Yet the girl Mary had been adamant – Richard Wildman had taken his own life. I chased my own thoughts in circles as a demented dog chases its own tail until, after hours of hunting, I felt ready to throw myself on a granadoe too, so viciously did my head pound.

I needed to speak with Hotham. Alone. I would find out from him who among the royalist boys had strung him up and as I did, I'd slowly tease his own confession out of him.

I returned through the square and past the church, then stood in front of the surgeon's house for an intolerable time, divining which of the many windows hid Jacob Hotham himself. I watched as Edmund Carew went in and later as Edmund Carew came out again, and after him the other boys who had gathered at Hotham's bedside. I'd thought they'd given up for the day but promptly another gang of boys arrived, exchanged words with Carew and then disappeared within. Hotham had friends in this camp then, I was certain of that, but now a new certainty leapt to mind, one I could not fight down: none of the boys who came to tend the cripple were the kind I would have sought to be companions of my own.

There seemed little hope of getting inside and cornering Hotham, at least not in daylight hours, so instead I thought to sniff around the dead boy Fletcher. Fletcher, only so recently pressed into service, had not yet fought in any battle and so I didn't expect to hear many tales from the common soldiery; but he was a local boy. The other locals would know him and might have a story to tell. Thomas Fletcher, I thought, must have had a mother.

There were few women left in Crediton. Aside from Miss Cain, the only ones I'd seen who remained were old and withered, the kind soldiers protect as cooks and cleaners and do not torment. At the surgeon's house I asked a woman old enough to be my own mother after Fletcher and where he'd lived. At first she didn't want to tell me but I didn't think she had a secret to keep: hers was merely the common suspicion of a woman whose world has been upended. I was able, with patience, to convince her I didn't mean to cause any trouble, that I had a vested interest in making certain Thomas's memory was honoured. She gave me directions to a cottage at the southern edge of the village on the Exeter road and I realised I must have passed it every day on my way to Fairfax's farmhouse.

I walked the familiar lane, watched on either side by soldiers in their camps. There were dogs here and a mongrel worked up a din as I passed the yard where it was roped to a tree. The cottages between the church and the edge of the town were set farther apart, and in the spaces between them, camps had been built. Enterprising soldiers had constructed walls of ice and compacted snow so that in places it seemed that each cottage bled into its neighbour. Some of the camps had roofs of a sort where the men had trained the snow in such a way that it crept out from the cottage walls and sheltered them beneath.

Halfway there I had the feeling of being followed and

turned to see a lad, no older than seven or eight, traipsing after me with his hands outstretched. He walked barefoot, his trousers ragged things, his shoulders and torso wrapped in a cape that billowed open every time he took a lurching step. When he saw me looking he stopped dead, lifted up his cupped hands and suddenly nipped away between two cottages. Too young to be pressed – but it hadn't stopped the New Model ousting him from his home. I was beginning to lose count of how many spies had been set to watch me. Warbeck watched for Cromwell, Purkiss for Fairfax and now, after last night, perhaps another. Was it Carew and his gang? Had I blundered too close to whatever secret they held? If so then I greatly wished they might do me the kindness of telling me what it was. Or perhaps the boy hadn't been following me at all.

The cottage where Thomas Fletcher had been born and raised – and from which he'd been snatched and shoved into a Venice red coat – was at the end of the lane, nearly on the edge of Crediton itself. As I approached I saw that a soldier loitered outside. His coat seemed smarter and certainly less frayed than I'd seen in the rest of the camp, but he didn't stand as firmly and statuesquely as the guards had done outside Fairfax's farmhouse. I'd passed him before, I realised, or another man like him, standing watch on this spot. I'd walked this way each time to Fairfax's house and each time a man had been here. At the time I'd thought nothing of it. Now I thought a great deal. A guard meant that something was inside and now I wanted very much to know what that something was.

I walked slowly by on the opposite side of the lane until I was certain this was the Fletcher place. The soldier watched me with the dull interest of the intensely bored. Snow rose in a great drift against the low stone wall that bordered the cottage. I turned back and approached him; when I looked him up and down, I saw he had a dagger in his boot as well as the sabre at his belt – but that was not what held my eye; I was more concerned by the fact that his boots were spotless, with barely a scratch on them.

'What do you want?' he barked as he gathered himself. 'Can't you see this is private property?'

'Black Tom sent me,' I said.

He was still. 'Black Tom?'

I nodded. 'It's nothing to bother yourself with. You know it was the Admonishments two days ago. We're rounding up wastrels, cleaning up the camp.'

He was a thickset man with wild black eyebrows that dominated his face. Beneath were piggy eyes and a crooked nose. Up close I might have taken him for any old pikeman in camp – he was certainly ugly enough to have had his face staved in in many a battle or brawl; it was only from a distance, in his fine red coat and cared-for boots, that he seemed distinct. I wasn't sure if he believed my story but I was certain he hadn't entirely dismissed it. Not yet. I decided to drive for the kill before he had time to think on it too deeply. 'It won't take more than a moment. But you wouldn't want me reporting back that some sorry bastard got in my way, would you?' I stopped. 'Son,' I said, though he was at least my age if not older, 'if it's a girl you've got hiding in there, it won't matter to me. It's meant to go reported but we're all men here, aren't we?'

He was silent for a second but then he broke. His mouth widened in a toothy mockery of a smile. 'Ah, don't fool with me!' he laughed. 'There's no girl in there unless you count old Mrs Miller. And if she was a girl, it was in another century. There's no one hiding out here. I see to that.'

I started forward, taking his merriment to be assent for me to pass, but his face changed at once. He stepped smartly back and his hand rested on his sabre again. Behind him the shutters were tightly closed on all the cottage windows. 'I'm sorry, Mister . . .' His eyes were on me, questioning.

'Falkland.' There seemed no point in pretending otherwise.

'Mister Falkland.' I thought I saw a slight glint of recognition. 'The intelligencer. I'm sorry, sir, but you can't pass here without Black Tom's say-so. Go on, get about your business.'

So he'd been warned. By whom? 'The boy who blew himself up with a granadoe lived here,' I said.

I thought I saw a genuine sympathy now. 'Aye. A tragedy, that was. Poor Mrs Miller. Took him on as if he was her own after . . .' His face hardened again. I could see him thinking he'd said too much.

'Who warned you I'd be coming?' I asked.

He wouldn't bite but I thought his answer telling enough. 'None come past me, Mister Falkland, save with Black Tom's blessing.'

I wished him a good night and left him at his post, head spinning anew. Something inside this house was under the supervision of Fairfax himself. I couldn't see how or what this might have to do with Fletcher's death, or that of any of the other boys, and yet surely there was no coincidence? I hurried back to Miss Cain's house and accosted her in her kitchen. 'There's a house towards the end of the Exeter road,' I gasped, out of breath. 'A man stands guard there every night!'

The look she gave me was one of curious amusement. 'Poor Tom Fletcher's house? Yes, and every day too.'

'You knew him?'

She almost laughed at me now. 'Master Falkland, do you imagine before this army came upon my home that I sat upon my back doorstep with my eyes closed and never once went to church or market? Poor Tom used to live with his mother in that cottage. His father was gone two winters ago, fighting for the King.'

'Dead?' I asked.

'Dead,' she replied. 'It took the longest time. They had a surgeon take off his leg but it didn't matter. In the end they sent him home to die. I told you most of the women fled when the army came. Tom's mother wanted to run too but Tom made her stay. Then, when the soldiers came, they made her take men in her house. She tried to resist. She barred the doors, just her and Tom inside. They let her go at first. You could hear them whispering up and down the lane about the mad woman making her home into her tomb. But eventually they got sick of sleeping under the stars. They forced themselves in.' She looked away, paused a moment and then her eyes found mine. 'We all heard well enough what happened. Tom tried to fend them off but he was a slight little lad, that one. Not much more than skin and bone, and not much of that. They locked him outside while they did what they did to his mother. Oh, they didn't go unpunished. You've seen one of them already, dangling from that tree in the middle of the village. But it was enough for Tom's mother to just disappear. Nobody knew where she took herself. Tom vanished too, disappeared into the army. Pressed. I saw him maybe twice after that, both times coming out of the church in a soldier's coat that was far too big for him.' Her words finished with a sigh of heavy melancholy. She turned away from me, back to busying herself with her pot.

'Kate, what are they doing in that cottage? Fairfax himself has set the guard on it.'

'I've heard nothing much. I've heard people see old Mrs Miller go in and out but she's a spiteful old witch, that one, and doesn't talk to anyone else.'

'Where will I find her?'

Kate directed me to a cottage on the west side of Crediton. Outside, the November twilight was already turning to night. I would, I supposed, have to wait until morning but I desperately wanted to know what secret Fairfax was hiding in there. That was the King's man in me coming out, who'd fought against Cromwell and Black Tom and their militias for too many years.

'Kate . . .' I hesitated to ask her but I needed help. 'Does Fletcher's cottage have a back door?'

She didn't look round. 'Yes.'

'I only ever saw the one guard at the front. But I would need someone to distract him . . .'

'You'd have me walk up to a soldier in the dark of night and engage him with idle talk while you break into the house? And what, Master Falkland, do you suppose he will think of that?'

The question hung in the air between us. He would think she was propositioning him. 'I'm sorry,' I said after a moment.

'You'll be done and gone soon, Master Falkland. The rest of us have to weather this invasion for months yet.'

'Perhaps one of the camp followers . . .'

She turned and touched my arm then brushed past me into the hall. I was surprised to see that she was smiling. She went upstairs and returned with a candle and a lighted lantern with a hood. 'There's another way, Master Falkland. Come. I'll show you.' She wrapped a heavy cloak around her shoulders and stepped out into the night.

At first the path she led me was a familiar one, past the market square with its defiled cross and the church. As we passed the graveyard she turned down an alley, dark as pitch, that made me think of the first night I'd come this way where the man had dropped his rosary. It was, I thought, the same alley. 'Miss Cain, when you first set eyes on me did you really think I was here to hunt for witches?'

She hushed me. The alley exited into a narrow lane with packed banks of snow pressed to either side. It was clear this road was well used in daylight but now it was deserted. 'Keep your ears about you, Master Falkland. We've learned it's best to keep to the High Street after dark.'

I heard a burst of laughter from inside one of the cottages. Thin curtains of flickering light filtered out between ill-fitting shutters. Kate hooded her lantern. With the clear night sky above us full of stars, we had enough to see by. Almost at once Kate turned into another alley every bit as narrow as the first, then struck across some open ground where the snow rose up to my calves. There were tracks here, footsteps, but too few to have beaten a path. We followed them and then she began to pick her way across virgin snow. She turned once to put her finger to her lips. A pair of jesters we might have seemed to anyone who saw us, creeping in exaggerated steps through the snow, lifting each foot high and placing it gently down, but no one did. The fires and lanterns of the camp were distant, and though I could see figures moving in the tents and timbers against them, they were far too far away for me to see who they were.

We reached a wall as high as my outstretched hand. Miss Cain stopped. As I looked about, I thought I knew where she'd led me: we were at the back of the Fletchers' house, at the end of its walled yard.

'Lift me up,' she whispered. I must have looked bewildered. 'Over the wall!'

I peered around the corner. Barely three paces along the side of this walled yard was an arch with a door. It seemed a far easier means of entrance and so I eased my way through the snow until I stood before it but there was no latch, no handle, nothing. I pushed gently but it didn't move. I didn't dare rattle it hard.

Miss Cain, when I returned, regarded me with a steady gaze. I bowed my head. I should, I understood, have listened and known better. I put my back to the wall, bent my knees and cupped my hands, indicating that Kate should step in them. She did and I lifted her. She was lighter than I thought she would be, or perhaps Newgate had not stolen as much of my strength as I'd imagined. As she pressed herself against me, fumbling the snow from the top of the wall and dropping it now and then on my head, I found my thoughts tinged with unwanted desires. For all the years I'd marched with the King, my Caro was all I'd ever needed, the only woman I'd lain with and the only one I ever would. I made myself think of her as I held Miss Cain higher. Then at last I felt her weight ease as she lifted herself away and over the wall and heard the soft rustle of snow from the other side. I stood a moment, waiting for the thump of my heartbeat to slow, then crept back to the door. I was waiting for her as she opened it and we stared at one another for a moment – I could not say why. In the night her face seemed dark and her eyes uncommonly wide. She grabbed my arm and pulled me after her and then carefully shut the door and latched it. We stood before one another like thieves, so close we were almost touching. 'Kate . . .' I don't know what I meant to say to her then; but before I could frame another thought she quieted me with a sharp 'Shh!' and moved to the cottage door. It was as well, I think.

The back door to Tom Fletcher's old home opened without a squeak. I pushed through while Kate carefully lifted the hood from our lantern and turned the shutters so that light spilled only in a narrow shaft ahead of us – by this means we would have light to see by and the guard outside would know nothing of it unless we were fool enough to shine our lamp through the cracks around the door or the shuttered windows at the front of the cottage. Our hands touched as Kate passed me the lantern. Had we not had a need for silence, I would have told her she would make a fine intelligencer. Perhaps I would have told her more but a man with a pistol stood guard not far from the cottage door and I doubted he would hesitate to use it if he detected us. Here was no place for idle talk.

We were in a scullery. There was a small range but it didn't seem to have been lit in many days and the cottage was as cold inside as out. I crouched and fingered the ash but it was icy. There were no provisions in the cupboards and no water in the pail. A tin pot sat on a stove but it was bone dry. Indeed, it appeared to be covered in a thin film of dirt and dust. I was left with the empty feeling of walking through somebody's mausoleum. There were, I knew, a great many houses across the kingdom that had been abandoned since the battles began – some left behind by young men gone off to war, some abandoned in a fevered rush by families fleeing in the face of the fighting – but I hadn't expected to find one in Crediton, not in a place where so many soldiers slept in crudely constructed camps.

I turned and pushed at the door that led to the front of the cottage. It opened into a tiny hall from which led a staircase to rooms above and two doors: the one in which I stood and a second room. I turned to the other door and cautiously pushed it open. The air was just as cold. As I crept onward, a rich and bitter smell I couldn't place swirled around me, making me gag. Heavy shutters blocked out all but the thinnest sliver of starlight. I set the lantern down, taking care to face it away from the windows. Against one wall, opposite a hearth as cold and empty as the first, stood a tall contraption. At first I took it for a harpsichord or even a church organ, but as I brought the lantern closer I quickly understood it was nothing of the sort. The frame was polished oak and within it sat an iron plate, with another plate suspended above it by a great shaft. A heavy lever protruded from the uprights of the frame allowing the second plate to rise and fall – and revealing behind it a sequence of other plates that could be dropped and shifted into place. I approached it slowly, half-circling it as a man might do on observing an enemy outpost. The base of the contraption was built out of iron slats with handles for each so they could be slid backwards or forwards, or from one side to the other.

I reached out and touched the iron plate. When I drew my finger away, it was black with ink. I felt Kate, the presence of her close behind my shoulder. 'What is it?' she whispered.

There came a sound as of footsteps on the floorboards above. I hooded the lantern and eased myself to the window, then lifted a latch to peer between the shutters. The guard was standing where I'd seen him before, bored and cold and shuffling his feet, untroubled. The noise didn't come again. The world outside was still. The wind, perhaps. Or a bird on the rooftop, or rats.

Satisfied that we were alone, I re-latched the shutter and turned back to the contraption. I dropped to my knees and peered around it with the lantern. Crates lay piled under-neath and around it. I hauled one of the boxes into the middle of the room, careful not to let it drag. It wasn't sealed and when I unmasked our light and shone it inside, I saw stacked a dozen copies of *The Soldier's Pocket Bible*. I lifted a copy and opened the cover to read the verses inside but there were no words at all. I flicked through the first pages and still there was nothing. I dropped the book and picked up another. This one too was blank.

Again I heard a footstep and this time there was no doubt of it. One, two, three, four. I froze and felt Kate quivering beside me. I fancied I could almost hear the race of her heart. I turned very slowly so her face was inches from my own and then leaned closer still until my lips brushed her ear. 'Go,' I whispered, almost soundless. 'Go back outside. Go home.'

I sensed her hesitation.

'It's one thing if they catch me here. If they catch you then it's another.' As she started to move I caught her for a moment and touched a finger to her cheek. I meant to thank her but my words somehow lost themselves and so I withdrew and watched her go while I stayed frozen still and listened. The footsteps above had stopped again and I didn't hear Kate as she crept away. Everything fell to silence. I knew I should follow as soon as I thought she must be gone but a curiosity held me fast. I peered underneath the contraption and looked into the next crate. There, as I'd expected, I saw hundreds of tiny scraps of metal. When I reached in, I found my hands full of letters and apostrophes, of full stops and quotation marks. I let them slide through my fingers back into the box and stood, my hands sticky with the residue of ink. The contraption before me was a printing press. I'd not seen one before, though perhaps that was ignorance on my part; it sometimes seemed that there were as many printing presses in London as scholarly young men. Yet the question presented itself: what was a printing press doing in Crediton, far away from the frenetic push and pull of scholarly debate?

I heard the footsteps again and hooded the lantern at once. They seemed to be getting louder this time and came at irregular intervals, as if of a man dragging himself along and having to stop to tend to an injured leg, or hauling himself along on a railing.

The staircase. Someone was upstairs and now they were coming down. I'd hesitated too long. The only way out was through the hall and that meant I would surely be seen. There was the window but that was scarcely big enough for me to squeeze through and the guard would certainly hear. I cowered back into the corner in the deepest shadows I could find. My eyes were drawn back to the crate of pocket Bibles underneath the printing press. It hardly seemed possible that they should be printed here but I'd already seen the way this New Model worked, the frightening efficiency with which it operated: men little more than commodities to be tallied up on a warmonger's ledger. I reached into the box and lifted a book, dropping it into my pocket. The book was bound. Why bind a book before its pages were printed?

The footsteps stopped. I retreated deeper into shadow, crouched in the corner of the room where the lip of the printing press might hide me, and fixed my gaze on the door, waiting for it to open. I braced myself. As soon as I saw the shape of any shadow enter the room, I'd run them down, push them aside and make off the way I'd come, as quick as I could. In the dark, no one could possibly see my face. Fairfax might guess who the intruder to his press had been but he couldn't be sure. It was a relief to know that Kate, at least, was safe.

No one came. I seemed to have been squatting there an interminable time when I heard the cottage door open. Whoever had come down the stairs wasn't coming to the press but was leaving altogether. I eased across the room to the windows, cracked open a shutter and looked out. A hunched figure stopped for a moment to exchange a word with the guard then moved slowly on, heading back to the town while the guard turned smartly and hurried for the door. The hunched figure had heard us then. I ran into the hall and through the scullery as fast as I could, all thought of stealth abandoned. I heard the front door open as I bolted through the back and outside. Miss Cain, I saw at once, had not heeded my advice and gone home but was waiting for me behind the wall – I took her hand and pulled her away as fast as I dared. I hissed at her, 'Quickly! Hide!'

Behind us I heard the guard rush out into the yard as we rounded a corner and dived together into the shadows of a low wall. The night was dark enough and the shadows deep enough that even if he came looking I thought we might hide here and not be seen for as long as we were quiet and still. I strained my ears but he didn't follow. After a few long moments I thought I heard the closing of a door and the click of a latch.

'What was it?' Kate asked. 'What are they keeping in there?'

'A printing press. They make those pocket Bibles here.' I took her in my arms and this time held her tight a moment. 'Thank you, Kate. Thank you. Now go home. I have another matter to attend to.'

She clung to my arm as if reluctant to let me go. 'Master Falkland, I have . . .'

I pulled away. Whoever had been in that house with us, I very much wanted to speak with them and I'd already put Miss Cain in enough danger. I left her there in the night and hurried away.

CHAPTER 18

I returned as quickly as I could, running back across the field and through a different alley, leaving Kate in my wake. When I reached the road I stopped. Looking back towards the cottage it emptied into the sprawling encampment, but I could see no figure wending its way through the tents and lean-tos. In the other direction, towards the church and the heart of Crediton, three figures shuffled away. The closest appeared to be hunched and so I took that to be the man from the cottage; but as I came closer I saw it was a woman wrapped in a shawl, waddling away like a fattened duck. Beyond her stood a soldier in a slovenly red coat, flicking a stone up and down, his eyes flitting manically over the lane, while further on another man in a long black coat hurried past the church, throwing looks over his shoulder. At times he broke from a hurried walk to a canter, then slowed again. I left the woman and took after him, careful that I shouldn't let him know he was being followed, but perhaps I came at him too swiftly, for only halfway from the church to the square he risked a glance over his shoulder, fixed me with a look and broke into a run, darting along the narrow lane that ran beside the graveyard. I gave chase at once; when I turned the corner I saw that the end of the lane was blocked by a low wall of ice and a soldiers' camp that sat behind it. The man fleeing ahead of me vaulted over the wall, kicking the camp apart as he thundered through. Three men were gathered around a fire in the shelter of a timber frame over which ice had grown and snow had settled to form a deep roof – as the man ran past, he tumbled the ring of stones that walled in their fire and unsettled the snow on their shelter, dousing it. The soldiers jumped at once to their feet and hurled oaths and curses; distracted, I slipped on the ice and sprawled headlong. When I rose again, the running man was gone. I raced to the wall and stared past the three men at the sprawling encampment ahead. I could see a dozen different figures now, silhouettes in the night against the camp fires, but all of them too far away to be my man.

'Which way?' I demanded.

'Who are you?' one of the soldiers returned, reaching for a blade.

'The man who came this way! Ah to Hell,' I cursed, 'I don't have the time . . .' I vaulted the low wall of ice just as the runaway had done but I was evidently not as sprightly as him for I caught my boot on the lip and went tumbling forward. All that stopped me from falling over was a stone wall that reared up and smashed me in the face. I flailed through the soldiers, too desperate to pay much mind to the blood that trickled from my nose, and stumbled on into the wild sea of the encampment before me; but my ship had already set sail. The man was gone.

Disconsolate, I took the oaths of the soldiers camped around me and added a few of my own. I carefully levered myself back over their icy wall and trod back along the lane beside the graveyard. The road in front of the church was as empty as I'd last seen it, with only the old woman still shuffling towards me, hunched under her shawl; but when I came to stand in front of her, she reeled back as if I'd lifted my hand to drive it into her face. I suppose she'd seen such behaviour often enough from the soldiers here.

'Forgive me,' I began. 'I did not mean to startle you. I'm looking for a man.' I took her for a local, for no camp whore could have been this wizened and old. Wrapped up in woollen cloaks against the cold, she was tiny and frail, shrunken in her dotage. Her face was a wrinkled mask and it peered at me with alarm.

'Plenty of men,' she muttered. 'More men than the Lord knows what to do with.' She stumbled back but managed to keep her footing. Nor did she drop the bundle in her arms, wrapped up in cloth and clutched close to her breast.

'He was in this lane only a moment ago. I believe he came from *there*.' I pointed around the turn of the road at the cottage from which I'd stolen. The camp guard still loitered outside, propping himself lazily against the stone wall. 'You may have seen him before.'

The old woman followed my gesture. Her eyes lingered oddly over the cottage.

'The old Fletcher house,' I began, sensing something.

The woman blinked up at me. 'I didn't see him,' she said. 'I didn't see anything.' She tucked her head down, stepped around me and began to shuffle back up the lane.

I caught her easily. Something felt wrong. 'You must have seen him,' I began. 'I gave chase to him only a moment ago and right before your eyes!' I had my hand on her shoulder and she was tense beneath it. She whirled back and it must have come as a surprise to her to escape so easily, for she immediately lost her balance. She staggered and crashed into the corner of a wall and the bundle in her arms slipped out of her grasp, landing intact in the snow some feet away. As I moved to help her and offer my apology, her eyes lit with a fire and she let fly with a string of invective, cursing me and every other soldier in the camp. I stepped back, surprised by the demon I'd unwittingly unleashed. Still muttering of every vile thing she wished the Lord would send to repel us, she tottered past me and reached out to pick up her bundle.

I saw her hands then. At first I thought she was wearing gloves, threadbare things that opened in patches to show her pale wrinkled skin underneath; but then I understood that I was wrong. Her hands were stained. They were pale in patches but with a blackness worked into the open skin around her fingernails and the creases in her knuckles.

Black ink.

I made as if to help her up and, though she wriggled away again, I was now certain. 'Forgive me,' I said. 'My name is Falkland. Might I have yours?'

She stumbled away from me and hurried on down the road.

'Please,' I called. 'I must speak to you.'

'A moment gone you were wanting to speak to a man. Now it's me? You youngsters don't know whether it's summer or winter.'

It had been some time since anybody called me a youngster. 'I'll not waste any of your time.'

'You're wasting it already.' She turned abruptly along the road that ran before the surgeon's house. A little way past it she stopped and turned again towards a cottage door. As she reached for the handle I rushed to her side and took it myself, closing my fist over the top of her hand. Instantly she squirmed away. I leaned a little closer as she opened the door.

'I need to speak with you about the printing press.'

She pushed between me and the door, opened it and waddled inside, and without hesitation I followed. Once she'd gone over the threshold, she looked back. I could hardly see her face any longer, hidden in the shadows of the hall, but I'd not gone three steps when there came a chorus of cries from within and a tide of squabbling children poured out of a doorway along the hall and began tugging at the old woman's hems, yawning and rubbing their eyes. There were three boys and a girl, and I was certain there were more elsewhere in the cottage, for surely this amount of din could not have been made by such a small group. The youngest could barely walk and was being helped along by the eldest, a girl who might have been seven or eight. In the gloom I was startled to see how she looked like my own Charlotte. She had the same long nose and sad eyes and she wore her hair tied back in the fashion that Charlotte had always begged her mother to make – two tails plaited together at each side.

It had been too long since I last saw any children. I didn't know, until that moment, that such a thing could trouble me but I felt a great lurching in my breast. When I tried to speak, something was stopping me, like a mangled cork forced back into a bottle of wine. In my own youth I'd never imagined having children. I was to be a farmer, married to the land, and I didn't think much beyond that. When Caro came into my life I still didn't aspire to fatherhood in any real way. Indeed, I would have been content for Caro and I to live out our days without the smiles and squalls of sons and daughters; but when my son John was born – and after him Charlotte – all of that changed. I knew myself suddenly for a man who, in some dark corner of himself, had always wanted fatherhood. And as I watched them grow, I'd known no greater joy. Over the years of war through which I'd barely seen them I'd pushed all that away. It caught me now, rising up from somewhere deep, hard enough to bring a tear to my eye. They were children when I left them. By now they would be children no more.

The little ones squabbling at the old woman's hems stopped when they saw me and retreated behind her as if this tiny, frail creature was herself a fortress. They risked only little peeps around her legs. It was a horror to me that I could frighten children like that. I knew they took me for a New Modeller, the sort of man who had marched into their small world and turned it into a wintry Hell, and so I didn't blame them; it was better that they were frightened of this sort of man than open and trusting. Yet still it cut me to the quick.

'Away, away!' the old woman shrieked. 'Soon, sweethearts of mine.' She swept the children along the hall and into one of the rooms that sat alongside it. For a moment she disappeared with them and I stood alone in the darkness, listening to the muted chatter through the walls. The children were eager to tell her things but she hushed them before any could form a full sentence. When she reappeared, I saw her hands were empty of the bundle she'd been carrying. She had only a rag in her hands with which she was desperately wiping the ink away – or else kneading it further into her skin.

'Well then? What do you want?' She hobbled along the hallway into the scullery at its end. I followed. The windows here spilled more of the wintry moonlight into the room. The glass was frosted by ice so that only vague shapes could be seen of the world outside.

'You were in the Fletcher house.'

'I have a business to be,' she snapped. I was shocked to hear how viciously one so old could snarl. I supposed she'd had many more years of practice. 'Not like you. *You're* nothing but a sorry intruder . . .' She stopped, as if daring me to interject. I was silent. 'I heard you,' she said. 'Don't think I didn't. I'm old, not deaf. I knew there was somebody poking around. Do you know that place used to be a *home*? I know it doesn't mean a lot to men like you but this used to be a good place. A safe place. Oh we had our trials and troubles just like everybody else. But – well, this is a different world now.'

'Mrs . . .'

'Miller,' she returned, with the same wolfish bite. 'Beatrice Miller.' The guard outside the cottage had mentioned an old Mrs Miller and let slip that she had taken Tom Fletcher under her wing. The only surprise was that I had found her there in the dead of night.

'You have me wrong, Mrs Miller. I'm not with the New Model.' Saying it reminded me of what Fairfax had said to me when last we met: that I was not a pressed man but still a prisoner.

'You play a fine part, Mister Falkland. You dress like one, you talk like one, you even force your way into our homes like one.' There was little I could say to that given she was speaking the truth. 'Oh, don't look at me like that!' she sighed. 'I'm too old to play games. Too old to be polite to *soldiers*. King or Parliament, it doesn't matter to me. It isn't going to be my world much longer. But those poor children in there . . .' She waved a hand dismissively. 'Ah, what would you care? Spit it out, Mister Falkland, and then be gone – what do you want?' She studied me carefully. She had a waspish look about her still, as if at any moment she might subject me to her poisonous sting.

'Might I see them?' I asked.

If it was a surprise to her that I asked, it was even more of a surprise to me. I tried to quell any thoughts of John and Charlotte because I knew from bitter experience down which roads that would take me: where were they? What had become of our home? Had John run away to war as I often feared? Had Caro and Charlotte remained untouched by marauding soldiers?

'Why would you want to see them?'

'Please,' I began, my voice barely a whisper. 'Sometimes a man just wants to see something decent.'

I think she understood. She nodded curtly and shuffled me out of the way so that she might get to the door through which the children had gone. 'They're not mine,' she said, as if such a thing were even possible. 'The girl's my daughter's but she's gone now. And the rest – just boys from the village. They have to go somewhere.'

'You mean their fathers were pressed?'

'Pressed or runaways or . . . Those poor little ones had to come somewhere, so they came here. They tried to put soldiers in this cottage but I wouldn't hear of it. This place is for the children.'

I had to smother a smile when I imagined it: old Mrs

Beatrice Miller, answering the door to a raft of New Model pikemen and telling them there was no room for them to lay their heads. I had little doubt that a woman as proud and fearsome as this could repel the advancing soldiery, however diminutive her size, but somehow I fancied it had been the idea of half a dozen squalling children that had driven them away.

She opened the door and went through first. I followed. The room was gloomy but some candles had been lit to buoy the pale moonlight filtering in through the frosty window. It was small too, some wooden seats arranged around a hearth and a big deerskin rug covering the floor. I knew it instantly for a children's play room for there were toys scattered about: a doll, a wooden horse, a branch chipped crudely into the shape of a sword. The children were all here and they froze as we entered, yawning faces snapping around to look at us with big, innocent eyes. When I realised there were more children here than had met us in the hallway, I felt strangely shrivelled inside; Crediton had been a good place once but it was doubtful these children would see it again.

Mrs Miller lifted a finger and pressed it to her lips. The smallest boy – who until now had been huddling close to the girl I'd taken for his elder sister – looked set to start sobbing. He opened his arms wide, reaching out, and the old woman hobbled over to lift him up, whispering words I couldn't hear but which seemed to soothe him. I saw the bundle she'd been carrying lying on the deerskin rug. It had fallen open and its contents had been investigated thoroughly. They were papers. Papers with words printed on them and a woodcut impression of some malevolent face consumed in fire. In the dreary light I couldn't make out the words. I crouched and reached out to take one but a hand slapped down onto mine from the eldest of the girls. I saw that she had a stack of the papers beside her on the floor where she was sitting. On top of her little pile sat a thimble and thread, the sort that might be used for darning a sock.

'Might I see?' I asked her.

The girl shook her head fiercely. I considered that, were I to reach out and take one of the papers from her, she would sink her teeth into my arm and not let go until she tasted blood. Such is the fierce pride of children.

'I can't do it alone, Mister Falkland.' Mrs Miller sounded different now. Gone was her ferocity, gone was her bile. She handed the little boy back to his sister and tried to usher me out of the room. I stood fast. 'Please, Mister Falkland! I know what I promised but I can't. Haven't you ever made a promise you couldn't keep?'

I promised once that I would never stop thinking about my wife and children, that I would be back as swiftly as possible and would always protect them. I supposed that was a promise I'd broken but I had no idea to what Mrs Miller was referring; yet she looked at me with something verging on terror. I had an unsettling feeling that it wasn't sympathy that had made her agree to show me the children; it was fear of what I might have done had she refused.

'I would like to see the papers,' I began. I didn't want to let her know she was wrong about me, not yet, not until I'd found out the reason for her fear. This time, when I bent down, no one struck my hand aside. I took a paper from the bag and lifted it to a candle, cupping my hand around the flame. I studied the printing. The words 'YOU WILL BE

DISCOVERED' were printed in thick black lettering at the top of the page, still sticky to the touch. Beneath was the woodcut of the malevolent face – all eyebrows with dark slits for eyes and a cruel pursed mouth underneath springing forth from a fountain of flame. It was difficult to judge whether this was a person being consumed by the fire, somebody trying to escape it or some sort of devil being birthed.

I turned the paper over. There was nothing on the reverse; but when I studied the room more carefully, I saw that several other children had piles at their sides with thimbles and needles and threads perched on top. 'I want to see the rest,' I said.

'Sir?'

'The rest!' I said, my voice climbing in pitch. 'There has to be more. What are these children stitching together if it's only one leaf?'

Mrs Miller took a handful of pages and passed them to me, then swept the children into one corner of the room and put herself between me and them. 'You have to understand,' she said. 'It's my hands. They're . . .' She lifted her hands to show me but I was too busy scanning the pages of what was to be the pamphlet to pay her gnarled fingers much attention. 'Finished,' she breathed. 'Done. Some mornings I can hardly hold a spoon. How am I supposed to do all this stitching alone with fingers like this? They do good work, sir.'

Her last words brought me back to the present. I held the pamphlet hard and looked at her. 'You do the binding of the pocket Bibles as well?'

She nodded but there was a flicker on her face now as if,

for the first time, she was starting to question me. Why, she seemed to be thinking, did I not already know?

'And nobody knows these children are doing the stitching?'

'Nobody but you, sir.' When she next spoke her voice throbbed again with the simmering rage I'd had from her out in the lane. 'And I beg you,' she went on, though there was no begging in her tone, 'you must keep it secret. These children cannot starve. These children must be here to see the end.'

'The end?'

'Of the war,' she said. 'They must survive.'

'So they pay you to bind their books and stitch up their pamphlets, is that how it goes? And with their coin you feed the little ones?'

Her face crumpled. Whether she was trying to hide tears or rein herself in from clawing out at me and filling the air with curses, I could not say. 'They must go on paying,' she said. 'If not for me, for the children. Do you have children of your own, Mister Falkland? Are you at least a godly man?' She stopped. I was glad of it, for her words were running together to make a babble. 'Bethany, come. Explain yourself to Mister Falkland. Tell him your story. If he has a heart at all it will be exposed if only you tell him . . .' She pressed in on me and I flinched away.

'In the name of God, woman, be quiet!' I rounded on her. Had I been a different sort of soldier then I might even have lifted my fist but I'd seen too many soldiers reaping their spoils of war to ever lift my hand to a woman, no matter how incessant she was with her shrieking. With a hush at last, I began to read.

> I doe in the presence of Almighty God, Promise, Vow,
> and Protest, to maintaine and defend, as far as lawfully
> I may, with my life, power, and estate, the true re-
> formed Protestant Religion, expressed in the Doctrine
> of the Church of England, against all Popery and
> Popish Innovation within this Realme, contrary to the
> same Doctrin, and according to the duty Allegiance; as
> also the Power and Priviledges of Parliament.

The words were familiar enough though I judged there
were subtle changes. For the most part it was the late
Protestation, part of the traditional oaths that all members of
the Church had to make. I'd seen the oath before in the days
when I first came to London to join the King's armies with
Caro's father and I quickly realised what was missing. There
was mention of Parliament here but no mention of the oath
to the King as rightful head of the Church. Whoever was
printing these pamphlets had cut it out. When I understood,
I admit I reeled a little, for such a thing could not make
sense. Come the spring the King would have to come to
terms – I had no doubt of that now having seen the power
simmering in this New Model – but he remained the ruler
of both kingdom and Church by divine right. Not even
Cromwell and Fairfax would dare counter that. Neither man
was a heretic.

I looked at the next page. Here were more woodcut
pictures, more flames, more malevolent faces. This time they
were not people who appeared out of the fire but fantastical
creatures the like of which I'd not seen in the real, physical
world, and doubted any man in the kingdom had either. If
such creatures did exist, it was only in the stories of seafarers

and explorers – but here the beasts were given names: *Jarmara* was a savage-looking dog, *Newes* a polecat with impish features.

Another page opened with big, bold letters and beneath them a picture that was familiar. In the woodcut stood a simple prince, drawn in stark lines with his mouth wide open in a scream beside an upturned dog, a carcass with its legs sticking in the air, and a man standing above it with a musket on his back.

The words read:

DOGS ELEGY or RUPERT'S TEARS

For the late defeat given him at Marston Moore, neer York, by the Three Renowned Generalls: Alexander Earl of Leven; General of the Scottish Forces, Fardinando; Lord Fairefax, and the Earl of Manchester, Generalls of the English Forces in the North.

Where his beloved Dog, named BOY, was killed by a Valliant souldier who had skilled in NECROMANCY.

Close mourners are the witch, Pope & DEVILL, that much lament yo'r late befallen evil.

I'd heard this story before. Prince Rupert's terrier, so they said, was whelped by a Water Witch. It was the kind of story that might have been believed in Yorkshire, where men are simple and superstitious, but never in London, Oxford or Manchester where men are not given easily to mindless terror. I pushed the papers into my pocket along with the blank pocket Bible. 'Why did Thomas Fletcher blow himself up with a granadoe?' I asked.

Mrs Miller turned to the children. She crouched down as far as her aged knees would allow her and made them a rush of promises as she shooed them away. All the same they seemed to take an age to finally leave the room, the littlest one having to be pried away. When we were alone, she looked at me with the most contempt I'd ever seen, all of her wrinkles creased up, her eyes sunken deep into her face to tell me what she made of me.

'You're not from *them*, are you?'

'You can start by telling me who *them* are, and we can take it from there.'

The old woman didn't look at me. Instead she flittered around the room, gathering up the piles of printed pages and stacking them neatly in a corner. 'Mister Falkland, I'd have been better off running, finding a place your sort wouldn't come, some remote farmhouse, somewhere with a sheep for milking and a hen for eggs. But . . .' She paused. 'In the end, sir, I've been here all my life. I've seen people come and go. I thought the New Model was just another season.'

The way she said it was perfectly clear: she was now of the opinion that the New Model was not just something that would come and then go. The New Model had changed things forever. I feared she was right.

'Poor Tom. They had him thrown in with a gang of pikemen. He was drilling with them and . . . He was a boy, you understand. A delicate one at that. No muscle on him. A whole head shorter than any other lad in Crediton. And there he was, trying to hold a pike twice as tall as him, tumbling every time he tried to join a drill. I watched him one day. He couldn't have lasted a march with this army, let alone a battle. I'd started taking the children by then. They found their way from all over. It started small but . . . Well, children whisper, and it was better they have a place to go to than end up serving common soldiers like squires. Tom heard too. He'd come here sometimes. Not for food or shelter or . . .' Her words trailed off as if she could not contemplate the sadness of it. 'He just wanted something familiar. Somebody from the old world.'

'Did he say anything that made you think he might . . .' I faltered. I did not know how to phrase it.

'Throw himself on a granadoe and blow himself to bits?'

I nodded.

'Don't be daft. If I'd have seen it coming I might have stopped him, don't you think? They quickly kicked him out of the pikemen. He couldn't ride a horse so he'd never make a cavalryman either. They set him to guarding the gunpowder stores. All he was fit for, they said, but it suited him well enough. They'd taken over the church—'

'I've seen it. Stacked up there like they want to wipe the building off the face of the kingdom.'

'They consider it a blemish. They'd banish our good priest from the camp altogether if they could. I think they were too superstitious to do it – and these the very people calling us papists and witches and worse.' She kept moving around the room, picking things up and putting them down again, as if arranging them in some sort of proper order whose design seemed to me no different to the one the children had left behind. 'Then some new soldiers moved into the Fletcher house. Young ones. Until then it had been older men, forty years old and more. I wondered what was going on so I found myself going down there. Well, you've seen it yourself. They caught me snooping but it didn't matter. I could help them, I said. They needed someone to stitch the papers together. Someone to bind the books. They told me they'd even pay me. The New Model doesn't want for money and I had the children filling the house by now and hated the sound of them crying for empty stomachs. What else could I do?'

She seemed to invite my derision, but stitching up a few pamphlets was hardly a crime. I imagined far worse things happened in this bloated camp almost every day.

'It was no great secret, so I found, that they were making those pocket books of theirs in that house. One day I was coming out of there, smuggling out some papers for the children to help me with the stitching, when Tom was standing there hisself, all alone in the middle of the lane with the snow piled up around his boots. I'd never seen him look so full of anger. Like a boy three times his size. He came pounding down the lane, wanting to know what I was doing, what was going on in his house. I told him it was those books they all had, begged him that it didn't matter, just to come home with me, but there was something terrible behind his eyes. I wondered had he been drinking? I don't suppose he'd touched a drop before in his life but, whatever it was, something had given him fire. I tried to catch him at the church that night but he'd locked himself into the cellars with all that gunpowder and refused to come out.

'I didn't see him for a few days after. Then I went down to the house one morning to gather more papers, things I could bring back for the children to stitch, and there he was. The other soldiers seemed to know him this time. They didn't treat him badly, not near as bad as I've seen in this camp. I think they thought him a nonsense. Something to be forgotten. Or tolerated – like boys sometimes do their younger brothers. They had him taking out their pamphlets, Tom and some other boys his age, sharing them with soldiers all across camp. They got wine in return and a soldier can buy almost anything he likes if he's got a full skin of wine.' She looked immeasurably sad. If I hadn't realised it before, suddenly I saw how very old, how very tired, she truly was. 'I didn't worry about little Tom Fletcher after that. A boy has to become a man and find a way to live in the world. Especially when the world doesn't know how to treat itself. These are the end times, Mister Falkland. You'll have seen it yourself. I was only happy Tom had found a way to live with it.'

'Until he turned up dead.'

There were tears shining in her eyes. I'd not meant to make her cry. I stepped forward, thinking I might put a consoling hand on her shoulder, but she shuffled back and left my hand hanging in the air.

'They still distribute the pamphlets?' I asked.

She nodded. 'It went more slowly after Tom died, but yes. There's a pamphlet tucked inside every pocket Bible and more besides.'

I could hear the children gathered in the hallway like dogs punished by their master, scrabbling at the door to be let in, all ready to grovel. I opened it and the flood of them almost swept me over as they came past on either side and even through my legs to get back to Mrs Miller. The oldest girl moved more slowly than the rest, considering me with a withering eye. I wanted to tell her: this isn't my fault; I didn't make your nanny cry; I didn't throw her friend on top of a lit granadoe.

'Mrs Miller,' I said. 'The printing press and the books, then, they are well known?'

She nodded. 'Black Tom hisself has spoken of it.'

'I will not tell anyone of *your* secret, that you bring these papers out of the old Fletcher house for your children to stitch. It is no concern of mine at all. But it's not only the pocket books you stitch, is it? The pamphlets you have with you now with pictures of devils. They are not *The Soldier's Pocket Bible*. I will ask one thing, Mrs Miller: who is it who pays you? Who prints them?'

She was smothered by the children. They formed a protective guard around her. I had a terrible feeling I could have used a guard of my own. 'I dare not say,' she whispered.

'Black Tom?' But I saw at once that I was wrong. A ghostly tremor moved in my spine and the image of a face floated into my vision. It wasn't a face I wanted to see. 'This soldier. Does he have wild black hair? A strange kind of grace?'

Mrs Miller nodded. 'You've met . . .' She breathed a little sigh, almost one of relief. 'Well, sir, you'd do well to pretend your paths never crossed. Edmund Carew might look a soft enough man, but meeting him is the biggest regret of my long, long life.'

CHAPTER 19

The house was silent when I got back. In the scullery, Kate Cain had some watery soup on the boil even though it was now the dead of night. She'd waited for me. Her face, still swollen, showed her bruises more darkly than I remembered. Still, she welcomed me fondly and stirred up whatever had settled at the bottom of the soup for me to have my fill. There was rabbit in there and it sat welcome and warm in my stomach. I made sure she ate as well.

'Is Warbeck here?' I asked her. Her glance to the ceiling was answer enough. 'Kate, I must ask you a question.'

'You can ask,' she returned, 'but I won't promise an answer.' She spoke with a smile.

'They asked you to spy on me,' I said. 'That much I know. But I must ask you – have they asked you to spy on anybody else in this camp?'

The question seemed to throw her off guard. She'd been standing at the oven and turned, cautiously, with her green eyes twinkling behind her beaten mask. 'I'm indebted to Black Tom. I'm indebted to Purkiss, even though it was his commands that did *this*.' She gestured at the markings on her face and I winced, for shame. 'Without what they pay me, I'd . . .' She turned away from me again. 'I'd be one of the

Admonished, Falkland. A camp whore!' After she barked out
the word she seemed to wrestle with herself. At last she let
out a deep sigh. 'You already know, Falkland,' she said more
softly this time, coming to sit beside me. 'All the men I keep
here, I'm sworn to spy on them. There were others before.
Now it's you and Master Warbeck.'

'I had thought,' I said, 'there might be others now.'

She shook her head slowly. We faced each other now and
my legs formed a guard around hers. I took her hand. 'What
have you found, Falkland?' she whispered.

I did not know. I had found – a story. A connection. The
fact that Edmund Carew knew both Hotham and Tom
Fletcher seemed much more than coincidence and I'm not a
man who cares much for the vagaries of chance and fate.
Perhaps I was that way once, but now there must be a reason
for everything that happens. To admit there was no reason
would be to admit that it was just cruel fate that took me
away from my dear wife and children – and to admit that
would be to admit nobody was to blame. I wasn't ready for
that.

'Have you seen this?' I asked. I let go of her hand though
she seemed unwilling and it took me a lingering moment to
tease my fingers free. From my pocket I produced the pages
of the pamphlet I'd stolen away from the children of Mrs
Miller. 'The dead boy Tom was distributing it.'

She looked at the pages for only a moment before she
handed them back. 'Falkland,' she said. 'It's incomplete.'

'Incomplete?'

When she didn't quickly reply, I faltered. She shuffled
away from me and looked shamefaced. 'Falkland. I don't
know what the pamphlet says because I cannot rightly

read.' She paused. 'Don't look at me like that. I'm no lady of letters, but I've never pretended to be. I'm a servant, Falkland. To men like you.'

'You have me wrong,' I said. 'I'm a farmer.'

'A farmer?' She snorted: 'Perhaps you were a farmer once, Falkland, but look at you now! You're an intelligencer for Oliver Cromwell himself! You'll never be a farmer again. A common man might rise to be a politician but he doesn't return to the land.'

Perhaps she was right but it was a terrible thing to know that this, now, was how the world looked on me: not as a farmer, lost in the city as I once was; nor as a common soldier, pressed into service and rising, however unwillingly, through the valour of combat. I was a man in the employ of the nation's oppressors. I could barely stand it to think that an honest, decent woman such as Kate would see me in such a way.

She took my hand again, gently, perhaps sensing the loathing I felt for myself in that moment. 'The pamphlet,' she said, 'Might it mean something to your investigation?'

I nodded. 'I've a terrible feeling it might mean everything.'

'In that case, Falkland,' she said, drawing herself high, 'I cannot tell you what is in the missing pages . . . but perhaps I can show you the pages themselves.'

She led me up the stairs. They creaked and complained underfoot but we took them lightly for we were not alone in the house. At the top was the small room with the single pallet where Warbeck laid his head when he passed the night here at all. In the second room, Miss Cain slept. Now she led me through that door. The windows were shuttered and the air thick with motes of dust but she lit a candle that spread fingers of light across the room. Against one wall there stood a bed, dressed down with blankets folded at the end, and against a wooden chair stood a scabbard with no blade inside. An embroidery hung on the wall, a biblical verse picked out in black stitches with flowers growing up and down the frame. Caro had one just the same, a work she'd slaved over as a young woman and expected to pass to our daughter and our daughter's daughter for generations to come. Standing here I felt as if I was at the frontier between a long, happy past and a long, uncertain future. This had been Miss Cain's family's home once; come the spring, perhaps there would be no family to survive.

'Shut the door,' she said.

I did as I was told while Miss Cain skirted the bed and lifted her hems and knelt to open a chest around the other side. In it were folded clothes, some tied with string. I saw a green tunic, a woollen shawl, a dagger buckled inside a glittering scabbard. These, I deduced, were family trinkets, things she'd somehow managed to deny the New Model. On top of them all were pieces of crumpled paper.

'Here,' she said. She smoothed them and passed them to me across the stark bed. I took them. My fingers touched hers. We held the pose.

She let go of the pamphlet but I let go of it too and it fluttered onto the bed between us. 'I was the King's man,' I breathed. I could hardly force the words out. 'Not Cromwell's. But I spoke up against my King once. Believe it or not it's the reason I'm here. Cromwell told me he needed a man of good conscience in a place like this. He did not mean Crediton. He meant the New Model.'

There seemed a new spark in her eyes. 'What did you do,' she began, 'to speak up to your King?'

'I had a man hanged,' I said, refusing to swallow the words however ugly they seemed. 'A ravisher. I did as Cromwell would have done, though the King told me not to. I thought afterwards that I might lose my head for it but at the time I didn't care. I didn't want to serve a king who saw it fit to let his soldiers . . .'

My voice was trembling. Those days in Yorkshire would always be a part of me. They had, I thought, been directing my movements ever since. Had I been a coward that day and done as my King expected then I would have been hanged at Newgate. There would have been no reprieve. I wanted to think it would have been better that way but I couldn't. And it wasn't because I was thinking of my wife. It wasn't because I was thinking of my son John and my daughter Charlotte, no matter how much I loved them. It was because I was here in this room, staring at Miss Kate Cain with her short black hair and her emerald eyes, studying the crumpled contours of her face where the soldiers had taken to her with their fists.

'I would hang them for hitting you,' I quaked. 'Purkiss and whichever men he brought with him. Fairfax for sending them to do it. I'd hang them up in the town square. I'd draw and quarter them.'

'Falkland,' she whispered. '*William* . . . They did not . . . They did no more than you see. Purkiss and his sort, they're not good men but nor are they bad. They're simply men.'

She reached down and picked the pamphlets up from the bed and handed them back to me. 'I found them in the scullery of the Fletcher cottage as I made my way out. I

waited for you. I tried to give them to you. I thought . . .'
When I took them I felt her fingers again. This time I
clasped her wrist with my hand and she didn't resist.
I moved forward, one knee on top of the bed, and she
mirrored the movement on the opposite side. We were so
close that I could feel the warmth of her breath, her lip dark
and bulging where a soldier's hand had struck her. My own
hand danced up her arm until I softly stroked the marks. She
winced as my touch feathered her but stopped herself from
retreating. With my other hand I cupped the back of her
head. Her hair was like down, like the soft fur that topped
my daughter's head on the day she was born.

My lips were almost with hers when I drew quickly away.
I rose, the pamphlet scrunched in my hand, and hurried to
the door. I stood on the threshold. Her words, I thought,
might have described all the thousands of men that made up
this New Model: not one thing and not another; not good
and not bad; neither roundhead nor cavalier.

'He would be a bad man if I found him now,' I admitted,
turning to take another lingering look at her, still hovering
over the bed. 'Miss Cain, I beg your forgiveness.'

I turned and walked the passageway and down the stairs,
back to the sanctity of my own room – but as I went I
couldn't keep myself from hearing, over and over again, the
whispered words that followed me. 'Falkland,' she said,
'there's nothing to forgive.'

I lay alone for hours after that, unable to sleep and yet unable
to bring myself to read the pamphlet in my fingers. I didn't
hear anything thereafter. I supposed Miss Cain had gone to
her bed for the night was already long in the tooth. Yet

whenever I closed my eyes I imagined a different night. Catching myself dreaming of it was a curious form of punishment, like being outflanked by two opposing armies with no possibility of escape. The fleeting images I had of Kate, pinned underneath me or else arching above, were a torment themselves; but a torment greater still were the pictures that punctuated them – of the country church where I was wed to my Caro, of the grey afternoon when I was summoned with weary joy by the midwife to be introduced to my firstborn son.

I must have lain there for an age before the pictures ebbed away and left me. It wasn't only a weariness that assailed me. It was a foreign kind of empty desolation. I skirted the edge of sleep but it wouldn't take me. I got to thinking I was less a man than I was a ghost already. I walked in a world that wasn't my own. I had no allegiances. I had no great love nor great hate for the people I had around me. I was an island. And then, very slowly, my thoughts returned to the boys: to Richard Wildman and Samuel Whitelock, to Tom Fletcher and even Jacob Hotham who stood apart from the rest, a roundhead strung up just the same as those poor cavaliers. Something bound these boys together. At last I heaved myself up from the bed and drew close to the guttering candle. In the dead heart of the night I unfolded the papers Kate had brought for me and assembled them into the pamphlet they were meant to be.

On the front was the familiar woodcut drawing of the malevolent face in the flames. Inside were the passages I'd already read – the oaths of allegiance, carefully rewritten to omit Parliament's allegiance to the divinely appointed King;

the proclamation of Boy's death, so mockingly worked up with NECROMANCY and DEVILL in bold lettering. At the centre of the pamphlet was a discourse I'd not yet seen. It drew my eye instantly. At the top of the page were the words ON THE DISCOVERIES OF WITCHES. The lettering beneath was small and dense with only odd words leaping out of the page: POPISH WICKEDNESS and INCARNATE SOULDIERS were only the most prominent of a dozen and more such phrases.

I read from the top:

ON THE DISCOVERIES OF WITCHES

In answer to several QUERRIES LATELY delivered to the Judges of the Assize for the County of NORFOLK
And now published by MATTHEW HOPKINS, Witch-finder for the BENEFIT of the WHOLE KINGDOME:
EXOD. 22.18. 'Thou Shalt Not Suffer A Witch To Live'

I had a feeling like Hell itself in my stomach. It wasn't the soup Miss Cain had served nor my tempestuous carnal imaginings. I'd not heard of this Matthew Hopkins before, nor of any man fool enough to name himself witch-finder, but I'd heard the word right enough. My father once taught me that the worst devils are the devils that men make up. It's not lore that any churchman or nobleman would suffer gladly, but there was wisdom enough in it. This wasn't the first time I had heard of witches or witchcraft around this camp. It was what Kate had thought of me when Fairfax had brought me to her door.

Certain Querries answered by his stalwart companion John Stearne, which have been and are likely to be objected against MATTHEW HOPKINS, in his way of finding out WITCHES:

Querie 1. That he must needs be the greatest Witch, Sorcerer, and Wizzarde himself, else he could not doe it.

Answ. If Satan's kingdome be divided against itself, how shall it stand?

Querie 2. If he never went so farre as is before mentioned, yet for certain he mett with the Deville, and cheated him of his Booke wherein is written all the Witches names in England, and if he looks on any Witch, he can tell by her countenance what she is; so by this, this helpe is from the Devill.

Answ. If he had been too hard for the Devill and still got his book it is to his great commendation and no disgrace at all: and for judgement in Phisiognomie, he hath no more than any man else whatsoever. The secrets of Divinning Witches are not themself Witchecrafts. There are methods for Men to Employe wheresoever Witches are found.

There was more. Much more. The type was so tiny that I fancied it made up almost half of the pamphlet even though it was only printed on its innermost leafs. It wasn't a surprise to me to know that men like this Hopkins, styling themselves the vanquishers of devils, might be abroad in the kingdom as

it faltered. There will always be men to prey on the super-
stitions of the weak and never more than in a time of war.
What gave me the strongest feeling of foreboding was a
question for which I could not have an answer: why did
Hopkins' pamphlet form a part of this work put together by
New Modellers? What did Carew and Hotham have to gain
by distributing his message around the camp?

I read on:

Querie 3. From whence then proceeded this his
skill? Is it divinely gifted or was it from his profounde
learning? Or from much reading of learned Authors
concerning that subject?

Answ. From neither of both but from experience.

Querie 4. If there is no divine gift should all Men
not be their Witche-finders?

Answ. A Man of great will shall find his way as
Witche-finder. He pleads with all Men to be watcheful. Men must be watcheful for Witch spots which doe
not bleed no matter if a blade be administered.
Though it be meanly esteemed of, this is yet the surest
and safest way to judge.

I meant to read on, for now there was something compelling
about the answers Hopkins gave as narrated by his
companion John Stearne. It sounded to me like the same
vindictive railing I'd seen in this camp and indeed across the
country – of one kind of man taking joy in torturing another.
Yet as I squinted at the papers, a sudden sound tore me
away. I stood up. The sound came again and I had the
instinctual sense that I was cornered as I'd been outside

Abingdon when I was finally captured.

The sound came again and I realised that somebody was tapping very softly on the shutters across my window. My hand went to my hip but I had no dagger there and never would have while I remained in this camp. I crept to the shutters and lifted the latch to see who was outside. I will admit that a large part of me feared a rock thrown through the window or for musket fire lighting the night. At once the very idea seemed laughable – an assassin does not announce himself by tapping at a window as though he's your long-lost love; still, my heart pounded in my breast, its thunderous rhythm instructing me that I was too old and weary to fling myself about like a young man.

I drew myself up and craned out into the night. The sky was overcast and swollen with snow. Indeed, thin flakes were falling already, presaging a tumultuous fall to come. I could smell it in the air. In the street in front of me stood a figure. At first I could make out little but his frame, tall and spindly. He wore a coat fastened high around his neck and great gloves that made him appear bigger than he was. He had no hat but his hair was frosted with sparkling crystals of ice.

'Who goes there?' I hissed. I could see only a vague outline of his face. He had a nose like a hawk.

'Are you the intelligencer?'

That word was beginning to grate, no matter if it was true. All the same I told him he was correct.

'Sir, you must come with me.'

'Come with you where?'

'Sir, please . . .' His voice seemed suddenly frayed and I wondered if his baritone commands of only moments ago had been an act he was finding hard to continue. 'Must I beg?'

I risked glances up and down the street. All was dark and I could see no other man abroad, not even a camp guard making his rounds. From here I couldn't even see the light of the fires that surrounded Crediton. The world appeared strangely at peace. 'No,' I said, 'not beg.' I paused. The man shifted uneasily from one foot to the other. I still couldn't see his face. 'But what is this about?'

His voice broke. It was only then, in the way he croaked his words, in the way he had to force them out, that I knew he was genuine. 'Thomas Fletcher,' he finally said. 'We saw you by his old home. We heard you were . . . asking questions. If you want to know how he died, you'll come with me.' He paused once again. 'Please, sir.' Again his voice faltered. I could not tell whether he was dread fearful or distraught. Either way, I owed it to those dead boys to hear what he had to say.

I nodded my assent and closed the shutters.

Alone in my room I took haste to dress myself and put on my boots, forcing my swollen feet into each one. Thomas Fletcher, they told me, was not a boy with many friends. What friends he had were his family and they were gone already. I didn't know who the soldier in the street was but I was certain of one thing; he was not the sort of man to befriend a small, cowardly boy like Thomas Fletcher.

I crept along the hall and up the stairs past Warbeck's door. Outside Miss Cain's room I stopped. My hand hovered on the handle. I wanted to push in, to wake her and tell her where I was going, yet I hesitated. The worst of it was the reason – that a very large part of me wished I'd returned here some hours before.

I tapped on the door and turned the handle. I could hear her breathing now, soft and steady, quietly asleep. I eased into the room. At once she stirred.

'Falkland . . . ?' she whispered, rising and turning to me. She was wrapped in a shawl but wore little else. In the gloom I couldn't see the swollen patterns of her face.

'Miss Cain,' I began, 'I'm sorry to have woken you.'

She rubbed her eyes and showed no alarm that I'd crept into her bedroom in the dead of night. As I came closer she reached out a hand and touched my leg. I was suddenly glad of the man waiting down by the door.

'There is something I must do,' I said.

She drew away. I sensed her puzzlement.

'Kate, there's one thing you might do for me.'

'What is it, Falkland?'

'Miss Cain,' I said. 'I shall need a knife. A dagger would be best but a blade from the kitchen would suffice.'

CHAPTER 20

The soldier in the street was impatient. He stood some distance from the house and beckoned me to join him. As I approached, I felt for Miss Cain's scullery knife secreted at my back and did as I was told; it was only as I came close that the starlight finally pulled his face from the shadows and I recognised him: Lucas, the surgeon. It had only been days since I'd seen him, a man no older than twenty-five suddenly in charge of all the invalids the New Model coughed up, but it seemed much longer. If he knew who I was or recognised me from that day as I did him, he was working hard not to show it. He barely fixed me with a look as he turned and began to shuffle away.

'You treated Thomas Fletcher,' I began, 'after he was found?'

He mumbled something I didn't catch and led me along the street, past the inn and the chestnut tree with its hanging man. Over the rooftops I could see the spire of Crediton church and then at last the glow of red and orange from the fires pitting the encampment.

'Did you treat the hanged brothers too?' I asked.

I was getting used to the idea that he didn't want to respond when he stopped, dug his heels into the snow and turned. It was only a half-turn, just enough for me to make out his lips. He kept his eyes downcast. 'There wasn't any treating to do,' he said. 'I'm a surgeon, not a sorcerer.' He was trembling, and not simply from the cold.

'Not a *witch*,' I breathed, remembering the pamphlet.

I stirred a reaction in him but not one I expected. His face screwed up and his eyes lifted and for a second it seemed as if his gaze was locked into mine. There was terror in those eyes. It was the terror of a little boy on a dark night, camping out with his father with a head full of stories of devils and their familiars. It seemed laughable that a grown man could recreate such an expression, but there it was.

'You should not talk of the dead,' he whispered.

He led me on a familiar route along Main Street. The snow began to fall in ribbons of white. The further we walked, the more thickly it came down, until I wondered if we'd crossed the frontier one storm makes with the next. I was thankful there was no wind to whip it at my face but it was hypnotic. There's a magic in falling snow. It makes all the world seem the same, even if underneath one patch of ground is vastly different to the other: one corner for the roundheads, one corner for the cavaliers; one corner for the Puritans, one corner for Catholics clinging to their rosaries and praying not to be discovered.

We passed close by Mrs Miller's home and came through the last of the Crediton cottages. The sprawl of the encampment tents spread out before me. Even at this hour of night it felt like day, for the whiteness of the snow made the tents visible to the very horizon, brought close by the encroaching blizzard. There was movement in the camp too as soldiers, stirred from restless sleep by the snowfall, rushed to stoke their fires and make sure they saw it through the night. Men can get used to the worst deprivations. I'd learned that in prison.

We followed a weaving trail through the tents to join a track I'd taken once before on that very first night with Miss Cain. She was without doubt a better escort than the surgeon Lucas but at least I knew where I was going. It already seemed so very long ago.

We left the camp and crossed the acre of land beyond its border. We plunged above our knees into the snow. Drifts were building again. If the blizzard continued through the night then in places those drifts would climb as high as my head by morning. In the distance I saw the witching tree. Thinking of its name like that set new mechanisms whirring in my head. The word *witch* seemed, all of a sudden, to have different and less idle meanings. It was probably trees like this that Matthew Hopkins used to string his sorcerers up while baying crowds gathered round. Tonight the tree was a black silhouette crowned in deeper and deeper white. As we approached it seemed to grow more stark, to leap out at me, pitch-black against the swirling snow.

Twenty yards away and with the falling snow a shifting curtain between us and the old oak, Lucas put out his hand and bade me stop. No sooner had I done so than the snow began to settle on me, frosting my eyebrows and eyelashes, caking my skin.

'He's waiting,' Lucas said.

I squinted. There was another figure in front of the tree. That was all he was to me now, but something made me move my frozen hand to the handle of the knife at my back. My fingers were stiff but they closed around it tightly. It was enough to know I could draw it if I needed. 'You're not coming?' I asked.

Lucas shook his head. 'I want no part of this, Falkland. Besides, the cold will kill us as easily as a granadoe being lit.' He shivered.

I nodded and left him behind. It took an age to cross those measly twenty yards. The snow had not been walked upon – where the man at the tree had come from, I couldn't yet tell – and I had to kick my way through. Where the granadoe had exploded, the depression in the land still showed, the snow piled higher in the crater so that I plunged suddenly and stumbled, falling into what felt like a pit. When I recovered my feet, the snow in the crater reached my waist. I fought my way free but the ice clung to me and I could feel it seeping into my bones.

The figure waited on the opposite side of the tree but moved around as I approached. I was glad we didn't stand beneath the very branch where the brothers and Hotham had hanged themselves high. I stopped my eyes from even glancing that way; I was cold enough without having to bear another chill.

'I'm glad that you could come.' The voice was measured. Calm. I knew it at once.

'Carew,' I whispered.

'I'm glad to meet you again, Falkland,' he said, extending his hand. 'Would that it were in less trying circumstances.' His voice didn't tremble as I knew mine would, in spite of the cold. He moved nearer but I couldn't see his face. All around us the world was illuminated by snow – but here, underneath the crown of white lodged in the branches, we were only outlines in black. He held himself like a lord, less

like the roundhead pikeman I'd first taken him for and more
like the fey cavaliers with whose image they mocked the
King's army. He had the vestiges of a London accent –
though it seemed to my ears a tone relentlessly rehearsed
– and when I took his hand, I found it limp this time, the
touch too light. Perhaps it was only that both of our hands
were frozen inside our gloves but something seemed awry in
that pose.

'I was told you knew things about Thomas Fletcher,'
I said. 'So what's this about? And why the forsaken hour?'

'A sorry tale.'

'A tale that might easily have been told in front of a fire
with ale in our hands and pottage on our plates . . . .'

'And have the whole camp hear?' he replied, rising in a
shrill peak but holding back from laughter. 'No good could
come from that.'

'The surgeon's quarters then. Surely we might have
spoken there?'

I was suddenly aware of the pamphlet still stuffed into
my pocket. I pictured Carew and Hotham working the press,
arranging the letters, fixing the paper. In my head, Thomas
Fletcher scurried around them, obeying orders thrown at
him from left and right.

'Jacob would have been disturbed,' Carew replied. 'And
there are too many boys lying there. I don't want the story
told too freely.'

'I know you knew Thomas, Carew.' A wind flurried up,
throwing a veil of snow between us, and for a moment it
robbed my breath. 'But you know I know as well.'

'I wasn't sure you had recognised me.'

In truth I hadn't. It was only as I looked at him now that

it occurred to me: he had exactly the same lean, willowy figure as the hooded man I'd chased from the Fletcher house before I was drawn, instead, to old Beatrice Miller. Carew had been there all the while. And Beatrice Miller had known it too and quietly never said a word. Somehow it felt as if we were parrying blades, with me forced onto the back foot. 'You might have told me,' I ventured, 'when I first came to see Jacob, that you knew Fletcher as well. You were not honest, Carew. Why was that?'

I could see him weighing up the words he was about to say. 'You must forgive me, Falkland. These are trying times.'

'All the same, it was a lie. You told me you knew only his story, yet all the while he was your messenger boy, delivering your –' I checked myself from saying pamphlets: there was still a chance I didn't know that part of the story – 'Bibles to the soldiers.'

'That was how White Tom and Jacob knew each other.' Carew came closer to me. I hated to admit it but I was thankful. Together we formed our own windbreak, turning against the worst of the chill. No longer did we look at the witching tree; instead, we gazed over the endless white. 'We didn't know it was Fletcher's house. Not to begin with. He was just some simpering royalist whelp who started loitering around. But we had our use for him. We were turning out more books of verse than we—'

'The printing press,' I interjected. 'Where does it come from?'

Carew's lips curled. He seemed to be enjoying a joke at my expense. 'Why, Falkland,' he said, as if the answer was so obvious that a child might have known it. 'It belongs to the New Model.'

'The army has its own press?'

'How else is it to lead its soldiers? We are not barbarians. We are –' and here he could not but grin, for he was driving a stake into what he presumed was my unending loyalty to the King and Prince Rupert – 'not *minions*. There can be little opportunity for a printing press when the army is campaigning. But in a winter like this the contraption has a part to play that is much, much bigger than any individual soldier.'

There was truth in this. He didn't know that I already understood, but he wasn't only talking about Bibles and books of pocket verse. The pamphlets, I was beginning to understand, were as much a way of controlling the men, cut from disparate towns and disparate militias, as was drilling and the rule of soldier's law. The pamphlets cut away all mention of the King from the traditional Oaths. They filled their pages with images of Prince Rupert as a devil and his dog as his familiar and other such. These were not idle thoughts. These were careful manipulations. Yet as I looked at him, I was suddenly aware of how young he was. War is a time for young men to make bold, to climb high, to be ambitious and stake claims from which they can build their future lives. I suppose, in a way, that was what I'd done, though I'd not planned on it and didn't care much for where it had brought me. All the same, Carew did not seem to me to be a man in any way in charge of this army. For all his airs, he was common soldiery.

It dawned on me then that perhaps Cromwell wasn't the astute tactician he seemed. If a weapon as powerful as the printing press – for, make no mistake about it, this was a weapon far more powerful than any granadoe – was left for boys to employ, then the New Model was not as clever as he believed.

'Why you?' I asked.

The question must have caught him off guard. 'Falkland?'

'Why are you running the press?'

'Not me,' he said. 'Jacob. He is an esteemed sort of man. Knows the presses inside and out from his days in London. He fancied himself a poet, you see. Or, if not a poet, a polemicist. When we came to camp he was asked to help in the binding of the Bibles but it quickly became clear that he was much more useful than that. He asked me to aid him.' Carew paused. A shiver ran through him; we'd been out in the cold too long. 'He's fortunate that he did. If I'd not been working the press with him, I would not have been there to save his life.'

I remembered what Carew had told me the last time we met – that they had been working a watch around the camp, that Hotham had taken himself to the witching tree where we now stood and strung himself up there only for Carew to have a vision from God and come running with his fellows to cut him down. My eyes began to stray back to the branch from which the rope had dangled but Carew ploughed on:

'It was because of Thomas Fletcher,' he said. 'It was all because of him. You know, by now, that the house we use for printing was where he grew up. Well, he came there often. We took pity on him at first. He was hardly more than a boy and certainly he didn't have the ideas and thoughts that might belong to a man. So we thought it little danger to take him in. We did not let him near the press but he was useful enough as a messenger—'

'And a courier.'

Carew ploughed on, heedless of my interruption. 'He became something of a little brother to us. One night we had a wineskin and offered it to him. Do you know, I believe that until that moment the only wine to ever touch his lips had been from some secret communion in that treacherous little church of theirs. Still, he took to it with aplomb. You will think it cruel but it became a game for us, to taunt him and see how far he might go. We decided to share some stories. Jacob is a man with many stories to tell and I will admit to having my own tall tales, but Thomas Fletcher – well, a more naïve, hopeless boy you'll never meet. You see, Falkland, it became clear to us that Thomas Fletcher was *innocent* of things a soldier must not be innocent of. I don't mean killing a man . . .' He said it with a lascivious grin, his mouth open a fraction too wide like a glutton contemplating his supper.

'I know what you mean, Carew,' I said.

'There are lots of sorts around here to take that innocence from a boy. So we took him to see a girl we knew.'

It didn't strike me as right that a boy like Carew, so fiercely Puritan in his outlook, would have fraternised with camp whores. I remembered distinctly the way he'd looked on the Day of Admonishment, not baying like the rest of the crowd but somehow pleased nonetheless. I met his eye. 'Then I'd like to talk to her. Who was she?'

I had it in mind that he'd answer 'Mary,' and before he'd even spoken the word, ideas exploded and reformed in my head. If Fletcher had wandered into the same ménage as Richard Wildman and his brother then perhaps there was something other than their Catholicism to draw all these boys together after all: three boys enamoured of the same whore? Jacob Hotham the one who spun the spider's web . . . ?

Carew must have sensed something for he paused before going on. 'Her name, as I recall, was Beth. She was a dark little thing. I hear she's been following us since long before Naseby but, as you'll warrant, I had little interest in making her acquaintance. She was pleased to take Thomas in. We thought perhaps they would not do anything. Thomas Fletcher was certainly the sort of boy who would rather be cuddled than treated with a man's proper respect. But he took to seeing her. He even had a little pay, now, to shower her with gifts.

'It was our fault, Falkland. We took him to the wrong whore. She had her suitors among the soldiers and there was one who fancied her his property. We didn't know it until after but he was the one who brought Fletcher to this spot. He was the one who struck a light against that granadoe. Thomas Fletcher was not a suicide. He was murdered.'

I let it sink in. The bitterness of the winter had grown up around me and I felt rooted to the spot. Not even the fire I felt at hearing this story could thaw me out. 'Hotham?'

'He tried to hang himself as penance.' Carew nodded thoughtfully. 'I think he thought it fitting.'

'Yet you . . . you did not feel the same thing?'

'I have a different way of looking at life than Jacob Hotham, Falkland. I was not the one to light the granadoe. I regret what we did but I will not burn in Hell for it.'

At last I lifted my boot from the snow. My left leg felt dead but I flexed it over and again until it screamed out – then, at least, I knew it was alive. Hotham hanged himself as a penance? I found it hard to countenance.

'You look pained, Falkland.'

'If all you say is true, why not come forward?' I turned around and took two faltering steps away from the tree. As I turned I was drawn to the branch where the boys had hanged themselves. If it seemed unfair that Thomas Fletcher had come to such an ignoble but ordinary end, it seemed more unfair still that, at the end of everything, the deaths were not all tied together as I'd thought. I'd been sent here to investigate suicides, and suicides were all I'd found. There was nothing more remarkable in this camp than too many frightened, starving boys, plucked from every last corner of the kingdom, flung into one place and told to exist.

Then I saw the rope hanging from the branch. I'd climbed up that trunk only a few days ago. I'd nervously edged along the bough and inspected that rope. I'd lifted its severed end and run my hands up and down its length. I'd tried to imagine what it might have been like for those boys. I'd fingered the frayed end and wondered who had cut the last one down.

But now, when I looked at the rope, I saw no severed end. I saw a loop of rope tied in a slipknot. I saw a noose freshly ready.

My eyes fixed upon Carew; and as I did I saw a harsh resolve fix upon his face. I knew, then, how all this story was merely another lie. This story of some whore and a jealous boy was just that – a story – and a poor one too, and Carew knew from my look that I'd seen through it. The reason he'd called me here was suddenly clear. 'Carew,' I said, my voice quiet with condemnation, 'Fletcher died *after* Hotham had been cut down.'

He seemed untroubled that I'd seen through him. 'The

other two,' he whispered. 'Those two papist boys? They were more ... complicated. I'm sorry, Falkland, that it comes to this. I'd hoped to avoid it, truly I did.'

In his hands he held a dagger. In the darkness beyond the tree stood three other men. Suddenly I wasn't cold any more.

CHAPTER 21

'Carew,' I said. The word came out strangled, ripped away from my lips by a sudden gust blowing past. 'Think carefully about what you're doing, Carew. Somebody finds me strung up here, they won't think it's suicide. They won't think I was one of your royalist boys beaten and beaten until he couldn't take it any more.' I stepped back, spreading my legs to get a firmer grounding. It had been too long since I was in a fight. Even at Abingdon when they captured me there had been little of it left. I reached to the small of my back for the knife I'd hidden there but felt only my naked flesh. It had fallen away when I plunged into the crater the granadoe had left; I'd been too frozen to notice. I looked about for anything I might use to defend myself but all I saw was a second knife on Carew's belt.

'Beaten?' He laughed. 'Who has been beaten?'

'You'll bring Hell on this camp, Carew.'

He came a step closer, mirroring my every action. In a sudden reflection of snow I glimpsed his eyes. They didn't have the calmness I'd seen in them before. Now they were wide.

'You do know who sent me here?' I asked. I didn't like invoking the name but the three other figures were close to

Carew now and I felt as if an unstoppable wave was about to pound me down. I'd never been to sea but I had the vivid idea that this was what it was like to be shipwrecked. 'Cromwell isn't the man to ignore it. He sent me as his investigator. Killing me is like . . .'

'Perhaps,' Carew said, his voice barely a whisper, 'that is precisely the point.'

I didn't have time to consider what he meant. They came forward together as if ordered by words I couldn't hear. Two of the other figures broke away, vaulting through the deep snow to come at me from behind, while Carew and the last of them advanced from the front. I had only my fists to protect me but, nevertheless, I whirled, desperate to keep them at bay, stretching out as if my forearm itself was a sabre with which I might cut them in two. I cast an eye back for Lucas – I didn't think he was a part of this – but he was gone or lost to the snow. There seemed little point in crying out.

Like a snake coiling around its prey, the others encircled me. All the while the face of Carew hung in front of me. 'You would bring me out here,' I said, 'to tell me your tale, only to string me up anyway? Carew, you're not thinking . . .' I saw the way he held that dagger in his hand. Here was a man not used to trading blows. The men with him were more battle ready – I judged them second-rank pikemen; too strong and stocky to waste as fodder in the front row – but Carew was the one with the dagger. I could use that to my advantage.

'Only when you would not believe it,' said Carew.

As one they began to close. When they were only feet away I sprang and launched myself directly at Carew, coming up from underneath him so I could sweep his dagger arm out of the way. To his credit he hung on to the blade even as I forced his arms above his head and barrelled him backward. Together we plunged into the snow. Straddling him I had the better of it, but it wouldn't last long before the other men were on me. The snow hampered them, though, and I risked bringing my fist back to smash into Carew's face. As I hit him we sank further still into the drift. I drove a fistful of snow into his mouth. He bucked back, trying to throw me off, but now he was choking. I wrestled the dagger out of his hand. It dropped and vanished into the snow. I seized the blade from Carew's belt and rolled away; even as I did, the first of his henchmen was on top of me. I kicked out with the flat of my boot and pushed him back. He didn't topple over – he was no fool – but it gave me enough room to haul myself to my feet. Thankful that the tree was at my back, I used it to drag myself around. There was no way I could fight them off. I had one on either side while the third helped the choking Carew back to his feet. 'Do you boys have any idea,' I gasped, 'of what you're doing? You might as well put the rope around your own neck. Cromwell will see you hang.'

'What does Oliver Cromwell care about a King's servant?' one of them spat.

'Little enough, but I think he cares even less for soldiers who don't obey orders,' I said. 'You've seen what he does to ravishers.' I waved Carew's knife at the closest of them. They shared a look.

'We're not going to ravish you,' smirked one.

I fixed my eye on him. 'You're not going to get the chance.' Before Carew and the other pikeman could join the fray, I lunged for the man on my right. He had a dagger of his own, a longer blade than mine, but I had the element of surprise. I swiped and then jabbed, cutting left as if to parry his own blade and then went for his chest. Twice his age, I was still too fast for him. My blade sank in. Yet, when I drew it back, no blood dripped from its end. There was no tear in his tunic, nothing but a faint wrinkle where I ought to have spilled his life. I marvelled at the dagger. For the first time I realised that it sat too lightly in my hand. I weighed it and something seemed to rattle in the handle, something I'd not understood before. With the fingers of my other hand I tested the blade. It retreated, as if by magic, into the hilt, disappearing until all but an inch of blade was hidden away.

Wordless, I dropped it at my feet.

'Take a hold of him,' Carew said hoarsely. 'We've been out here too long.'

I swung my fists but they grappled me and held me fast to the trunk. At first I couldn't feel their hands around me, so bitter was the cold, but they dragged me out and threw me to the ground. I landed hard, all the breath forced out of my chest. I gasped and heaved but all I took in were the mouthfuls of snow they fed me. Two of the men wrenched my wrists together behind my back and began to bind me. It took only a single blow after that for the world to fall out of focus. They hauled me upright and, hanging between two of them, heaved me into place beneath the great bough.

The noose hung some distance above my head but I heard awkward grunting in the tree above and understood that one of the men had scrambled up to ease my passage.

While Carew looked on, the other two pushed me high. My
legs were held fast so I couldn't kick out and I would not
scream – there was no point and I would not give them the
satisfaction. I bucked and twisted and toppled us all into
the snow but they soon had me up again. It would not, I
noted grimly, be as easy as the last time I'd escaped a
hanging.

They hauled me up a third time. The world came
beautifully into focus. There were the rolling white fields.
There was the encampment. There was Crediton and
somewhere there was Miss Cain. Carew gazed at a point
above my head. I didn't look up – I knew he was looking at
the noose. I looked, instead, at him. It had felt different on
the morning they hauled me out of Newgate. I was ready for
it then. If anything, though I might not have admitted it
even to myself, it was what I wanted. All my desire had been
bled out of me – by the King, by the wars, by roundheads
and cavaliers. All of it was the same to me. But now I wasn't
ready any more. Now I didn't want to die. Now there were
people who needed me. Yes, my family, wherever they were
and whatever they were doing. But more than that I meant
the dead boys: Whitelock, Wildman, Fletcher; for I was
certain now that everything Carew had said to me was a lie. I
even thought, as they hoisted me higher and the noose
brushed the top of my head, that I was beginning to
understand. I had that pamphlet in my pocket. Somewhere
beneath me there was the knife with the retractable blade.
The images of both seemed to swirl in front of my eyes,
tempting me to draw some conclusion, tempting me to
shout it out loud. I knew it was Carew. I was certain I knew
why. I almost knew how.

A light like a tiny orb of fire split the darkness. Riding on the back of it there came a sound – thunder, in miniature, the crack of a musket. I froze. The men underneath me froze too. They hadn't yet got the noose around me.

The sound came again, this time from a different direction. Another flash of musket fire. Another noise like thunder harnessed and thrust out of a barrel. The second shot came too quickly for there to be only one person out there, filling his weapon back up before aiming and releasing fire.

I took my chance. I thrust myself left and toppled from the pikemen – no matter that I landed on the ground hard enough to shatter half my ribs. The snow cushioned my fall, betraying me only where one of the tree's roots broke through the surface. I rolled away gasping for air. This time the pikemen did not grapple after me. They were too busy whirling around, trying to discern where the ambush was coming from.

Bound as I was, I squirmed away like a snake across the snow. Once I'd reached the trunk I used it to haul myself up.

'Stop!' Carew bellowed. He wasn't shouting at me but at the pikemen who seemed about to scatter. 'There can only be two of them or they'd have shot again. Let's get this . . .' Out of the gloom somebody grappled Carew from behind. A diminutive forearm curled around to constrict his throat and he began to buckle. I fancied there was a dagger – one with a real blade this time – pressed into the small of his back. As he went to ground, I marvelled at what I saw. Miss Kate Cain stood above him dressed in soldier's clothes far too big for her slender frame, a kitchen knife in her hands.

One of the pikemen had run, vanished into the whiteness. Two still remained. They stopped as they saw who had forced Carew to the ground. From the snow he called out to them. There was only a second of hesitation before they shared a look and began to advance.

'Falkland!' Miss Cain exclaimed. 'Falkland!'

My hands were still bound. I threw myself away from the trunk. I was between Miss Cain and the pikemen and I began to run. I saw the retractable dagger in the snow at my feet, still by the base of the tree. I couldn't pick it up but kicked it high instead so that it landed beyond Carew. I charged on, reached Kate and hurried past her.

'Leave him!' I called. 'Get away! Back to the camp! They can't risk following us there . . .'

'No,' Miss Cain replied, her voice so calm she seemed not to care that the pikemen were rampaging towards us. 'Not yet.'

Another pealing of thunder. Another flash of white muzzle light and one of the pikemen gasped and stumbled. He looked down at himself and sank to his knees. He'd been shot in the chest. Out of the gloom emerged Warbeck, dressed up in his red Venice coat with leather gauntlets and metal bracers on his wrists. He had a vicious look in his eye. As the other pikeman kept on, Warbeck threw away his musket and drew out a sabre.

'Get him out of here,' he said. All his foppish sweetness was gone. 'I'll hold these.'

The second pikeman stopped. Kate lifted her foot from the small of Carew's back and rushed to my side. She took my hand and tried to lead me back across the field but I resisted. 'Kate, the dagger! Carew's dagger.'

Warbeck was backing away. 'Go!' he barked. 'They won't follow. I'll see to that.' Carew floundered in the snow until he found his feet. Kate scooped up the dagger with the false blade and began to run, hesitating only to help me along. Halfway across the field we stopped and she loosened the ties at my wrists. I could hardly feel my fingers. She cupped them to my mouth to breathe some warmth back into them. We stood there beneath the freshly falling ribbons of snow and listened out for what was happening down at the witching tree. All we heard was silence: long, unending and pure.

Back at the house, Kate dropped the latch and heaved a chair from the scullery to stop the handle from turning. She bade me sit and, in the light of the candle, reached for my neck as if to inspect me for bruises. As her fingers, ice cold, touched me, I took hold of her wrists and folded them back against her breast. I promised her the rope had not marked me.

'Damn them, Falkland,' she said. The light of the candle waned suddenly and I couldn't tell if she was crying; but when the flame surged back into life I saw it wasn't tears but pure rage that was making her shake. 'You should not have gone!'

She was right. It had been foolish to follow the surgeon into the snow. Yet now I understood. Now I had the pieces of this shredded tapestry woven together. 'How did you know where I was?' I asked.

'I watched you going down the lane . . .' She stopped. 'I was afraid . . . because who comes knocking at windows in the middle of a night like this, Falkland? Who? Not honest men, that's for sure.' She looked away. 'I thought you were a fool.'

It seemed she was right.

'I must have woken Master Warbeck. He wouldn't let me follow you alone. And now he's . . .'

I put my hand over hers. 'We don't know anything.' I couldn't bring myself to see her grieve over a man like Warbeck; although it occurred to me that he had perhaps saved me twice now from Carew and his gang.

'I wouldn't regret it.' Miss Cain looked up. In the candlelight her eyes were alive. Some of the rage had seeped out of her and now she looked in control of what was left. The anger hardened inside her like a freshly cast sword plunged into a blacksmith's well. 'If he were not to come back tonight, I wouldn't regret it for a second. Let the snow cover him up. Let wolves find him for all I would care. He's never been welcome in my house.'

I stood. She had wine, red and watery in a jug, and I poured cups for both of us. It wasn't until I gulped it back and felt its warmth that I realised how cold I'd been or how much my fingers trembled.

'Who were they, Falkland?'

'It was the surgeon took me there,' I said. 'To meet a man named Edmund Carew.'

'Do you know him?'

'They said they had news about Tom Fletcher. He spun me a story about some camp whore and a soldier who wanted revenge. I should have known it.' My hand let go of the cup and it clattered to the tabletop, spilling its dregs. Instantly I was shaking again. 'A sorrier story I've never heard. I should have seen through it at once but I didn't.

Only when I saw the fresh noose they'd made ready for me.'

'Falkland,' Miss Cain said, her voice even, 'they may come for you again.'

'I know it.'

'They know where you live.'

I did not mean to but I snapped, 'They may also come for you. I won't put you through it. I'll be gone.'

'That's not what I meant!'

There was silence between us for what felt the longest time. 'Carew was looking after Hotham, the third boy to hang,' I said at last. 'They knew Fletcher from the printing press. They worked it and made him serve as they made old Mrs Miller serve. They had him delivering . . . I thought it was Bibles but it wasn't. It was this.' I produced the pamphlet she'd given me. 'Have you heard,' I said, 'of this man, Hopkins?'

I opened the pamphlet to the correct page and spread it out. The candlelight spilled over it and lit the pictures of devils and familiars in terrible orange light. As the flame moved they appeared to dance. It was a trick as magical as any the man Hopkins must have been using to catch and try his witches. Miss Cain hovered over it. She traced the inky pictures with her finger but, before she could speak, there came a sudden sound of wood hammered against wood, of somebody grappling hard to get through the front door. We froze and then I took her knife and pushed past her through the scullery door.

'It's me they've come for. I shouldn't have brought this on you.' I faced the door with only the glow of the candles behind me to light my way.

'Falkland!' The hammering on the door came again. The

voice was Warbeck. I strode forward and kicked the chair so it fell and unlatched the door. Warbeck came in fast, the naked sabre still in his hand, and he only scabbarded it when the chair was back against the door. 'They didn't follow,' he said. 'I saw to that. But who's to say how many more there are?' He flashed me a nasty smile. 'Did you see the bruise on that other pikeman's face?'

I shook my head. I had not.

'I fancy you landed a blow or two on him when he took you in that alley two nights back. Got a good piece of him.'

'We should go to Fairfax,' I said, but Warbeck shook his head. He pushed me out of the way to come down the hallway, stopping his stampede only when he saw Miss Cain in the scullery door. He poured himself a cup of wine and told Kate to get a fire going. 'No Black Tom, not yet. There's no more sleep for us tonight,' he growled. 'So Falkland – have you got Cromwell's answer for him?'

I looked at the table where the pamphlet still lay. 'I fancy the answer is in there,' I began.

Warbeck and Miss Cain looked back at it.

'What became of them?' I asked.

'The one I shot will die if he's not dead already,' Warbeck replied, his eyes lingering on the pamphlet. 'The others loped away as soon as the opportunity presented itself.'

'Into camp?' I asked.

Warbeck nodded. 'They didn't much like the look of my sabre but they didn't seem terrified as though they'd been found out in some scheme that would get them hanged. It's a troubling thing, that. What did he want of you besides to see you dangle from the very tree you came to investigate?'

He scoffed at me. 'A poor report *that* would make to Cromwell.'

Miss Cain finished at the fire as I sat. She came to stand at my back, rested her hands on my shoulders and leaned into me. I produced Carew's knife. In the light of a new candle I turned it over, marvelling at the way the orange flame flickered along the contours of the collapsible blade. 'It's Carew's dagger,' I said. 'But not the one he drew on me.'

I turned to the pamphlet's pages about Hopkins, the roaming Witch-finder General, and began to read aloud. '"Men must be watcheful for Witch spots which doe not bleed no matter if a blade be administered. Though it be meanly esteemed of, this is yet the surest and safest way to judge." I think,' I said, 'that this is our answer.'

We froze, all three, at the sound of another hand on the door. Whoever it was they quickly passed but they were out there. They were letting us know.

'I've seen already,' I went on with a level look at Warbeck, 'what this New Model is. A bastard army, sweeping across the kingdom, rounding up whatever boys it can find, no matter what their allegiance, no matter what their ideals. Roundhead or cavalier, Catholic or Protestant, it doesn't matter to Cromwell.' I looked at them plainly. 'But I fancy it matters to Fairfax and it certainly mattered to these boys,' I said. 'It matters to the soldiers who organise tourneys in the squares. It matters to the lads who secretly go looking for the Mass, for communion or confession. It matters to the camp whores who sneak out at night to plant crosses in their lovers' graves to steer them on their way to Heaven. Cromwell overlooked one thing when he set about making this monster. A soldier's body might be bought by regular pay and regular food but his spirit cannot be bought so easily. I said as much to Fairfax last night. He understands the truth of it.'

In that instant I relived again the moment when King Charles told me to look the other way, told me that soldiers did what soldiers did, that one ravisher in our ranks was not an aberration.

'There was something the camp whore said. Mary. She was a lover to one of the boys who hanged himself, the one named Wildman. He spent some time away from her, stewing in envy, and when she saw him again she said he was changed. I expected to hear how he was murdered by some Puritan gang, most likely by Carew, but she swore he took his own life. He said to her . . .' Here I struggled to remember the exact words though the image was burned into my mind. 'He said he would rather hang by his own hand than die at somebody else's pyre. I took it to mean he couldn't face another battle when the spring came around but it was more than that.' I lifted up the dagger and teased the point with my finger.

'They talk of it all over camp and it's in here too,' I said, tapping my finger to the pamphlets, 'how every royalist is a Catholic, how every Catholic is in league with devils. That story they tell, of Prince Rupert's little dog Boy – as if that yapping little terrier is anything more than an over-grown rat . . .' I admit it: I hated that dog, even if it was no witch's familiar. I looked at Warbeck again. 'Do you remember the day we arrived? Do you remember the soldier who came out of his hut as we entered that night, how he looked at us with a face as though he'd seen the devil himself? Do you remember the two men in the alley by the church who turned and fled? Where I found the rosary? Why, even Kate, when Fairfax brought us to the door, thought we were here to hunt witches. The camp is rife with it. How? Fairfax can talk of rumours and of dancing girls with the itch if he likes, but what if some of the soldiers here have decided to make this army how they see it *should* be? You've seen yourselves how ardent some men are. How much passion! We were all there on the Day of Admonishment. We've read their books of soldier's verse. What if Carew and the other boys running that press decided that something had to be done?'

Warbeck's eyes boggled but I saw he understood. 'What you're suggesting is preposterous!' he exclaimed, showering us with spittle. A speck must have landed in the candle flame for it sizzled and flickered. 'This is an army – a united army!' He couldn't take his eyes off the pamphlet. I caught once more the reek of his rotten breath.

'So united that half its officers are under suspicion?' I said. 'Some of them even having to be spied upon . . .' I said that more pointedly than I might have done, for we all knew what I meant. 'So united that Cromwell sends his own man and does not trust his general?'

'So they start printing these pamphlets,' Kate said. 'With pictures of devils and witch-finders and instructions on how a man can tell a witch for himself.'

'It says it bold as day – this Matthew Hopkins is a witch-finder through his knowledge and experience, not through any sorcery of his own.'

'And they have that boy Fletcher distributing the pamphlets?'

I nodded. 'The stories start to take hold. Royalists are

being spat on already. It only takes a little push, another bastard telling that story about Boy, for the idea to start breeding. Royalists, Catholics, devil whores – they're all the same thing. What's needed now is some *evidence*. Just a little. Something that proves beyond any shadow of a doubt that there are sorcerers inside this camp . . .'

With a suddenness, I lunged and stabbed Warbeck in the arm, right where it met his shoulder. The blade disappeared, seemingly sinking into his flesh. Warbeck's eyes flew wide. He lurched back and jumped to his feet, reaching for his sabre, and then stopped.

'Falkland!'

I pushed the pamphlet towards him. 'According to what is written here,' I said, 'you are a sorcerer, a plaything of the devil.'

I showed him the blade. I watched the wonder in his eyes as he looked at the wound he thought I'd given him, as he touched it with his fingers and found they came away dry, that he was not injured at all, not even marked. Miss Cain took the knife and pressed it slowly into her own palm. She trembled, for now she understood what I had realised back under the tree.

Bitterly, Warbeck pushed me aside. 'Don't suicides go to Hell, Falkland?'

'You can hardly call it suicide,' I spat. I could not stop my mind from straying to that terrible moment when Wildman and Whitelock felt the rope around their necks; I'd so nearly joined them. 'I'll wager Carew looked among those he knew to be royalists and Catholics. Most would be too level-headed to be tricked. They'd find the young ones, the most naïve, the most susceptible. If you drag a man to the edge of a cliff and tell him to jump then it's a fool who jumps. But Warbeck, if you tell him to jump or be damned, if you make him *believe* . . .' I slipped the dagger into my belt and took a final slug of wine. 'And then when hundreds of Puritan boys around you have seen how a few royalists truly *are* in league with the devil, how long is it before the lynchings start? How long before the only evidence anyone needs is a rosary or a crucifix or a whispered word in the dark?'

I marched into the hallway. Miss Cain hurried after. 'It doesn't explain Hotham,' she said. 'If what Carew said was true, if it was Hotham running the printing press, then why would he end up hanging from that branch as well?'

I kicked the chair out of the way. 'It doesn't explain Fletcher either. But if you have a thread, at least you can follow it. Perhaps that part of Carew's story was true. Or perhaps Wildman's friends wished to show that they, too, were capable.' I remembered their words: *we do not consider the scales balanced*.

Kate seized my arm. 'What will you do?' she demanded. 'You can't go out there again!'

'I'll do what I was sent here to do. I'll reveal what happened to those boys. I'll make my report to Fairfax and then to Cromwell.' I stopped. I fancied I could even feel the rope chafing my neck. 'Then my debt is done. Then I'm gone.'

I opened the door with a flourish, half expecting to see Carew and his pikemen ranged around. All that I saw was whiteness, the hypnotic snow still falling gently down. Before crossing the threshold I stopped. 'Miss Cain,' I said. 'I have to cross the camp. I have to reach Black Tom. Once it's with him they have no cause to come after us. Stay here with Warbeck and open the door to no one until morning.'

Warbeck had come out into the hall as well now. He shook his head. 'Are you mad, Falkland? Now you'll close that door and listen to me.'

CHAPTER 22

In the hallway, Warbeck held me fast. He spoke more words in those few minutes, I think, than over all the days of our journey from London, and yet, as he related his tale, I could not see how I could claim any one part of it to be a surprise. Cromwell had indeed sent an intelligencer to survey the New Model Army but *I* was merely a cloak. While Black Tom had his eyes on me, Warbeck was at work, the real intelligencer.

'We'll go to Fairfax in time,' said Warbeck when he was done, 'but I'll watch and wait a while and see what this Carew does before I burst through Black Tom's doors.'

And the boys, the suicides, the witching tree? Cromwell could hardly care. What were they to him? Merely a convenient excuse. But to me, now, they had become something more.

'Find where Carew camps, Falkland. Keep your eyes on him.' Warbeck turned away from me as if we were done, but we were not. I caught his shoulder and spun him back to face me.

'I will do no such thing,' I told him. 'Whatever you and Cromwell have hatched between you, I mean to go to Black Tom. I mean to confront him with what is happening right under his nose. At his own press! And I will not be moved on this by anything short of a musket ball.'

Warbeck regarded me coldly. 'If needs be, Falkland. I would prefer not, but if needs be.'

'And will you shoot me too?' demanded Kate.

I pushed for the door. 'I'll go alone,' I said.

'And if Carew and his gang come while you are gone?' Kate asked.

Warbeck bared his teeth and graced us both again with his rotten breath. It took all his will, I think, to relent. 'We go together then. All of us. But Falkland, I implore you to caution! Do not barge in to Black Tom's house full of half-grown accusation!'

We exited the cottage, finally, onto the lane. I was still in Crediton, the same as it ever was, but now I felt as if there were eyes all over me, watching from the narrow lanes between the cottages. We came to the square where the dead man hung. I thought his hollow, crow-pecked sockets followed us across the untouched snow. In his shadow we stopped. Behind us trails of footprints were imprinted deep into the white blanket of fresh snow. Though flakes still twirled gently over the town, they would not come thickly enough to mask the way we'd gone. Our tracks were plain and so were several others that had come this way before us. If we were not yet being followed then it was only a matter of time.

'I'll meet you at the farm!' hissed Warbeck. He doubled back towards the inn and its stables and I fancied I knew why. I did not much like what I thought it meant: Warbeck was preparing to run.

We didn't see another soul as we slipped through the

middle of the town to where the hulk of Crediton church still sat. Along the lane running to the north – the one that would take us to the hanging tree – lights glowed in the windows of the surgeon's house. I stopped dead, hidden in the shadows at the end of the lane as two figures emerged and hurried towards us. For a second it felt as if we were outmanoeuvred – the church on one flank, the surgeon's house on the other. I pulled back, casting my eyes for a place to hide. 'We'll have to find another way around,' I said, my eyes still fixed on the men heading towards us.

Kate scurried us away towards the graveyard. 'He's still in there, isn't he?' she whispered. 'Jacob Hotham?'

'Hotham and the rest, if I'm right. Carew already knows I was in his printing press. He knows I have his dagger. It won't be long before he understands that I've pieced it together. He'll think I'm going for Jacob.'

'And?'

'There's a time for everything,' I whispered. 'Perhaps he won't be watching for us to go to Black Tom instead.'

We retreated behind the church by one of the thin, winding alleys around the back of the graveyard, up the cobbled shambles where a butcher's shop sat silent. In the narrow alleys among the cottages behind the church were places where the snow hadn't reached any real depth and others where the wind had piled huge drifts we were forced to scale as we went. We followed the garden plots where villagers had once kept their vegetable patches, chopped their wood and cared for their chickens, and emerged from the edge of Crediton on its southern slopes. The encampment was sparser here where the winds could howl in from the moors and bury men in snow as they slept, but the tents still spilled around. Between them, low border fires burned inside circles of rock.

'Where does Carew camp?' Kate whispered as we edged around the town, keeping to the dark tract of land between the end of the cottages and the first of the tents. I hesitated to answer. I didn't know and regretted now that I'd not followed him already. He'd come this way when I'd given chase earlier tonight. If I was right then he bedded down in the old Fletcher house close to his printing press – or else in the surgeon's quarters where he could keep watch over Hotham. Nonetheless I was wary. Here and there I could see soldiers unable to sleep, tramping the feeling back into their toes, bending low to stoke their fires or else keeping their lonely, meandering watches. Any one of them, I supposed, might have been Carew or his pikemen. Any one of them might have relayed a message. How many did he have already drawn to his cause? I had no way to know.

Kate led me away from the bulk of the camp, pressing steadily from the town. In this way we came to the small frozen river that, further downstream, ran close to Fairfax's farmhouse. Perhaps the ground here had been boggy before it froze – whatever the reason, there were no tents so close to the river. The snow was heavy and we had to plunge through it but at least there was little danger of being seen. We reached the field where the horses were corralled and crept around it. A little stone structure squatted on one side with a great bonfire heaped in front; it was more important, or so it seemed, to guard over these horses than any of the boys in the camp. We crossed the little bridge and I saw from the tracks in the snow that others had crossed not long before us. Ahead, Fairfax's farmhouse loomed at us at the top of a gentle slope. Even though the way wasn't steep, somehow it seemed to lord itself over the encampment. There were fires burning inside and a thin plume of smoke rose, dissipating quickly in the snow.

The sky shifted, came apart and closed again. The snowfall strengthened.

'Come on,' I said. Again I felt eyes watch us along the way but it wasn't until we came into the grounds of the farmhouse itself that I had cause to pause. From this distance, through the twirling snowflakes, I could see two men stationed outside the farmhouse door. A third stood at a distance, warming his hands over a low fire, sheltered from the snow by what used to be a chicken coop.

'Do you see?' I asked.

Kate drew close to my side. She pressed against me and I was thankful for the warmth. Her eyes found mine. 'What?' she asked.

'The snow,' I said. 'Kate, look at the snow.'

The snow around the entrance to the farmhouse was carved up, criss-crossed with the tramping tracks of the guardsmen as they moved back and forth to stave off the bitterness of night, their footsteps dulled and softened by later falls. Yet there was another trail, one that cut across the full expanse of the grounds. It ran from the low stone wall heaped up with snow where we were standing to the door of the farmhouse itself. The prints were crisp and deep, more defined than the confusion where the guards had tramped.

'One of the guards?' Kate offered. 'Caught short?'

'Perhaps,' I said.

'Or Black Tom, out on some errand?'

'Fairfax should be sleeping.' I studied the tracks. 'Besides, these are the prints of a man heading within from without, and in some hurry. Someone has come this way before us.'

'But who . . . ?'

I looked at her intently. 'Find yourself somewhere safe,' I said. 'Wait for Warbeck. But please don't go far. I've needed you already tonight.'

'I was there, wasn't I?' she said. I thought she was challenging me but she did so with a smile.

'I may yet need you again.' I turned. I had a mind to follow the stone wall, circle the farmhouse before the guards knew I was there and judge it from every angle I could. Fairfax, I was sure, was within; but I knew now that he was not alone.

I had only moved a short distance when I spied another figure hurrying along our tracks from the bridge. I tensed, ready to ambush him from behind the wall if I must, but as he approached I saw it was Warbeck. I waited for him to come closer before I revealed myself, then pointed to the tracks in the snow. He understood at once as I thought he might.

'Carew?' he asked.

'I don't know yet. Go to Kate!' I told him. 'Don't let her out of your sight.'

He laughed at me. 'I think not! If Carew has gone to Black Tom then everything is changed.'

'What do you mean?'

Warbeck gave me a pitying look and began creeping closer to the shuttered farmhouse windows, lurking in the shadows to hide from the sleepy watch of the two wandering guards. My heart demanded I should take Kate and be away, take her somewhere safe. But in the end I'd come too far for these boys to abandon them at the last. I followed him without further word, though I fancied Kate watched me for the longest time, at least until I'd gone out of sight round the back of the farmhouse.

There were no guards stationed outside the back door. Here the night was truly silent and the snow untouched but for Warbeck's footsteps. I followed them as best I could. I didn't have time to fear I was being watched – we were leaving a trail any halfwit could have followed if they happened upon it – and, as I came to the first broad window, I crouched low to scuttle underneath. The curtains were drawn in the bay but there was light inside. I fancied there had been a fire whose embers now glowed in the hearth. I crept close, pressed hard against the icy stone, and listened for voices on the other side. When I could hear nothing I edged to the handle of the back door and cupped my fist around it. Gently I turned it but the door, held fast by latches on the other side, didn't move. It wasn't until I released my hold and fell panting against the stone that I realised how rigidly I'd been holding myself. My breath made a mist around my head and I could hardly see.

The lights were brighter in the second window. I reeled through what little I knew of inside the farmhouse – the entrance hall, the big, stark chamber where Fairfax first received me – and wondered if I was now crouching outside the very same room. From this corner of the farmhouse I could see the back of the stone shed where Fairfax had the captive he wanted strung up for the boys' suicides. I supposed he must still be inside, huddled up under blankets thick with his own filth. Unless the cold had finally taken him.

'Falkland!' I barely heard Warbeck's hiss, and even when I looked I couldn't see him until he shifted a little and waved. He'd found himself a corner of blackest shadow right under that other window, pressed up against the wall, so dark as to make himself invisible.

I shifted. Outside the stone cell a man was moving, another camp guard unable to stand sentry without pacing for the cold that gnawed at his bones. Instinctively I kept myself close to the wall, steeped in its shadow, desperate not to be seen. There were voices within. The more I held myself there, the more they came into focus. I pressed myself into the wall so I could hear them better.

'He's outside.'

My heart thudded. The voice was familiar: Purkiss; and I thought for one dreadful moment that he was talking about *me*, that Purkiss somehow knew I was here. I looked one way and then the other, yet all I saw was pure white snow. I told myself I must be wrong but it did little to still my pulse.

'You woke me for this?' The second voice was Black Tom. I'd have known that thick Yorkshire burr anywhere.

'I thought you'd want to know.'

'Very well,' Black Tom grunted. 'Bring the bastard in.'

I heard footsteps. More voices, too faint to make out the words, the rattle of a door being closed and then a third voice came from the room, high and haughty, everything Black Tom was not. 'Sir,' it began. 'I beg thanks for receiving me. I am afraid I bring ill news.'

Carew. From the moment I'd seen that trail of footprints across the virgin snow, I'd known who had woken Fairfax in the middle of the night. Known it but hoped it wasn't so. I feared I already knew what story he was about to spill.

'If it's bad news, lad, I'd rather you spat it out.'

'Very well, sir,' said Carew. 'It is the intelligencer. He knows about the pamphlets. He knows about Hopkins. Sir, I think he knows about Wildman and Whitelock, and I think he can prove it.' Carew paused, as if steadying himself to receive a mighty blow. 'General, he has my dagger.'

There was silence. Even the snow seemed to hang in the air around my head. Then, like the cold, sharp shock of stepping onto thin ice and plunging into a frozen pool, there came the roar. From the voice I knew it to be Black Tom, but I've rarely heard a man sound so much like a devil, even on the battlefield with granadoes exploding and sabres flashing all around. 'How did it come to it?' he thundered.

'General, we did as you bid. We lured him down to the tree and told him a story to satisfy him.' Carew paused. I thought I could hear, for the first time, a wavering in his voice. 'But he didn't believe it. He had others with him. I'm afraid there was a skirmish.'

'Your ambush was ambushed?' Black Tom's voice was full of scorn.

'Sir, with the utmost respect—'

'Think very carefully about what you're about to say, Edmund. People who profess to show respect rarely mean it.'

Carew was silent. For the longest time, nobody said a word.

'How much does he know?' Black Tom asked.

'He's been to the printing press. He has the dagger. And you already know, sir, that he followed the whores out of camp.'

'Then he knows the whole sorry tale.' There was silence. 'Did he speak to Jacob?'

'We've been watching Hotham closely, sir. He's not returned to the surgeon's.'

'It's only a matter of time,' Black Tom said. 'Carew, you were trusted with this simple task. I had high hopes for you.'

'I had my own hopes too, sir.' For the first time, Carew sounded contrite. Then a sudden flourish of pride surged in his voice. 'General, I won't lie down for this. We had your assurances that Cromwell's man wouldn't be a hindrance. The man you forced to confess, you promised that would be an end to it.'

Black Tom grumbled, 'He wouldn't accept it. This Falkland is a man of bloody-minded conscience. That's what Cromwell's letter said. For once dear Oliver was not simply spinning a yarn.' Fairfax paused. 'Damn that man! A general sleeps with his army. He does not run off home at the first sight of snow! Yet he has his fingers here, even now!' He paused. 'This is my army, Carew. *Mine*. Cromwell can have his lords and his chambers and his robes. He can have his cavalry if he must – God knows he puts the fear into every royalist in England when he rides them. He can name himself the new King for all I care, go marching up and down his hallways in Westminster. But he does not get to control *my* army, and come spring when we force the King to his knees, my army will be a *godly* one!'

The third voice joined the conversation. Purkiss with his rough tones. 'If I may, sir,' he began, 'this is not finished yet. Falkland has the pamphlets. He has the dagger. But . . .' He paused. I could almost imagine the smile spreading across his features. 'Sir, you see how the snows have fallen tonight. He's not sent word to Cromwell, not out into this storm. There's still time.'

'Time for what?' barked Black Tom.

'We must find Falkland before he can alert Cromwell.'

'And then? He cannot be made to forget what he knows. I doubt you'll either beat or bribe him into silence now.'

'I think we are past that, sir.'

Here the voices hushed, becoming almost indistinct. I wheeled back through all they'd said. I began to think. Perhaps there were places in this monstrous camp where I might go unnoticed. There were still devout royalist boys here. Wildman and Whitelock's friends, perhaps others. In an army of this size it might be easy for a man to disappear.

I gazed out into the blinding white. I could run. They had nothing on me. If Carew was taking his orders from Fairfax then I was not truly here to investigate the suicides of two poor boys. I was here as an agent of Cromwell, and to what end I was only just beginning to understand. I was no intelligencer. I was the same as a letter meant to be intercepted by the King, or a small force sacrificed to dupe Prince Rupert that the New Model was moving somewhere they were not. I was a pawn in a game and I no longer knew the rules.

I might have run then but the voices returned, as belligerent and distinct as ever before. Fairfax's voice rose again. 'No. We are not murderers. The woman, Kate Cain. She'll harbour him,' he said. 'Put her under lock and key. Falkland has a fondness for her. If she won't tell you where he is, perhaps he'll come to bargain for her safety.'

My fists curled.

'And we're not brutes, Purkiss,' Black Tom said. 'Do not hurt her this time.'

Footsteps tramped away. They were heavy and sounded loudly through the walls.

'He must not leave camp, Carew. The second he leaves camp, the game is lost. And I will not command Cromwell's army of mongrel dogs. Come the spring we will go out as good, godly men – every last one of us, every last heathen saved – or we will not ride out at all. Bring him to me. Some way or another we'll find an accommodation.'

I would have liked to have marched in there and then and told him that no, we would not. I might even have understood his fervour, but three boys were dead and however much Fairfax claimed he was no murderer, Carew had meant to hang me. Nor had I forgotten the bruises on Kate's face.

I crept around to the front of the house to watch Carew go. I fancy Warbeck did the same but went the other way. I didn't see him; but outside the door Purkiss had waited for Carew. I heard them both clearly now.

'You said Falkland had others with him. Who were they?' asked Purkiss.

'The woman he lives with.'

Purkiss snorted with derision. 'Miss Cain? He ambushed you with Miss Cain . . . ?'

'And the other one who came with him.'

'Warbeck?'

'I don't know his name. He shot one of my men.'

There was a pause. I thought perhaps Purkiss understood in that moment what I'd come to understand earlier that night – who it was who was truly Cromwell's intelligencer here. 'All three have to be stopped,' he said after a time. 'And Miss Cain might be kept quiet, but not the other two. None of them must leave the camp.'

'Sir, what would you have us do?'

'What you must.' He took a long look around at the snow-covered landscape. 'On a night like this, anything might happen to a man not tucked safely up in bed.'

'Sir?'

'You know what's needed, Carew. See to it. Start with the house. And Edmund?'

'Sir?'

'Black Tom will know but it mustn't stand glaring before him. Take them away from the camp when you're done and let them be found in their own time. Set upon by royalist deserters from Exeter or some such. That would do.'

'Miss Cain as well, sir?'

I didn't hear Purkiss answer. I feared he simply nodded. Carew left and I remained, crouched in my shadows there for a long time after he was gone. Purkiss went back inside. Presently the lights were extinguished.

In one pocket I had the dagger. In the other, the pamphlets they'd used to spread the story. I had a mind to creep inside and find a different dagger – one with a true steel blade – and plunge it into Fairfax's heart. He'd known all along. More – he'd been the architect.

I fancied for a moment that I could see a cavalryman in the distance, coming up from beyond the southern fringe of the camp. It was only the way the snowflakes were falling that made a mirage, but all the same I pictured him riding from the night towards me. I saw myself and Warbeck coming that way not so many nights hence. I saw the

terrified faces of the men who thought I was this Matthew
Hopkins, the Witch-finder General, coming to Crediton to
burn the whores and the Catholics. Carew had only been
playing at his game, fumbling as an amateur. If Fairfax
brought this Hopkins here to set about his business in
earnest then he'd have a hundred Puritan boys as his eager
apprentices and a thousand would burn. Catholics and
royalists – devils and witches, all the same.

I crept away to the wall and circled around the guards
until I found where Kate had hidden herself, shivering. I
lunged forward and grabbed her and pulled her close to me.

'Falkland!' she gasped. 'I might have shrieked!'

We held each other close in the frozen darkness. 'Where's
Warbeck?' I asked.

'I'm here,' came a voice at my neck. 'You heard all?'

I nodded.

'So now you and I leave this camp for good.'

We began to retrace our steps, hurrying as best we could
in the thick snow, hunched and crouched through the fields
until we reached the bridge, hoping not to be seen. Warbeck
led us across the ice of the frozen river and off through the
camp, keeping away from the farmhouse track and then the
lane. Our footprints in the snow would give us away if
anyone saw us but the camp was huge and I didn't imagine
Carew and Purkiss setting to search the whole of it, not on a
night like this. As we ran I told Kate what I'd heard. 'They're
coming for you,' I finished. 'You have to leave Crediton
now.'

We followed the way we'd come all the way across the
camp and into the graveyard alley beside the church. As we
reached the lane at the end, a soldier marched past. He

didn't see us and didn't break his stride but I felt sure that at such an hour he must be one of the camp guards sent looking for us. Carew had surely reached the town ahead of us but he'd have to gather his men and it would take him a moment to break into Miss Cain's house. The next place, if they had any sense, would be the stables. I judged we'd not have long before they knew we were gone.

Kate was at my side. Pointedly, I did not hold her tight. She followed the pikeman with her eyes and needled me between the ribs. 'We should be moving.'

I nodded.

We beat back down the alley beside the graveyard, losing ourselves between the houses in the dead parts of Crediton where the soldiers didn't camp. I wanted to go back to the house to find provisions and a weapon – even something as simple as a kitchen knife – but already we were too late.

'You've seen how much of a mongrel this army is yourself,' I said. We were past the back of the market square now and creeping through gardens and alleys. We'd have been quicker to use the lanes and already my heart was pounding. If Carew reached the stables before us then I was sure we were done for. I still had no notion how many men he'd drawn to his cause. 'Cromwell built it this way because this is what he needs it to be, this is how he's going to win the war and force the King to come to terms. But Fairfax isn't the sort of man for a compromise. They don't breed them like that up in Yorkshire. I should know – they tried to kill me up there too many times. I don't know whether he ordered Hotham and Carew to start mongering the idea that a witch-finder is coming to expose all the devilry in camp or whether the idea was their own and

Fairfax merely their sponsor. Carew used his dagger to prove there were witches and sorcerers in the soldiery. That's what drove Wildman and Whitelock to finish it all. They thought themselves good Catholic boys but suddenly they were waiting to be exposed as witches and devils like Prince Rupert with Boy.'

'That was why the desertions . . .'

'Soldiers always try and desert, especially in winters like this. I met some on the road. Yet . . .' We stopped. At the end of an alley another soldier hurried past along the lane. There were more of them on the prowl tonight than I'd seen on any night before. The hunt had begun. 'Thomas Fletcher knew what was happening,' I said. 'I'll wager he learned it wasn't just Carew, that Black Tom was ordering it. Perhaps they dragged him to the same tree and threw him on one of the granadoes he was entrusted with guarding. Perhaps they wanted to work up a mystery around that place. Perhaps they thought it had a beauty about it . . .'

We reached the square where the ravisher hung. Warbeck gestured at us to hold back.

'What about Hotham?' asked Kate. 'If he was working with Carew then why—'

'I need to speak to him,' I said.

Warbeck hawked up phlegm from the back of his throat and let it fly into the snow at our feet. 'You can't be serious, Falkland!' he exclaimed. 'Tonight? With the whole camp about to—'

I ignored him and looked only at Miss Cain. 'I'd run,' I said. 'I would. I'd run and I'd take you with me and to Hell with roundheads and cavaliers. But . . .' It was Whitelock I was thinking of. It was Wildman. It was little Thomas

Fletcher himself. 'I have a son. In another time perhaps he'd have been swallowed up and turned into a New Modeller with a Venice red coat and a pike at his side. And if this witch-finder comes to camp, if they're set on turning good, honest lads into witches and devils just to *purify . . .*' I almost choked on the word.

Kate shuffled closer to me and lifted her fingers to cup my chin. At her touch I calmed. 'I know,' she whispered. 'I know. But Hotham is in the surgeon's quarters. You can't mean to . . .'

I glanced at Warbeck. 'A horse and a mule are saddled in the stables. Two can go, not three. Warbeck will take you somewhere safe. Hotham is the only one who can tell me how it ends. There's a reason he was hanging from that tree.' I hesitated. I was aware for the first time of how the snow had stopped falling. 'I'll need a diversion . . .'

Kate trembled. She stepped out of my embrace, her eyes gleaming in the winter night. She opened her lips to speak but Warbeck hissed at us to be quiet. We all froze as yet another camp guard hurried across the square, breaking his march as he started to run. When he was past, Warbeck seized my arm. 'Come on, Falkland! We haven't got time for this!'

We dashed across the corner of the square and raced for the alley beside the inn. From somewhere down the street I heard a shout. Warbeck must have heard it too and hurled himself forward with abandon, skittering through the snow. 'Faster, Falkland!' Hue and cry rose up behind us. Warbeck stumbled and sprawled into a drift. He floundered a moment before righting himself as Kate and I caught him up. He'd left the stable door open, the horses ready and waiting, and took no time to vault into the saddle. 'Come on, Falkland! Take the mule and let's be gone!'

I shook my head and pushed Kate forward. 'Take Miss Cain, Warbeck. Keep her safe.'

'Don't be a bloody idiot. You heard Fairfax. She'll survive well enough once we're gone.'

I doubted that. 'I heard Purkiss too.' And I'd already seen what he could do. 'Kate, go!' But she didn't move.

'The devil take you both!' swore Warbeck. 'We've no time for this.' He kicked his horse forward and charged out of the stables. I heard a man shout and then another and then the crack of a musket.

'Do you see now?' I picked Kate up and dropped her struggling onto the back of the mule. 'Now *go*! Before it's too late!'

'Falkland . . .' She looked at me in despair. 'Don't die, Falkland. They're not worth it.'

I slapped the mule and watched Miss Cain disappear into the night. Then I looked for a place to hide.

CHAPTER 23

I'd expected Carew's men to burst into the stables at any moment and didn't imagine my feeble skulking amid the hay and shadow would avail me for long, but for once I met with fortune. Warbeck's flight must have distracted them: only two men came, and only as far as the door. I saw them make a quick count of the horses and then withdraw. They must have thought I'd fled too. I was glad I heard no more musket shots. The snow, I supposed, had dampened their powder and dimmed their sight.

When no other men came I crept out of my hiding place and moved with silent care around the back of the cottages beside the square, keeping to the darkest shadows as best I could. I returned at first to Miss Cain's house and watched from the opening of a thin track on the other side of the lane. I saw a man come out, one of the pikemen Carew had brought to ambush me at the tree. He left the door wide open and marched off along the lane, close enough to have seen my breath misting around my head if only he'd cared to notice. I slipped inside behind his back and stood just past the threshold, ears straining, but I heard no other sound. I crept up the stairs to Warbeck's room, quiet as I could. They wouldn't imagine, I hoped, that any of us might return, but

Warbeck was a walking armoury and I'd not seen him carry that much about him tonight. I was rewarded: under the bed I found a pair of muskets and a cavalry sabre with scabbard and belt. I'd hoped for pistols but the sabre would do. I left the muskets. On a night like this they'd be of little use.

Back in the lane I slipped into the alley where Carew's pikeman had ambushed me and set off across the cottage gardens until I reached the back of Main Street and looked out onto Mrs Miller's cottage. I wondered fleetingly if I might find shelter there but then thought better of it. Beatrice Miller wasn't one to take such a risk.

Further down the road was the surgeon's house with a pikeman standing outside. Candles still burned behind the shutters. I'd noted Hotham's window on the day I went to see him and remembered it now. Light flickered there too. Did that mean he had someone with him?

A figure exited the house and joined the pikeman as I watched. Carew. They turned down the lane and stood there, facing the church with their backs to me. After a moment I took my chance and flitted across the lane, crouching in the shadows of Beatrice Miller's door. Carew was carrying a sword at his side. I wondered, feeling for my own, if he knew how to wield it. I crept closer. It seemed odd that Carew and his pikeman simply stood out in the falling snow on a night like this, as though they were at a loss for what to do. My impression of Carew had not been of a man who experienced such feelings. They still had their backs to me and were talking with quite some animation. They kept their voices low but as I crept closer I began to hear scraps of words. Something about Black Tom and Cromwell.

I was about to move for the steps to the surgeon's house itself when another two figures hurried out of the night. I recognised Purkiss from the way he walked and I froze at once, crouched against the wall. I fancied that if I was still then they wouldn't see me even if they happened to turn my way, but all I had to hide me was the darkness and my coat. The four of them spoke for a moment and I guessed that Carew must have told Purkiss of our escape, for Purkiss swore loudly and shook his head. 'Black Tom will have to know, Carew. You were supposed to stop them!' I didn't hear Carew's reply but whatever it was, Purkiss poured out his scorn. 'In this weather and with such a start? You'll never catch them. You'll never even find them.' He turned on his heel and trotted away. Carew stared after him. I took my chance and eased into the shadows of the steps leading up to the surgeon's house and crouched again, out of sight. I heard Carew and the pikeman tramp through the snow towards me as they went back inside. The pikeman passed through the door. Behind him, Carew paused a moment; I felt certain he somehow sensed I was there – all he had to do to see me was to look down beside the steps. I tensed, ready to fight, but then heard him walk on and close the door behind him. The lane was empty again.

I waited and counted my breaths to a hundred, then mounted the steps myself, eased the door ajar and peered through the crack. The surgeon's hall was dark. I listened and heard nothing at first, then the creak of a board from the upper floor and a low murmur of voices. I slipped inside and waited again. The house fell silent; and I'll admit that I'd feared to find a half-dozen of Carew's men on guard here, but it seemed they'd all been drawn away by

Warbeck's flight. I cursed myself now for sending Kate away with him. I didn't fancy much for her chances if Carew got his hands on her in the camp but I *had* heard Black Tom order Purkiss not to hurt her. Out in the darkness, away from Crediton, Carew's men would murder her in the most horrible way. I didn't like to think on it. I feared I'd sent her to her death.

Light filtered down the stairs from a lamp on the balcony of the upper floor. I might hide away in the dark of the hall but there was no possibility I could ascend unseen if anyone was standing watch outside Hotham's room. But I'd come this far. I couldn't turn back; and so I walked to the stairs without any thought of trying to conceal myself, my hand on Warbeck's sabre. To my surprise the balcony was empty. No one stood in my way or called out to challenge me. Carew must, I supposed, be in the room with Hotham himself.

A stray thought troubled me then: why had Carew stayed in Crediton if he thought we'd escaped? If he'd sent men to ride after Warbeck and Kate, why hadn't he gone with them? Or was Hotham too much a friend to abandon even when everything they'd worked for stood to be unravelled? I pushed the door open to Hotham's room, sure I'd see Carew waiting for me, but no – Hotham was alone. A candle burned by his bed. He was awake, his eyes open, and he saw me clearly. He didn't make a sound. Perhaps he couldn't. I closed the door behind me.

'Do you know who I am?' I whispered.

Very slightly he nodded. His eyes never left me and they told me he could hear me and that he understood me, that behind his mangled body was a mind still alert. He opened his mouth a little as if trying to speak but all that came out was a strangled hiss of air.

'Show me, however you wish, where I have this wrong,' I said. 'You printed pamphlets claiming that Catholics and men who fought for the King were witches and had turned to the devil. Was it Edmund Carew or was it you who had the notion of the false dagger?' I stared at him but his eyes didn't move. 'Yours, I suspect, but Carew was the one who found those boys. He has the eye for it, I dare say, to find those boys whose minds are not so strong. Where did you do it? Did you take them down to the tree where they used to go for their confessions and hold them down as he stabbed them with his dagger? They thought they were going to die but you had something far worse in mind. I have to guess now but I'll give you the benefit: you wanted them to desert. Just run away and be gone. Them and all the others like them. But Richard Wildman didn't. When he thought this witch-finder of yours was coming, he didn't run. He hanged himself. And then his brother did the same.'

Hotham looked away for an instant. I had the truth of it then. 'I'd like to think that what happened to you was something you did to yourself out of remorse when you knew what you'd done. Edmund Carew says you did it after Tom Fletcher died but I know that to be false. It wasn't remorse at all, was it? Whitelock and Wildman had friends. Tom Fletcher, when he found out and realised what you'd done, when he realised that he'd been a part of it, he told them. After Whitelock, they came for you. They were going to do to you what you'd done to their friends, but Carew and the others came in time to save you. Was there a fight?'

This time his eyes didn't flinch. They blazed back at me, full of anger.

'That's why Carew never left your side after he cut you down. Because he thought they might come at you again. That's why he blew poor Tom Fletcher up with a granadoe, because Tom was the one who'd told them.'

'In fact, Falkland, it was Wildman's friends who hanged poor Jacob,' said Carew softly behind me. I hadn't even heard the door open. 'Not Whitelock's.' I didn't feel the dagger at my back but I knew it must be there. Suddenly I understood: Carew had known I was here all along. Perhaps he'd seen Warbeck and Miss Cain ride off alone or perhaps it was mere instinct, but he knew that I'd stayed. I fancied then that he'd seen me lurking beside the steps as he'd come into the house. He'd chosen to wait for me here rather than face me in the street.

'Black Tom wants to see you,' he said.

This I knew to be a lie but Carew had no means to know he'd been overheard on the porch of Fairfax's farmhouse. I supposed he meant to do away with me somewhere along the way, in the dark where no one would see; I was sure he didn't mean to run me through here in Hotham's room if he could help it. I raised my hands. 'Then that suits us both, since I also want to see him. Shall we both stand before him, Edmund, and tell him the truth from start to finish? I fancy he won't shed a tear over two Catholic boys driven to hang themselves. I wonder, though, if he'll have something to say about Tom Fletcher murdered by a granadoe.'

'Come on, Falkland.' This time I felt the press of the dagger and this time the point was real. I cast one last look at Jacob Hotham but his eyes gave away nothing. Perhaps he regretted what he'd done but I thought not. I think all that he regretted was what had been done to him in return.

Carew backed away. 'Slow now, Falkland. Don't turn around.'

I stepped backwards after him, out through the door and into the corridor to the balcony over the stairs. It was a simple mistake he made, one of a young man who hasn't seen his share of real fighting. He had a dagger at my back, not a pistol. I let him nudge me forward a few steps to let him think I'd come meekly and then I ran, and as I ran I drew my sabre.

He wasn't as foolish as I'd hoped, though. As I reached the balcony across the stairs I thought I saw men in the darkness of the hall, perhaps four or five of them – certainly too many to bull through to the door. I ran past the stairs instead of down them and an instant later I knew I was right. A flash of light lit up their faces amid the boom of a pistol shot. I didn't feel its burn so it must have missed me but I didn't see where it flew. The corridor ahead sank into darkness.

'After him!' shouted Carew. 'Don't let him get away!'

I whirled around, looking for escape, but Carew was pounding after me. I crashed into the first door I found, tumbling over empty cots, reaching for the shuttered window. I fancied I'd take my chances with a jump to the lane and pray for the snow to break my fall, for I was no match for four men with pistols and knives and Carew was right on my heels. I already knew he was faster than me.

The shutters were latched. I spun around and Carew was right there. I had no choice. I turned to face him and stretched out the sabre. I don't know what I thought. To drive him away, I think. To hold him back; but I did neither of those things. Perhaps he didn't see it in the gloom but he ran headlong straight onto the point of the blade. I felt it drive into him, just beneath his breastbone, carried deeper by his weight as he stumbled forward. He fell at my feet and groaned.

'You bastard, Falkland.'

I let the sabre go and leapt away, uncertain how badly he was injured and with care for the dagger still in his hand. Footsteps were pounding up the stairs. My hands were shaking as I unlatched the shutters and threw them wide. I heard them at the door as I leapt from the window. My knees slammed into my chest as I crashed into the snow below, knocking the breath out of me. I rose and stumbled away as I heard them at the window, their shouts: 'Murderer!' Another pistol cracked. My ankle ached, twisted in the fall, but still I ran as fast as I could along the lane and across the end of it, into the darkness of the alley beside the church, the very alley down which I'd chased Carew at the start of this endless night. I didn't know where to go or how, only that I had to be away. I ran as fast as I could, remembering the wall of ice at the end; this time fear gave strength to my legs and I vaulted it without falling. I was in the sprawl of the camp itself now. I even thought that I might get away but then I heard the cry across the night. 'Murderer! Stop that man!'

I knew then that I was doomed. I should have stopped as soon as I was in the camp and hidden. In the darkness amid the falling snow perhaps they would never have found me; and if I'd not frozen in the night then perhaps I might have made my escape in the morning. But I ran, and a man running headlong through a camp full of soldiers is easy prey. I don't think I even saw the man who took me down. He came from the side while I was too busy casting my eyes behind me. I sprawled into the snow and pushed him away, flailing at him with my fists.

I didn't see his friend either but I felt his blow as he clubbed me down.

CHAPTER 24

Four times they tried to kill me. They came for me on those blasted northern moors and I lived. They cut swathes through my fellows at Edgehill and somehow, deep in dead men, I came through. They routed my company outside Abingdon and cornered me in the thick of night when I had nowhere to run to and nobody to watch my back, but even then it wasn't my end. They let me loose in the world just to have another chance of running me down. Yes, four times they tried to kill me.

Fourth time lucky.

They weren't Carew's men who battered me to the ground that night but they were no more gentle because of it. They beat me down and beat me again until I lost my senses. I have a dim notion they dragged me through the snow. They must have done. The next I knew for certain I was in a cell that stank of filth. It was difficult to know how long I'd been lying there. They'd bound my ankles in chains but, by some strange mercy, had not bound my hands. Even as the days passed, they never did that. Endless times I slipped in and out of consciousness, waking only when a camp guard appeared with thin helpings of pottage and handfuls of snow. I knew where I was. I was in the stone shed behind Black Tom's farmhouse but Black Tom himself never came. The other man, the one Black Tom thought might serve as our scapegoat, was gone. Dead, I supposed. The cruel irony was that, lying there, I couldn't even remember why I hadn't simply shaken Fairfax's hand, accepted his falsehoods and ridden off to discover what had become of my wife and children. In the end that was all that mattered. Not Whitelock and Wildman. Not Fletcher, no matter how wretchedly those boys had died.

After the third week of it, I began to feel myself wasting away. My body had been living on borrowed time ever since they released me from Newgate. I felt I'd been dead since I first shook Oliver Cromwell's hand. Sitting here now, smeared in my own filth, images of Kate drifted sluggishly across the backs of my eyes. I hoped she was safe, that she'd escaped and that Warbeck had found some honour buried in his black intelligencer's heart. For myself I knew there had never really been a chance of being free.

By then my body was revolting. I had pains even where they hadn't beaten me. I was slowly starving. My guts were telling me to eat, to cram the very earth into my throat, but I wouldn't. I lay there and listened to the sound of the wind around the stone walls, judging the snowfall by sudden changes in the quality of the air. I didn't understand why they didn't simply kill me and be done with it, what kept them from putting the rope around my neck, from declaring me a murderer and hanging me in the square. Perhaps this witch-finder Hopkins was already here, dealing out his godly justice, proclaiming boys right and left to be witches and sodomites for the devil. If that was delaying my hanging, if their gallows were too busy for me, then I didn't care to think about it. I didn't want to know. By then I didn't know if it was day or night. I didn't know if I was dead or alive.

Just as I had in Newgate, I lost track of the days. It must have been the fourth week when the door of the prison opened, as it sometimes did, and a camp guard entered, stooping low so he didn't bang his head. Outside there was struggling sunlight behind him, though I couldn't say if it was dawn or dusk. The snow around the entrance was dirty and packed hard, so I knew there had been no fresh fall in the last few hours. It filled me with rage that I still noticed the details. It meant there was some little part of me that hadn't quite abandoned all hope. Like my gut with its niggling pains, that mule-headed part of my soul just kept clinging on.

I'd been lying on the ground, only the rags of an old red coat between me and the frozen earth. I hauled myself up to my elbows as he came in. It was then that I noticed another damnable detail. The guard wasn't carrying a bowl. This time he wasn't here to bring me food.

'Now?' I asked, hopeful.

'I hate to do it to you, Falkland, but you'll have to put your hands behind your back.'

It was difficult to stand. My legs were weaker than in that winter in Oxford when I was fixed with a splint. All the same I did as I was told. I faced the other way and he bound my wrists with coarse twine.

'You're still eating this filth?' he said, kicking one of the bowls he'd left behind some time ago.

'I'm afraid it will ruin my main course,' I said, still facing the wall as he fiddled with my chains.

'We haven't starved that tongue of yours, then.'

He was right and I hated him for that. Whatever was left inside me that still wanted to live, it just couldn't be knocked down.

'Are you ready?'

I nodded and began to turn. 'Don't you want to put a sack over my head?' I asked.

'A sack?'

'It's the way it was before,' I shrugged.

He led me to the door of the cell. After its constant gloom the world outside was blinding bright. I cringed. For what seemed to be the first time in long months the sun had broken through the snow clouds and its dazzling rays were reflected from deep mounds of white all around. I couldn't see. 'I've been here before,' I said. 'A sack over the head is the way these things work.'

'Falkland, just keep your lips tight and walk.'

I walked uneasily but I had to keep moving because he was marching behind me, one massive stride for every two shuffles of mine. In that way we crossed the snow and came to the front of the farmhouse. Two camp guards stood outside the door as they had on the night I came to confront Fairfax. They stood aside as I stumbled on, though one of them at least had the dignity to look dissatisfied about it. He propped himself lazily on his pike and spat into the snow as we went through. The heat within hit me like a wave. In the hallway I didn't know where the fires were burning but it rushed out to engulf me. After so long in the cell I felt smothered. The warmth didn't reinvigorate me so much as make my body remember what it had been missing, making every last inch of me tingle.

I blundered to a halt.

'Not now, Falkland,' the guard said, propelling me forward with a hand in the small of my back. 'On.'

I stumbled through broad doors into the hall where Fairfax had first received me. The room was as stark and empty as I'd last seen it. A great fire leapt and crackled in the hearth.

'You won't have to wait long,' the guard said. He retreated back the way we'd come and closed the door behind him. I listened out to hear it lock but there was no sound. It didn't matter. I was far beyond running now. I shuffled over and crouched at the fire. I wanted to hold my hands out in front and warm them but they were still tied behind my back and so I had to make do with basking in the glow like a grass snake on a rock. I'd been crouching there some time, taking a perverse delight in the way the heat made my body prickle, when I heard the door open. I didn't bother to stand. I didn't even look. I assumed it would be Fairfax, come to send me on my way.

'That's the way, Falkland,' came a voice I found all too familiar. 'Defiant to the end. If the King himself were to lead you to the top of a cliff and then demand that you didn't jump off, you'd throw yourself straight onto the rocks below, wouldn't you?'

I turned.

Cromwell had been different in London. Here he was dressed every inch the soldier: a madder red coat with white stylings, leather gauntlets and thick woollen trousers over which armoured tassets were fixed in place as if we were about to fight a battle.

'You might act more pleased to see me, Falkland.' He pulled out a dagger. 'If I may?'

I nodded and turned my back to him. I didn't flinch as he marched at me and brought the dagger down between my wrists, severing the twine. I brought my hands to the front of my body and massaged them in the fiery glow.

There was a long silence.

'Tell me,' I said. 'When you sent me here – how much did you know?'

Cromwell raised an eyebrow. I knew he was toying with me as a cruel teacher toys with the stupidest boy in his school. I no longer cared.

'I know you didn't send me here because of the suicides. How could a man like you – even one who writes so many letters of condolence – care about a couple of dead cowards? You sent me because you knew. Didn't you? Why are you even here? Why not simply let Fairfax hang me?' I asked. 'I've played my part. He'll never bring Hopkins and all his endless Hells now; and there, I think, it could have ended. That's what I would have done.'

'Really?' Cromwell looked at me hard. I hated the way the smile spread across his face. 'Whereas I would think that a man with any sense to him wouldn't let an asset like William Falkland down so easily. So here I am, not here *for* you perhaps, but here *because* of you. Black Tom wouldn't have hanged you anyway. You've earned his respect, though not in a way that will ever have him call you his friend. But he has his honour, Falkland, whatever you might think of him. More so than your King.'

'Miss Cain,' I began, voice trembling. 'What did you do to Miss Cain?'

'She has a position in London now.'

'And me?' I hardly dared to ask.

Cromwell came forward, extended his arm and wrapped his long-fingered hand around my own. My fingers felt brittle and cold in his clasp and the gesture felt awkwardly uncomfortable. I could not say which of us liked it least, yet he didn't quickly let go. 'Might I beg another moment of your time, Falkland?'

I tried to tease my hand away but he was holding me fast. I was too weak.

'We are about to embark on life in a very new world,' he said. 'The New Model will live on regardless of kings and ministers. There can be no disbanding any more. The army itself simply wouldn't allow it.'

I managed to extricate my hand as a servant appeared with a bowl of broth and a tankard of what looked like cider. I was shocked to see that the broth had great hunks of meat floating in it – chicken, if I wasn't mistaken. My stomach started to cry out. Damn it but even my gut was creeping onto Cromwell's side. 'What does it have to do with me?' I asked.

'You've shown your character, Falkland,' he said. 'You might do so again.'

I took a spoonful of broth into my mouth. It burned me from the inside and I spat it back into the bowl. 'You promised me my freedom.'

'And so free you are. Take care not to lose your way and you could be home by . . .' For once Cromwell's smile seemed real. 'By Christ-tide, Falkland.'

'Then I could ride out of here and never see a soldier again?'

Cromwell shrugged but there was something about his patient demeanour that sickened me. 'If that's what you want,' he said. 'But I fancy you'll return after Christ-tide and serve us a little longer.'

'And that's it? Out of nowhere you come and I'm free to go?'

'Yes, Falkland.' He nodded. 'You're free to go. You have my thanks.'

'For what?' For the life of me, I could not see what I had done that mattered save to a few Catholic boys pressed against their will into an army that didn't want them.

'You've saved my army, Falkland, from a zealous purge that could have destroyed it. This war could yet have ground us down for years.'

I rather thought it already had. I put the bowl and tankard down in the hearth and made to march past him. 'I'm done,' I said. My eyes were suddenly aglaze. It must have been the soot and smoke stinging me and causing them to water. All I could see was my Caro, my boy John, my little Charlotte. Fairfax's farmhouse had become a ghostly apparition around me. 'I'll find my own way from here.'

I was almost at the door when he called out. 'I'll see you soon enough, Falkland.'

I didn't turn round, and whatever else he might have replied, I didn't care to listen.

Acknowledgements

With thanks to my editors Ali Hope and Flora Rees. To Sarah Bance and Darcy Nicholson for the copy-editing and to the proofreaders and production team, whose names I've rarely known. A special thanks to my agent Robert Dinsdale and to Sam Childs, without whom William Falkland would not exist.

I've always had a penchant for the Hollywood noir of the forties and fifties, and if William Falkland evokes something of the Sam Spade and Philip Marlowe then that's probably no coincidence. The setting lends itself well, I think.

If you liked this book and would like to read more of William Falkland, please say so. Loudly and to lots of people.

Keep reading for an exclusive extract from
the next in the William Falkland series

the Protector

headline

I had foot-slogged my way for six months across half the country and back again. I had found nothing except a numbness, and the stale dregs of straw-strewn taverns in the villages I passed. Uxbridge, this one, I think.

'I'd wager she got bored and run off with some other fellow.'

Six louts sat around a table together. I did not see which of them said it. They were watching me, listening to me foul drunk on watery beer, wine-slurred and moon-faced, waxing loud of my missing Caro, ranting and railing at the smoky air and the vicissitudes of a fickle and heartless fate. I had barely noticed their presence in the tavern until that lucid moment. I saw them now. They were laughing.

She wouldn't do that. Not my Caro.

They looked back at me as I turned, and their laughing fell off their faces. Among all the things I am, I am a large man and a soldier, and have been so for too many years. I have killed men, and I have seen men die. As I took a step towards them they rose from their table and bunched together, ready to stare me down.

'What did you say?' I could tell from their eyes and their exchange of glances which of them had spoken.

'I said I'd wager your wife tired of your talk and has run off with some other fellow, you sot.' He stood across their table from me – given courage, perhaps, by the knowledge I would have to pass through his friends to reach him. I did not feel so inclined. I raised my foot and smashed a kick into that table, slamming it into him. He howled, as did I, a roar of such fury and despair that I could not imagine it was my own. I would have jumped after him and pulled him out and beaten him half to death, I think, but instead I staggered and fell, unbalanced by drink as I was. I floundered to find my feet and a boot connected with my ribs, and then another. I barely felt them. I stumbled against the wall, almost fell into the fireplace, and lurched a drunkard's punch at the nearest of the men who now set upon me. Another and another. I lashed with my feet. I try, now, not to imagine what a sight I made, flailing limbs, the mournful snarls and howls of a pitiful fury. Perhaps I gravely injured a stool or two before they had me. The air filled with shouts, a thick cloying smoke of them. The men seized me between them. They carried me out to the street and held me up, and beat me and beat me again. Blow after blow. I felt them in the distance. I saw the fists fly at my face, knuckles clenched, bloody and raw from the blows before. I remember most clearly of all the moment before my eyes closed. The spittle-flecked, twisted faces. The fist like a knuckle of ham.

It was not the last. I felt a handful more, like the shake of distant drumbeats through the air, but I was no longer among them. I had taken myself to another place and another time. I was in my house. My empty home, and where once had been laughter and smiles and movement, now was cold, still air. The table stood bare, and I sat alone. The pans were neatly hung in the kitchen. The blankets folded in the closet. There were clothes in the dresser. Old dresses my Caro had once worn. In the room where our son John had slept, I found shirts and smocks I had never seen before. They were years old, but already for a boy taller than the lad I remembered. He would be starting to grow traces of his first beard now. He would be almost a man, old enough to pick up a pike or a musket. Old enough to fight. In a corner beside my daughter's bed I found an old cloth doll. Discarded. The girl I remembered had loved that doll. She'd taken it everywhere, but it was a child's toy, and she would be sixteen years now, and all childish things long forgotten.

Six years since I had left them for the King's banner. Outside, snow lay heavy on the ground, but no one had lit a fire in these hearths for months. I ran my hand through the dust by the fireplace where we had once sat, and my fingers came back thick with it. I wrapped myself in blankets and lay on the bed that my Caro and I had once shared. I shivered myself to sleep, and in the morning I left again and did not come back.

In the place and time from which I had come, in the summer evening outside an Uxbridge tavern, the men beating me had gone. For a moment I knew where I was again. There were others looming over me now, two faces in soldier's coats; and then I slipped between them to the past once more, and they were Cromwell and Thomas Fairfax. They would force the King to terms before the year was out, they said. I no longer cared. My home had abandoned me. My family had waited as long as they could, but I had not come back in time. I had tried to tell myself, in all the days that followed, that I would find them again. That they would be alive. They had left our home with a quiet determination, with no sign of haste or fear, and my Caro was strong and wilful. One way or another she would survive. I told myself she had found some haven where she and Charlotte would be safe from marauding soldiers, where my son would find good honest work and never wear a soldier's coat as I had done; but it was a fragile hope, and somewhere I had lost it.

Did I throw it away? Did I simply misplace it? Did it quietly slip into the dark one night as I slept? I couldn't say, for at first I didn't notice it was even gone.

CHAPTER 1

I opened my eyes and strained to see. There was no window in the cell where I found myself, but somewhere there was candlelight, and it was enough to show that I was alone. I heard the heavy tread of boots on stone coming closer. My head pounded. I was not, I confess, at my best. I tried to recall how I had come to be in this place, and found I could not entirely be sure.

The boots stopped at the door to my cell. I heard voices outside.

'He's a surly bastard. Are you sure you want him?' I thought I had perhaps heard that voice last night.

'Not greatly, but I have my orders.'

The second voice I knew better, though it was one I had not heard for nigh on six months. A deep, syrupy baritone, almost musical. A voice I had once imagined belonged to a thespian or a minstrel or to some courtly fool too cowardly ever to fight, but I had long since learned the error of that impression. It was a voice I had not wanted ever to hear again. Henry Warbeck. Cromwell's man.

The air around me stank. I could not imagine a more noisome reek. Animal filth, rank and foul.

A bar lifted on the other side of the door. Reluctant iron hinges squealed open. Two men stood in silhouette against the light outside, one making way for the other.

'Hello, Falkland,' said the syrupy voice. 'Dear Lord but you smell rotten.'

'Warbeck,' I croaked. 'Am I in hell, then, and the devil has sent you?' I tried to rise and found my legs too unsteady. The dim world of the cell around me seemed to swim and shimmer. I managed as far as hands and knees and then had to stop. I feared I might vomit. It was a shameful thing for Warbeck to see me like this.

'Grief, Falkland. Do you even know where you are?'

'Uxbridge, I think.'

Warbeck hissed his disgust. He turned to the guard who had opened the door. 'Get him out of here.'

The guard hesitated, torn perhaps between the authority in Warbeck's voice and some sense of other duty – or so I thought until I saw Warbeck reach to the purse on his belt, and it was then that I understood that the hesitation was simply an invitation. I heard a jangle of coin. I staggered to my feet. I would not, I told myself, have some jailer drag me out of here. I would walk on my own.

The guard came in. He took my arm. I flinched, ready at once to shake him off, but I sensed an unexpected gentleness in his hand, and so I let him steady me. I have been in more than one jail in my time, and I have never come to expect kindness. The soldiers who supervise Cromwell's prisons are taught to view their charges with scorn, that their prisoners are somehow lesser men and less godly, though in truth they are simply less lucky.

'Mister Falkland, is it? Come on then, Mister Falkland.'

The guard helped me to the door. Warbeck uttered a grunt of disdain and turned away ahead of us.

'You need a bath, Falkland,' he said.

I had imagined myself, until now, to be in some prison built to cage men, but as I walked through the door I saw this was not the case. Four more low stone rooms opened onto either side of this dingy corridor. On one side the doors were closed, but on the other they were open. The first room was empty, save for a covering of muck and straw, but in the next lay a sow, suckling a litter of pigs. They could not have been more than a few days old.

'Yours?' I asked the guard, whom I began to suspect was no guard at all.

'Aye.' He sounded proud, as I suppose any man would be to have such a treasure.

Warbeck opened the door at the end of the corridor. Brilliant light flooded in, far too bright. I squeezed my eyes shut and cringed, feeling my way blindly as the guard helped me on. I knew when we crossed the threshold. The sunlight was bright and warm. A glorious English summer's day in this year of Our Lord sixteen forty-six.

We left the pig-farmer's sty, and my 'guard' was, I think, more than happy to see the back of us. Warbeck had come on horseback. He had brought a second mare, and I am ashamed to say that my first dismal efforts to mount the animal were comical at best, I who was once a cavalryman under Prince Rupert himself. When Warbeck had finished pouring scorn with his eyes and I had finally settled myself in the saddle, he led us to the centre of Uxbridge, to a tavern of some size. He walked me in through a back door – I was at least able to dismount without sprawling across the stables

– and took me upstairs to a room, and, shortly, to a bath. I suppose I might have considered myself fortunate he didn't simply hurl me into the nearest pond or brook. I have done the same and worse with drunks in my time.

I sank into the lukewarm water. I was still intoxicated, yet I was no longer so far gone as to feel no shame. I had made a fool of myself the night before, and paid for it in bruises and a bloody lip. I was lucky it had not been worse. Warbeck might ask me, as indeed might any man, what had brought me to Uxbridge. He might ask me why I had drunk myself stupid and then entered into a fight with a man I'd not laid eyes on until an hour before, a man too well equipped with friends.

I cupped my hands and lifted the water to my face. It was already murky. I stared as best I could at my own reflection, trying to understand what nature of man looked back. Hollow, haunted eyes. Straggly hair, half of it grey around the sides of my head. Not much on top. The beginnings of an unkempt beard, untouched for nigh on two weeks now.

Behind me, the door opened. I recognised the tread of Warbeck's boots from my pigsty prison.

'Are you sober yet, Falkland?'

'What do you want, Warbeck?' He'd pulled me from a prison cell before, a darker one than today. Back then it was Newgate, where I'd been due to hang, just another royalist soldier to be rid of, but Warbeck had taken me away. He'd stuffed me in a carriage with a sack over my head, all the way to Parliament, and now here he was again.

'Cromwell wants you.'

That was all that had saved me from Newgate. Cromwell had heard of me. I had had a use.

'I have more pressing things,' I said now.

'You can tell him that yourself, Falkland. Once you're fit to meet him.'

'I have a family to find. Tell him to go to hell.' I heard the emptiness of my words, and perhaps Warbeck heard it too, for he didn't reply at first. I sank a little deeper into the tepid water and closed my eyes. I heard him breathing, slow and steady and, when I listened closely, with a slight rasp. Warbeck wasn't entirely well. I couldn't put my finger on what it was, but he'd been this way since we'd first met. I'd had a hood over my head at the time, and the rotten reek of his breath lingered in my memory.

I heard him open his mouth. The wet smack of his lips. I knew what would come next. Threats. Something to remind me of how little he cared for someone who had once fought for the King. But he surprised me.

'Your family weren't waiting for you when you reached your home in Launcells, then?' he asked.

'It's a truth I've learned in the long years of this war,' I said, 'that a man should never have hopes, for nothing so crushes him as the dashing of them.'

Warbeck waited a heartbeat or two. I heard his breathing change. 'If that's your answer, Falkland, I'll be very happy to take any money you might have to pay for your incarceration last night. Otherwise you can go back to where I found you. It's a nice enough sty for a pig, I suppose. There might be a magistrate from St Albans come by in a couple of weeks, but I dare say they won't wait that long. Another couple of days and they'll kick you onto the streets penniless and ragged and covered in filth. Is that what you want?'

I had taken a beating. I hurt. I was missing my purse. I

had nothing. In truth, I'd had very little to begin with. I hoped I'd given the rest of them a bruise or two to remember me by. I feared I had not.

'Get yourself dressed, Falkland,' Warbeck said, after another moment of silence.

'How did you find me?' I asked.

I heard him hawk up a gob of phlegm and spit it to the floor. 'It wasn't hard. I've known whole companies of militia stumble more quietly through the kingdom than you do. A blind deaf mute on a lame mule might track you down.'

He left, his boots tapping across the floor. I sat in the filthy bath, drifting through the torture of the last months, my futile wanderings from one failure to the next, and it was only when the water was cold enough to make me shiver that I was able to pull myself away. I scrubbed myself clean, though the dirt clung to me with the tenacity of despair. I dressed, and immediately I stank again. My clothes were filthy. When I stumbled out, Warbeck was waiting with a pitcher of milk and a hunk of stale bread. I drank the milk and felt my stomach churn, sour and unwelcoming. The bread was as hard as wood. I should have saved the milk to soften it, but Warbeck was in no mood for further delay. He grimaced at my sorry state and hurried me outside. A fresh pain stabbed between my eyes, while I screwed up my face against the brightness of the sun. It was as well that I had once been a cavalryman and knew my way to mounting a horse almost in my sleep. At least this time I didn't fall. Warbeck led us on, and my mare did as all horses will do if not otherwise steered, and men too: it followed. I dozed as the sun rose through the morning, slumped on the animal's back and grateful for Warbeck's silence, my mare vexing him now and then when she stopped to snatch a mouthful of whatever passing vegetation caught her fancy. I did nothing to hurry her along. I barely noticed the lanes and villages through which we passed.

By the middle of the day my head had begun to clear. I chewed at that piece of bread a while, and gradually became aware that we had not reached the fringes of London as I had imagined, but were in fact deep in the countryside with hills all around us. I drew alongside Warbeck.

'Where are we going?' I asked him.

Warbeck gave me a look as if mildly surprised to find me still alive. 'To Cromwell, Falkland. Was that not clear?'

Author Q&A

What inspired you to start writing this series?

Oh, all sorts of things. I was drawn to Falkland as a character, and a certain atmosphere that I think pervades *The Royalist*, and the English civil war seemed a very apt setting, the murkiness of it, the blurring of lines, the lack of any real clarity once you look hard at what any of it stood for. All sorts of motives, some idealistic, some purely material, seem meshed together on both sides, and I think that ambiguity has a very modern feel to it which I like. But a part of it, too, was probably the fact that a long time ago I was half mugged by a gang of friends to spend a summer in the Sealed Knot, lugging a pike across a battlefield, living in permanent chaos, and drinking an awful lot of mead.

What do you enjoy most about writing Falkland? Is there a little of you in him?

I have a real fondness for the cynical detectives of film noir, the weary pragmatist who carefully hides his soul, and Falkland fits right in that mould. He's so damn tired of it all, wise enough to see the pointlessness of a lot of it, and yet deep down he's an idealist. He never quite gives up on that, never quite stops trying, and just about manages to define and live by his own code. He certainly has his faults, but there's a generosity of spirit to him too. I don't know if there's anything of me in that, but there's certainly a good chunk of how I'd like to see myself.

Your scenes are so rich with historical details, sounds, sights and smells. How do you go about your research?
Wikipedia is a good start for the dry facts, but the internet doesn't give you the taste and the smell of things. For me, 'research' turns out to be all sorts of little bits, really, added together. I've spent a fair amount of time in very cold places, and I certainly drew on that for the winter camp in Crediton. Numerous battlefield re-enactments, not for the battles themselves, but for the camp afterwards, the practicalities of what you can and can't do and how sometimes you get by as best you can with whatever you happen to have, how it is when a lot of people are squashed together in a small space. I went to a renaissance fair once and bought a packet of seventeenth century stew mix and made it and ate it just because it was there (what I discovered, by the way, was far too much clove and nutmeg). A lot of 'research' is gathering bits and pieces from everywhere, going to places and looking at them without any real plan as such, doing and seeing new things, having an interest in the world and its history, and then closing your eyes and sinking back into the character on the page and trying to really feel and see and smell and taste the world around them.

Which characters have been the most interesting to evoke on the page? Are you daunted by tackling a 'real-life' character in Cromwell?
Falkland, obviously, and I have a special fondness for Henry Warbeck too, who's never quite what you think he is. But in writing made-up characters there's always the liberty of

making a persona from whole cloth however you like. Of the 'real' characters I found Fairfax much more interesting to write than Cromwell, in part because he doesn't appear on the page so much, but also because he's not a particularly well-known figure. That presents the challenge of taking dry biographic material and bringing it to life, making him strong and strident and yet true to what's recorded of him, and doing it within the restriction of a few scenes. Cromwell is another matter. Yes, he was more daunting, but that wasn't because of who he really was so much as how well-known he is and how diversely he's been portrayed in the past (which covers a wide spectrum – my kids, for example, see Cromwell as an out-and-out villain because *Horrible Histories* told them he banned Christmas). It's quite a challenge to evoke a character in a way that's both true to their known history and to a modern perception of them that is, in some ways, quite different.

My favourite of the historical figures I've used, by the way, is John Milton. He was immensely fun. He's in the second book though.

What is your favourite book and who is your favourite author?

I don't have any firm favourites, and whatever answer I could give today would be different in six months from now. George RR Martin's *Game of Thrones* (the book, not the TV series) blew me away. Books that have lingered with me for a long time include Toni Morrison's *A Mercy*, *Catch 22*, *Zen and the Art of Motorcycle Maintenance*, *Steppenwolf*, and those are just a few of them. I might just go for Jane Austen. One book that was certainly influential in the writing of *The*

Royalist, though I read it a good few years ago, is Ariana Franklin's *Mistress of the Art of Death*.

What are you currently reading?
Altered Carbon by Richard Morgan. (Very) different setting, same love for noir detective stories.

If *The Royalist* was turned into a movie, who would you choose to play the central cast?
I like Robert Carlyle for Henry Warbeck, Tim Roth for Cromwell and Hilary Swank for Kate Cain. Falkland is harder. Robert Mitchum, maybe, if I can go back far enough. If it has to be someone alive, Liam Neeson might fit the bill, but I'm going to be a little dull and go for Russell Crowe.

Can you tell us about the next Falkland novel, *The Protector*?
I can tell you that it revolves around Falkland once more being co-opted by Cromwell to solve a rather delicate mystery, this time an abduction with political implications. I can tell you that it involves an old mystery in a country house, a murder or two, that most of the main characters from *The Royalist* make a return, and that John Milton was an absolute treat to write and tries to steal every scene.